By Mary Rosenblum
Published by Ballantine Books:

THE DRYLANDS

CHIMERA

Mary Rosenblum

A Del Rey Book
BALLANTINE BOOKS • NEW YORK

A Del Rey Book
Published by Ballantine Books

Library of Congress Catalog Card Number: 93-90515

ISBN 0-345-38528-4

Manufactured in the United States of America

First Edition: November 1993

For Ellen,
whose enthusiasm
and tons of hard work
matter.

I'd like to thank the members of the 1991 Oregon Coast workshop, who read and commented on the first draft of this manuscript. A special thanks goes to Sage Walker and John Gibbons, who put a lot of effort into this project.

Chapter One

"Mr. Ishigito." Jewel bowed as she entered the small man's virtual office. He was wearing a classic business Self: bland smile, not-too-tilted dark eyes, hair knotted into a sleek club that could not possibly stay so smooth in the flesh. Don't think about that. She bit her lip, let go quickly, and forced her lips to relax. "I appreciate the time you could spare me from your busy schedule."

"Please be seated, Ms. Martina." Ishigito bowed formally. "How may I be of service to you?"

Be cool. Jewel seated herself in a chair of polished teak, aware of sleek wood beneath her thighs. In actual, she was sitting on a plastic chair in her bedroom. The knowledge intruded, and she shoved it away. The room was very Japanese, all clean, uncluttered spaces, with a single branch of cherry blossoms in an earthenware jar. Custom designed and expensive, because Ishigito was very inside. Very big. Jewel tried to relax, hoping that the body language edit in her office was projecting a Self full of seamless confidence. If Ishigito read her nervousness, he might figure that her package contained a hidden risk, and he would pass. She struggled for calm, but it eluded her. Beyond the unreal walls of this office lay the corridors of Erebus Complex, and beyond that the freezing desert of Antarctica. Mr. Ishigito might be short and fat, with a pimple on his chin. He might be sitting in a public VR cubicle outside a bus station in Duluth. The image intruded, and Jewel struggled with a terrible urge to giggle.

She was blowing it, and she knew it. Before she had even made her pitch. With a sinking feeling, Jewel studied the faint aura that shimmered around Ishigito: soft magenta. Her office was interpreting his edited body language as moderately positive, but her office was a cheap model and probably couldn't read his editing for shit. "I am honored that you could spare me this time." Jewel

1

touched the crimson wax seal that lay on her desk. "This Secure File represents a package that should provide a healthy margin of profit for Epyxx." And had cost her a lot of expensive Net time to set up. Don't think about that, either. Jewel leaned back, struggling to keep her body language relaxed.

"I may be interested." Ishigito inclined his head a fraction of an inch and cleared his throat. "I can spare you a few minutes, Ms. Martina."

Steady magenta. Still reading positive. Was this damn cheap office worth *anything*? "I received an advance report on the latest ozone survey from the Zurich Center for Environmental Control. It will be released in two days and will reveal that the melanoma risk factor for the northeastern United States has risen by nearly one percent in the past six months. The demand for high-quality sunscreen will certainly increase." Jewel snapped her fingers, and a large white screen appeared in the air beside her desk. "If you will look at the figures, you will see that projected sales of high-end cosmetic-grade sunscreen in the region exceed the immediately available local supply."

This was the moment, the hook. Jewel felt herself sweating and struggled for a smile that projected seamless confidence. "A Thai pharmaceutical company is overstocked with the required base at the moment. Labor costs are quite low in Thailand since last year's revolution. Projected leasing costs for necessary manufacturing hardware and soft support fall well within market norms. The manufacturing can be done there. The political situation is stable enough for sound short-term investment." She tapped the virtual screen, and numbers appeared, scrolling slowly down the white surface. "The first product could reach northeastern cosmetic companies within thirty-six hours. A profit margin of seven percent is a conservative estimate. I have already optioned the necessary hard and soft support."

It was a nice, tight, custom-manufacture package, small-scale but profitable. She sat back, hands folded, remembering not to hold her breath. She was sweating under her skinthins, but her office would edit that out. Her Self—a blond, slightly Scandinavian model—would be smiling at him, sure of herself . . . sure enough that his office couldn't see her sweat? Stop *thinking* about it. Jewel let her breath out slowly, but the tension didn't go away. Mr. Ishigito was a midlevel node in the Epyxx corporate web. If he brought her information package—if this deal worked and she made him money—it was an entrance.

You needed an entrance in the universe of global brokering. There were plenty of brokers, all hungry to put together packages for the big corporate webs. Here is the market niche, there is the raw material source, and over here is the best deal on hardware and labor, all optioned and ready to sign. Take it and run, and I get fifteen percent, thank you. Newcomers were an unknown quantity, a risk in a game that carried enough risks already. And she was a raw newcomer, pushing in on her own instead of slipping in as some broker's carefully groomed protégée.

And she would damn well do it on her own, thank you. She had gotten this far. Jewel realized that her smile had grown stiff. *Relax!* She stretched her lips, feeling as if her face were about to crack.

The node frowned at the blob of crimson wax, but made no move to touch it. "Your numbers interest me, Ms. Martina." Ishigito nodded at the screen. "You have a sound premise, but upon considering the margin of profit involved and the absolute numbers, I must apologetically decline." He got to his feet, still smiling, and bowed. "I'm sure that you will find a client for this particular package. Perhaps we will have the opportunity to do business at another time."

"Perhaps we shall." She returned his bow, her smile plastered to her face—so what if it was stiff? So *what*? "Thank you for your time, Mr. Ishigito. I know you are very busy."

He ushered her through the door of his office with more polite, meaningless words. No, they weren't meaningless. They translated to "Don't bother me, amateur." His door closed firmly behind her, and Jewel stood in her own cheap, off-the-rack office again. "Shit!" She clenched her fists, tears and anger struggling in her throat. "I was so *close*." And if she didn't sell this sucker, it was going to mean a big hole in her account. It had taken expensive hours of Net time to put together—never mind the cost of the security certification. That ozone tip had been so *hot*. The Worldweb, a mosaic of a million small companies, formed, broke apart, and re-formed with the shifting winds of demand and supply. You either rode the crest of those winds, guiding those patterns, pitting your information and guesses against those of other nodes . . . or you worked for somebody else. You belonged to them. As she belonged to Alcourt. "That bastard." Her voice trembled. "Exit office . . ."

Water! Jewel gasped in terror as blue ocean closed over her head. Ice stalactites speared down from a frozen ceiling, and a gray-green seal slid by. Cold . . . freezing . . . she was trapped in a subsea ice cave. Jewel's chest spasmed, her trachea clenching tight in a drowning reflex. For one agonized moment of panic she clawed for that distant white ceiling of ice, terror a beating wing in her head.

Then sanity caught up with her, and she grabbed for her virtual lenses. The seal had swum close, and it metamorphosed suddenly, becoming a red fox perched on a thick lump of bottom ice, green eyes glinting like gems, grinning at her. Jewel ripped off her lenses.

White light made her blink, and she gasped in a breath of blessed air. She was in her room, of course, facing the futon sofa where she slept, the tipped-over chair prodding her calves. No water to drown her, no ice ceiling to trap her. Breathing hard, Jewel dropped onto her sofa. For a moment she had been drowning in an icy sea— her body had thought so, anyway. She pushed sweaty hair out of her eyes and shivered. The cold had been an illusion, but her flesh had believed it. She rubbed her arms, goose bumps ridging her skin.

Someone had done this to her on purpose—the green-eyed fox. He—or she, or it—had crashed her office and had diverted her into another virtual. That fox had laughed at her terror. Jewel clenched both fists, swallowing down the hard lump of her rage. The most likely culprit was one of the infinitely spoiled children who lived in this place. They *lived* in virtual, and the trick had a childish feel to it. A prank.

If one of the children here had played it, there was nothing Jewel could do about it. She swallowed bitterness. She was an employee here, not a resident.

Not yet.

"Jewel?" The voice came over her audio implant, brusque and impatient. *"I'm awake."*

The boss. Harmon Alcourt. "I'm coming," Jewel said, stifling her sigh because he might be listening in. He usually slept longer than this. If the little fox bastard hadn't dumped her into his freezing ocean, she might have had time to try another web contact.

But none of them was as inside as Ishigito. She had blown her big chance. Jewel slapped the palm lock on the inside door of her tiny apartment, folding her anger like a piece of cloth, tucking it away in the deep places of her mind. Anger was a privilege of wealth. And of poverty. On the tough road from one to the other, you couldn't afford it. Jewel folded her gloves and lenses, stuffing them into her uniform pocket. The rear door of her apartment took her directly into a hallway in the Alcourt complex. It closed behind her, locked tight by Security. Only Security could unlock it, because this was, after all, the Antarctic Preserve. Only the center-most nodes in the Worldwebs lived here, the men and women who shaped the economic structure of the whole planet. They took no chances. None.

Jewel straightened her uniform as she hurried down the corridor, smoothing the red medical-aide patch on her coverall. It was the key that had let her enter at all into this world of power and wealth buried beneath the frozen skin of Mount Erebus. But she would get no farther unless she opened a door to the Worldweb, and that didn't seem very likely at the moment. Jewel smoothed her short, thick hair back from her face, wincing at the cost of the wasted virtual time. Her skinthins—a cheap model—itched beneath her uniform coverall. Alcourt kept his rooms warm, perhaps because it was so cold outside. Harmon Alcourt was one of the most central nodes in AllThings Web, so he could live however he wished. Jewel unsealed the front of the skinthins and tucked the neck down out of sight beneath her uniform.

He napped in the solarium, so she took a shortcut through a leisure room. Empty sofas, recliners, and floor cushions clustered artfully amid flowering bougainvilleas. A housekeeper skittered across the floor, silently lifting dirt from the handwoven carpet with a localized electrostatic charge. It had been designed to look like a giant blue beetle. Jewel sidestepped it and walked into the midst of a bougainvillea. Even after a whole year here she still flinched when she walked into a holo.

Alcourt liked illusion. Whole rooms were nothing but holograms projected into recessed doorways that led nowhere. Jewel ran her fingers through a tumbling fountain of unreal crystal water. Did he do it simply to watch strangers bang their noses on invisible walls or walk around a bush that was nothing more than a smear of colored light on the air? Perhaps he simply enjoyed manipulating people, as the web he belonged to shaped and manipulated the economies of a hundred nations.

"Jewel? Where are *you?"*

Alcourt sounded petulant, in a bad mood. Jewel hurried down the hall beyond the living room, past the grand dining room with its immense table and dozen chairs—holo—and the library, thick and claustrophobic with dark furniture and walls of expensive leather-bound, press-printed books—real, and he never opened the books. The next doorway displayed a holoed garden.

It was new, and Jewel paused for a quick glance. The previous day massed clumps of flowers had bloomed between brick paths. Today textured stones, ocher sand, and cactus filled the space. A rattlesnake basked on a rock, and a small lizard perched on a dead branch of sage. It flicked its tongue out at her and streaked away, almost too fast to see. Jewel shivered suddenly, shaken by an unexpected memory of heat, sand, and dust that coated her throat and made her cry. Then it was gone. I never went into the desert, Jewel thought. But she had remembered . . . something, and the memory had shaken her. Uneasy, she walked the last meters to the solarium's wide door. The memory had had a childish feel to it. As if she had been very young. Jewel slapped the door open, angry at this brief bit of intrusion and, beneath that anger, a little afraid. The past was dangerous. Jewel looked over her shoulder as the door whispered closed behind her, as if something might be following her from that holoed desert.

The corridor was empty. Of course. Illusion. She shrugged as the hot Carib sun scalded her shoulders. If she had been in the desert once, what did it matter? That part of her life no longer existed. She had made sure of that. Jewel breathed sea-scented air, hurrying now, ignoring the screeching gulls that dove at her head. Holo, of course, but the sand was real, slippery and white underfoot. Waves broke on the beach in an unreal welter of blue-green water and foam, hiding her footsteps as she approached the recliner set up in dappled palm-frond shade.

Harmon Alcourt, most inside node of AllThings Web, lay facedown on a padded lounger, basking in his harmless artificial sun. He looked sixty—a well-muscled, tanned sixty. He was much older—how much older even she, privy to his every physical twitch, didn't know. His dark hair was carefully peppered with gray. Fetal cell treatments and cosmetic surgery gave him youth. His tan came from melanin augmentation, not from genetic heritage or ultraviolet damage. Young body, but he was *old*. She could see the years in his eyes—and on the readouts of her machines. He was pushing the limits of technology's ability to give him life and health. In virtual, he was forty, and ruthless.

"You took your time." Alcourt didn't bother to lift his head.

Sulky, this evening. "I'm sorry, sir." Jewel soothed, because when he was in a mood like this, that was what he wanted: comfort, in a mother's tone. Give the clients what they want. Rule one. "I stopped to look at your new garden," she said.

"I brought Chen in to do it." Some of the sulkiness had evaporated from Alcourt's tone. "I met him several years ago at a gallery showing. His last gallery piece was so-so, but he's the best in the field with holo. Have you ever dropped into any of his pieces on the Net?"

"No, I don't think so." Of course not. Jewel palmed the biotherapy console beneath the lounger, and it blinked acknowledgment of her clearance. "I've never had much time for Net art." Or interest, or money to waste on such luxuries. "Are you ready for neurostim?'' She started the unit's self-test and reached for a warmed towel.

"I suppose so.'' Alcourt rolled over and propped himself on one elbow, not bothering to hide his genitals. "Did you like the garden, Jewel?''

His sudden intensity caught her by surprise. "It's . . . very nice. It's realistic.''

"You're lying to me.'' Alcourt grabbed her wrist suddenly, pulling her closer. "I was watching you on Security. You didn't like it, did you? Tell me why.''

"You're mistaken.'' She had recovered and gave him slightly widened eyes and bland innocence. "I guess I liked the old garden better. It was more colorful.''

"You're still lying.'' His eyes held hers, as unreadable as the dry sky above the 'burbs. "You know, you weren't adopted by the Walsh family as an infant. Those records are fakes. Good ones, but not good enough to fool my Security. Did you grow up in the desert, Jewel? Is that why you flinched in there?''

He knew. Jewel stared at him, tongue thick and suddenly clumsy. He *knew*, and she'd been a fool to think he did not. But she shouldn't have gotten this job—not *here*—not with a faked personal file. She had paid that engineer so damn much to go in and tailor her file. Foolish to think Alcourt wouldn't own someone better . . . "You . . . you're mistaken.'' Jewel struggled for words and breath. "Really.'' Hopeless, you idiot. You're fired. "Of course I was adopted.''

"Oh, stop.'' He made a petulant face. "We don't need to play this game, and you were the top-ranking aide when I hired you. Whoever you are.'' He still held her wrist, and now he ran his fingers lightly up the inside of her arm, as a lover might. "I want to know, Jewel. I want you to tell me what scared you in there, what your demons are. I want to know *you*.'' He stroked her arm, eyes glittering. "I want to know who you are.''

"I—don't understand.'' Which was the truth. Jewel tried to free her arm, but he wouldn't let go. His eyes glittered with something like lust. "What exactly are you asking me?'' She glanced involuntarily at his genitals, wondering if it was sex he was after. His penis lay slack in its nest of youthful curls.

He followed her glance and laughed softly. "Not sex, Jewel Martina. I'm asking for truth, and sex is the greatest deception of all. I've never asked you to sleep with me.'' He smiled crookedly. "Would you have said yes? Probably, because you would expect me to fire you otherwise, and you want this job. So you'd trade the pretense of love for it, wouldn't you? I don't want that. I want *you*.''

Emotion surfaced briefly in his eyes, vanishing too quickly for Jewel to identify it. "I am very powerful." He sat up, still holding her, fingers digging into her flesh now. "Power sticks to you. It hardens into armor, and after a while *you* are forgotten. There is only the armor, and no one cares what might be underneath. They talk to the Harmon Alcourt they see—they talk or challenge or try to flatter *him*. And I'm forgotten. Me, the real man, the flesh man. I exist for very few people in the world. David Chen, perhaps. You. A handful of others." He raised his eyes slowly to her face. "You see *me*, not the virtual. You see me inside and out with your monitors and machines. Sometimes I . . . think you know me better than anyone else, for all your knowledge is bought and paid for. I want to know you. I want to know the part that you hide, the dark years that my Security can't pry into. Tell me, Jewel." His voice was a whisper.

"I . . . I can't." Jewel looked away from his shadowed eyes. They were gone, those years, boxed up and put away in the back of her mind. Damn that desert and the video eyes here! Sex she could handle. Jewel swallowed a twinge of panic. She would have lain down if he had asked, made love to that artificially youthful body. Nothing free in this world, and that price she would pay if he asked.

Not this one.

She could not.

"You're wrong." She met his eyes, straightening her shoulders, chin lifting. "I lived with Linda Walsh and her mother from the time I was a baby. I don't even remember visiting the desert. You're mistaken, Mr. Alcourt."

For an instant anger hardened his face and flashed like sheet lightning in his eyes. No one said no to Harmon Alcourt, and Jewel's stomach clenched as she waited for him to fire her, break their contract, and send her back to the States.

With a grunt, he threw himself back on the recliner, one arm across his eyes. "Check the sciatic group," he said sharply. "My left hip bothered me during my squash session today."

Warily, Jewel called up the holo of Alcourt's reclining body. It glowed in the monitor box, a shimmering smear of color representing muscle and nerve activity. "I see some simple muscle strain . . . Image enlarge," she directed the console. "Lumbar region, dorsal, right rotation." Perhaps it was over, this strange conversation of his. Perhaps he would forget and never bring it up again.

Sure. What did he *want*? Jewel peered at the image as it expanded; warm reds and yellows swirled, streaked by cooler greens and blues. "There appears to be some slight deep tissue trauma," she said. "Muscle strain, perhaps. Nothing serious. I'll use an anti-inflammatory and give you a sonic message after therapy."

"I played squash with Banacek. He's always out for blood and has the finesse of a bull elephant." Alcourt grunted as Jewel probed the inflamed area with her fingertips. "That's the place. Ouch. I've got a new tech working for me. He's good—better than anyone Banacek has. I think I'll have him sneak a twist into the interface. Make Banacek run a little, but not enough to throw our win-loss ratio off." He smiled slowly. "It'll be fun to watch him pant. He's so vain about his stamina."

He was speaking casually, but there was an edge to his tone. Illusion and reality. Jewel sprayed a light mist of anti-inflammatory across the affected area, relieved at the change of subject. The squash game had been in virtual, but muscles could be overextended just as easily in virtual as on an actual squash court. Alcourt would manipulate the virtual, but not enough to beat Banacek. Jewel wondered about that as she ended the session. Why fix the game if you didn't want to win? She began to remove the remotes. Illusion and reality overlapped in this place; sometimes it was hard to tell one from the other. Her lungs had tried to keep her from drowning in an imaginary sea, and Alcourt had strained a muscle reaching for an illusory ball. Had Alcourt's strange words been illusion? Or reality? He knew about her tailored file, and that was an ugly reality. Very ugly. The price for Net piracy was high if you got busted, even if you had simply paid someone else to do it.

"Your serotonin levels are slightly elevated," she said, marveling at her calm tone. "I entered a dietary change into the House."

"Serotonin? Now what? Always something going wrong." A hint of fear colored his tone. "Keep an eye on the bloodwork, Jewel. I want a twenty-four-hour watch on the remote samples. No surprises, understand? Never mind the massage." Alcourt sat up, brushing the last of the remotes from his arm. "I'm going to swim. Castor can give me a massage later."

Castor had night duty this week. "I'll make a note of it in the log." Jewel draped a cotton robe over his shoulders as he stood. "Is there anything else before I go off-shift?"

"No." Alcourt belted the robe tightly around himself, a hint of anger in his face. "I have an assignment for you." He paused briefly, his eyes on her face. "Define love for me. I'll expect you to have it for me by your next shift. Don't be slow next time I call you." He turned his back on her, stalked across the pristine sterilized sand that had been flown in from some tropical beach, and disappeared through the doors.

Jewel stared after him. Define love? Her lips twisted suddenly. Love was a thing for children who could dream and pretend that the dreams were real. She had never been that young. Maybe she would tell him that. She snatched up the towel he'd dropped and flung it onto the recliner. Maybe he was just upset today because of the serotonin levels. Sometimes she thought his body frightened him. Perhaps because he couldn't control it, not completely. Not forever, no matter how much medical intervention he could afford. Jewel shut down the console and left the disarray for Housekeeping, relieved that her shift was ending. Maybe this weird mood would be over by tomorrow. She hurried past the desert garden and met Castor, who was just coming to log in.

He waved at her, tanned and muscular as an athlete. "Good morning," he said, although it was evening, and grinned as if he had made a terrific joke.

"He needs a massage after he swims," Jewel told him. "Muscle strain. It's in the log."

"Of course. You never forget a thing, do you, my dear?" He smiled at her, a slick, smooth smile that didn't reach his eyes.

"Of course not." She gave him his smile back in spades as he brushed past her.

They had never gotten along. She ranked slightly higher than he in the medical-aide data base, and she had flatly turned down his invite to bed. He was muscular and handsome, a gene-selected Nordic phenotype with red-gold hair and enhanced blue eyes, the son of a minor web node. The muscles and the tan came from the spa. Castor got his kicks in virtual sports, surfing the Pipeline or skiing down Mount Everest—the more dangerous, the better. A walking illusion, she thought as she palmed the connecting door to her apartment. A perfect match for this place.

Security opened the door for her and closed it behind her, locking her out of Alcourt's space until her next shift or until he called her. Jewel stretched, arms spread wide, trying to loosen the tension in her shoulders. Security watched her stretch. You couldn't breathe here without *someone* counting your respiration rate. It had bothered her at first—she had slept in a shirt and underwear for a month. She had stopped noticing it after a while, but today she felt it again—eyes watching her, peering over her shoulder.

When had she been in the desert? Why didn't she remember it? Beyond the fake windows in her apartment, a holoed summer afternoon was softening into evening. More illusion. "House, blank windows.'' They darkened obediently as she stripped off her uniform and the virtual skin she wore under it. She had intended to eat dinner and prowl the Net, fishing for a buyer for her package, but the idea of wading through illusory offices and parties depressed her suddenly. She pulled on casual tights and a long-sleeved tunic. It was all illusion down here: the illusion of privacy, when Security watched your every move, the illusion of freedom, when you did whatever it took to keep your precious job, the illusion of intimacy, when your soul was up for sale. Jewel wandered over to the kitchenwall, brought up the inventory on the little wallscreen, and scowled at it. Stick a meal tray in the microwave, get on the Net, and stop fussing about illusion, she told herself.

Alcourt knew that she had paid for a tailor job on her file. What the hell did he want from her? Something, or he would have fired her, even turned her over to the cops. Instead, he played games. Suppressed anger stirred in her belly, banishing hunger. Jewel ordered a pack of vat-grown orange juice from her kitchenwall, drank it down in four long swallows, and left her apartment. Her main door opened onto Mirny corridor. Erebus Complex occupied the network of old lava tubes beneath the icy hide of the volcano. It had frightened her at first to live so close to the beating heart of a volcano. They could predict an eruption long before it could happen, but sometimes the weight above pressed down on her until she felt cornered and trapped, squeezed flat by dirt and rock and the weight of Security's eyes.

The door to the entrance bay was marked only by a single icon, a snow-covered mountain peak. It opened for Jewel, admitting a breath of chilly air. The ceiling arched over her head, and ice glistened on the walls. Her breath plumed; she had been stupid to forget her jacket. Shivering, Jewel hurried across the slippery floor, past a bank of snowcats. The door of her rented locker stung her fingers as she opened it. The slick folds of the ice suit raised gooseflesh on her skin, but the thermal fibers warmed almost instantly as she pulled it on. Gloves, goggles. She checked her battery pack and stepped into the thermal boots.

In spite of the light folds of the ice suit, she felt clunky and hampered as she palmed the door. As it opened, she felt a sudden unease, as if someone were watching her, creeping up on her. Jewel glanced around, but the bay was empty except for the cats and a few motorized sleds. Movement? She squinted, then decided it was her imagination—leftover nerves from Alcourt's mood. The door opened, and bright outside light stabbed her, darkening her goggles instantly. Cold bit her in spite of the thermal suit. Deadly cold and hard alien light. Jewel walked out onto Erebus's flank, onto hard whorls of wind-carved snow that squeaked beneath her boots.

It was sunset, although at this time of year night would fall only in the Complex corridors. A soft pink light hazed the Ross Sea far below. Ice drifted in slushy shoals, and the white-fanged horizon bit the cold sky. McMurdo was invisible from here. She might be the only living being on this entire continent, and that solitude comforted her. She didn't feel clunky out here. Jewel let her breath out in a slow sigh as she followed a narrow path northward along the flank of the volcano. This was her space, her path, made by her feet only. No one went outside—not here, anyway. Few of the Erebus residents went out at all. They did Antarctica in virtual—climbed Mount Terror or alvined the Ross Sea. They were afraid. Antarctica could kill a person in a few minutes, no matter how much of the Worldweb he or she controlled. Technology could not always save a person out here, and they had never lived outside technology's safe womb.

You could die out here, yes, but you could die in the 'burbs, too, and for less reason. Here you had only yourself to blame for being careless. Out here death was honest.

Jewel had reached an outcrop of black lava. A twisted spire of wind-carved ice jutted up from the edge of the rocks. As she reached it, the wind dropped suddenly. The sudden stillness was almost tangible, a thing that could be breathed, almost touched. Ice tinkled musically, and sudden tears filled Jewel's eyes. Out here she was . . . herself. Nothing more, nothing less. Neither yesterday nor tomorrow had any meaning. There was only here and now. She stroked the slick curves of the ice spire with a gloved hand, letting the silence soak into her.

"It's beautiful, isn't it? And utterly real."

The strange voice shattered the moment, too loud in the unusual silence. Jewel started, and her boot slipped on a patch of ice. Frantically she scrambled for balance, falling, her knee slamming hard onto a ridge of lava rock. She cried out as pain knifed up and down her leg.

"I'm sorry." A shadow of movement above resolved into a suited man climbing swiftly and easily down the rock face. "I didn't mean to startle you. Are you all right?"

"No." Jewel struggled to her feet, tears of pain blurring her vision. Who the hell are *you*? she wanted to yell. This is *my* place. She took a step and gasped as her knee buckled beneath her.

"Easy." He caught her, supporting her weight even though she tried to shake him off. "Lean on me, and I'll help you back. Maybe you should go down to the infirmary."

"I'm going to." Jewel clenched her teeth. He was wearing a leased suit, which made him staff, not resident. She didn't recognize his voice, but that didn't mean anything. A balaclava mask and goggles hid his face. "I think it's just bruised," she said between clenched teeth. "I'll be okay once I get back inside."

He was barely taller than she, slender and wiry, but he supported her weight easily. He kept his face turned to the sunset-stained vista of the Ross Sea as they made their slow way back to the entrance bay. Almost there, he paused, as if he were reluctant to go back inside. "We can't tame it," he murmured. "We can foul it, we can damage or destroy it, but we can never bend it to our will, no matter how much tech we use." He was speaking softly, as if he had forgotten that she was there. "You can't really do this world in virtual. You can get close, but . . . it's too extreme. Too big, too cold. Too alien to truly capture. Out here on the ice all our pretty illusions seem so thin, so trivial."

"Yes," Jewel said softly, her irritation at his intrusion suddenly vanishing. That was what had brought her out here. "No one owns this place, no matter what's on file in the Net. Maybe that's why they're afraid of it."

"You're not afraid?"

"No." Jewel looked into the dark eyes behind the stranger's tinted goggles. "I'm not afraid." It was illusion that frightened her, not reality.

He was nodding, and his eyes looked as if he were smiling. "That's your private place, isn't it? The rocks? Your sanctuary? It's a beautiful view." He bent his head in a slight bow. "I won't go there again."

"It's all right," Jewel said, and discovered that she meant it. Because he understood. "You can go there anytime." As if she owned the place, as if she had the right to deny him. Jewel winced at her words, but he was nodding.

"Thank you," he said gravely. "I appreciate your sharing it with me. Let's go in." His eyes crinkled as if he was smiling. "I don't know about you, but I'm cold."

Cold, yes. Instantly she became aware of her aching toes, the chill that went clear into her bones, never mind the thermal suit. Leaning on him, she limped through the door and into the bay. It was cold. Shivering, she pulled off her warm suit, realizing suddenly that she didn't know this man's name, didn't know who he worked for. She turned, mouth open to ask, and stopped in surprise. He was Asian and a stranger, with a wiry build and a braid of black hair that came down to his waist. Jewel's eyes widened as he stripped his suit down over his shoulders. A filigree of silver fibers glittered on his skin, covering hands, arms, neck, and the planes of his face.

He was netted.

It was like skinthins, only the Kraeger net was part of your skin. It was the ultimate connection to the virtual and was only beginning to catch on. Most of the children in the Complex were netted, few of the adults. It was a sign of privilege: they had been bred and born for the virtual universe of Worldweb. They were branded for success from birth, because it cost a *lot* to implant a Kraeger.

He belonged to Alcourt's world, not hers.

Jewel became aware that he was holding a dark green tunic in one hand, his eyebrows raised. Gooseflesh covered his naked arms. "Can I put it on now?" he asked with a crooked smile. "I was planning to take a boat out on the Ross Sea this afternoon to go look at the bergs from the waterline. Would you like to come?"

The anger in her gut expanded suddenly, banishing the chill in the air. He talked to her as if she were a peer, and it was a game, because she wasn't. He must have known it out there on the ice. Jewel clenched her fists. Alcourt had demanded to know why the desert garden had upset her, and she had refused to tell him. Because that much he did not own.

And now she had given something away to this silver-skinned man out there on the ice.

"No," she said, her voice as cold as the glacier outside. "I can't go." She slammed the locker door and fled, her throat knotted, furious at him, at herself for being careless, at the whole damn world of illusion down here.

Chapter Two

Sitting in front of the terminal in the solarium, Jewel ran through the last twenty-four hours of biomedical data on Harmon Alcourt. His biochem profile fell well within normal diurnal variation curves. A slight spike late the previous night in adrenaline levels indicated stress. Bad deal in the web? Jewel wondered if he knew how accurately she could read his day from his blood chemistry. That segment there was his morning exercise regimen. That one had enough stress component to indicate more web time. This was sleep; his serotonin levels were still a little high.

She called up the next screen. Implanted hardware broadcast Alcourt's stats twenty-four hours a day. Jewel stretched and yawned, lulled by the afternoon light from the artificial Carib sun and the whisper of holoed surf. So much of her job was boredom, waiting to be called. If Alcourt should suffer an arrhythmia—unlikely with his medical and genetic profile—or any kind of trauma, the hardware would immediately alert both herself and Castor as well as the Complex infirmary.

Unbidden, a memory rose in her mind of the crowded waiting room with grimy walls and ancient fluorescent lights whose flicker always gave her a headache. The local fed-med clinic.

Guaranteed health care for all and, like the guaranteed public education, pretty much worth shit. The adults there were always silent, withdrawn into a private space of fear and illness. *Will I qualify? Or am I too old—too low on the employment curve?* The children acted out those unspoken worries, crying, squabbling, translating fear into noise. The room was so thick with tension that Jewel could barely breathe, but if she got up to go outside, Mama grabbed her wrist, clinging to her with fingers like bony claws, as if Jewel might suddenly tear loose and run away. *Don't leave me,* she would whisper. Her eyes would be full of fear, and her nails would make marks on Jewel's wrist. She sweated the smell of sickness, sweet and cloying, and the small sores on her neck and arms made Jewel cringe when she touched them.

Jewel shuddered, blinking the screen back into focus. No expensive implants and anticancer treatments on fed-med basic. Not for someone on a welfare card. Not for someone with positive drug tests in her medical file. Jewel pushed her hair out of her eyes, glowering at the ghostly reflection of her face on the blue terminal screen. Why this memory? Why today? It was the damn desert garden, that was why, with its resident ghosts. Every time she walked past, it reached out to her with hot, dry fingers and squeezed her throat with the memory of fright and tears.

"Jewel." The neat curves and numbers disappeared from her screen, to be replaced by Harmon Alcourt's face. *"Come into my office, please."*

Trouble? She couldn't read his flat, two-dimensional image. Jewel reached into her coverall pocket for lenses and gloves. She and Castor always wore skinthins on duty. Alcourt required it. A small uneasiness moved in her belly, even though she couldn't think of anything she might have done wrong. He almost never called her into his office space. She was his medical aide. She dealt with his flesh, in the flesh, in the solarium or on the massage table. His virtual, web life was a separate existence. They did not overlap except in the biomed profile on her terminal screen.

She windowed the profile away and stood, wincing because her bruised knee still hurt. Pulling on her lenses, she found herself standing on an Oriental carpet in an elegant foyer. A carved oak door in front of her was closed. She looked around, surprised; last time she had seen this space, the decor had been antique Moorish. An arched ceiling of leaded glass let in soft gray light, and rain pattered gently onto the panes. Flowering trees clustered around a small stone basin, heavy with large pink and lavender blossoms, and water trickled over the worn lip of the basin to disappear into a bed of small moss-covered stones.

"Nice, isn't it?"

Jewel jumped. She hadn't heard the door open. She had heard the water and the sound of rain on glass, so her subconscious had expected to hear hinges squeak or wood whisper against the carpet. It occurred to her that he had made the door silent on purpose, that he enjoyed surprising people, the way he enjoyed seeing them walk around his holoed bushes. "It's very nice." Jewel picked up one of the polished pebbles. Gray-green moss blurred the rich earth tones of the surface, beaded with tiny droplets of water. "It's so *real.*'' She dropped the pebble into the basin and watched rings waver across the still surface.

''It's a Chen piece. He's doing a whole series of designs for me.'' Alcourt ushered her into the familiar office, with its polished agate desk, and sat down behind it, smiling gently at her.

This was the Alcourt the web knew: forty, athletic, full of energy, confidence, and power. He would never ask her to define love. Shit, she had forgotten all about that. Jewel looked down at her clasped hands to hide her expression. Maybe he would forget. This man frightened her, and the actual Alcourt never did. Which was another trick of illusion, but it was hard to catch a glimpse of the real Alcourt in this virtual persona. He had said something about that, something about armor.

''You should get yourself a Chen office.'' Alcourt picked up a carved-ivory letter opener. ''They're very creative, and he backs them with excellent software. I can have him do one for you.''

There was a malicious edge to his tone. Jewel glanced at him from beneath her lashes, wondering what game he was playing. He knew very well that she couldn't afford a custom office of any sort. To hell with games. She lifted her chin. ''What did I do wrong?'' she asked calmly.

''Wrong?'' He frowned down at the letter opener in his hands. ''This is an antique. I own the real piece.'' He spun the delicate blade lightly between his fingertips. ''It's carved from poached ivory, from the tusk of the last wild-stock elephant. It's quite valuable. You could say priceless, but there is a price for everything, isn't there?'' He laid it down. ''I put together a neat little package yesterday.'' The malicious edge was back in his voice. ''I like to do the basics myself once in a while. Just to keep in practice. According to reliable numbers, a market niche for sunscreen should be opening up in the northeastern U.S. in a few months. I've got manufacture and distribution in place.'' He steepled his fingers on the desktop. ''AllThings will make a nice little profit. What do you think of that, Jewel?''

Her package. She had sold it the previous day to a low-level node in PanEuro. But if Alcourt had moved first, profit, if there was any, would be slim. Her fragile reputation would suffer if PanEuro lost money on the deal. How could he have *done* this? Stunned, Jewel struggled to control her expression. He couldn't have accessed her actual package—it had been safely stored in a secure archive until the PanEuro node had purchased it. Had Alcourt listened in on her interview with Ishigito? Was her office security *that* crappy?

No. Jewel's face felt as still as wax. Ishigito's office would have caught a ghost even if hers had missed it.

Alcourt had done this to her on purpose.

"Do you know why I hired you, Jewel?" He leaned forward, smiling. "Partly because you are one of the highest-ranked medical aides available. But there was another reason. You know what you want, don't you, Jewel? You're willing to sell your ass to get it, but it's a contract, not a surrender. You expect a return on your investment. You're like me in a way." His smile disappeared. "You really think you're going to make it in my world, don't you?"

Jewel held his stare, cold inside. "Yes," she said. "I will."

He nodded as if he approved. "You've come a long way, Jewel Martina, and your determination is a rare thing. Most people of your class settle for complacency and escape either into drugs and virtual or into the boredom of subsidy, which is just another virtual, isn't it?" He shrugged and picked up the antique letter opener again. "I could break you," he said meditatively. "I have the time and resources to make sure that you lose even your aide status, that you never get beyond a federal subsidy. It wouldn't even be a challenge." He bent the letter opener slowly until it curved into a filigreed arch. With a tiny *snick*, it snapped. Alcourt examined the halves, his face impassive. "There's a certain . . . aesthetic in breaking something priceless." He tossed the two pieces onto his agate desktop. "Don't ever forget that."

"Are you forbidding me to broker while I work for you?" Jewel whispered, willing her voice not to tremble.

"No, or I would have said so quite clearly." His perfectly shaped eyebrows rose into twin arches. "You were sloppy. When you're sloppy in the Worldweb, you lose, and there is always someone else waiting to take your place. That is a very valuable piece of advice, my dear. Appreciate it. You can go."

The office vanished, and Jewel found herself back in the foyer, in front of the stone basin. Illusory water trickled onto mossy pebbles, and the soft sound of rain on glass filled the air. Jewel closed her hand very slowly into a fist. *There's a certain aesthetic in breaking something priceless.* Oh, yes, he could destroy her easily enough. But he had slapped her instead, the way one might slap a whining child. He had not been warning her. He had merely been . . . what? Demonstrating his power? Reminding her how insignificant she was? How the hell had he found out about that deal? Jewel yanked her lenses off. The bright sunlight of the solarium made her blink as she took off her gloves. Red half-moons from her nails marked her palms. Jewel wiped her hands on her coverall, then called up Alcourt's biochem screen.

His profile suggested excitement. Sexual arousal looked like that in numbers. "Exit to log," Jewel said tightly.

So Alcourt had enjoyed their little interview the way he might have enjoyed a quick tumble in bed. Perhaps that was the only reason he had gutted her package: so that he could call her into his office, tell her about it, and watch her reaction. Perhaps he had recorded it. Perhaps he would play it over and over, savoring her expression as he tore her package and her hope to shreds. It had been such a good tip, those ozone numbers. A real windfall. Humiliation and anger filled Jewel with vague nausea and made her voice quaver as she began to dictate her daily summary. Someday, *someday*, he wouldn't be able to do this to her. No one would be able to do it. She got up to get a drink of water, because if her voice trembled, he might hear it when he reviewed the log.

She didn't want him to hear it.

"I don't believe you." The PanEuro node steepled her fingers on the polished glass slab of her desktop. Her name was Suriyana. Thai? Indonesian? She wore a vintage Lauren Bacall Self.

"You accessed the token file. The package was *certified*." Jewel didn't try to keep the desperation out of her voice. "He must have been monitoring my filespace while I did the research."

"You *do* have security?" The node's lip curled. "I find it hard to believe that Harmon Alcourt would waste that much time on such a trivial package."

"My security is obviously inadequate." Jewel bowed, struggling with her anger. What do you *want* from me, lady? "I'm transferring your full payment back to your account." The mauve walls of the node's office seemed to be closing in on her, squeezing her. "I apologize for any . . . inconvenience my security leak might have caused you." She made her voice humble. "I hope we can do business in the future."

The office vanished, dumping her unceremoniously back into her own space. *Bitch!* Jewel blinked back tears, wanting to scream or smash something. She hadn't had to warn Suriyana, could have let her find out that someone else had contracted for the labor and marketing sources she had expected to use. Maybe she *should* have let the node take the fall. Except that Jewel's reputation would have been shot forever if a rumor went around that she'd sold the same package to two different webs. Do that, and the webs blacklisted you forever. *Bastard,* Alcourt. The tiny *snick* of the breaking letter opener seemed to echo through her room. Suddenly she couldn't take this labyrinth of deception anymore. Grabbing her jacket, fighting back tears, she burst out into the corridor, needing the harsh, healing solitude of the ice.

Outside she almost didn't take the path that led to her outcrop, but in the end she did. The lava crags were empty—no sign of the netted stranger, but why should there be? Jewel told herself that she was relieved, but she felt restless anyway, irritable. That PanEuro bitch had had no reason to be so nasty. She hadn't lost squat on the deal. A sneaky, gusty wind whirled ice crystals into the air and whined around the tortured spires of rock. Far below, a newly carved berg lifted jagged white peaks in the Ross Sea. What would it be like to stand in a rocking boat and look *up* at one of those silent, floating mountains? She had never told anyone about the ice, what it meant to her.

Thin, bitter clouds banded the horizon, bruise purple against the fiery orange of sunset. There was no comfort here today, just cold and a vista of emptiness. *You're willing to sell your ass,* Alcourt had said. Jewel took a slow breath of air that had no scent, just the burn of cold. If you had been born in the 'burbs, or the refugee camps, or on the streets of the city, you did not have anything to sell because someone already owned you—the subsidy board, or fed-med, or the dude who sold you your dose. Selling was a step up. It implied that you owned at least part of yourself, that you got something in return. Alcourt didn't know that because he didn't have to. Neither did the netted stranger.

Jewel turned her back on the cold rocks. The wind followed her back to the bay entrance, prying burning fingers beneath her balaclava, making her sore knee ache. A delivery was coming in, and the muffled thunder of heelo blades followed her down the corridor as she left the bay. More supplies. They came in daily and at great expense. In her own corridor Jewel slapped her palm against her doorplate. There would be other tips, she told herself, other chances.

Yeah, sure. She unsealed her coverall as the door closed behind her, had peeled it almost down to her waist before the intruder registered. "Shit!" She yanked it back up over her shoulders, although she still had on her skinthins, anyway. "What the hell are you doing in my room?"

A man crouched in front of her built-in drawers, looking up at her with mild annoyance, as if *she* were inconveniencing *him*. He had a young face—early twenties, no older—with a loose tail of white-blond hair that trailed forward over his shoulder. Jewel's initial rush of fright warmed to anger. In this clean world of no privacy, you didn't have much to fear from violence. Wounds made in this place didn't bleed visible blood. "House," she snapped. "Report an intruder."

"You really don't have to call the cops." He sat down on the floor, arms crossed on his tucked-up knees. "I wasn't stealing anything. I was just looking." He tilted his head, eyes laughing at her. "If you'd stayed outside as long as you usually do, you wouldn't even have known I'd been here."

"Intruder reported. Security is observing," the House announced in its mellow voice. "Do you wish to file a complaint?"

"Better not." He grinned at her. "I might be the lover of the innermost node of Epyxx, and you might end up in deep shit."

"I don't care who you are," Jewel answered, but there was a painful truth in what the little bastard had just said. After her disturbing interview with Alcourt that afternoon, she was no longer entirely sure where she stood. He might dismiss her if someone complained. "House, no complaint." She averted her face. "File a complete visual-audio record in my personal filespace."

"Visual/audio recording and saving."

"Smart move." He settled himself more comfortably on her floor. "You're lousy in virtual, you know. Ishigito read you like a script. Even with that crappy office you should have done better." His green eyes glittered. "You threw away a hot option, lady. Waste of prime info."

Jewel stared, remembering a grinning fox face and green eyes. "You skinny freak." She took a quick step forward. "*You* did it to me—the underwater virtual. You *bastard*!"

"Careful." He leapt to his feet, laughing at her again, although he put her small table safely between them. "I told you, I could belong to someone very big."

"I thought I was drowning, you prick."

"Blame David. That was his piece. I was sort of testing it for him. I guess it passed, huh? Look, I'm sorry if I scared you, but I had to do it. You blew it so *bad*, you really deserved it." He boosted himself on the corner of the table and faced her, one foot flicking restlessly. "Old Ishigito was watching you sweat. A three-year-old could tell you were hungry to close that package deal and scared you were screwing up . . . and shit, you sure were. So he put you off. He'll lose a few yen on sunscreen, but next time you'll shave your commission if that's what it takes to get him hooked. He's gonna jump you through some hoops, lady, and make yen off it." His grin revealed pointed white teeth. "He was calling up bio on you while you were showing off your numbers, but your office is such a clunk job that you didn't even know. He's got you *down*."

"You were *ghosting* me," Jewel said between her clenched teeth. "Inside my filespace." *Got* him. "I think I'll file a complaint with Security, after all." She smiled at him sweetly.

"Yeah, you're recording, aren't you? I guess you can screw me if you want to." He didn't seem very worried. "So let's deal, okay? I'll give you a few tips on getting around, and you wipe the record. It was just an accident, my wandering into your filespace."

"Oh, yeah. Like you accidentally wandered into my room?"

"Well, I *was* checking you out. It's kind of a thing with me, knowing the flesh." For a brief instant he looked almost embarrassed. "Gets me into trouble, too. Maybe I should give it up for Lent or something, huh?" He rolled his eyes. "That plastic Self you got is too shitty for words. The blond snow-queen look went out last year. You'd be okay with your flesh self." He swept her with a head-to-toe glance and made a face. "Not too bad. That gypsy face of yours might even catch on. The bod's too skinny, though."

"Get out." Jewel slapped the door, standing aside as it slid open. "If you ever show up anywhere in my private space again, I'll file charges. And use this recording to back it up. Do you understand me?"

"Private space, huh?" The grinning youth rose lazily to his feet. "Your filespace is about as private as one of David's interactives. You got a ghost haunting you nine ways from Sunday, lady."

"A ghost?" Jewel hesitated, wondering if there was any point in believing one word from this punk. "No one's been in my filespace except you."

"You're cute when you can't decide whether to be pissed or not." He tossed his head. "You better believe you got a ghost. He, she, or all of the above are practically living in your space. Where do you think your hot little tip about melanoma risk came from?"

"It came from a friend of mine. I met her during my internship," Jewel said slowly. But small doubts were surfacing, tiny questions that she had ignored because there had been no reason to take them seriously. Like why Carolyn had suddenly decided to renew their very casual friendship. Like how her boyfriend had managed to get the hot tips he had been feeding Carolyn and why Carolyn had passed them on to Jewel instead of selling them to a talk peddler herself. The face was Carolyn's, but in virtual you could look like anyone. That was why you had a good office—to tell you when the person you thought you were talking to was someone else. "Why bother?'' she said out loud, and flushed, realizing that she halfway believed him.

He laughed. ''Two and two adds up to four, huh? I guess you're not stupid, after all, even if you can't do squat in virtual.''

''Knock it off,'' she snapped. ''Who the hell are you, anyway? And why are you bothering me?''

''I'm Flander.'' He tossed his tangled hair back over his shoulder again. ''I'm a VR artist, and I'm one of the best operators in the Net. Maybe *the* best. I'm bothering you because I'm curious. Your ghost is good, and I can't figure why he or she is wasting time on you.'' He shrugged. ''I mean, what have you got to boost? Not much but that shitty office, and who wants *that*? You got to work on your body language or get a better office, lady.'' He strolled over to her kitchenwall. ''You want some tea?'' He ordered, grimaced at the tea bag that dropped into his cup, and then filled it from the hot water dispenser.

''Please feel free to help yourself.'' Her sarcasm was lost on him. Jewel frowned, uneasy. Why would anyone bother to feed her market tips? A setup came to mind immediately. But a setup for what? As the fox man had said, she didn't have much to steal. Revenge? For what? She had learned very early that enemies were expensive luxuries. Like lovers. ''All right, fox.'' She let her breath out in a slow sigh. ''I'll make a deal with you. Tell me who's in my filespace, and I'll wipe the House record.''

''Deal.'' He handed her a steaming mug of tea. ''Listen, you've gotta get better at reading Selfs or you're dead in the web. You can even figure a good edit job if you're sharp—enough to know when you're getting screwed or when your connection is maybe the cops or the competition. Shit, David doesn't even bother with an office, but David can read anybody. He's kind of talented that way.'' He shrugged. ''Sometimes you got to forget that it's all just a program, and sometimes you got to keep it right on the front of your lobe.'' He took a swallow of tea and grimaced. ''What kind is this? It's shit.''

''I don't know. It came with the kitchen. I don't like tea.'' Jewel upended her mug into the sink.

He was right. She wasn't good in VR. Her education had taken all the money she could scrape together. A public education from the Net—free for the masses, and aren't we wonderful—got you absolutely nowhere. Anything more cost, and what she had wanted cost big.

She had paid a lot for the aide patch on her shoulder. And there hadn't been anything left over for playing games in make-believe universes. Body language didn't matter in an applied-neurotherapy-techniques classroom. You only needed a hood and gloves. Skinthins were toys for the rich. Alcourt had given her skinthins as part of her uniform, and they were her first pair. They might be her last if he blew out her tailored file. She would lose her patch. Jewel's hand went to it on its own, the silk threads rough beneath her fingertips. The only way out was the web.

And this fox was telling her she wouldn't make it without a better office. And she couldn't afford a good office until she had made more money, and apparently she wasn't going to make money if she did not have a good office.

One of those nice, closed, endless circles. Kind of like the 'burbs. With a ghost in her filespace, don't forget that. A ghost could strip her account bare in a nanosecond. "Shit," she said softly.

"Yeah." Flander's eyes had gone dark. "That's life, isn't it? And if you go down, you stay down unless someone comes along to pick you up by the scruff of the neck. Mostly, no one bothers. They just step over you." He bared his teeth at her. "You got the talent, lady. You just don't know what to keep track of, what the other dude's office is looking for. You can do okay without a decent edit protocol as long as you know what they're reading for. I think I'll give you some pointers."

"Oh, sure." Jewel leaned her hip against the counter, trying to make some kind of sense of this guy. "For a price, right?" she asked warily. "Up front? That's the next line, isn't it?"

"Nah." He hopped lightly down from the table and was at the door before Jewel could speak, quick as a fox on his feet. "For free." He grinned his fox grin, teeth glinting. "Your ghost is pretty good, and I'm going to have fun tripping it up. I don't get too many challenges, so I'll owe you. A few tips'll settle us."

"Modest, aren't you?" Jewel snorted.

"I don't have to be. I'm the best." He winked and vanished like a shadow through the doorway.

Of course she couldn't possibly believe one word of all this. Jewel chewed thoughtfully on her lip. She knew him, kind of. He had street written all over him, so how the hell had he gotten *here*? Well, hell, *she* had gotten here. He had something to sell to somebody down here. She shrugged and turned her back on the closing door. Immature, a punk . . . and maybe as good as he said. He had crashed her virtual, had dumped her into his ocean, and her security hadn't even noticed.

For that matter, he had broken into her room, and Complex Security was a hell of a lot better than what she could afford for her personal filespace. "House?" She frowned. "Review stored visuals onscreen. Last hour only, fast forward, no sound." She looked at the flat, blue square of her terminal screen. The room appeared, translated into two dimensions. No fox brat. Jewel frowned as she watched herself open the door, quick-march in, and talk animatedly to the empty air.

Damn. The little bastard was as good as he had said. Jewel wondered what would happen if she told Security someone was pre-editing the video tracks. If the brat had left evidence behind, he would be seriously up the creek. If not . . . She shook her head. She had a feeling he hadn't, but she could try holding it over his head if he bugged her anymore. And maybe, he could teach her something. She needed it. He was right.

"We'll see." The words sounded too loud in the empty room.

Why was someone ghosting her filespace? And why had they handed her the melanoma prediction? A "*who*" might clear up both answers, but she couldn't come up with anything no matter how much she racked her brain. Restless, she prowled her small space, closing the drawer Flander had left open, dropping the dirty cups into the recycle slot. His fox Self fit, she thought sourly. It was as if a wild animal had prowled the room, sniffing and pawing at her things, not doing any damage but leaving its spoor behind. This room had been a retreat, a place of safety and privacy of a sort. She didn't invite people here casually. The room felt strange now. Violated. Or maybe it was just her worry about who was looking over her shoulder and why.

Questions, worries, and she didn't have any answers. Not yet, but maybe this fox would sell her some. Flander, that was his name. Jewel stripped out of clothes and skinthins, wrinkling her nose at the sour-sweat smell. She tossed them into the sonic cleaner in the kitchenwall and went into the bathroom, wrapped in a towel because the echoes of Flander's presence still lingered. She showered quickly and put on clean clothes: a loose gray-green shirt, cut long enough to hide her butt because she wasn't cruising, and orange tights with a tracery of fiberlight embroidery up one leg. The colors brought out the olive tint in her skin, but down here it was okay. An ethnic face didn't get you killed or even hassled very much. Jewel sighed and smoothed back her hair. She needed a beer at the TimeOut. There would be people she knew, other aides who might know about this fox brat and who he belonged to.

She could ask about the netted Asian dude with the braid. If she wanted to.

With a shrug and a last wary look around, Jewel left her apartment. "House, record and file any intruder," she said before the door closed. Probably a waste of time, but it might give the fox a little trouble if he tried to get back in. She had to find out who was in her filespace—if anyone was there. Jewel let her breath out in a sigh. Extra Security cost big. And she was already spending to the limit for Net time.

Damn, damn, damn. She walked quickly down Mirny. At least she could afford beer. One or two, anyway. That was about it right now.

Chapter Three

Mary Rosenblum

David Chen sat down on a thick ledge of virtual ice and propped his chin on his fist. The vast ice cave arched meters above his head, its farthest reaches lost in shadow. Thick spires and buttresses of clear blue ice jutted from the walls, polished to a wet sheen, carved into fantastic whorls and arches. A thin slick of water puddled on the smooth floor, and the metronome tick of dripping water rang through the cavern. David shivered in the chill, although the cold was only suggestion, an electrical tickle of modulated frequencies and amperage changes transmitted by his intradermal net. Because he was sitting in an ice cave, he felt cold. If he had been sitting in a desert scene, he would be sweating, his flesh fooled into reaction by the visuals.

It was pretty damned easy to fool the flesh if you got right down to it. And not only in virtual.

David sighed and ran his finger along the ragged gouge that zigzagged across a graceful curtain of ice. This piece hadn't been out on the Net long; only a few people had stumbled onto it yet. Chips of broken ice lay on the floor beside a virtual hammer and chisel. More tools lay on the ice beside him: hammers, an ice pick, a wire brush, rasps. Whoever had gouged the ice curtain had smashed one leg of a fragile arch and hammered cracks into some of the buttresses.

The damage swirled rage across the surface of the ice like oil rainbowed across a puddle. David tilted his head, surveying the effect. It changed the direction of the piece. He got to his feet, tugging at the long braid of his hair. Try this . . . With one finger he smoothed away the small cracks that radiated from the gouge. Better. It gave the damage more impact. He wandered through the cave, softening or erasing some of the chips and cracks, deepening others, leaving some untouched. Carefully, he enhanced the edges

27

of the shattered arch so that the broken pieces gleamed like icy daggers in the muted, directionless light.

Perhaps a human figure or two, frozen into the ice . . . He reached into the largest of the buttresses and began to shape a face. It took on form: a man trapped in the ice, frozen in an eternal struggle to scream. Yes, this piece was taking a dark and angry turn. Because of his unknown collaborator? Or was some of that anger seeping up from inside him? He withdrew his hand from the cold grip of the ice, staring into the face of the trapped, frozen man. Yeah, some of it was his own. He reached into the ice again.

"I'm sorry to interrupt you," his House program spoke up. "But Shau Jieh would like to talk to you."

Shau Jieh? David frowned and let his hand drop. His youngest sister was one of the few people for whom his House was instructed to interrupt him in his studio. He sighed. This piece was starting to *work*, and for a moment he hesitated, half-tempted to have his studio tell her he wasn't home. Within the ice the trapped man's lips were drawn back from his teeth as he strained in anguish for a last glimpse of vanished sky.

She would know if he told the studio to lie. She always knew. "I'm coming." David sighed, deciding to leave it for now and see what happened next. "Exit," he said. A doorway opened in the ice wall, and he stepped through into the light and air of his studio. A black and white cat leapt down from an old-fashioned steam radiator and arched against his leg. Absently, David reached down to pet it, feeling cat fur beneath his fingers because that was what he *saw* and his brain had to interpret the stimulation from his net somehow. Sometimes he wondered if the flesh world was any more real. You touched someone, and your brain interpreted *hair* or *hand*. Your endocrine system reacted, and you thought *sex* or *love*. But what was really there, behind the visual and tactile? Anything?

Enough. David tossed his braid back over his shoulder, annoyed at himself. His sister's visits always did this to him—turned him introspective and cynical, as if he had to examine himself for her, grade himself. Or something. David reached for the ice-cave doorway and squeezed it down to a canvas, a painting of an ice cave done in thick brushstrokes of blue and white. He racked the canvas among the others that lined the wall. The cat had leapt back onto its radiator and was contentedly washing its face. "Exit to office," he said. A plain birchwood door appeared in the studio wall.

"Hello, Youngest Sister." He held out his hands as he came into his office, glad to see her in spite of her interruption.

"David." She embraced him, smiling, a finger width taller than

he, although she looked shorter. "I love to come to your office."
She ran her finger across the surface of his desk. It was a thin slab
of milky jade mounted on salt-bleached driftwood. "It's so lovely."

She used the Self he had designed for her: her own face, but done
from memory so that recall softened and shaded realism. *It's too
beautiful,* she had said when he had showed it to her. *I don't look
like that. You do to me,* he had said, and it was true. Shau Jieh was
the only one of his three elder half sisters with whom he had ever
been close. She had not been angry when he had left the family
firm to pursue his art. She had guessed how much it had cost him
to walk away, and she got along with Flander, too. More than the
rest of his family did, anyway.

"So, how are you?" David drew her over to the thickly piled
carpets beneath the fern wall. Orchids bloomed amid the feathery
leaves, brushing Shau Jieh's face as she sat down beside him. "How
is our father?" he asked. It always amazed him how easily he fell
into formality when he talked of the family. *Is he still angry at me?
Do you think he'll ever forgive me?* Those were the questions that
he wanted to ask her. That's us Chinese, he though wryly, although
actually he was only half-Chinese. Always too formal.

Shau Jieh smiled with his brief laugh, but her eyes brimmed with
sympathy. "Fuchin is tough," she said. "He'll live to be a hundred, you'll see. He still runs the firm with a grip of iron. Poor Dà
Jieh." She pretended interest in a delicate cymbidium blossom.
"She has a hard time making him listen to reason."

Which meant that no, Fuchin had not forgiven him for quitting
the firm. And that Dà Jieh was in trouble. Again. David sighed.
"Youngest Sister, what's wrong?"

"You read me so easily." Shau Jieh bent her head over the orchid.

"I read you so easily because you let me." David lifted her chin
so that she had to meet his eyes. "Don't play the shy blossom with
me, Youngest Sister. You flutter around Fuchin like a mindless
butterfly, playing dutiful daughter. But *I* know better. You're the
only reason Chen BioSource still exists. If you didn't always defuse
the family politics, it would have come unglued a long time ago."
He smiled. "Dà Jieh owes the existence of her precious company
to you, and she'll never admit it. So what kind of help do you need?
I hope it's not money, because I won't have much until after the
next gallery show, and then only if it's a success."

"No, I'm not asking for money. You're right, of course. Eldest
Sister is never going to admit that I'm anything but a butterfly.
Sometimes that's to my advantage." Shau Jieh smiled briefly, but
her eyes were worried. "No, money won't help this time." She

fingered the cymbidium absently. "I think Dà Jieh is manufacturing illegal drugs in her lab."

"Dà Jieh?" David stared at his sister, wanting to laugh. "My so-upstanding, righteous sister?"

"Don't, David." Shau Jieh drew a long breath. "Last year went badly. Dà Jieh put all our resources into a new strain of krill, specifically designed for seeding into Tanaka Pacific's Antarctic ocean lease. Everything else was put aside because it would double their harvest in less than a decade and they were willing to pay a lot for it. It was a safe venture, Dà Jieh told us. Because the genetic combination was an accidental discovery and no one would think of trying anything like it."

"Only someone did." David felt a weight settling onto his shoulders. This was almost a replay of eight years ago, only then Dà Jieh herself had leaked her own research notes to destroy Chen Bio-Source. She had done it because Fuchin had intended to give the controlling interest to David. He had bribed Dà Jieh with his share of the firm and had walked away from the family forever. Because he could not do art and run a company, too. And because Dà Jieh cared as much about the company as he did about his virtuals. Dà Jieh was the son Fuchin wanted, not David. Only David doubted that the old man would ever understand that.

Shau Jieh was nodding as if she had been following his thoughts. "Oceans BioTek came out with an almost identical model," she said sadly. "It was ready months before ours. You know how careful Dà Jieh is with her trials."

"And you didn't have a solid contract because Fuchin hates to deal with Japanese firms," David said bitterly. "So Tanaka bought BioTek's model. Why does this make you think Dà Jieh is tailoring drugs?"

"She loaned the company enough money to cover our debts." Shau Jieh would not meet his eyes. "Investment windfalls. And she is . . . protective of her research lab."

"She never lets *anyone* into her lab. What else is new?"

"David, stop *fighting* me. You know how much custom neuroviruses bring on the market. She could do that in her lab. Easily. And the penalty is death. Death." She clenched her fists. "Don't you care, David?"

"Shau Jieh. Youngest Sister." David put his hands on her shoulders—gently, but she gasped and widened her eyes as if he had shaken her. "I do care," he said in a low voice. "I think I proved that eight years ago."

"I'm sorry." Shau Jieh opened her hand, looking sadly at the ruined orchid on her palm. "I know you care, but I'm so worried. I love her, even if she is difficult at times. She has so much *pride*. It drives her, and . . . she made a mistake with the krill. It was Fuchin's mistake, really, but she's made it hers, and now it's eating her. She'll risk anything to make it up." She dropped the crushed blossom onto the carpet between them. "The money didn't come from investments," she said softly. "I checked, and they're fakes. Very good fakes, but fakes—meant to cover up the real source."

"*You* checked?"

Shau Jieh blushed. "I hired Flander to check. I thought he might have told you."

"No, he didn't tell me." David got to his feet and paced across his office. It felt too small suddenly, claustrophobic, a closet space of unreality. "I don't understand. What can *I* do?"

"Talk to her, David."

"What?" He stared at her. "You can't be serious. She won't listen to me." His sister's body language was unedited, and he examined her face, hoping for hesitation, for a sign that she didn't really mean this. Her expression was implacable. "Shau Jieh, I can't do it." He sighed and sat down again. "You don't understand what . . . happened between us."

"That you caught her setting up Selva Internacional's lawsuit against us? That you trapped her into obedience with the gift of your company shares?" She smiled at his shock. "I have always been able to read *you*, Little Brother. And I have always been able to read Dà Jieh. I guessed what had happened, even if you wouldn't tell me." She took his hand, stroking his palm gently. "She will hear you, and it will shock her that you know. It will make her angry, but it will make her see what she is doing with new eyes. Clearer eyes, I hope. Will you do this for me, David?" Shau Jieh's voice trembled just a hair. "I love my sister."

It was Shau Jieh who had made his life tolerable as a child. Without her, he would have drowned in the bottomless swamp of his father's expectations. "All right." David sighed, knowing that he would regret this. "I'll talk to her, but I don't think it'll change anything."

"Thank you, Little Brother." David raised his hand to her face and kissed it gently. "Do you need money?" Her eyes searched his face. "I could lend you some."

"No, I'm not broke." His smile felt strained. "The last couple of gallery shows didn't do as well as expected, that's all. We . . . haven't had another offer yet. We'll get one, one of these days." From a smaller gallery, perhaps.

"I'm sorry. David, your gallery pieces are so *wonderful*."

Not wonderful enough. How much of that was Flander's absence? Flander hadn't put much into the last two pieces. He had been spending most of his time in the Net, playing games that he didn't share with David. David swallowed, tasting bile. How much of their combined talent actually belonged to Flander? He lay awake some nights, wondering and hating himself for wondering. It was what they did together that mattered, not who contributed how much.

"I'm working on something new," he said quickly. "Interactives. I start with a created milieu—the latest one is an ice cave— then I put it on the Net. It's open; anyone can get in. But I don't advertise where it is. People find it and drop in. I've left tools available so they can experiment. Make some changes. I shepherd things along a bit, work the piece in the direction it seems to want to go. It's interesting." He shook his head, remembering the shattered arch and the resonant anger. "The pieces are constantly in motion. They're never the same for long. It's . . . frightening to have so little control. And it's exhilarating." He smiled. "I never know what I'm going to find."

Shau Jieh touched his cheek. "I love to watch your face when you're talking about your work," she said softly. "I know I asked you to do a hard thing. Thank you, David."

He kissed her gently on the forehead, as if she were a child instead of a very competent woman who perhaps saw the flesh world more clearly than any member of his family, himself included. Perhaps one day he would ask her what she thought of himself and Flander. Perhaps. "Wish me luck," he murmured.

"I wish you much luck," she said in precise, formal Mandarin. She bowed, her eyes still worried above her smile. Then she walked through the door of his office and closed it behind her.

David sighed again, wishing that she were here in Antarctica or he were in LA and they could go sit together somewhere, just sit and *be* there, in the flesh. Yes, flesh was real. You had to believe that it was real, because if you didn't, then life was nothing but a handful of deceptions and what the hell did any of it matter? He spread his hands on the jade slab of his desk. The inspiration that had moved him in the ice cave had evaporated, leaving in its wake a thin restlessness. He should call Dà Jieh. The thought of speaking with his eldest sister made his stomach clench, but he had promised.

Without warning a red fox darted out from beneath his desk. It leapt up onto the desktop with a flick of its tail, sat on its haunches, and grinned at David. "Yo." It lolled its tongue out over its white teeth. "I'm back in the flesh, and you look pissed. What's up?"

"Hello, Flander. Exit," David said. The office vanished, and the pastel walls of their leased Erebus apartment appeared around him. Flander was standing in front of him, head tilted, frowning as he pulled off gloves and lenses.

"You look upset. Your sister always does that to you." He tossed his unruly hair back over his shoulder. "She's the best of the lot, too. Maybe you ought to change your access code, tell 'em all to take a hike." He tossed gloves and lenses onto one of the floor cushions and wandered over to the kitchenwall. "Tea?"

"The rest of them never bother me, and I like Shau Jieh. No tea, thanks." David dropped onto a cushion beside the low ebony table in the middle of the room. "She told me she hired you," he said slowly. "To check out our sister's investment portfolio. You didn't tell me."

"You didn't ask me." Flander stared into his mug of tea. "Hey, you wouldn't believe what these kitchens stock for tea if you don't custom request. It doesn't come off any live bush, that's for sure. Maybe they use old penguin feathers or seal shit." He sipped his tea and nodded. "I didn't tell you because it was *my* contract." He rolled one eye David's way, and David could almost see fox ears flatten. "You didn't tell *me* when you took that contract with Alcourt to do holos down in this frozen shithole. In the flesh, no less. Like we're fucking *mechanics*."

"I did tell you." David looked away, lips tight. "As I recall, you were doing kickers at the time. That might have had something to do with your not remembering." The new tailored neuro-viruses were hot on the illegal drug market. Kickers. The cutting-edge operators used them. In effect, the kicker chemically isolated part of the mind; the operator could then download data directly from the Net, using a photostimulation pulse focused on one eye during the virtual connect. The effects were individual and intense as the brain processed the massive dump of information. Results varied from flashbacklike intrusions and blackouts to permanent psychosis and catatonia.

"Alcourt offered a *lot* of money. You didn't have to come."

"David, you're still pissed at me," Flander said softly. "I quit, remember? I promised you."

"Yeah, you did." Wanting to believe him, David traced the delicate grain of the polished wood with one fingertip. Dead tree flesh. He took his hand away abruptly.

"Hey, come on. Quit." Flander knelt behind him, putting his

hands lightly on David's shoulders. "I know I haven't been doing much with our stuff for a while. I got into messing around in the Net . . . and I just kind of let it take over. I'm sorry I left you stuck, but I came down here, okay? I've been working on the holos with you, and I *hate* holos. You're the one who's good with holos." His voice had gone low and rough. "Look, I know I don't think about anybody but me sometimes. I'm sorry, David, I am, but I don't think I'll ever be much different."

He was massaging the tight muscles of David's shoulders and spine with his long, slender fingers. David sighed and leaned his forehead on his fist, knowing that the touch was partly manipulation, a way to distract him from his anger. Flander had grown up on the street, selling whatever could be sold. He knew all the subtle and less subtle ways to use the flesh to get what he wanted.

No, it was not entirely manipulation. There was a trace of anxiety in his touch, too, a child's nervous worry at incomprehensible grown-up anger. It scared him when David got angry, never mind that sometimes he needled David unmercifully. It was as if he needed to prove to himself over and over again that David wasn't going to throw him out no matter what he did. Sometimes, poised between love and the desire to kill Flander with his bare hands, David caught glimpses of the fragile, wounded child who hid beneath Flander's adult facade. Maybe one day that child would grow up, but it hadn't happened yet. Flander needed him. He needed someone, anyway.

And how much did he need Flander? How much did he depend on the crazy sparks of Flander's inspiration to catalyze his own work?

Too much?

Midnight questions again. David let his breath out in a gusty sigh. "You're right. I *do* get like this when Shau Jieh calls, don't I? Let's not fight." He leaned back against Flander's touch, making himself relax. "Thanks for doing the search for her, anyway. She's worried about Eldest Sister. Shau Jieh thinks she's selling kickers."

"Could be. She's making enough money." Flander's hands paused. "How long is this holo job going to take, anyway?"

"Not long." David looked back at him, hearing restlessness in his voice, feeling it in his touch. "You don't like it down here."

Flander's eyes flickered. "You can't get *away* from anybody in these damn tunnels. I feel like I'm trapped."

"Claustrophobia?" David read genuine distress in Flander's posture. "You could get a temporary suppression from the shrink."

"Huh-uh. I *like* small spaces. That's not it." Flander looked around, nostrils flaring as if he were scenting the cool, sterile air. "There's no place to go here. You can't get away from all these flesh bodies. I mean, you can go outside, but it's colder than shit. Hey, never mind." He shrugged and got lightly to his feet. "We won't be here that long, and I'll live. Here." He collected two more mugs of tea from the kitchenwall and handed one to David. "Have you noticed the aide who works for Alcourt?" He perched himself cross-legged on the table. "You've been over in his space."

"The red-haired muscle boy?"

"No, the woman. Jewel Martina." Flander combed his fingers through his hair, yanking at tangles. "She's a clod in virtual, but she's sharp for all that."

"I haven't seen her." David sipped his tea. "I want you to come over and take a look at the desert piece I'm working on. It's a holo-stationary mix, and it won't come together for me. Maybe something'll bother you and it'll shake loose."

"Yeah, okay." Flander shrugged and grimaced. "Maybe tomorrow, when this Jewel's on shift. You ought to meet her."

"How come?" David looked up and caught the glint in Flander's eyes. "What are you up to, anyway?"

"She's got a ghost in her filespace." Flander grinned his fox grin. "She halfway thinks it's me, but it isn't. I know who it is, but I'm not going to tell Martina yet. I want to know why this operator's wasting her time playing guardian angel to some nobody aide." His grin widened. "I think I'll find out."

It was a game. David sipped his cooling tea. They all played it, the men and women like Flander who lived in the Net and resided only reluctantly in the flesh world. Prestige was the coin of their universe. They counted coup when they could, doing no particular damage, just tweaking people, letting others know that they had been in and out of their spaces, untagged. David stared into the amber depths of his tea and stifled a sigh. Well, it might keep Flander happy while they finished the holo work for Alcourt. Flander was always happy with a new puzzle to unravel in the Net. David let his mind drift.

He had worked yesterday's virtual recordings into the ice cave, but he needed more imagery. Perhaps he would go back out onto the ice tonight, staying well clear of that woman's private rock pile. He still couldn't figure out what he'd done to piss her off. David shook his head, smiling wryly. He'd been recording when she had showed up at the rocks, and he had a great visual of her reaction to his voice: head lifting, body turning. He had shut down as she fell, so he had only that brief vignette, a startled moment of surprise and defiance. That was *her* place; you could see it in every movement of her body. He wished now that he had recorded her in the entry bay as she stripped out of her suit.

Her profile was incredible: a strong sweep of nose beneath a high forehead, prominent cheekbones, and a wide mouth. In no way beautiful by this year's standards and certainly not a gene-selected package. But she was striking. He couldn't place the phenotype, had thought Hispanic at first, but now he wasn't so sure. Her face had a Mediterranean flavor to it, with maybe a few Mayan genes from Guatemala to give her that nose, all mixed and toned down with a solid dose of Caucasian blood. He wondered suddenly how she would fit into the ice cave. She wouldn't be trapped in the ice. Not her. David tugged at his braid, running over that quick, defiant lift of her head, envisioning her within the ice wall. The ice cave was part of a glacier, and maybe she commanded its flow as it scoured the surface of the planet. No, she powered it—demon and angel with a single soul. A heart of ice and heat enough to melt the whole glacier; yes. That might just work . . .

"Show me." Flander's green eyes were fixed on David's face. "Show me what you're seeing," he said softly. He touched David lightly on the knee. "It's good. I can tell."

David smiled slowly. "Not yet," he said. "But it's getting there." He reached for his lenses and tossed Flander his set. "Put your gloves on," he said. "And I'll show you."

Chapter
Four

Jewel dreamed, knowing she was dreaming; she was floating somewhere, a disembodied pair of eyes, or awareness, or memory. Huddled beneath the ragged sleeping bag on the mattress below the window another Jewel, a skinny, tanned-dark Jewel with a thick braid of hair, cuddled spoon fashion against Linda. Floating, watching, she was also aware of the warm press of Linda's back against her just-starting breasts, of the curve of Linda's buttocks against her bony thighs.

I don't want to dream this, the observing Jewel thought—not in words but in a brief, sharp chord of sorrow and pain and nostalgia. Then she was sliding into the sleeping Jewel, sucked like smoke into the feel of warm skin and cold, slippery fabric, into the twinge of pulled hair where her braid had caught beneath her shoulder . . . Jewel blinked awake, that watching Self fading out like a note of music in the air, half-heard, half-remembered. Jewel reached for the white plastic container that she had tucked between mattress and wall, then froze as Linda murmured and wriggled deeper into the covers.

Don't wake her. Don't make a sound or Rio will hear. Not Kerry, Linda's mom. She slept like the dead after her shift, snoring so loudly that you could drop the house on her and she would never wake up. Clutching the container against her chest, Jewel tiptoed past the bedroom where Rio and Kerry slept, holding her breath, not scared exactly because Rio did not scare her with his sticky paws and his big grin, even if he scared Linda. Jewel slipped out through the door, which had been broken in a fight a month earlier and not fixed yet. It was cloudy outside, gray and soft, never mind that it was almost summer. She stood barefoot on the cracked concrete porch in front of the old tract house, prying at the lid of the container. It looked just like the tubs of soy paste that Kerry got at the subsidy center. The name *Martina* had been scrawled on the top with a marker.

Her mother's ashes.

The lid popped off, and she nearly dropped the whole thing. Mama's ashes filled maybe half the container, gray and coarse like dirty sand. There was so little left . . . Fascinated, she poked a finger into the stuff. Gritty. She made a face. Linda wanted her to hike way out to the old cemetery on the hill and find a place to put her mother's ashes. She wanted to do a funeral, and she wanted Jewel to cry.

But Jewel couldn't cry. She jammed the lid back on and ran down the long street, past the burned-out foundations left over from the street war with Little Cambodia, past old Robert's garden with its barbed wire fence and the dog that would go for your throat or for your balls, or at least that was what folks said. Linda didn't understand that her mother had been dead for a long time, had left behind a flesh ghost, an empty shell that lived only for the next dose. Jewel hopped over a tangle of rusted metal and half-burned plastic in the street and dodged around a clump of thistles growing up through the cracks in the asphalt. At the corner she stopped and looked back.

The house squatted on its foundation, its roof sagging in a weary slump, mangy like a dog's back with patches of missing shingles. Kerry would sleep till noon after her all-night cleaning job, sprawled on the mattress that stank of piss because something was wrong with her bladder and the clinic couldn't or wouldn't do anything about it. Rio would be up before Kerry. He would be surly because he had been drinking backyard booze the previous night. Another day, same smells, same words. It had seemed like a safe place after their life on the streets—a place to stay. And Linda was a friend, which was a new thing, a precious thing. But it wasn't safe. They just lived the same day over and over again, and it would never stop, never be tomorrow.

A thick surge of loathing rose in her throat, and Jewel gagged suddenly, imagining herself vomiting blood into the dust—thick, shiny, bright-red blood. "No way." She straightened, wiping her dry lips. "Not us, do you hear?" She raised her voice, not sure whom she was speaking to, not sure if anyone was listening. Maybe no one was listening. Jewel wrenched off the container lid. "We're not going to get stuck here!" She shouted the words at the blank blue sky. "Do you hear me? We're getting out, Linda and I, and we're never coming back!" The ashes fountained into the air as she flung them at the sky, pluming on the morning breeze, sifting to the earth again like a blessing . . . or a curse. There wasn't much left when you died. Only dust and empty space. "I swear it." Gray dust coated her palm, and she wiped her hand across her cheek, marking her face—with death or life, take your pick. "I swear it!" she yelled at the sky, and blinked awake.

In her bed in Erebus, of course, not under a sleeping bag on a mattress . . . Gray light seeped through the holo windows, the first hints of the artificial dawn. Jewel sat up abruptly, catching a whiff of her own sweat. She had been almost twelve that day. Linda had just turned eleven. Jewel touched her cheek, half expecting to feel gritty ashes beneath her fingers. *I swear it . . .*

Jewel flung the sheet aside and padded naked over to the kitchenwall. Why this dream? She ordered coffee, tapping her fingers impatiently while she waited for it. She never dreamed about the 'burbs, didn't think about them. Or about Linda. It was Alcourt's desert garden—that was what was making her dream. It had summoned the past, conjured it to haunt her in an instant of remembered heat and thirst. Jewel sipped her coffee, burning her mouth, letting the flood of taste and pain drive the dream fog out of her head. Get a pill from the infirmary, she told herself, but she didn't like drugs. They had claws to snag a person. Damn Alcourt and his desert. Damn Chen for making it so *real*.

The light had been growing in the windows, fake dawn brightening to fake morning. There was something on the floor in front of the door, a shape of wrongness. Jewel sucked in a quick, shocked breath as it came into sudden focus. A body, curled into a loose fetal ball. Pale hair gleamed as the windows brightened, and she recognized him suddenly; the fox, Flander.

Oh, my God . . . She stumbled across the two meters of carpet, and dropped to her knees beside him. He was twitching, his body shaking with hard, fine tremors. Grand mal seizure? She lifted an eyelid; pupils wide but reactive. Shit, why *here*? She scrambled to her feet, angry, afraid, because if this guy mattered to people and they got pissed at her, she could be in deep trouble. She yanked open the cupboard beneath the terminal and grabbed the medical remotes.

Shaking out the tangle of leads and fabric with a flick of her wrist, she wrapped the neck cuff around Flander's throat, then sealed it. Air hissed softly as it inflated and vitals popped up on her terminal screen. Pulse 165, systolic blood pressure less than 90. Jewel sucked in a quick breath. *Dying.* How did he get in here? The terminal beeped: the microcatheters in the cuff had failed to worm their way into his jugular vein. Of course. With his blood

pressure that low, his venous system was in a state of collapse. This
was *major* shock. The tremors had stopped. Cold, Jewel watched
his chest rise, fall, rise again . . . He stopped breathing.

"Medical intervention initiated," the House voice murmured.
"Stand by, please."

Flander was bad enough that the remote program had tapped one
of the Complex's full-fledged MDs. No time. Jewel grabbed Flander's chin and titled his head back. Tongue clear . . . She breathed,
watched his chest rise and fall, breathed again. It was hard to force
air into his lungs. She breathed again.

"This is Dr. Chirasaveena." A clear, slightly high-pitched voice
came from the speakers. "I have dispatched a transport crew to
bring the patient into the infirmary. I need an ID, please."

"His name is Flander." Jewel gasped between breaths. "I don't
know him." Breathe . . . "He's in shock. No respiration. I
need—" Breathe. "—epinephrine."

"I see." Dr. Chirasaveena's voice chilled. "I've dispatched—"

"*Now!* I'm a licensed aide. Check. He'll be dead in a minute."
Breathe. "I accept responsibility for it, okay?" She was not going
to let the fox die just because this prick wanted to cover his ass.
The terminal chimed.

"Your epinephrine is available in your kitchenwall." The doctor's tone was icy. "Your acceptance of risk has been filed."

She bolted to her feet, ignoring him. The syringe was waiting
for her—every kitchenwall was equipped with a secured supply of
emergency medication. She stripped the cover from the needle. No
time to try for a vein; with pressure that low, she would never hit
one in time. She opened Flander's mouth, pulled his tongue up.
Lots of vascularization here. You got a quick high from using a
street patch under here, priming it with a little DMSO. An old
trick. Lips tight, she injected the epinephrine.

Flander gasped as it kicked in, then shuddered. Come on, fox.
Jewel tossed the syringe aside. You don't get to die on *my* floor.

The House chimed. "David Chen is at the door."

Jewel blinked. David *Chen*? As in Chen desert scene and expensive offices? Flander had said he was a VR artist, but . . . David
Chen was the David he'd mentioned? Jewel realized with a sudden
jolt that she was still stark naked. Flander drew a shallow, gasping
breath. Where the *hell* was her robe? There, down on the floor
behind the futon. She grabbed it. "Let him in."

He was through the door before she could get it wrapped around
her. Silver threads glittered in his tawny skin, and the thick black
braid hung down over his shoulder. The stranger from the ice.

Jewel's eyes widened. *He* was David Chen? His eyes flickered in an instant of recognition, and he nodded. Then he sidestepped her with quick grace and sank slowly to his knees beside Flander.

"He said he was clean," he said softly to no one or everyone. He touched Flander's face gently with silver-netted fingers. "I believed him. Is he going to live?"

Calm voice, tortured eyes. He thought it was an OD. Maybe. The seizure suggested kickers, and he might be deep enough into the Net to be doing kickers. But something had sent him into shock, and kickers did not usually do that. "A team is on its way," she said. "To take him to the infirmary."

He understood her evasion for what it was. Jewel looked away from his anguished face. She recognized the look in this man's eyes. You saw it in the 'burbs, in the eyes of mothers or lovers. It was grief, a tired, angry, hopeless grief for the blade or the OD that was going to happen. It was grief for tomorrow and the heavy knowledge that no one, not even God, could stop that final tomorrow from coming.

It was not a look she had expected to see, not on the face of this man with silvered skin, heir to the virtual world where anything was possible. Jewel let her breath out in a rush. "He'll be all right," she said, although even here that was not a sure thing.

"I hope so."

Meaningless conventional words, and they both knew it. Jewel turned as the door opened to admit the transport team, followed by a gurney. The two techs bent over Flander. Their terse professionalism shut out David and Jewel, pushing them away from Flander like the expanding skin of a tough, invisible balloon. Jewel found herself pressed back into the corner beside the futon with David. He stood stiffly, almost unaware of her as the gurney settled to the floor beside Flander. The techs ran an endotracheal tube down his throat with smooth skill and hooked him onto the respirator. David made a small sound in his throat as they shifted Flander onto the padded deck of the gurney and strapped him down. One of the techs cursed softly as he struggled to get an IV running. The other was applying patch 'trodes, slapping them onto Flander's head and torso. He would have a hard time dying now, even if he wanted to. When he got to the infirmary, he would be safe, assuming he had adequate medical coverage. And down here he must. It was a given.

"I'm coming along." David stepped forward.

The taller of the two techs shrugged and whistled two notes. The gurney lifted itself and trundled after them like a ponderous, obedient dog. David walked along beside it, one hand resting lightly on Flander's shoulder. The door closed silently, and it was over. Faint morning bird song filtered through the fake windows. Dewdrops sparkled on grass, and a robin probed for worms on an unreal lawn. "Blank windows," Jewel snapped.

So that was David Chen. *The* David Chen. Jewel stared at the soft gray of the empty windows, remembering the sound of his voice when he had said *You have to be here*, out on the ice. Strange words for a man who lived in virtual. Jewel shook her head, realizing that her hands were trembling a little. Reaction and low blood sugar. She was used to quiet, orderly dying, not this. Not in her bedroom. What the hell had brought the fox here to OD on her floor? She didn't need this. Jewel let out an angry breath as she prowled through her tiny apartment, retrieving her skinthins from the back of a chair, ordering more coffee from the kitchenwall. Chen's face haunted her, his expression as he squatted beside Flander. Jewel pulled on her skins, frowning. She'd thought that you left that kind of grief behind when you escaped the 'burbs. What place did it have in these privileged corridors? What did netted artist David Chen know about it? She stepped into her uniform coverall.

"David Chen is at the door," her House intoned.

What now? Jewel squashed a twinge of apprehension. She had done everything right. "Let him in."

He stepped through the door before it had finished opening. Shadow pooled beneath his cheekbones, giving his face a tight, gaunt look. Dark circles hollowed his eyes, and he looked as if he had lost pounds of weight in the last half hour. "Come in," Jewel said, and felt immediately stupid, because he was already in. *The* David Chen. The emphasis blurred the memory of the man who had shared the ice with her and had waited patiently for her to finish staring at his netted hide. "Would you . . . would you like some tea?

"Thank you." He sat down at the table, dropping into the chair as if his legs could no longer support his weight. "Did Flander say anything about what might have happened?"

"No." Jewel handed him a steaming mug. "He was already unconscious when I woke up. I would have told the doctor. I'm sorry."

"Of course you would have." David gave his head an impatient, sideways shake. "I apologize. I was up all night working, and . . . I'm not quite tracking anymore. I'm sorry to bother you." He looked around with a slightly dazed expression as if he couldn't quite remember how he had gotten here. "They kicked me out of the infirmary. I can't see him . . . until he's stabilized. I should go back to our apartment,'' he finished reluctantly.

The fox was his lover. Jewel went back to the kitchenwall, not so nervous anymore. David Chen, maybe, but his pain was real familiar, oh, yes. She ordered a breakfast plate and stuck it into the microwave to thaw: bagels and salmon spread—fake salmon even here, because she wasn't about to waste her pay on real farm-raised and certified toxin-free fish. ''You'd better eat something.'' She plunked the plate down on the table in front of him. ''It might be a while.''

''That's what they said. Thanks.'' He took a bagel and stared at it. ''I went out recording yesterday,'' he said in a flat, exhausted tone. ''I stayed away from your rocks. I'm sorry if I insulted you in the bay the other day.''

''You didn't,'' she said, and earned herself a brief, sharp look. ''All right, you did. Sort of.'' Because he had talked to her like a peer and had known that she was not. ''It wasn't important.'' She picked up a bagel and bit into it.

''Things like that are always important.'' He stared at his own bagel with a slightly puzzled expression, as if he couldn't quite identify it. ''I was recording, yes, but I didn't get much of you. Mostly parka.'' He tried for a smile and almost made it.

He thought she was pissed that he had recorded her? ''I didn't even know you could record.'' She blinked. ''I never thought much about it, how you get the scenery for virtual. I guess I thought someone just . . . made it up. Like a painting.''

''It works something like that.'' David shrugged. ''I start with recordings, sort of like a palette of colors, only I'm using visual/tactile/audio.'' He laid the untouched bagel down, turned his hand over, and stared at his open palm. Reflected light ran silver across the fibers in his skin, and a fine white scar curved across the base of his thumb. The silvery fibers looked thicker at the edge of the scar.

''What happens when you cut yourself?'' she asked, curious. ''I don't even know how a Kraeger net works.''

''They inject a dividing ovum with engineered epithelial cells. The fibers are actually part of my epidermis. They grow back with the skin if I get injured.'' He rubbed the scar gently. ''The subdermal jewels and the primary interface chips are added later. They collect the signals from pressure, temperature, and muscle-tone changes, boost them, and transmit.'' He smiled faintly. ''I carry a lot of embedded hardware here and there.''

He had lost a little of his glazed look, as if the tech lecture had taken his mind off Flander for a few moments. Embedded hardware. Jewel suppressed a brief shudder. Linda carried implanted monitors in her flesh. She was a licensed surrogate, carrying contract babies for women who were wealthy enough to hire out the physical discomforts of pregnancy. They had fought about it the night she had told Jewel, but it had been too late. She had signed the contract, and the surgery was already scheduled. Jewel stared at the blanked windows without seeing them. She had gone into a teaching model, had watched a team of surgeons implant the necessary hardware into a woman who had looked like Linda. There were a lot of ways to sell your body. Jewel put down her uneaten bagel and discovered that David was watching her.

"The main reason I came by was to thank you," he said. "For your prompt action. I think—it was close."

Yes, it had been close. If she had slept another fifteen minutes . . .

"ODed?" Jewel pushed away the rest of her bagel, not hungry anymore.

"Yes." A dark history coiled inside that single syllable. "It upset you," David said softly. "I'm sorry."

Yes, it had upset her. Jewel tried to hide her surprise; she hadn't realized it until he had said it. It had brought back too many old memories. Maybe it was that desert—it had all started there. "I've got to get ready for work." A lie, but it gave her a reason to escape this silver-netted man who had opened the door to yesterday. She retreated into the bathroom and closed the door, staring at her reflection in the mirror as she combed her thick, short hair, waiting for him to take the hint and go.

Her skin was tawny, light enough to pass for suntan in the white neighborhoods. Her face was the risk, not quite Hispanic, not quite white. Her mother had had light hair and blue eyes. *You look like your father,* she had said, and even as a small child Jewel had heard the lie in her voice. What the lie covered up, she had never been able to find out. Screw the past. Jewel tossed her comb down. Forget it. Get back into the Net again. You look ahead, not back.

Yeah, get into the Net and find out how much damage Alcourt had done her.

Jewel shoved the bathroom door open, expecting to find the room empty, because a three-year-old would have gotten the message. It wasn't empty. David sat slumped at the table, head pillowed on his forearm, sound asleep. Even in sleep he looked strained and exhausted. She opened her mouth to call his name, to wake him, then closed it without speaking. Love cost. It was a pricey luxury, like good skins or virtual time. Like a Kraeger net. David's eyelids fluttered, and he made a small sound of protest in his sleep. Jewel sighed. The infirmary would call him through her House when they had reclaimed Flander from death. No privacy in this place—they would know where he was.

The room was still nighttime cool. Jewel sighed again, took the tumbled spread from the futon—the spread she had used to cover Flander—and draped it across David's shoulders. Now it *was* time for her shift. She took one last look around her invaded, compromised space, then palmed Alcourt's door. Security opened it for her and closed it behind her, locking her into Alcourt's bright world of illusion.

Afternoon sun filled the holo windows of the private infirmary room. David sat beside Flander's bed, watching him sleep. Hooked, snared, tethered to life by catheters and leads, Flander was being dragged slowly, inexorably back into the world of the living. David stretched his tight shoulders, head aching from his brief sleep in Jewel Martina's apartment. He hadn't meant to fall asleep, had no memory of doing so. Her House had wakened him with subsonics and the infirmary's summons. She had already left to go to work or simply to escape him, he didn't know which.

At the head of the sterile white bed the console hummed to itself as if it were pleased at yet another victory over death. Catheters dripped colorless fluids into Flander's veins, and more tubes carried away the excess, as if Flander had become nothing more than a living filter, straining a few nutrients and necessary chemicals from the flow of liquid. At least they had been able to remove the respirator tube. Flander was breathing on his own again.

He had nearly died this time. David shifted on the chair, vaguely aware of his full bladder, the uncomfortable press of the chair seat against the backs of his legs. Holo windows showed him a cheerful scene of green pastures and a line of willow trees in the distance. Pure white sheep grazed on the lush grass, and lambs frisked. It was only a so-so rendering, but David felt a sudden fierce longing to step through that window out into the grass, to walk to that willow-edged creek and stare down at his reflection in the water.

Where could you find a scene like that? Not in the icy landscape above their heads. Not in the dry reality of diminishing rain, vat-grown soy, and fake meat. Jewel Martina's windows had been blank. He had noticed them when he had woken up and had wondered why. He touched Flander's cheek gently, reassured by the console's soft hum of triumph. Flander looked thin on the white-sheeted bed. David could see every rib, and his bones looked fragile, as if someone could snap his arms and legs bare-handed. David's father had looked like that after his heart attack, small and shrunken on the white sheets. He had never quite recovered. In the family scenes Shau Jieh had downloaded to him, Fuchin had always looked so *old*. As if his heart attack had sucked the strength from him.

Or had it been the loss of his son that had aged him? He would never understand that the David Chen he had created, the dutiful, obedient son he had believed in, had never really existed. David sighed. Two David Chens could not coexist in the same world. One of them had had to end—David Chen the son or David Chen the artist. He had made his choice to save the family company for his father. He had destroyed the lesser virtual to save the greater. No, that was a lie. He had made the choice as much for himself as for his father. And he wondered sometimes if he had made a mistake. Perhaps Fuchin would grieve forever for that lost virtual son.

"Thinking about . . . your dad?" Flander's whisper was barely audible.

"It's about time you woke up." David bent over the bed, shaken by the intensity of his relief. Deep down inside a hidden part of him had not been sure, no matter what the doctor had said.

"You couldn't have been what the old boy wanted. You would've tried . . . and hated it . . . and he wouldn't have been any happier. And the real part of you would . . . have died." Flander lifted a hand to David's face, faltering, as if the catheters taped to the back of his wrist were lead chains.

"How did you know I was thinking about Fuchin?" David took his hand, careful of the tubes.

"You get this . . . sad look. Like it's your fault, and it isn't, only you won't let yourself believe it." Flander moved his head restlessly. "What happened?" He plucked at the tangle of tubing. "I can't . . . remember."

"You ODed." David looked away from his pale face. "On a kicker. You went into anaphylactic shock. Jewel Martina found you in her room when she woke up."

"Jewel? Why'd I go there?"

"I don't know." David laid Flander's hand gently down on the sterile white sheet.

"David? I'm . . . sorry. I promised you I was through."

David kept his eyes on that thin, long-fingered hand with its tracery of blue veins.

"I meant it . . . but I *need* it. I can't handle the flow without it, can't you understand?" He touched David's arm, a spidery, importunate scratching on his skin. "I can almost let go, get out of the flesh, you know? People can . . . hurt me in the flesh," he whispered. "Not even you can stop it, David."

"That was a long time ago. When you were a kid."

Flander moved his head in a weak negative, but he didn't let go of David's arm.

"You've lived with me for eight years," David said gently. "I haven't let anyone hurt you." But Flander's eyes were closed, and he didn't answer. David sighed. Flesh was a weakness to Flander, a vulnerability that David had never quite understood. Once he had asked Flander, *What happened to you, before I knew you?* thinking that together they might get to the root of that fear. *Don't ask,* Flander had said. *Just don't ask me, please?* And his eyes had been the eyes of a cornered fox, ready to bolt or bite.

So David had let it drop. Now he brushed a wisp of hair back from Flander's face, wondering what would have happened if he had pried at Flander's fear. Healing? Maybe or maybe not. He'd been afraid that if he pushed, that cornered fox would bolt.

"I'm awake." Flander's eyelids fluttered open. "How soon do I get out of here, anyway?"

"A couple of days." David managed a smile at his familiar, reassuring impatience. "The doctor wants to keep you under observation for a while."

Flander scowled and tugged at one of the IV catheters.

"I still have to finish that desert holo for Harmon." David made his voice cheerful. "By the time you're ready to get back to work, I'll be through with it. Then we can finally get started on that new gallery piece."

"Yeah." Flander squirmed again. "Listen, can you get Jewel to come visit me?"

"Jewel Martina? I can ask her." David raised his eyebrows. "How come? She doesn't seem to think she knows you."

"She knows me better than she guesses." Flander gave David a sideways look. "You know, you ought to talk to her. You'd like her. Like I said before, she's a together lady for all she's a klutz in the web."

"We met."

"Oh . . . yeah. I forgot." Flander let his head fall back on the pillow. "I bet she was pissed," he said faintly.

"Yeah. She was pissed." David stared at the gamboling lambs, wondering who she had lost to an OD. Someone important. Her image hadn't quite worked in the ice cave, but he knew her better now, and now it would work. Yes . . . "You owe her a major apology.'' He looked down at Flander. ''And stay out of her space. She's a private person.''

''So I'll apologize. I need to talk to her.'' Flander fingered the catheter again.

''About your friend the ghost in her space? Don't touch.'' David took Flander's fingers away from the tubing. ''You're going to set off a dozen or so alarms.''

Flander did not answer. His hands had gone limp in David's grasp, and his eyes had closed. Asleep? A little worried, David touched Flander's throat, reassured by the steady pulse of blood beneath his fingertips. The console hummed to itself, singing a song of life. No alarms, no hurrying staff. Asleep, then, and he needed it. David took his hand away from Flander's throat and stood up. He would go put in a couple of hours on Alcourt's pesky desert garden. Maybe it would work for him this afternoon.

David paused in the doorway. Flander's head lay turned to the side on the pillow, his features slack. He had the look of a drowned man, a body washed up on a snow-white beach. *Stop it.* David shook himself, but the image persisted. This time he had lived. Next time? He and Jewel Martina had both known that there would be a next time. They had both known what the final outcome would be.

Yes, she had lost someone this way. He wondered who it was and how much she blamed herself. He shook himself and hurried off to hunt for the soul of a desert beneath the frozen skin of a volcano.

Chapter
Five

Jewel closed the door of the solarium behind her, tired to the core of her being, tired in a way that had nothing to do with the flesh. Alcourt was a pain today, preoccupied, full of a controlled, needling rage. It was an immature version of his cold anger in his virtual office, like a kid's temper tantrum. Not as frightening but more wearing. She let her breath out in a sigh. His biochem profile was erratic, and nothing she tried stabilized him. Which upset him, of course, because he could access his own files and did, and he could interpret the numbers nearly as well as she could. Which made his mood worse, which screwed up his biochem even more. And he blamed her. Of course.

"Shit," she said out loud, not caring if he was listening in. Right now she didn't give a damn.

Only she did care. Jewel pressed her lips together. She gave one hell of a big damn, because reality was reality, and she needed the next paycheck to pay for her Net time, so swallow it, honey, and shut up. Think about something else. Like the fox. She had messaged David Chen the previous night to find out how Flander was doing. She had intended it as some kind of closure—He ODed on my floor, and now I've asked about him, so we're quits. But David had been in his apartment or had been monitoring his mail. He had answered her in realtime, telling her that Flander wanted to see her. About her ghost, David had said.

Her ghost. Another headache, as if Alcourt's mood were not enough.

She didn't want to go see the fox, didn't need to sit by his bed and try not to notice death hovering at his shoulder. She didn't have to do it—she didn't work for him or for David Chen, and Alcourt could probably care less if she was rude to his artist.

There was a ghost in her filespace.

It might be nothing more than Alcourt, playing games.

Or it might be a lot more. She couldn't afford the Security to check on the ghost herself or wall it out. The fox owed her, she told herself, and if he was willing to pay up, she was willing to take it. Jewel hesitated as she approached the desert room. Every time she walked by, she felt as if something or someone were watching her. She had dreamed about Linda again last night. The 'burbs were a desert in their own way, and Linda was lost in them. No, not lost. Linda had made her own choice to stay. Jewel shook her head, as if her thoughts were flies that could be chased away. No flies in these clean rooms. Only memory.

A shadow moved in the desert room, a flicker at the bare edge of vision. Jewel looked, the hair on her neck prickling for no reason at all. There were video eyes everywhere, and nothing could really hurt her. Nothing there. Of course . . .

Wrong.

David's holos merged the physical rock and sand with a sweeping holographic vista of mesa, sage, and sky. In that unreal distance something moved, a shadowy drift of tawny motion that vanished before her brain could sort out the image. A huge cat? Jewel shivered, then laughed at herself. So David had added some wildlife to the scene. To keep the lizard company. Or maybe Alcourt had asked for it. Maybe lions and tigers would start leaping out at unwary visitors. Escalation in a private war of illusions? And who was the enemy?

The desert floor was empty now, baked by sun, filled with the dry whisper of the wind. The lizard wasn't out on its rock, and nothing moved. On the far side of the corridor Jewel could see into the holoed dining room. A vase of fresh, pink tulips stood on the polished, unreal table. Too much illusion in this place. Jewel looked once more into the desert garden and discovered that she was holding her breath.

No glimpse of cat fur and stealth. The lizard was back on its rock, flicking its tongue at her. Big deal. Jewel shrugged, tired, irritable, and sick of tricks. Was Alcourt watching her on the monitors, smiling at her flinch? She was tired of jumping through hoops. Jewel stomped down the corridor and slapped her palm against the doorplate, bursting out of Alcourt's space and into her own room.

Only it *wasn't* hers. Not yet. Alcourt owned it, too.

Go and see the fox. Find out who the hell was playing games in her filespace before she lost everything she had worked so hard for. Jewel walked through her silent apartment, past the windows where an unreal evening sun gilded an unreal green lawn. She didn't stop to change out of her uniform; a medical aide patch would give her a little bit of leverage in the infirmary. As she turned down Mirny corridor, a suggestion of movement behind her caught her eye. She turned, but there was no one there. The corridor was empty, its pastel walls blank and shadowless in the bright, directionless light.

Why did the afterimage on her brain suggest a huge, slinking cat?

Because she was tired and there were too damn many holos here. She didn't look over her shoulder again on her way to the infirmary. Not once.

Jewel did not like the infirmary. It was a small facility, pleasant, carpeted, and decorated with holos designed to soothe the spirit, because this was Erebus Complex, after all, and not a fed-med clinic. Jewel followed the nurse down the short hall to Flander's room, walking stiffly. In spite of the luxury, it reminded her too much of the clinic where an unsympathetic doctor had passed sentence on her mother. Perhaps it was the smell. The fed-med halls smelled of piss and disinfectant and suffering. This place smelled of flowers, but beneath the sweetness the smell was the same.

"Good thing you showed up now and not later," the nurse said as they reached Flander's door. "The patient is scheduled for release tonight. After the doctor checks him over." He palmed the door open.

Flander had a whole room to himself. He looked thin and fragile on the white sheets, his arms strapped to the bed frame with gently padded restraints. Tubes snaked from the backs of his hands to the squat guardian console at the head of the bed. Remote monitors patched his scalp and torso like leeches, and dark shadows stained the skin beneath his eyes. He grinned at Jewel, though. It was a faint echo of his fox grin but recognizable.

"About time you showed up." He tugged at the restraints. "Make them take these off, huh?"

"They're there because you pulled the IVs out again." The nurse spoke to Flander as if he were a disobedient child.

"Jewel's here." Flander winked at her. "She'll make me behave."

Light words, but his eyes had a trapped-animal look to them. "I won't let him touch anything," Jewel said to the nurse.

He frowned. "You better keep an eye on him. We had a hard time getting the drips restarted." He released the restraints and stalked out of the room.

Jewel sat down in the wood-framed, cushioned chair beside the bed. In the clinics the chairs were plastic and mostly cracked. "You're a jerk," she said.

Flander rolled one eye at her. "You've got your lines wrong, lady. You say, 'Poor thing, how are you feeling?' and I say something clever, like 'awful.' "

"David feels like shit."

"Don't lecture me, okay?" He plucked at the catheter taped to the back of his hand. "I *know* he feels like shit, all right? I know a hell of a lot better than you do just how bad he feels. And I feel like shit for making him feel like shit. Is that better? Are you satisfied? Oh, yeah, and I'm sorry I passed out in your room. I want out of here." He tugged at the tubing again, winced, and glanced nervously at the door. "I *hate* places like this."

He didn't hate it; he was scared. She knew what fear looked like in this kind of place. She knew what it smelled like. Dark hematomas blotched his skin where he had torn out the IV tubing. "If you don't like it, lay off the home-cooked kickers." Jewel didn't try to keep the disgust out of her voice. "Then you won't end up here."

"We're full of sympathy, aren't we? I didn't do home-cooked shit." Flander bared his teeth. "All right, I've done it before, gone into something that looked good and was crap. I mean, you can't really get into VR without the kicker, not like I need to. But this time the stuff was *real*. Custom fit to the body chemistry. No major risk. This time it wasn't my fault." He looked up at the corner of ceiling and walls, his lips tight. Then he fumbled at Jewel's wrist, clutching it weakly. "Someone tried to kill me," he said softly.

"What are you talking about?" Jewel let him pull her closer, not sure if he was putting her on, half expecting him to laugh and toss a punch line at her. "Who? Why would anyone try to kill you, Flander? You're such an angel."

"Shut up." Flander's nails dug into her. "Not out loud, lady, and I'm not joking, okay? They'll be listening, and I don't know who. If I knew *who*, I'd do something about it."

Drug demons were dancing in his brain. Jewel pressed her lips together, pissed at Flander, who was going to catch up with the death he was chasing sooner or later; pissed at David Chen, who had the bad sense to care about him; and pissed at herself for being here at all.

"You can't tell David," he said softly. "He might believe you, and this isn't his problem. He'll just get hurt if he tries to mess with it, because he doesn't know his way around for shit." His eyes bored into hers, glittering like backlit emeralds. "If . . . they do it, next time, I want him to know that I didn't kill myself. He'll blame himself if he thinks I did it, and it's not his fault. Tell him that. Tell him that he's the only good thing that ever happened to me in my life, and I give him shit for it. And I'm sorry." His eyes darkened and took on an unfocused glaze. "He's a hot artist," he mumbled. "He doesn't need me, he just thinks he does. I don't want to hurt him . . . Don't . . . let him . . . mess with it."

"It's all right." Jewel's eyes narrowed. Was that a sedative kicking in? "They're going to send you home later. David's coming to get you."

"It's not . . . all right."

"Who are you afraid of?" Jewel asked, but his eyes had closed.

Jewel laid his hand down gently. Getting to her feet, she prowled to the head of the bed. Standard console. They were never voice-controlled because doctors and nurses didn't want patients to overhear their commands. The touchscreen was mounted on the back side, out of patient view. She frowned for a moment, then touched up the menu. Current medication . . . ah. With an effort, she did not look at the corners of the ceiling where Security had surely mounted its optics.

Yes, someone had just sent a hefty dose of sedative down the tubing and into Flander's veins. She didn't know the prescriber's ID code. One of the doctors? Why sedate him when he was about to be sent home? When he had a visitor? She touched the screen blank again.

The door opened. "What are you doing?" the nurse snapped. "Don't touch that."

"I was just looking." Jewel shrugged. "His blood chem has certainly improved." Jewel walked back around to the side of the bed and sat down in the chair. He had known before he had opened the door that she was at the console. So he had been watching. "I told Mr. Chen that I'd wait here until he came for Flander."

"I'm sorry." The nurse's eyes flickered from Jewel to the console, then to Flander's sleeping face and back to Jewel again. "Dr. Chirasaveena's on his way, and he'll want to examine the patient in private."

"Does he usually examine his patients while they're sedated?" Jewel rounded her eyes, presenting a mask of innocence to the man's scowl.

"I don't know." His voice went very smooth. "*I'm* just a nurse."

And you're just an aide, so what the hell do *you* know? Jewel smiled sweetly for him: fuck you. He got the message. He had a fiberlight inlay on his left cheek: a dagger and a rose that glowed bright silver and magenta against his darkening flesh. I didn't say a word, sweetheart, so you can't, either. Security is watching and listening, and who knows, Alcourt *might* file a complaint if you're rude to me for no reason. "I'll be going, then," she said as she got to her feet. "I'll tell Mr. Chen that he's sleeping peacefully."

"That's fine. Do that." His eyes skewered her, cold as ice.

Jewel smiled again for him and for Security, watching the dagger wiggle as he forced a return smile. She wondered what his ID code was. Who had sedated the fox, and why? Too much illusion here, and maybe some ugly reality. Jewel shifted restlessly, wondering if she should try to stay. A holo window in the wall showed her lush grass and fluffy sheep. It looked flat and artificial after the powerful reality of David's desert.

The nurse was tapping his foot, waiting for her to leave. What could he do right here, under Security's watchful eye? She walked past his scowl, chin up. Maybe she was getting carried away. Flander was scrambled by whatever drug he'd done. Paranoid. The console had probably been programmed to sedate him any time his blood chemistry indicated agitation. He had been agitated enough, and this was not her business.

Thinking this, she stopped at a corridor terminal and leaned into the privacy shell. "David Chen, please," she said. "Personal mail." And hesitated because she was buying trouble. She didn't know shit about David Chen except that he liked to walk on the ice, too, and that he cared about this crazy fox. And that wasn't enough. She had learned a long time before that it paid to keep a low profile. Jewel opened her mouth to cancel the message. Too late. The screen blinked and filled with David Chen's face.

"Jewel?" His head was tilted slightly, as if he were looking upward, backed by an out-of-focus tan blur. "Were you trying to reach me?"

Was he monitoring all his messages? She hadn't expected a real-time response. "I just visited Flander." She paused, groping for an evasion, trapped by his onscreen face and the terminal cameras that were feeding her image and indecision to him. "I . . . need to talk to you." The words came slowly, reluctantly.

"How about right now?" His eyes were worried. "I'm working on Harmon's desert. Can you come here? I've been editing holos, and it'll take me some time to get them sorted out and filed."

That damn desert. That was why his head was tilted—he was looking up into the security eyes mounted on the wall. And he couldn't see her face because there wasn't a wallscreen in that room, and this booth wasn't equipped for holo transmission. Jewel closed her eyes briefly, pissed at herself. She could tell him right now and stay out of that bloody desert. Only maybe someone had been listening in on her visit with Flander, had perhaps ordered that sedative to shut hm up, and this was a public connection. Jewel shook her head impatiently, wondering if the fox's crazy paranoia was contagious. "I'll come by," she said, and sighed. "If Mr. Alcourt will let me in."

"Thank you," David said gravely. "I appreciate it."

Her last hope was that Alcourt's door would not open for her. She wasn't on shift, and he might not let her in. You didn't just walk in and out of his space.

No such luck. The door opened obediently to her palm, letting her into the entry and the room full of holoed bougainvilleas. Slowly she walked down the hall to the desert doorway. David sat cross-legged on the sun-scorched, expensively real desert sand, naked above a pair of gray tights. His chin was propped on one fist, and he was wearing virtual lenses.

He stretched out a hand, pointed, made a grabbing motion, and then pulled off his lenses. "Thanks for coming by." He rose in a single lithe motion, eyes on her face. "I know you're off-shift. I usually file edits as I do them, but this scene is beating me. I get sloppy when I get frustrated." He tossed his braid back over his shoulder with a twist of his head. "How was Flander? Restless?"

"Yes, but someone gave him a sedative." He was watching her intently. Jewel edged into the room, searching the sun-scorched landscape. No sign of a cat. "That mountain lion startled me this afternoon." Mountain lion? she thought with a twinge of unease. Why mountain lion? It had slipped off her tongue, but she hadn't really seen anything more than a shadow.

"I guess it's a good thing they've got him sedated. Flander's not cooperating, from what I've heard." David sighed, rubbing at the marks the lenses had left on his face. "I'm supposed to keep him in bed and plugged into the remotes." David laughed shortly. "Ordinarily I'd have to sit on him, but the threat of going back into the infirmary might keep him down. So what's wrong, Jewel?" His smile vanished. "What's so important that you didn't want to tell me from a public booth?"

He was reading her as if he were an office. Jewel flushed. "Flander told me someone set up that OD on purpose." Oh, shit, it was such a *lame* excuse, and here she was, passing it along. "And no,

I didn't believe him,'' she said quickly, pissed at the fox, pissed at herself for listening to him at all. ''And I still don't think I do . . .''

''But?''

She looked away from his dark, intent stare. ''But—someone sedated him while he was telling me,'' she said reluctantly. ''There was no particularly good reason to do it. Although it might have been some kind of programmed medication regimen. That might explain it. But I thought I'd better tell you . . .'' She gave up, tired of stumbling over her tongue.

''Watch out.'' He put out a hand as she stepped backward. ''That rock's real—don't trip over it.'' He frowned, not at her but at something only he was seeing. ''He makes excuses. He makes up stories like a little kid,'' he said softly. ''But it could be real. He . . . ghosts around in the Net. He steals information for the talk market. He doesn't tell me because he knows how I feel about it, but I know he's doing it. He lived with a woman when he was a kid—one of the top operators in the Net from what I've picked up. A serious pirate. He learned from her, and I don't think he'll ever quit ghosting. Money's not the issue. I'm not sure what is.'' He tugged at his braid, eyes on her face. ''This garden makes you uneasy, doesn't it? Why?''

''It shows, huh?'' A small pool of water glimmered next to her beneath a screen of thirsty willow. Frowning, Jewel picked up a smooth brown pebble and tossed it into the pool. It splashed into the water; droplets spotted the stones at the edge of the pool, and rings wavered across the still surface. She leaned over to touch the water, feeling nothing but warm air. She stared at her dry palm. ''How did you make the rings? And the drops?''

''There's a chip inside each pebble.'' David gave her a crooked smile. ''The pool senses the pebble and generates the rings. And the splashed water.''

''I'm impressed.'' She tossed another pebble into the unreal water, watched more rings spread. ''This room . . . reminds me of something, and I don't know what. Something happened in the desert a long time ago,'' she said slowly. ''I'd forgotten about it until I walked into this room. I still don't remember what it was, and I'm not sure that I want to remember. It scares me.''

''I think you've just given me what I need.'' David stared into the sun-baked distance, frowning a little. ''Yes, I think it'll fix this,'' he said softly. ''Maybe.'' He shrugged and gave her a crooked smile. ''I guess I'd better tell you that I borrowed your likeness. I've been working with an interactive, and I used your image in it.''

"My image?" She blinked. "I don't understand."

"It's part of an ice-cave sequence. If you'd like, I'll download the address to your filespace." He cleared his throat. "As long as I've put the time into creating a physical likeness, I thought I'd have Flander install it onto one of his offices. He does a good custom office when he feels like it, and he was grumbling about how you had a cheap model. It's a fee for using your image, a little more than usual because I used it without your permission. I hope it's enough."

He was offering her something that only the Alcourts of the world could afford to buy. Jewel touched her cheek, hesitating. David Chen had made a judgment about her—about what she was, what she meant to this ice cave of his—and he had put that judgment into the Net. Strangers would look at her. She lifted her chin. It was only her image. A trick of illusion, like the bougainvilleas. And she needed a good office. "I accept," she said. "You can use it."

"Thank you." He bowed slightly, as if she had just done him a favor. "What mountain lion holo were you talking about, by the way?"

"The one in here." Jewel nodded at the distant rocks. "It was slinking around earlier."

He was shaking his head. "Not mine," he said. "Maybe Harmon was playing with something he had on file, but if so, it was a temporary overlay. No mountain lions in my desert. Wrong ecosystem. Which I guess is a silly conceit, considering that this is all make-believe, anyway." He was staring at the real stone where the unreal lizard sometimes sat. "Flander told me once that I'm too stuck on reality. He's right, but it sells well in the decorator market. Flander's the one who takes off on the crazy tangents. He's a genius, even if he doesn't like to hear me say it. Our art works because it's a combination of my reality and Flander's inspiration. I don't think either of us would do half as well on our own. And he's trying to kill himself."

I want him to know that I didn't kill myself, Flander had said.

"Why?" Jewel asked.

"I don't know." Very deliberately, David smashed his fist down on the lizard's rock. "Maybe it comes from his past," he said softly. "Maybe it comes from inside himself. Maybe it comes from me."

He'll blame himself . . . and it's not his fault.

"No," Jewel said. His hand was bleeding. A thick drop of blood fell, making a small, dark spot on the ocher sand. "It doesn't come from you."

"Doesn't it?" He whirled and seized her arm, eyes blazing. "And just what makes you so sure?"

His grip hurt. "Flander told me," Jewel said coldly. "He said you were the best thing that had ever happened to him and he gives you shit for it. Let go of my arm, please."

He released her abruptly, going as pale as if she had slapped him. "He said that?" He looked out into the desert, his eyes as opaque as bits of obsidian. "I don't know if it's true or not." He wiped his hand on his thigh, leaving a smear of blood on his tights. "I'd better get this editing saved, since I'm supposed to be at the infirmary in half an hour."

"Good night," Jewel said.

He was putting his lenses on, and he didn't answer.

Outside, the corridor was empty and silent—no sign of either Castor or Alcourt—and for that she was deeply grateful. With a sigh of relief, Jewel palmed her private door and escaped. The fox was David's burden, and he was welcome to him. She stripped off her coverall and peeled out of her skins. David's grip had left a bloodstain on the thin fabric just below her elbow. She tossed them into the cleaner on her way to the bathroom and stepped into the shower.

He cared too damn much about the fox, that was clear. He cared too much, period. Jewel turned her face up to the spray, letting the warm water wash off the sticky residues of the day. She soaped and rinsed herself, frowning. Maybe that was why she had told David about the desert when she had refused to tell Alcourt. Alcourt had wanted to enjoy her reaction; David had wanted to understand it.

It occurred to her that the expensive office was a gift, a thanks for plugging Flander into the remotes in time. If he had offered it to her as a gift, she would have refused it. Gifts carried a hidden price tag, and sometimes you found out too late that the gift was not worth the price.

Jewel shivered, although the jets of air blasting from the dryer nozzles were warm. She felt transparent around David Chen. Maybe he could read minds.

No, or he would have known what kind of drug the fox had done.

It was past dinnertime, too early for bed. Jewel thought about going down to the TimeOut for a beer, but she didn't feel like being around people tonight. She put on a loose shift, then ordered a realtime exterior view into the windows. The icy slope of Erebus filled the room with a harsh orange light that made her squint. Out of sight, the sun burned its way along the horizon, never sleeping, banishing darkness and dreams. No mountain lion had ever walked on that frozen snow. Where had it come from? One of Alcourt's tricks? Had he been playing games in David Chen's desert? Of course, she told herself—but the words brought no comfort.

It had been there and it belonged in that desert no matter what David said. It belonged in *her* desert. Her past. She was sure of it, and that certainty scared her. What made her so sure it was a mountain lion? The alien light stabbed into the room, filling it. Jewel prowled into the kitchen, not hungry, too restless for holovid, not interested in one of Castor's virtual adventures, thank you. She drank a glass of water, deciding to go to the TimeOut anyway. By now the crowd would have thinned out. After a beer or two, maybe she could sleep.

"David Chen is at the door," the House murmured.

What now? She almost told the House to say she wasn't home, but in spite of the bright, unforgiving light, shadows lurked in the corners, furtive and catlike, waiting to slink closer. "He can come in," Jewel said, suddenly wanting company, conversation, *someone*, even sharp-eyed David Chen. Maybe he could tell her where holo ended and ghost began. Sure.

"Thanks for letting me in. I know it's late." He was wearing a green tunic over his tights, and he carried a covered plate. "The doctor won't let Flander go until morning. Flander's pissed as hell. But Chirasaveena said he'll only have to stay on the remotes for a few days after his release, so that helped." Shadows still darkened his eyes in spite of his cheerful tone. He lifted the cover on the plate. "These are phoenix-eye dumplings. My sister downloaded the recipe to my kitchen when I first came here. She worries about what I eat." He gave her a tentative smile.

What was he *doing* here? The tiny cups of crispy dough held some kind of spiced filling. Jewel picked one up, her stomach growling at the rich, garlicky scent, reminding her sharply that she hadn't eaten since her light lunch. She took a tentative bite, her mouth filling instantly with the flavors of shrimp and ginger and others too subtle to identify. "These are wonderful," she said with her mouth full.

"Classic dish." David bowed. "We Chinese love food and family." He looked at her sideways. "It's a flat-out apology. For my . . . rudeness in the desert. I'm not at my best when I'm frustrated about a project—that's not true. I was angry."

"I was pissed at you, too."

"Yes, you were." David gave her a quick, thoughtful look. "Why?"

The harsh light from the frozen skin of Erebus filled the room, banishing illusion, compelling truth. "Because you love the fox," Jewel said. "Because you can afford to love him."

"And you can't afford love?" David's eyes pinned her.

She looked away, angry all over again, because that was not the issue. "You started this," she said bitterly. "You and your desert."

"I don't understand."

"Neither do I, all right?" She had shut yesterday behind a thick door. Somehow his desert had opened it. "I think you'd better go." She handed him back the plate. "Thank you for the food."

"Excuse me," the House intoned. "A Susana Walsh-Reyna is calling. Shall I put the call onscreen?"

Susana Walsh-Reyna? Jewel felt a rush of giddiness, as if the floor had moved beneath her feet, as if Erebus were erupting.

Linda's daughter.

Something had happened to Linda. Dear God, how could *anything* go wrong, with all the hardware Linda carried? How had she gotten Jewel's address . . . it couldn't be her . . . "Yes," Jewel heard a voice say. Her voice, but so strange that she wondered if the House would ID it. "Put her onscreen."

The face on the terminal's screen shocked her. She had been expecting a child, but the thin girl who faced her was fifteen, maybe sixteen. Had it been that long? She was dangerously tan, her face slashed with a diagonal band of white untanned skin. Turf mark. 'Burbs kid. Her coppery hair was pulled tightly back across her skull and bunched into wired braids at the back of her neck. They fanned out in stiff loops, accentuating her jutting cheekbones and the hollows of her face.

She looked like Linda.

"Aunt Jewel." She didn't smile. "You got to come back."

"What?" The words made no sense, none at all. "What do you mean? What do you want?" Jewel groped for words. "Where's Linda?"

"Home," Susana said coldly. "I wanted to *look* at you, and the house isn't wired for visuals, remember? This access costs, lady, so listen. Carl got hit by a car. He can't walk, and Linda's coming unglued. She losing it fast, do you read me? She needs help, but *she* won't ask. So I'm doing it."

Help? Linda had been the strong one, the rescuer. Carl paralyzed? He had been the reason they'd drifted apart . . . Jewel shook her head, not really able to comprehend it. Linda was part of memory, part of yesterday.

A shadow from that desert?

"You mean money, right? You're asking me for money." The

words came at last, stumbling and rough. "I can send something. I—I'll need to talk to Linda."

"Screw money." Susana's eyes were as cold and hard as the frozen Antarctic sky. "She needs *you*, but you got out, and you're not dumb enough to come back, right? So, good for you. But I asked. Because Linda calls you sister, *Aunt* Jewel. Maybe she believes you're her sister, but I guess you know better. See you around."

"Wait!" Jewel said, but the screen had gone blank. Damn, damn, what did the brat mean? How could Linda need her? They had gone their separate ways years ago. Sisters . . . "House, place a call," she said, although it was late there, very late. "To Linda Walsh."

"Accessing." The House went briefly silent, then: "No realtime response. Do you wish to leave a message?"

The house probably had only basic service, if it had service at all. The lines were bad in the 'burbs, old telephone lines full of noise. Linda could be there right now. Jewel clenched her teeth, suddenly afraid. Afraid that Linda might answer, afraid of what she might see on her screen.

"House, yes. Leave a message."

"Linda?" Jewel drew a deep breath, wanting to look away from the cameras that were recording her face, transmitting it across the planet. "I . . . haven't heard from you in a long time. Susana called. She says that Carl is hurt." The words felt so *awkward*. Rough and lumpy as stones. "Listen, call me. I'll take the charge. It's free for me," she lied, remembering Linda's pride. Did she still have it after all those years in the 'burbs? The words were running out fast. What could she say? "Linda, I'm so sorry. About Carl. Please call me. House, end. Send it." How could Susana have gotten that old? Jewel covered her face with her hands, staring down at the thick carpeting between her spread fingers. "House, accept charges for any messages from Linda Walsh. Forward them to me with a priority interrupt."

"Understood." The terminal screen darkened. Nothing to do now but wait for Linda to call.

"Jewel?"

She flinched at David's touch. She had forgotten he was there. "I can't go *back*." Her words tumbled out, razor-edged. "What the hell good would it do? Carl hates my guts. I'm not going to comfort *him*, and Linda doesn't really want me there, fighting with him." She could send money from here. That would do the most good.

She needs you, Susana had said, with her young, so-certain judg-

mental face. Need? What did that child know of need? Linda was
a solid, rational woman. She had made her choice, just as Jewel
had made hers. She had chosen Carl, had shut Jewel out with that
choice.

Had she? Or had she chosen Carl because of Jewel?

No!

"You're shaking, Jewel. Sit down."

She let David draw her over to the sofa and dropped onto it as
he disappeared.

A moment later he was back, pressing a glass into her hand.
"This might help."

Wine, from the kitchenwall. Jewel drank some. "She's the
daughter of an . . . old friend," she said numbly. "It's been . . .
a long time. I was surprised to hear from her is all."

For a long moment David didn't say anything. Then he sighed.
"We get to thinking that the past is static," he said softly. "Yesterday is over, done with and dead. And then it shows up again,
right in front of us."

"We were friends." Jewel sipped more wine, willing the alcohol
to numb the memories that wanted to hurt. "When we were kids.
And after." For a while. "I lived with her after . . . my mother
died." Susana had Linda's face. "I'll download some money."
She needs you, Susana had said, but what did she know? It was too
late for that, could not be true. It was too *late* . . . "I can't go
back."

David didn't say anything, but he put an arm around her shoulders. Reading what? She almost asked him, almost told him to get
out, leave, because this wasn't his business. She drank more of the
wine instead and kept quiet. Because this *wasn't* his business, and
none of it mattered to him. All he was offering was comfort.

Linda had done that once: held her, comforted her, been a bottomless well of strength. Jewel drained the last of her wine and
closed her eyes. The alcohol was soaking into her brain, loosening
the tight knots in her muscles and her mind, fuzzing the memories.
She needs you, Linda's daughter had said. Money would help.
Money always helped.

Sleeping, Jewel dreamed. She was running through dry yards
full of junk with Linda, on their way to some wall or overpass that
Linda had picked out, because she always picked out the canvas.
Jewel always held the flash while Linda worked, watching faces
and lives take on life beneath her hands. They covered the gray
concrete or ancient brick with hope, brighter than the paint Linda

used. Jewel could almost believe in hope when she looked at Linda's bright scenes—almost. Tonight she was working on a red fox with eyes that glittered like emeralds. It bothered Jewel, that fox, although she wasn't sure why. Something was wrong. Movement—a painted mountain lion slid like a shadow across the concrete wall. Jewel opened her mouth to scream a warning, but it was too late. The lion leapt, seized Linda in its jaws, and vanished through the wall . . .

Jewel whimpered, struggling up from nightmare into gray dawn light. Arms around her, warm and comforting. Linda? Half-awake, her throat aching with tears and relief that it was just a dream, Jewel nestled into that embrace and lifted her face. Lips touched hers, brushing as lightly as moth wings, pressing harder. Sam? A sweet ache pulsed between her legs, and she arched her back slightly, pressing against the warm curve of his thigh. Jewel sighed, drew a slow deep breath, and opened her eyes . . .

She was lying on her sofa, head pillowed on David Chen's shoulder. Jewel stiffened and felt the answering twitch of his reaction. David, not Sam. This was Erebus. Susana had called.

"Good morning." David relaxed deliberately, smiling at her: a reassuring, neutral smile.

"I was dreaming." Jewel sat up straight, blood hot in her face. "About . . . an old lover."

"So I guessed." He grinned at her. "You fell asleep on my shoulder, and I guess I did, too." He yawned widely. "I've been working too many nighttime hours lately. Shall I get us some coffee?"

"It was the wine. I don't drink wine." Jewel straightened, feeling naked although she was fully dressed, pissed at herself for letting him stay. Last night the darkness had been full of ghosts. In the morning light she felt silly.

Light was growing in the window, revealing that unreal lawn with its cheerful birds. David glanced at it as he handed her a steaming mug, his expression preoccupied. "I've got to leave. I've got some business to take care of before I go over to the infirmary."

"Sure." Jewel sipped, wincing as she burned her tongue, searching for easy, comfortable words. Not finding any . . .

"I'd better go." David regarded her gravely, a hint of sadness in the set of his shoulders. "I'm sorry about last night. That I was in your space. And I'm sorry if my work had anything to do with it."

"It's all right." Phony words. "No." She shook her head, suddenly needing to tell this man the truth. "Thank you for . . . the shoulder. I'm sorry if I don't act very grateful." She looked away. "Your desert doesn't really have anything to do with anything. I was . . . looking for someone to blame."

David gave her one of his crooked smiles. "Sometimes that helps. If I can do anything, tell me."

"I'll do that."

He read that for the dismissal it was, lifted one hand in farewell, and left.

Susana, Linda, Sam . . . Yesterdays swirled through the room like dry, dusty leaves. Go back to sleep, Jewel told herself, but it was hopeless. Outside, the sun would be glittering off the ice, splintering like broken glass, violent as a hammer blow. She needed to go walk on the ice, let that violent light drive the ghosts and guilts and memories away. When she came back, she would download money to Linda's account. Money would help. Money was the real need, no matter what some emotional adolescent wanted to believe. As Jewel left the apartment, she looked over her shoulder to make sure David hadn't left anything behind.

Something moved beyond the unreal panes of the unreal window. A bird, she told herself, but it didn't look like a bird. It might have been the shadow of a huge cat flitting across the dew-wet lawn.

Chapter
Six

Dà Jieh's office was vaguely Japanese in style: a low table flanked by raw-silk cushions and a desk of pale polished wood. The walls were white stucco; a single spray of pink orchids in a crystal vase stood in a small, arched alcove. A Chinese scroll hung on the far wall—a piece of classic Chinese sumi, in which a few spare brushstrokes created a snow-capped mountain peak, twisted cherry trees, and a waterfall.

David recognized that scene. The real scroll hung on the wall of his father's apartment. David looked around at the empty office. The rest was a standard package, midrange in price. He wondered if Eldest Sister had chosen the Japanese motif as a thrust at their father. No. The scroll rustled beneath his virtual fingers, and his Kraeger translated the touch into the dry, crisp feel of rice paper. Fuchin never did virtual. Perhaps this office was more a reflection of his sister's unsettled feelings about their father than a deliberate provocation.

And perhaps he should stop reading so much into it.

He sighed, tired beyond fatigue. His two or three hours of sleep on Jewel Martina's sofa had been worse than nothing. And unfortunate. Their half-asleep kiss had upset her. David's mouth quirked. She reminded him of Fern Li. They had been lovers for a while, before they had mutually discovered that it wouldn't work. Fuchin had been furious—because Fern was Chinese and he wanted his dynasty. David shook his head, smiling wryly. He had crowded Jewel—just what he had warned Flander not to do. Whatever that call had meant, it had certainly summoned some painful ghosts for her. David stretched his neck, vertebrae crackling, wondering what she had left behind. Whatever it was, it was catching up with her.

He sighed. Sometimes yesterday came to unexpected life, lurching along, shedding graveyard clods, ready to seize a person by the throat. What had she said so bitterly? *You can afford to love?* As if she could not.

Could he afford it?

David touched one of the orchids, aware of the delicate petal like silk beneath his fingertips. Illusion. Illusion could seem so real—even to him. Flander would be released in an hour. David would take him home, and in the silence and privacy of their apartment, they would have to talk about it. The OD. That broken promise. A heaviness settled into him. Flander had always lived his own life, disappearing for days or weeks, returning without explanation. Daring David to challenge him? Testing? *Will you still love me, no matter what I do?*

The promise to quit kickers had been different. A statement, David had thought. An up-front aknowledgment of what they had between them, that life had some kind of meaning.

Maybe he had been wrong.

It scares me, Flander had said one night after a two-week disappearance. *You mean too much to me. Sometimes I've just got to run away from it. I've got to have some space.*

So David gave him space. He sighed. Jewel had almost believed Flander's murder-attempt story, but she didn't understand. Flander had broken something, and now, like a child, he was groping for someone to blame.

"Little Brother." A dark oak door opened in the stucco wall and his sister entered. "You must excuse me. I was busy in my lab."

"We Chinese are so adept with manners," David murmured. Her tardiness in greeting him had been a pointed message: You are not particularly worth my attention. He bowed. "We can save a lot of time if we don't play games."

"You should know about games," Dà Jieh said in a silky voice.

Games. That was how Fuchin referred to David's work—*playing games.* David would have been angry at her for that comment once, and she knew it. That's how I think of Flander's time in the Net, David realized and felt a pang. Perhaps he was not so unlike their father, after all. "There are worse ways to live," he said slowly. "I enjoy my games, at least."

She looked at him for a long minute, frowning a little. Her Self was a version of her own face, its flaws smoothed into a porcelain perfection. Like the face of a doll. He had not seen her in the flesh since the day he had handed her his company shares outside their father's hospital room.

"Perhaps you are finally growing up, Little Brother." Her hair swung forward like black wings on either side of her face as she bent her head. "So why did you come to see me?"

She was wary. He read it through the bored indifference that her office had edited into her body language. "I heard a rumor," David said carefully, "that you are tailoring custom viruses in your lab."

"Did you?" Dà Jieh's black eyes did not waver. "And who brought you this rumor? Your little fox-boy lover?"

"No." He met her stare. "But Flander did check out your supposed investments. Where did the money really come from, Dà Jieh?"

The porcelain mask couldn't quite hide her reaction. "Shau Jieh asked you to do this, didn't she? Our butterfly sister is always worrying. If she has nothing real to worry about, she invents something."

"She's worried about *you*." Anger stirred in his belly, and David fought it down. "She loves you. Are you ever going to understand that? Or does it even matter to you?"

His sister didn't answer. She turned her back on him and walked across the room to stand in front of the scroll. "Why did you leave the firm?" she asked abruptly. "Why did you give me your shares, Little Brother?"

"To save the firm. To keep you from taking that job with Tanaka." That wasn't the entire truth. David turned one hand palm up. In virtual his skin was smooth, without the silver threads of his Net. Perhaps he would change that so that the virtual David Chen and the flesh David Chen were exactly alike. Or perhaps they could never be exactly the same—the flesh man and the virtual man. Perhaps you were always two slightly different people. "I could never be what our father wanted," he said slowly. "I . . . would have failed him." He shivered suddenly because this was the core, the center, the real reason he had handed those shares to her.

Flander had known it. *You're always going to be scared that you'll let your old man down,* he had said once. David had gotten angry. Because it was the truth, he thought bleakly. He always knows what I'm trying to hide from myself. "I told myself that it had to be one or the other." He forced himself to meet his sister's porcelain stare. "I told myself I had to choose: Chen BioSource or my art. In art I could only fail myself."

For a long moment Dà Jieh was silent. "That is quite an admission," she said, and her voice sounded strange. "I think perhaps you *have* grown up, Younger Brother." She touched the scroll lightly. "I did some . . . design work on the side. You can tell Shau Jieh that the job is finished. Completed. There will be no others."

"What about blackmail?" David asked, because it had to be asked.

"I am not stupid." Dà Jieh's eyes flashed. "I was careful, and I am safe. The purchaser was a very inside node with PanEuro. She has a vested interest in disassociating herself from our little . . . transaction."

Kickers were not looked on with great favor in the inner labyrinth of the web. Word got around, and users found themselves slipping outside fast. People were afraid that they would become unpredictable, and in the lightning-strike world of the web, a moment of hesitation could cost you and your connections a lot. Or perhaps they were more afraid that it might give the risk takers an edge. Kickers were for the rogue operators, the pirates, and the serious ghosts. In any case, that unspoken rule might keep his sister safe. Perhaps the affair was nothing more than what she had just told him.

Dà Jieh confided in no one, and she was very hard to read. David didn't usually bother having his office analyze for editing, but he wished suddenly that he had. Maybe his office could read the nuances behind his sister's smoothly edited face; he could not. Even in the flesh he had never read Dà Jieh well. He stifled another sigh. "I'll tell Shau Jieh that she can stop worrying," he said. "She'll be relieved. Thank you for taking the time to talk to me."

"I entered your interactive on the Net."

David paused, surprised, his hand outstretched for the virtual door that would exit him into his own office.

"I tried to damage it because I was angry." Dà Jieh was looking at the scroll again, frowning.

"So that was you." David looked at his sister's perfect porcelain profile, remembering that resonant anger. It was in there somewhere, behind that porcelain mask, behind the flesh mask, untouchable and unknowable. His doing, or had it been there before he was born? Fuchin had named her Chen Yao Hwa, Shining Bright. And she shone with the brilliance of genius. But the name also carried the meaning of "ambitious." Fuchin, looking for a son to cherish, had ignored that aspect of his eldest daughter. Whom did she blame for that? Fuchin? David? Or herself? He felt a sudden pity for her and for Fuchin and his willful blindness. "I'm glad you entered the ice cave," he said slowly. "I'm honored that you've looked at what I do."

"How is Flander?" She tore her eyes from the scroll. "Is he well?"

"Yes." The single syllable fell into silence between them. David wondered if she had been keeping track, if she knew of Flander's OD and his hospitalization. Was this a subtle dig? A careful stab of the knife intended to cause pain? Enough games. "That's not true." David met her eyes. "Flander isn't well. He's under observation . . . recovering from a drug overdose." So now it's out in the open and we can both see the knife blade, he thought bitterly. Your turn.

Dà Jieh looked away. "I'm . . . sorry, Younger Brother."

"You needn't be. Flander makes his own choices." Bitterness crept into his tone even though he tried to keep it out. "I don't own him. I simply live with him." And with the results of those choices.

"This . . . project that I designed." Dà Jieh looked down at her hands. "It was extremely potent, designed for a specific individual. The neurotransmitter and endorphin response is intense. I assume it would be used to allow direct optical access to the Net." She frowned. "It could permit enough of an information overload to cause a serious disruption in the user's reality."

"Why are you telling me this?" David felt a small coldness growing in his belly.

"My . . . contractor gave me a gene scan, standard and certified." She wouldn't meet his eyes. "Afterward, some of the sequences bothered me. They were unusual, and they seemed . . . familiar. I hadn't retained the full code—for safety reasons. But I remembered two unusual sequences, so I ran them against the gene records I have on file. They correlate quite closely with Flander's code."

"What?" David whispered.

"The odds that the code was indeed his are very small. But it is not impossible." Dà Jieh opened the dark oak door behind her. "I can't give you her name, you understand. I have work to do."

An inside node in PanEuro had commissioned a custom-made, highly illegal kicker for Flander? Payment for what job? Flander knew the ghosts and information dealers, but web nodes kept a careful distance from the talk peddlers. They bought information, yes, but they never associated themselves with any one peddler too openly. Production shifted to new markets with the speed of electrons in the worldwide economic web. Information security made the nodes money, got them there first to claim the new markets. If word got around that a node dealt with an operator like Flander, the node could end up blacklisted—outside. Dà Jieh's node had taken considerable risk, never mind the legal penalty for commissioning a kicker.

Which suggested that Flander's part of the deal was seriously illegal. The cold had turned to solid ice in David's gut, heavy as stone. Time to talk about this. More than time.

"David?" Dà Jieh paused in the doorway that led to her private space. "I went back into your ice cave yesterday." Her dark eyes held his for a brief moment, then shifted away. "You are very talented," she said. "The node's name is Anya Vanek." The door closed softly behind her.

David stood in front of it for a long moment, staring at the polished wood. Dà Jieh had called him David. He couldn't remember ever hearing her use his given name. It was always Younger Brother or Little Brother, in formal Chinese style. She had taken a major risk herself, giving him the node's name. He glanced at Fuchin's scroll on the wall. *I don't own him,* he had told his sister when she had asked about Flander. But a part of David wanted to own him. A part of him wanted to possess Flander, body, soul, and talent, as his own father had tried to possess him. David had a feeling that Flander had read that wanting a long time ago. Maybe that was what had brought Flander into his bed in the first place.

It had been a surprise. He had hidden his feelings from himself, if not from Flander. Another failure in his father's eyes. David's lips twitched. Sometimes, in the middle of the night, he wondered how much Flander truly shared with him and how much his presence in David's bed was simply payment for room and board. Flesh was a liability to Flander. He was terrified of its vulnerability. At best, his body was simply something to sell.

Or to give away to a friend?

"Flander," David said softly. "What have you gotten yourself into this time?"

His sister's empty office didn't answer him. David bowed to the virtual scroll, opened the oak door, and exited to the real world to go reclaim Flander from the infirmary.

Dr. Chirasaveena met him at the infirmary's entrance and ushered him into a spacious office. Cactus-garden decor. A detached part of his mind wondered if the hot climate theme in holo decoration was a direct result of the freezing reality above their heads. Good holo work, but the resonance could have been stronger. "How is Flander?" David asked as he sat down in the offered chair.

"Recovering as rapidly as can be expected. I can foresee no obvious complications." Chirasaveena—a small, wiry man with a broad Thai face—steepled his fingers. "His . . . choice of life-style is unfortunate."

Such a polite euphemism.

"The laboratory finally identified the cause of the anaphylactic response. It was a protein chain derived from peanuts."

"Peanuts?" David blinked. "He's allergic to peanuts. He almost died once from eating peanut oil."

"That particular protein can cause quite a severe response." Chirasaveena sounded disapproving. "Pharmaceuticals of questionable origin are certainly a grave risk. I can suggest a number of . . . appropriate programs. I think it would be wise. If necessary, I will authorize legal guardianship for you."

If you showed up in a fed-med clinic with a drug-related condition and lived, you ended up in federal rehab. Which was jail, only worse. If you lived through *that*, you would try very hard not to come back. That was the popular belief, anyway. But this was Erebus, and by definition, people here were privileged. They got a choice. Or rather, David got the choice. He could have Flander committed to a private rehab program. For a long moment he hesitated. "I'll . . . consider it."

"As you wish." Chirasaveena averted his eyes. "You may call me any time you wish to discuss the procedure. Your remote biomedical interactive is directly accessed to Flander's treatment file. He needs to remain on-line for another two or three days. I'll inform you when you may remove the remotes." He rose, ushering David to the door. "We installed venous ports for the remotes. The patient may disconnect them briefly in order to facilitate bodily needs. The nurse will instruct you in the necessary sterile technique."

"Thank you, Doctor." David bowed. The thanks was genuine in spite of the doctor's cold tone. He had saved Flander's life, no matter how he felt about Flander's use of the virus.

Perhaps Chirasaveena had expected something else—defensiveness or a justification of Flander's drug use. In any case, David's thanks silenced him. He turned David over to a nurse, who showed him how to keep the catheter sterile when Flander unplugged to go to the bathroom. And then Flander was coming down the hall, walking on his own because he would not sit in a wheelchair, face pale, eyes glittering, twitchy with the desire to get the hell out of this place. David took his arm, feeling the quivering weakness that Flander had hidden well enough to fool the wheelchair nurse. He guided him through the pretty entry, out to the little electric car he had rented for the long trip down the corridors to their apartment.

Flander didn't protest. "God, I'm *out*." He sank back onto the seat. "I thought they'd hang on to me forever."

His face still had a glazed look, and he stumbled a little over words. Sedatives, David reminded himself. "They were glad to get rid of you," he said, turning down Amundsen. "You're not the model patient."

Flander gave him a sour sideways look—a fox showing its teeth—and didn't answer.

At their door David helped Flander out of the car. It shocked him a little to realize just how weak Flander was. He leaned on David's arm—he who never leaned, who touched rarely and wanted to be touched rarely. Their apartment looked strange to David, as if the decor had subtly changed. The cushions and the low table in the living room were still shoved haphazardly into the corner from his last entry into his studio. Every room in the complex was hardwired for virtual. A person could live in skins and lenses here.

Illusion within illusion, David thought suddenly. Jewel had said something like that yesterday in the desert room. The closing door shut David and Flander into the immediate bubble of the apartment, a bubble of unspoken words. Words that needed to be said out loud. David helped Flander to the bed, reading pain and weakness in the small tensions and hesitations in his movements. The words crowded around them like invisible moths, thickening the air until it was hard to breathe. Flander felt them, too. He dropped onto the bed, eyes closed, hand flat on the bed, palm down so that David could insert the remote catheter into the plastic port near his knuckles. The wall terminal chimed aknowledgment, blinked a brief display of numbers that Jewel Martina could probably read but he couldn't, then went blank. David taped the tubing to Flander's thin wrist.

"You can take it out, but you've got to do it right. I'll show you. Flander . . . why?" He sat down on the edge of the bed, not touching him. "It's time to tell me," he said softly.

"Yeah, I guess it is." Flander opened his eyes and stared up at the ceiling. "You think it's some kind of message, don't you? I made a promise and then I broke it, and that means I don't give a shit about us. That's it, isn't it?"

"No." David wanted to look away from Flander's glittering eyes but did not. "All right, yes, that's what it feels like. But that's not all of it. I don't want you to die. Can't you *understand* that?" He turned away, fists clenched. "You matter to me, whether you keep on living with me or not."

"David?" Flander touched his hand. "It's hard for me. I . . . don't matter much to *me* most of the time. This was special stuff. Custom fit. It kicked me loose from my flesh. I could let go, I could get into the Net and really *be* there, all the way there. It was a *door*, man. Nothing's ever done it for me before. Not like that.''

Custom fit? ''Did you get this from a PanEuro node?'' David faced him. ''An Anya Vanek?''

''Anya Vanek?'' Flander's eyes flickered, then his face smoothed. ''Yeah, she scored for me. It was . . . a payoff. For a job I did.''

And Dà Jieh had tailored it. Full of peanut protein? He tried to recall if she knew about Flander's allergy. ''A payoff for what?'' David wanted to grab Flander and shake him. ''What the hell did you do? Something major, right? My God. You can get the death penalty for piracy. What do you get out of it, the ghosting? Why *do* it?'' The words burst out, unstoppable, sharp-edged with old layers of anger and hurt. ''We make enough money—we'd make a lot more if you put a reasonable amount of time into our stuff. Is it more fun to make it stealing information? Or is it just a challenge? Because you're bored.''

''I don't know.'' Flander turned his face away. ''You decide.''

David got to his feet, breathing hard, as if he had been running. ''You and I live in a kind of eternal present, Flander. When I get too close to who you are, the person beyond the right-now, you-and-me Flander, you tell me to back off. And I always have.'' Because he was afraid Flander would disappear. David looked down at his clenched fists and opened them with an effort. ''I think maybe I've been making a mistake.''

Eyes closed, Flander didn't answer. David turned on his heel and left the room. He could call Dr. Chirasaveena, let him commit Flander to a private rehab facility. They would haul him away, by force if necessary, and then would use drugs, therapy, whatever it took to break him out of his self-destructive patterns. Psychic restructuring. Sometimes you could fix what was broken. Sometimes you couldn't.

Either way, Flander would see it as betrayal. It might save him and it might not. And if it did, what would be left of Flander, the artist, the lover he lived and worked with? Or was there anything between them at all? Maybe it was nothing more than his own self-delusion, David thought bitterly. Maybe it was a virtual he had created, a lover as unreal as his father's virtual of a perfect son. Yeah, he wasn't so different from the old man, after all. The empty living room nagged at him, scraping his mind like fingernails on a chalkboard. No, he decided, reaching for his lenses. Too much emotion right now. Vent it, get some cool before talking to Chirasaveena. ''Studio,'' he said as he pulled his lenses into place.

Bright light filtered through the skylight, catching the brilliant yellows in the half-finished canvas of sunflowers that stood on the easel. The black and white cat leapt down from the radiator and arched against David's leg; his Kraeger net gave him cat fur and the rough thrum of a purr. He stroked the cat absently, sorting among the racked canvases along the wall. There. He pulled out the ice cave and stretched the canvas between his virtual hands. It expanded easily into a door-sized rectangle of cold blues and greens, *became* a door. He stepped through, and the studio vanished behind him.

Ice arched above his head in white buttresses, and somewhere water dripped with melodic monotony. Someone had hacked a face into the wall. David eyed it. It was crude and without strength. It detracted from the powerful sweep of the ice rather than adding to it as Dà Jieh's rage had added. David wiped his hand across it, smoothing the rough carving to gleaming ice again. Someone else had carved a frozen stalagmite into a human shape. A naked woman embraced the ice like a lover, melting into it or perhaps emerging from it in an Escheresque either/or. It was powerful, although the shape itself was almost as crude as the face hammered into the wall. In a way, the crudity worked. Not quite enough, though . . . David touched up the rough places, tightening the planes of the woman's face, bringing the lines of the body together into urgency and adding a gloss of sexuality so that she and the ice flowed together/flowed apart. Yeah, better, but it had been good to start with. Pleased, David moved on to the trapped man struggling silently in his prison of ice. You could be trapped by love, able to see out but unable to escape. He shivered and reached out to add the glimmer of frozen tears to the man's anguished face.

Up ahead Jewel Martina's image spread her fingers in the ice, part of it and separate, powering it. He stood back, frowning, the memory of last night in his head. Not quite right . . . He had shaped her image from a visual record, with no knowledge of the woman herself beyond their brief encounter on the ice. He knew her a little better now, and that knowing changed his perspective. David tugged at his braid, then reached into the ice to reshape her face. Anger was there, old and dark. And fear? Yes. It seeped from her, a shadow within the ice, tainting the slowly flowing glacier. Where did your anger come from, Jewel Martina? And the fear? It caught up with you last night, didn't it? He blurred the boundaries between flesh woman and ice shadow until one merged with the other and the two were no longer separate. Yes.

"Jeeze, what you *did*."

Flander's voice. David turned and found the red fox sitting on a ledge of ice, tongue lolling. "What are you doing out of bed?"

"If I can go piss, I can drop in here for a minute. Skins won't hurt me. You're crazy to let people fuck with this." Flander laid his ears back. "David? How come . . . you don't walk on me?"

David had just asked himself that same question. He touched the ice, feeling slick cold beneath his netted fingers. "I'm not sure." He groped for honesty—for Flander's benefit or his own? "Maybe it's because I can't hide anything from you. You always know what's going on, even when I don't and . . . I guess I get tired of illusions." Or was it just because he wouldn't be as good an artist without Flander? Could that be it?

"You got to understand about the ghosting." Flander lowered his head, ears still flat to his skull. "Shy picked me up off the street when I was young. I wouldn't have made it without her. And she taught me the Net, and she taught me how to get around, how to hack Net time for myself. She took care of me, David." He hunched his shoulders, and his tail flicked nervously, spattering droplets of water across the ice. "She was a hot operator in the Net. The hottest. And it's like I *can't* quit. I got to do it." He flattened himself to his belly, eyes dark and unhappy. "I can't explain it better than that, David. I just *can't*, and I stay out of trouble mostly. And . . . I guess that's all."

Shy. Shy-Shy. David knew her, remembered Flander's street-chic mentor and protector. But she had not been real; she had been an autonomous persona Flander had created. Flander had brought her to life in a Pygmalion fantasy, a crazy phantom of a kid's needs and desires. She had been a good enough auto to fool even David for a while. Until he had recognized her for what she was. Until he had killed her for Flander. It scared him to hear Flander talk about her again.

Or had she been real once? Had there been a flesh basis for that fantasy? "What happened to Shy?" David asked softly.

"She made a lot of enemies." Flander twitched. "Goes with the turf. Someone . . . found out her flesh address. They killed her. It was before I met you," he said. "A couple of years before."

So. She had maybe existed, after all, the mother figure. The protectress, the heroine. Only she hadn't been able to save herself in the end. David tugged at his braid. Maybe this ghosting was just another re-creation of Shy, as the auto had been. Maybe he was keeping her alive by doing what she had done. Maybe it explained something.

It didn't explain the kickers.

"You see this?" Flander's ears had pricked. "Look who's been here."

He was staring at marks on the cave floor. David walked over and looked. Cat tracks? They had sunk into the ice like tracks in soft snow, and they were as big as David's hand. Lion tracks? A tiger? He followed their trace. They made a long arc in front of Jewel's frozen image, ending at a wall of ice. They didn't add much. David shrugged and wiped his palm across the closest print.

Nothing happened.

He blinked and tried again. "Erase," he said. The tracks didn't even fade.

"Forget it." Flander shook himself, spattering David with melt-water. "She went into your program. You'll have to go figure out what she did if you want to get rid of them."

"What are you talking about?" David swiped at the tracks one last time. "Who did this?"

"Serafina." Flander grinned a toothy fox grin. "She wears a mountain lion in the Net. She's a hot ghost, and she's Jewel Martina's private guardian angel. Don't ask me why."

Jewel had said something about a mountain lion. In his desert—but that was a holo job, not a virtual. "Did you tell her?" David asked Flander. "Does she know?"

Flander didn't answer. His front feet had splayed out suddenly, and his head was drooping.

"Exit," David snapped, and yanked off his lenses.

Flander swayed in the middle of the floor, feet spread, wearing a glazed, surprised expression. "Dizzy . . ."

David got an arm around his shoulders as Flander sagged, slid his other arm beneath his knees, and heaved Flander into his arms.

"I'm okay," Flander mumbled as David staggered back into the bedroom with him.

"Shut up." David lowered him to the bed, yanked off his glove, and pushed back the sleeve of his skinthins.

Miraculously Flander had disconnected the catheter properly. David plugged it quickly into the port, then looked anxiously at the screen. It remained blank. Dr. Chirasaveena wasn't sharing any treatment decisions with him. "I hope you don't have to piss," David said. "Because you're not getting up for a while. Got that?"

"Got it," Flander mumbled, and opened one eye. "You gonna tie me down or what?"

"If that's what it takes." David hauled a cushion into the room and sat down. He would call up a holo model of the desert and work on it from here. He didn't like remote work as a rule—he didn't get as thoroughly into a scaled-down piece—but he could do it if he had to. "Go to sleep," he said.

Flander didn't answer, and when David touched his cheek, he merely sighed and mumbled drowsily. Chirasaveena had probably sedated him again. And he would probably message David soon, chew him out politely for letting Flander get up. David sighed and called up the desert model.

He still hadn't made any clear decisions about himself and Flander. This was not the time. In the desert the tiny lizard flicked a minuscule tongue. He would have to ask Flander if he had told Jewel about her ghost.

Chapter Seven

"Ms. Suriyana." Jewel bowed in front of the PanEuro node's glass desktop. A crystal bowl of lilies stood on the corner. "You are very kind to see me." She kept her eyes down. Her office was shading her Self's body language with submissive signals, but it wouldn't hurt at all to reinforce them.

"I assume that I'm not wasting my time?" Suriyana lifted one perfect Bacall eyebrow.

Bitch. "I was pirated. I returned your fee." Think *humility*. Jewel spread her hands.

"By Harmon Alcourt?" Suriyana frowned down at a display on her desktop. "Do you have something usable this time?"

"Yes," Jewel said, laying a security certification seal down beside the lilies. "It's not large." Humble! "There's been a very recent increase in subsea vacations in the upper-income brackets. The trend is predicted to continue, which should increase demand for high-quality, custom-tailored scuba gear." She touched the seal lightly. "I've put together labor, material sources, and a plant site. If you move quickly, it should make you a small but significant profit." Damned right. She had spent a lot of expensive Net time checking this one out.

Suriyana touched the seal with one fingertip, as if it were dirty. Frowning, she stared down at her desktop, scanning the Token File she had just accessed, running the projections through her data base.

Realizing that she was holding her breath, Jewel forced herself to breathe normally. Take it, *take* it! she wanted to yell. I'm *giving* it to you.

"Your asking price is not unattractive." Suriyana withdrew her finger with a mild grimace of distaste.

Not unattractive, huh? It was a joke, a gift. Jewel made herself smile.

Suriyana tilted her head so that her blond Bacall hair swung forward over one shoulder. "I hope *this* package is secure."

"It is." Jewel met her stare. She had assembled this entire package inside a secure archive. That had wiped out her miniscule profit, but it was worth it to salvage her reputation.

"I'll risk it." Suriyana laid her hand down over the seal. This time she let her triumph show in her face.

"Thank you for your business." The fee had been transferred to Jewel's account, her office informed her. Teeth clenched, she snapped her fingers, transmitting the key that would allow Suriyana to access the Secure File and retrieve the data. "I hope your profit exceeds my projections."

"We'll see." This time Suriyana opened a door for her instead of dumping her out of the virtual. "I'll let you know."

"Stinking, lousy *bitch*!" Jewel yanked off her lenses and flung them onto the sofa. Suriyana knew it was a gift, a little financial groveling to pay for the sunscreen fiasco. "She could have been polite," Jewel yelled. And now she was late. Just to top it all off. Jewel grabbed her lenses again and slapped Alcourt's door open. Someday, one day, she would be on top. She bolted through the door into Alcourt's space.

The cleaner beetle scuttled across the carpet in the bougainvillea room, scavenging molecules of dust from the spotless carpet. Jewel's implant remained silent. Perhaps he had slept in or was busy in the Net. She felt herself tensing as she approached the desert garden, but it was empty. No mountain-lion ghosts. Sand and rock and thirsty plants baked in the unreal sun; not even the lizard was out on its rock. The solarium door opened as she approached, and Castor emerged.

"You're late." Castor grinned at her. "Going to make it up to me?" He stepped up against her suddenly. As she recoiled, he put his arm around her.

"Knock it *off*." Her elbow caught him square in his solid, exercised belly, and he grunted. "We settled this, remember?" She did not need this right now. "You didn't have to stick around," she said as she shoved by him. "You get to log off at shift end. It's my ass if I'm late, not yours."

"You're so right, sweetheart." Castor's face had gone red, and his smile revealed his teeth. "And it's not a bad-looking ass, even if you're part Mex. Don't waste it on the chink." His grin widened. "He's into boys. Next time you want a manly shoulder to cry on, just ask me. See you around.'' He gave her a jaunty wave, turned on his heel, and sauntered down the corridor.

Jewel stared after him, numb suddenly, her stomach contracting into a ball. He had *seen*. Somehow he had eavesdropped last night, had seen her asleep in David's arms. Jewel closed her eyes, a scene unrolling across the screen of her eyelids: Castor sitting in front of a video screen that opened like a window into her room. He had watched her face as Susana said *She needs you* . . .

This was too *much*.

Jewel shoved the solarium door open. It grated on the real pristine Caribbean sand, and she threw her weight against it, staggering as it gave suddenly, stumbling through into heat and sea breeze.

Alcourt lay on a recliner, naked and tan beneath the unreal, harmless sun. He turned his head toward her, shading his eyes from the glare. ''What's wrong with you? You look terrible. Shut the door.''

Castor had *watched* her. He had gotten into Alcourt's Security. It could happen. Alcourt had access to all his private space, and Jewel's apartment was part of that space. Her life was part of that space. She closed the door very slowly, very carefully.

''I'm talking to you, Jewel.'' Alcourt raised the recliner, his eyes on her face.

You're dead, Castor. ''I'm . . . sorry.'' She drew a deep breath, forcing calm into her flesh. Choose the right moment and tell him. If Castor was into his Security, Alcourt would be very, very interested. ''I had a . . . bad night.''

''Did you? Well, don't let it affect your judgment on the job.''

His tone bothered her—it had a needling edge. ''I never let anything affect my judgment.'' She smiled for him, trying to project cheery competence. The wind brought her a whiff of fishy decay, as if something had washed up on that perfect beach. ''I'll get started on your morning bloodwork.''

''I had Castor do it. See? I'm not angry at you for being late.'' Alcourt lay back a little, fingers steepled. ''I'm not such a tyrant, you know. Jewel,'' he mused. ''That's not a fashionable name, and it's not particularly ethnic. Your legal mother is registered as Caucasian, but we both know that's a fiction.''

''No, it isn't.'' The words popped out before she could catch them. That much was real—her mother.

''You don't have to play games.'' Alcourt closed his eyes against the sun. ''Your birth certificate is as phony as your adoption by Kerry Walsh. I'm not going to fire you for your file games, Jewel. I wish you'd believe that.''

He sounded genuinely hurt, but Jewel barely noticed. Phony? No. That much was real. *My Jewel.* She closed her eyes, hearing Mama's whisper in her ears, feeling her arms so tight that Jewel would squirm, barely able to breathe. *My precious Jewel, you're all I have. I'll keep you safe forever* . . . Forever. Forever had ended in cancer and drugs and the darkness of the ruined 'burbs house. "She was my real mother," Jewel said flatly.

"You're lying to me again." Alcourt picked up a pair of mirror shades from the sand beside the recliner and slipped them over his eyes. "I didn't buy your past, did I, Jewel? It's not written into your contract, and you don't give anything away for free, do you? You're like me in that. It's a good trait if you're going into the web." Alcourt's lips smiled beneath his shades. "What's the price tag, Jewel? What's the asking price for your soul?"

His voice had gone smooth and cold, mocking her. This was the Alcourt of virtual, the man who had snapped the ivory letter opener and tossed the pieces down in front of her, the man whose deals might affect the economy of an entire nation and who wouldn't care. Maybe he *was* the real Alcourt, and the flesh man with his fears and doubts was the virtual. "I don't understand what you mean," she said tightly.

"A lot of people are willing to sell their souls." The black, mirrored shades watched her. "For power. Or money, or sex, which are all aspects of power when you come down to it. Everyone has their price. What's yours?"

"I don't know." Jewel stared at the tiny twin reflections of her face in his shades. "What are you saying, please?"

"A part of you doesn't care if I fire you." Alcourt's smile had disappeared. "You hide it very well, but sometimes it shows. Perhaps I'm wrong. Perhaps I'd simply like to believe that there is someone on this planet who won't sell out for the right price." His lips smiled coldly. "Or perhaps that part of you *isn't* for sale and you *are* truly unusual, Jewel Martina. I want that part of you." He removed the shades again, dropping them into the sand. "I want you to give it to me as a gift. I . . . need it."

His voice had gone rough suddenly, and there was a hint of what looked like anguish in his light eyes. Jewel shook her head, confused by these shifts in his mood. It was as if there were two different men inside the same skin. She made a vague move toward the monitor, wishing she could call up his file. Maybe his chemistry would define him. "I . . . still don't understand what you're asking me," she said, and heard a hint of desperation in her voice.

He heard it, too, and held out his hands to her. "I'm a prisoner

here, Jewel, held captive by the virtual man I need to be in the web.
I don't dare leave, and no one really knows or cares about the flesh
behind the web node.

"I . . . want you to move in here. I have no children. I've never
wanted them, but now I want an heir. The flesh can't live forever,
and I find that I'm afraid to die. You're strong enough to have gotten
this far, as strong as I am, perhaps, but without my advantages.
You know what you want, and I'm offering you the means to attain
it. Live here with me. I'll teach you the web. See? I'm still trying
to buy you. The part of you I can buy, anyway. Perhaps I'm asking
you . . . to love me." His eyes held hers, full of shadows. "What
an old-fashioned notion, love." He laughed a soft, harsh note.
"I'm not asking you to be my lover. You can buy any pretty body
you want, and plenty will come to you for free, attracted to power
like bees to nectar. But I want you to carry our child, yours and
mine. I want to see tomorrow in the boy's face. I want to know that
there's something beyond death. Please," he said softly. "I haven't
said please to anyone in a long time. I haven't had to. I have a lot
of power, Jewel Martina. More than you guess. I don't want it to
end with me."

Her mind reeling, Jewel struggled for some kind of reply to that
crazy monologue. He sounded sincere, and that sincerity tangled
her words. The powerful isolated themselves, yes. Safe in this icy
fortress, he could very well be lonely. Jewel looked away. But there
were layers beneath that lonely voice. The other Alcourt—the very
inside web node—was there, too, peeking out from behind the
needy man in front of her. That Alcourt frightened her. *There is a
certain aesthetic in breaking something priceless,* he had said.

"I can't." Jewel took a small step away from his outstretched
hand. "I'm not what you want." Whatever that is, she thought. If
you even know. "You're seeing someone who doesn't really exist."
Her orderly, comprehensible world was crumbling around her, as
if Erebus had erupted silently. At any moment the ceiling might
crack, raining blocks of ice and burning lava down on them all.
"I'm sorry."

"Don't turn me down so quickly, Jewel Martina." Alcourt picked
up the shades. "This is what you've sold your ass for, isn't it?" He
gestured at the pure sand, the wheeling, holoed gulls. "You won't
get here on your own. With what I'm offering you, you can buy
anything you want. Real security, Jewel. Lovers. David Chen, if
you want him." His eyes glinted. "You're tired. Go home and go
to bed. Castor will take your shift. He won't like it, but he won't

let me see it. Because I own him, and he knows it. Someone will always own Castor. How about you, Jewel? Go to bed.''

It was an order, and she obeyed it instantly, fleeing Alcourt and his impossible, tempting, unbelievable offer.

''Jewel?''

She paused at the door and looked back.

''If you turn down my offer, I hope you understand that I can't retain you as an aide.'' Alcourt slid the shades onto his face. ''Do you understand?''

Say yes or get fired. ''Of course I understand,'' Jewel said through stiff lips. She had heard it before, thank you. ''Shall I take Castor's shift tonight?''

''That would be best.'' He nodded. ''Let's make that the deadline for your decision. Then we can discuss further arrangements.''

Dismissed, she left the solarium without another word, stumbling over nothing on the smooth floor of the corridor. Harmon Alcourt had just offered to share his world with her. Which was the stuff of fairy tales, and she'd *never* been young enough to believe in fairy tales. Jewel groped for the subtle cruelty, the joke that might explain his offer. He wanted her to carry his child, his son. This was what Linda did—hired out her uterus for money. No, it was more than that. He wanted something else, too, not just her DNA and her womb.

If she refused, she lost her place here. She slid downhill a little, farther from her goal.

What had he said at the end? Jewel found herself standing in the hall, staring into the desert garden as if it could give her an answer. He had said something else . . . A chill walked down her spine. Something about buying real security, about buying David Chen as a lover. She rubbed her arms, feeling gooseflesh beneath her palms, even though it was always too warm in these rooms. Maybe Castor hadn't broken into the Security file, after all. Maybe he had sat in the solarium while Harmon Alcourt opened a window into her room.

The cold on her skin was seeping through her flesh, and she remembered the tiny sound of the letter opener snapping between his fingers. Castor's mocking leer was a message. I own every moment of your life, Alcourt was reminding her. I can entertain myself with your tears and pain any time I choose. I have this much power over you.

And he was offering it to her?

Oh, sure. He had said it. What price for your soul? He had told her the price but not the terms of the contract. No, he wanted something, and the price he was offering was big enough to scare her. She was so tired of being scared. The chill in her flesh was turning to anger—cold, hard anger. Anger at Alcourt with his illusions and his games, at Susana with her childish ultimatum, at David with his damn comfort.

"Daughter." The voice came from the desert room, low and throaty. Like the purr of an enormous cat.

Jewel froze, wanting to run, knowing that it couldn't be anyone, not in the flesh—not in this place, where even her midnight anguish was observed.

"Come here."

The cat-purr voice plucked at her muscles. Jewel found herself stepping forward, through the doorway, into the unreal heat and dust of the desertscape. The lizard was out on its rock. It stared at her with beady, unreadable eyes. Beyond it a mountain lion crouched on the sand. She had expected it, and that expectation scared her more than the holo did.

"You need to get out of here." The lion rose and stretched fore and aft, pink tongue curling over white fangs. "Don't be tempted to go to Linda. It's not home for you." With a graceful bound, the lion leapt to the top of a rock outcrop, lashed its tail once, leapt again, and vanished.

Jewel stared at the spot where it had disappeared. Not it—*she*. Lioness, not lion, and the certainty with which she knew that increased her fear. Another of Alcourt's games, she told herself. He had listened in last night, had picked Linda's name from her misery, and was levering her with special effects. It was plausible. So why didn't she believe it? *Daughter,* the lioness had called her. It had not been her mother's voice. It was not that particular ghost, anyway, and in this place of illusion it would have its origins in technology. "To hell with you, whoever you are," she said out loud, just in case the trickster was still monitoring. "Keep your damn holos out of my space." She would have guessed Flander, but the fox was with David, under his watchful eye.

Alcourt. If not, who? And why?

The lizard had vanished—scared away by the lioness? With a jerk of her shoulders, Jewel marched out of the garden, down the hall, and through the bougainvillea room. But the bougainvillea had vanished and now pink and yellow roses bloomed in graceful arching clumps. Jewel waded through them, palmed the lock, and went into her own apartment. The room seemed as unreal as the lawn beyond the false windows. There were no walls here. She lived in a bubble of glass. Was Alcourt watching her right now? Sitting on his recliner with a glass in his hand, maybe smiling a little as she glanced warily around the room?

She walked across the floor, watching herself walk, watching herself look at the holoed windows. Flowers swayed in a gentle afternoon breeze, and a red-breasted bird hopped across the mowed lawn. She watched herself breathe, noticing that her respiration rate was elevated and a faint sheen of sweat was visible beneath her bangs.

"House, blank windows." This double vision was giving her a headache. "House, mail." She stared at the blank space where the illusory afternoon had glowed. "To Linda Walsh." She looked up at one of the eyes Security had mounted on the wall. It would focus on her face, shooting her image up into orbit. That arrow of words and emotion would ricochet off a satellite, then fly down again to the decaying house in the 'burbs where Linda still lived. Whose flesh would be the target?

"Susana called me," Jewel said clearly, carefully. "Linda, I'm so sorry about Carl." The words came easily, after all, smooth and conventional. "I am downloading some money into your account—"

"There is a realtime answer," the House interrupted apologetically. "From Linda Walsh."

"Jewel?" The voice came over the speakers, soft and slightly blurred, as if Linda had just woken from sleep. "Is that really you? The lines are bad today, and you sound so strange."

"Yes. It's me." Conventional words had abandoned her, leaving her groping. "Linda . . . how *are* you?"

"How am I?" Linda's voice came through the speakers too bright, almost shrill. "I'm fine. No flags on by bloodchem, and the kid's big for second tri."

"I wasn't talking about your contract." Jewel felt a twinge of unease. "I was asking about *you*. How is Carl?" She stared at the pickup as if she could conjure Linda's image in the air. Which she couldn't because the house in the 'burbs had only basic service, with no visual transmission, when it had even that.

"Carl's paralyzed." Linda's voice faltered. "Maybe he'll get better, maybe he won't. I told you—I know I did."

She sounded confused and too vague. Linda had always been so sharp, quick with repartee. It was Linda Sam had been after, at first . . . "No, you didn't tell me." Jewel swallowed. "Are you sure you're okay?"

"Oh, yeah." Pause. "I guess I didn't."

Jewel closed her eyes. They had gone to ground in the half-burned house in the 'burbs because Mama couldn't get around anymore and it was abandoned. The smoke reek had kept her awake that first night, and she had slipped out near dawn while Mama was still under, thinking maybe she could raid a garden or check out the vendors setting up at the local flea market for a handout. Linda had been sitting on the crumbled remains of the retaining wall as if she had been waiting for her.

"My mom's at work, " she had said without even an introduction. "Come and eat breakfast."

That was then. "Linda," Jewel said sharply.

Silence.

"Linda? Are you . . . having a tough time?" The words came out slow and thick, heavy with questions that could not be put into words. Jewel held her breath, listening to the small nonsounds of her apartment.

A faint whisper came from the speakers, like wind in dry leaves or a faint sigh. "Yeah," Linda said. "I guess I am. They got some fancy treatments that might let Carl walk a little, but fed doesn't cover it and I don't have the money. Look, I'll be up-front." Her voice didn't waver. "I can't pay you back, so don't call it a loan, okay?"

This time the voice was Linda's. Jewel closed her eyes and had a sudden vision of Linda in the black tights and T-shirt she wore when they were out tagging at night: one fist on her hip, head thrown back, a can of paint in the other. "How much do you need?"

A small silence came over the speakers. "About ten thou." More silence. "It might not work."

Harsh, hurting words, full of dying pride. Ten thousand would wipe Jewel out, leave her with almost no savings. Jewel blinked, but the T-shirted vision didn't go away. Linda had been so *strong*. A state official had come to the house the day after Jewel had scattered her mother's ashes on the wind. He had been tired, spiteful, and in no mood to be gentle. Someone had noticed Jewel's existence just long enough to file her as a state ward. She had spent a week of hell in the state juvenile refugee camp before Linda's mother had shown up to claim her, tight-lipped and angry. Linda had never told Jewel how she had levered Kerry into declaring formal guardianship of Jewel.

She would have died in the camp. Jewel stared at the blank windows. Her body might have survived the wire-fenced jungle, but *she* would have disintegrated, dissolved into the ugliness of that place. How much do you owe for your life? What is the monetary value of your soul? Alcourt had just asked her that same question.

"Linda, I'll download the money today, okay?" Jewel drew a quick, shuddering breath. "I called to tell you . . . that I'm coming back to the States." Not *home*—the mountain lion was right. It was not her home. "I thought I'd stay with you for a while. Until I pick up a new client and get settled." Going back. She had never meant to go back. "Is that all right?"

"All right?" Linda's voice was going vague again. "Yeah, it's okay, I guess. If you want to. I gotta go now. Carl's calling. Listen . . . let me know. When you're getting in. And—thanks."

"The realtime connection has been ended," the House intoned. "Do you wish to leave any further message?"

"House, no." She was so tired. "Are you listening, Harmon?" Jewel looked up at the pickup. "I am turning down your offer." My soul is not for sale, now or ever. "And I am quitting." Why give him the satisfaction of firing her? "House, access the U.S. medical registry," she said slowly. "Update my file to unemployed-active. Cross-reference Alcourt/Martina contract and file a personal hardship termination." This was her first personal hardship claim, so it shouldn't damage her standing in the registry. Alcourt's termination evaluation could damage her if he wanted to punish her. If he wanted to punish her, he could do it in a hundred ways—he had damn well proved that. Jewel shrugged, because what was going to happen was going to happen.

"House, purchase a one-way fare from McMurdo to Seattle, Washington. Immediate departure."

"Your file has been updated to active-unemployed with United States medical registry. One-way airfare from McMurdo, Antarctica Preserve, to Seattle, Washington, USA, has been purchased. Your account balance is 13,645 yen. The first available flight from McMurdo will depart at five-thirty local time and will proceed via Christ Church, New Zealand. Do you wish me to confirm space on this flight?"

She would have time to make that flight if she hurried. She wanted to hurry, wanted to flee this place, to absorb herself in a rush of escape. "House, confirm it."

"Confirmed. A shuttle will be at the personnel dock at three. Is there anything else?"

"House, yes. Download ten thousand yen into Linda Walsh's personal account."

"Please place your palm on the screen and recite your personal code."

The white outline of a hand appeared on Jewel's screen. Static crackled across her skin as she laid her palm against the cool glass.

"Verified. Ten thousand yen has been downloaded into the account of Linda Walsh. Your account balance stands at—"

"House, shut up."

Slowly she turned to face the private door that had let her in and out of Alcourt's rooms. When she put her palm against the lock plate, the door didn't open; Security had already locked her out. The safe walls of Erebus Complex had cracked, and the cold was seeping in. It was over—her stay here, her pretty illusions about the future.

No, she told herself fiercely. Not over. She could continue to work her way into the web elsewhere. She could put together a package from Seattle just as easily as from Erebus. This was not defeat. This was only a temporary setback.

Sure.

Jewel yanked her top drawer open and stood still. Alcourt's ivory letter opener lay on top of her clothes, broken into two neat pieces. She picked them up and ran her fingertip across the clean sharp edge where the ivory had snapped. *Priceless* . . . With a shudder, she tossed the pieces onto the floor, scooped up an armful of clothes, and began to pack.

Chapter Eight

Sitting cross-legged on the desert sand, David tugged thoughtfully at his braid. Finished. At last. He tilted his head, hearing the dry whisper of the hot wind against sand and stone, listening to the subtle song of the desert. He had imported the sounds of flute and skin drums, a wandering, subtle melody composed by a friend, muted and blended with wind sound, heard below the threshold of consciousness. David nodded slowly. It nagged at you, that desert song. It spoke of thirst and heat and the vast contemplative silence with which the desert would watch you die.

It was an uneasy place, this bit of desert. Full of his feelings about Flander? And Jewel's ghosts? He had woven them into it almost without knowing it, and the effect worked. David touched the sandy ground, staring at the tiny real grains on his fingertip. Bits of crumbled mountains . . . Jewel had left the complex the day Flander had been released from the infirmary. She had left without telling anyone—fired, the rumor went. He wondered if that was the whole story; he suspected that her past had reached out and grabbed her. She hadn't wanted to be grabbed. Perhaps that was what had attracted Flander to her in the first place—that they were both haunted by yesterday. David brushed the sand from his fingertips and got slowly to his feet.

He and Flander had started a new gallery piece. They hadn't meshed like this in months, rebounding off each other's inspiration, taking off on crazy tangents that sparked frenzied bursts of creation. The piece was good—one of the best they'd done. Maybe *the* best by the time it was finished. And because of that, the issue of the kicker had gotten pushed into the background, lost in the excitement of creation.

He had let it get lost because he was afraid to rock the boat. David clenched his fist, and the lizard darted beneath its rock.

Truth. It was a bitter seed in his happiness with their work. Time to face it? David tossed his braid back over his shoulder, uneasy because this completion felt symbolic. This holo had been his last piece for Alcourt. They could leave Erebus now, move on to something else. David had intended to message Alcourt and formally present the finished desert, but an unexpected urgency nagged at him. Across the hall massed pink tulips glowed on the table in the holoed dining room. Perhaps Jewel was right and there was too much illusion in this place. Perhaps there was too much illusion in his life. He would message Alcourt later. David headed for the main door, resolve hardening into a lump in his guts.

It was time. Security opened the door for him. Time to face Flander before it was too late. Time to face himself and his doubts.

Time, and more than time.

Nervous fear squeezed him as he turned down Amundsen corridor, and he fought it down. He palmed the door to their apartment, then burst through before it had completely opened. ''Flander?'' No answer. Asleep? He had been off the remotes for nearly two weeks, but he still tired easily. David crossed the room in three long strides and stuck his head into the bedroom. The bed was empty, rumpled, because Flander had still been asleep when David had left to work on the desert.

Damn. ''House?'' David swallowed impatience. Now that he had decided, he wanted to deal with this. ''Locate Flander for me.''

''Locating.''

The silence was lasting too long. Erebus System was state-of-the-art powerful. The hair began to prickle on the back of David's neck.

''Flander is not within the Complex's Security field.''

Not possible. ''House, search all exit logs,'' he snapped, but a knot was slowly tightening in his guts. Flander had been playing games with Erebus Security already. If he had been able to get in and out of Jewel's apartment without alerting Security, the Security was not going to see him unless Flander wanted it to. If he got caught, David wouldn't be able to save him. David clenched his fists slowly, furious, ready to wring Flander's skinny neck with his bare hands. Damn him. Playing his games, ghosting, because it kept his ghost—or goddess, or whatever the hell she had been—alive.

He could be down at the TimeOut. He could be out in the corridors somewhere.

But Flander read David, knew what David was going to do sometimes before David himself knew. He had known this confrontation was coming. The fox was quick to bolt. David let his breath out in a rush, hands dropping to his sides. Beneath the anger lurked a dark layer of fear. That one day he would not come back. "House, check all flights leaving McMurdo. Search for a reservation for Flander."

"No reservation has been made for that name or under that ID print."

So he was here somewhere, playing hide-and-seek with Security. David wasn't reassured. He could have gone out with a freight run; he might have sweet-talked some chopper pilot into hauling him along. Security was airtight only if you were coming *into* Erebus. He would show up in a few minutes, David told himself, but he was already thinking about going down to the freight dock to check around. Who else might know where he was? "House, mail, to Jewel Martina. Realtime request." He needed to ask her, see her face, read what he could. Maybe Flander was still ghosting her space; maybe he had dropped some kind of hint or was even on his way to see her.

"I'm, sorry. Jewel Martina will not accept mail from this address."

David stared blankly at the wall. "I'm screened out?"

He hadn't addressed the House, so it didn't answer him. Why? Damn it, *why*? David shook his head, impatience burning in him like a rising fever. Now what? He could review the video files for every entrance. Even if Flander had diddled the Security program so that it didn't find his image when it searched, the image was still there on file. Somewhere. David would at least know which entrance he had left by—loading dock or resident entry.

Why was he so sure that Flander was gone?

If he asked to review the files, Security would want to know why. David's impatience vanished suddenly, melting into a sense of dull futility. Deep down, in some unacknowledged corner of his mind, he had known that Flander was about to take off. David sighed. Everything had felt so good between them. Like it used to be.

Maybe that was the problem.

David walked through the thick silence of the empty room to order tea from the kitchenwall. Flander would come back when he was ready, he told himself. He always did. Flander's privacy was his own. It wasn't David's business where he had gone.

Maybe he should have made it his business. Was it too late now?

"I don't know," David said out loud. After a minute he dumped his untouched tea into the sink and pulled on his lenses. "Studio."

The pale walls solidified around him. The cat leapt down from its radiator perch, but David ignored it. He took the ice-cave canvas from its rack and stretched it open. What was Flander running from? Inside, the lion tracks were still there, melted deeply into the ice. Another face had been gouged into the wall. This one was bigger, ugly. The same hand had shaped it—with the sledgehammer, from the look of it. It drained energy from the cave. David slashed his hand across it, erasing it. He reached into the newly smooth ice wall and tore out a chunk.

Something was chasing Flander, had been chasing him ever since David had picked up the grimy kid from his doorstep. "Not me," David said softly. The ice walls echoed his words back to him in cold whispers. *Not me . . . not me . . .* They had the sound of a prayer. In a sudden gust of rage David squashed the lump of ice between his hands, digging his fingers into it as if it were flesh, as if it could scream and struggle. He formed a broad muzzle, shaping the ice crudely, with rough power. He added wide jaws and fangs that could crunch through bones and flesh, hook red ropes of guts from your belly. The slitted eyes were cold, merciless. It scared him, this monster, and it filled him with excitement, like a cold lust. David let those emotions seep through his fingers into a heavy mane and thick shoulders. Not paws, no. Try this . . . Oh, yeah, *that* was where it was going . . .

David worked until he was shivering with fatigue and imaginary cold, until he was as hollow and empty inside as a vase carved from ice. Then he exited, hoping for one agonized instant that Flander would be there, asleep on the bed or eating noodles at the table.

The apartment was empty.

David threw his lenses across the room. Then he went down to the TimeOut to fill up the emptiness with beer and find out if anyone had seen Flander anywhere.

Jewel stared through the window of the rail as it rushed eastward. The big mag-lev projects had been the last gasp of Seattle's old-days prosperity. Built late and to updated earthquake codes, all but one had survived the big subduction quake that had shattered much of the northwest coast. The Quake had been timely, Jewel thought with bitter irony. Before it the city had belonged to the gangs, the homeless, and the decreasing number of armed commuters who couldn't access their job via the Net.

But the thirsty 'burbs with their uncertain Net access and expensive commute were no longer an upscale asset. So when the Quake had provided convenient and instant demolition, wealth had moved in to rebuild the shattered city in a new image. Climate-controlled residence towers rose in sweeps of pristine ceramic and glass, self-contained gardens of clean air, recycled water, and armed security. Change had come to other urban centers less completely, accompanied by violence and bloodshed, but in Seattle the San Juan de Fuca plate got the blame for urban renewal. With its moderate climate and sleek new face, the city was a popular address for midlevel web nodes. The very rich—the Alcourts—lived elsewhere. In the Preserves. In pricey solitude.

The poor and Quake-disinherited had scattered like rats into the emptying 'burbs. Jewel looked through the gang-signed permaglass, sweating because the air-conditioning was down again. Below the grimy concrete span of the rail, small houses lined up in orderly rows, separated by tan strips of weedy dust. They were old, with roofs of crumbling shingles. Ancient cars, broken bits of furniture, piles of cardboard and plastic trash cluttered the old yards. A lot of the houses had burned to blackened shells in this neighborhood.

Within a block orderly green replaced the trash and the dust: Little Cambodia. Cambodian melon and baby corn were status dishes at parties in the city towers, and the rumor was that they paid off the city for extra water. Razor wire fenced the lush gardens. Cambodians, Eastern Europeans, Indonesians, Hispanics—the ethnic minorites clustered into tight communities out here. Mostly they worked in the service industries or security or were owners of some small family firm that might produce only a single specialized product, frequently by hand. A single street might separate one neighborhood from another, but the boundary was very real. More real than most international borders anymore. People did not wander aimlessly in the 'burbs, not if they wanted to survive.

Jewel barely passed in Linda's neighborhood. It was very white, and tensions ran high there. She looked too Hispanic, never mind that Mama had said she wasn't. Sam was Latino. He had offered her a home and she would have fit into his neighborhood—at least in appearance. But it had been another dead end, and she had said no. Jewel leaned her forehead against the vibrating permaglass, anger like a small stone in her belly. Anger at whom? Alcourt, for firing her? David Chen, for opening the door to the past with his damn desert? Susana, for walking through? Or herself, for not accepting Alcourt's offer? She grabbed for the seat back as the rail slowed.

It weighed her down, that anger stone, made her slow and stupid in front of her new employer. Which didn't matter, because the dying old woman didn't expect anything else and didn't care, anyway. To Jewel's surprise, Alcourt had given her satisfactory references. It had the feel of disdain; he had swatted her hopes as casually as he might swat a fly. He did not need to be vindictive.

Who do I throw this stone at? Jewel wondered, and closed her eyes. Perhaps she would simply carry it all her life, until she turned to stone herself. A young woman swayed down the aisle, eyes dreaming, moving to the music playing over her audio implant. She had a fiberlight rose embroidered on one cheek, pale in the afternoon light, and her skin had a soft, translucent look. Some of the street drugs did that—the hypnotics that blurred VR and reality. Jewel watched her get off, wondering what she would Net into tonight. Sex in one of the parlors that offered specialized hardware? Some pretty fantasy? It was probably more real to her than the delivery or personal service job she held during the day. The doors hissed closed, and the rail picked up speed again. It was almost empty now. The kitchen help, cleaners, the men and women who delivered prepared meals, the freshly cut flowers, love, health and cosmetic maintenance—they had all gotten off.

The rail slid up and over a low hill. Her stop. Jewel stood, bracing herself against the pull of deceleration. There were only two others in the car: gang, and white. She slung her carryall carefully over her shoulder and slid her hand into her pocket, fingers curling around the stun gun she carried.

"Hey, *chiquita*." The taller of the two gave her a bored leer. His face was burned dark brown, slashed with a lightning-bolt zigzag of untanned skin. Dark, ugly freckles spotted his neck and shoulders. "Sweet lips, you can't get off." He grinned, reaching into his lap. "I got somethin' you want."

Jewel pretended not to see the white thrust of his penis in his hand. She shot a look at the armed guard in the middle of the car, but he avoided her gaze. Paid off or just unwilling to intervene in anything short of rape or murder? Jewel tightened her grip on her stunner.

"What's wrong, baby? Too big for you? You need a taste of white meat, baby." They both giggled.

Play deaf. They weren't very serious, were just giving her shit. She tried for casual in her walk. See, guys? You don't scare me. I'll zap the hell out of you if you so much as move in my direction. *Read* it, Jack.

She could smell her own fear sweat and wondered if they could smell it, too, like wild dogs. Past them now, down the steps. She tried not to tense up, waiting for the sound of movement, ready with the stunner. She hopped down onto the platform, knees wanting to tremble for an instant. Made it. Jewel breathed a sigh of relief as the rail slid forward with a rush of displaced air. Maybe the guard would have intervened. And maybe not.

She slid her UV shades onto her face. At the far end of the platform an old man was closing the umbrella that shaded his home-made snack stand, getting ready to go home. Melanoma. She looked away from his face. A mall fronted the rail platform. The store-fronts were glassless and gutted, littered with empty shelves, trash, and junk too worthless to scavenge. A flea market had grown up in the empty spaces and out on the cracked sidewalk in front; people traded produce, hot food, meat, black-market antibiotics, clothes, and electronics. You could buy anything if you knew how to ask. Or anyone.

Jewel tucked her carryall with her work clothes safely under her arm—she did not dare wear any kind of medical uniform on the street—and cut across the baking asphalt lot. PARK AND RIDE, a rusty sign proclaimed. Bullet holes pocked its white and black paint, edged with rust only a shade lighter than dried blood. Paper and plastic trash shoaled along the Quake-cracked wall of the build-ing. She had missed the rush of morning shopping, when the scrawny, home-grown vegetables and newly butchered rabbits were cool and fresh. Perhaps they were cats, but you accepted rabbit because you didn't want to know. The hookers, jugglers, fire-eaters, dealers, and inlay artists came out after dark. Now the market was full of dust and evening sun. A drowsing dog stretched beneath a warped card table from which a crazy old woman with lavender hair told fortunes, peering at a tattered deck of tarot cards with cataract-clouded eyes.

"Child? Child?" The old woman waved a crooked, arthritic hand at Jewel. "Come here, dear. Come sit, and I'll tell you what's in store for you. A rich boyfriend, a lottery win." She grinned, revealing too-white fed-med teeth. "Come along now, child. Ev-erybody wants to know their future."

"No, thanks." Jewel tried to walk on past, but the old woman's hand shot out like a striking snake, closing tightly on her wrist.

"Stop now, hush." She pulled Jewel closer with surprising strength. "You shouldn't walk blind into tomorrow, child. No, not blind. And look, look, see what we have here." As she mumbled, her pale spidery fingers shuffled the ragged cards.

Magic, chemicals, and the lottery. Jewel stared at the bright pic-tures in distaste. Bright, cheap dreams of escape. The woman's face had been eroded by the sun and age into a thousand folded gullies. Harmon .' lcourt's face would never look like that. Neither would David Chen's.

"The hanged man, ah, yes." The old woman flipped a tattered card down on the table. A man swung by his bound ankles, hands behind his back. "This is a card of changes, child. The past will confront you. You have resisted it, but this is the time to face it, to accept and surrender."

A slight figure darted into the end storefront, a shapeless bundle tucked under one arm. Susana? Jewel squinted over the fortune-teller's shoulder. Yes, Susana, visiting the junk dealer who fenced stolen goods. She reappeared a moment later, her hair a coppery flash in the setting sun, skinny and tall. "I have to go."

"Not yet, child. You must hear this." Another card fluttered to the table. "Death." A skeleton bestrode a white horse. "Ah, but not of the flesh, child. This is death of the old Self. It is time to let go of fear. The more you resist, the more danger you will face, and this—" The third card fluttered down. "This is the empress." The old woman cackled. "Ah, yes, child. It is your mother you must face, oh, yes, I see . . . "

The robed woman on the card suddenly smiled, revealing the white fangs of a mountain lion. Jewel recoiled. "I—I have to go." A trick of the light. It was just a card. She fished in her pocket for a leaf of federal scrip and tossed it down onto the table.

"Oh, no. No money for this." The woman raised her milky eyes to Jewel's face. "This is a gift, child. And this: Listen to the lioness."

The lioness? For a moment, just for an instant, the old woman's pale, clouded eyes had gone clear. A stranger looked out and laughed at her.

Not a stranger. The lioness from David's desert.

Jewel backed away, telling herself it was imagination, fatigue, the bright sun and a long day.

"Tell your fortune, your future . . . Tell you your tomorrow; a new boyfriend, a rich one . . . "

Yes, imagination. Jewel walked quickly away from the old woman's singsong. Susana had vanished. The yellow dog opened one eye as she walked past and thumped its ropy tail in the dust. This was not Erebus; illusion in this desolate place was self-delusion and nothing more. But Jewel walked fast, sweating in the dry heat, catching imagined glimpses of a cat shape in the stark evening shadows.

More imagination.

Linda lived on top of a hill. Jewel had to slow down, sweating, as she plodded up the twisting street of cracked blacktop. A bicycle passed her, zooming downhill in a blur. The houses along this street had been big, with arched front windows and lots of decks. The decks were gone now, scavenged for firewood. Plastic and cardboard patched the broken panes. Once this must have been an expensive neighborhood. Now two or three families shared most houses. Two small girls peered at her from the shade of struggling fir. You didn't see too many kids out here. Jewel shifted her carryall to her other shoulder. This was a subsidy neighborhood, and the penalties for illegitimate pregnancies were stiff.

A faint breeze touched her, cool on her sweat-soaked back. A dense jungle of blackberry, stinging nettle, and brush covered the hillside. If there had been houses along here once, they had fallen down in the Quake or burned. Mounds of blackberry rose like small mountains. Jewel took the shortcut through them, ducking thorns on the narrow path. The shadows were thickening as the sun set, and Jewel felt a flicker of relief as the path opened onto the hilltop. A cluster of houses crowded the dusty space, surrounded by trampled dust that defied even the blackberries. These houses were older, not as big as the ones on the hillside. Linda paid rent to a woman who probably had no legal title to the house but who collected her rent with two husky gangies at her heels. Jewel wondered briefly who did own the house. She could find out if she wanted to spend money for the Net time. But what did it matter? The house closest to the path had burned. The shell still stood, but black smoke marks fanned upward from the upstairs windows. It gave the house a surprised look, as if it had raised smoky black eyebrows.

The old man who lived across the street from Linda opened his front door and peeked out. Jewel caught a glimpse of the pale oval of his face before the door shut quickly and silently. A rusting Triumph sat on blocks in the driveway, stripped of anything valuable. At night the man often got into the slashed seat, clutched the wheel, and made engine noises. Jewel had watched him one night when she couldn't sleep; his skin had looked white and translucent in the moonlight, like the shell of some cave-dwelling insect. Alcourt never came out into the sun, either. Would he look that white without his cosmetically altered skin?

Linda's house was quiet. Shutters cut from scrap plasticboard covered the front windows, shutting out the harsh afternoon sun. Sun-scorched grass whispered around Jewel's ankles as she crossed the yard and climbed the three cracked concrete steps. The door was ajar, and she could see into the sunken living room through the crack. It was Carl's room now—his entire world. He lay propped up by pillows on a sagging bed, naked from the waist up, his useless legs covered by a sheet. He had been a big, powerful man, proud of his muscles. Now flesh was turning soft, sagging on his bones, as if he were melting very, very slowly.

To Jewel's surprise, Susana was there. She must have run all the way up the hill, Jewel thought sourly. She was bending over Carl, her too-large tank top down over one heavily freckled shoulder, changing his urine bag. Hand raised to push the door open, Jewel hesitated. There was a tenderness about Susana's movements that Jewel had never seen before—as if Susana were the parent, and Carl an injured child.

Carl noticed her and grunted something to Susana, and the moment ended.

"Auntie Jewel." Susana straightened, bulging collection bag in her hand. "You're home early. Get fired?"

"Sorry, I didn't." Jewel stepped back as Susana brushed past her, close enough to bump her with the warm bulge of the bag. A challenge. Jewel hung on to her temper with an effort. "How are you, Carl?"

"How do you think?" Carl eyed her with dull resentment. "Listen, I got mail. Susana couldn't download it because the lines are bad, so Linda's gonna stop by the post office for the hard copy. It has to be my fed accident money." He plucked at the sheet across his legs. "The insurance bastards don't want to pay me because I'm a troublemaker. Myron was over today. He said that rumor's true—Sony-Matohito is gonna open a plant over on the west side."

"That's good, isn't it?" Jewel looked away from his feverish eyes, hating this hot, dim house. "It'll mean jobs. Do you want some water?" She picked up the empty pitcher beside his bed.

"Yeah. It's gonna mean jobs, all right." Carl levered himself onto his elbow to scowl at her. "I know what they're up to; they cut some kind of deal with the state. They'll pull workers off subsidy, and the state'll look the other way while they cut wages below minimum. You quit without cause and you can't get back on subsidy, so they got this slave-labor pool, just like that. That way, Sony-Matohito doesn't pay no more for good U.S. labor than it has to pay to the third-world geeks." He spit over the side of the bed. "Won't mean jobs for *us*, anyway. Salgado's tight with the governor, so you spicks'll get 'em, and maybe the tame geeks, 'cause Salgado gets payola from Saigon Town and Cambodia. Myron said Ray's calling a meeting of the Committee, because we gotta do something about this. I don't know how Ray got the chair. Shoulda been Myron's."

His voice pursued Jewel into the kitchen. *You spicks.* Anger twisted inside her like a directionless wind. When Linda had first met Carl, he and Jewel had hated each other on sight. They had had some screaming fights before she had split. Now his ruined legs silenced her, locked the anger inside her. She suspected he guessed it and needled her all the more because of it. Jewel stuck the pitcher under the kitchen tap. Race had no meaning in the Net; you could take any face and skin color you wanted. She dumped the water into the countertop filter, then stuck the pitcher underneath. Race didn't have much meaning in Alcourt's world, either. It had a hell of a lot of meaning here. Especially for Carl.

Susana breezed into the kitchen, halting with a wary lift of her head when she saw Jewel.

"I saw you down at the platform flea market." Jewel eyed her. "Skimming the loading docks again?"

"You're crazy. Me?" Susana shook her head so that her multiple braids whipped her cheeks. "I was here all day. You want to ask Carl? Hey, I even made soup for dinner." She nodded at the pot on the stove. "I'm a good little kid."

Jewel met her mocking stare. "You're not a subsidy kid, thanks to Linda. But you've already been busted once. If you're lucky, they won't put you into a juvenile camp next time they bust you. If you aren't, I hope you're a good fighter. You can't sell your ass unless you got something to sell."

The door banged behind Susana. Waste of breath. Jewel carried the clean water out to Carl.

"You picking on her again?" Carl scowled as she set the pitcher down. "Leave her alone. She's a good kid. She knows which way's up."

Sure. Jewel didn't answer. Susana was the typical 'burbs kid: boarding with the packs of teenagers that had taken over the streets, stealing, not doing drugs but maybe dealing on the side. She acted as if there were no horizon but the dusty dead end of this place, and for her there wouldn't be. She wasn't doing public ed, even. The public ed Net was shit, but there was no other way out. Not all the way. Jewel had figured that out early—the Catch-22. Education was the only way to make it, but the education you needed to make it cost too much. Closed circle. Shadows were filling up the room. Jewel opened the crude shutters. If you were lucky, you could work for one of the small individual firms that linked together to form the big webs. You could spend your life belonging to someone. The sun had set, but ruddy light filled the room, borne on a faint whisper of warm breeze. The color and intensity reminded her suddenly and vividly of midnight out on the ice. National politics were a

farce. The webs ruled the world. If you wanted to belong to yourself, you learned to manipulate the web. As Alcourt did.

"You're not listening to me. You got to keep on top, and Ray's
a fool," Carl growled. "Myron should of gotten the chair. The
Committee's got to stand up to Sony-Matohito, let folks know what's
going on, and Ray can't do it. He doesn't have the balls. LA pulled
that same wage shit, processing the bergs that Tanaka brings in.
And look what you got." His voice dropped. "Slavery, that's what.
We had a good thing, America. We threw it away, gave it away to
every piece of third-world trash who wanted to walk in and ask.
That's why they tried to take me out." His eyes glittered in the red
afternoon light. "Because they knew I was on to them. They knew
I could stop 'em."

Jewel pressed her lips together and poured him a glass of
water. He believed it—that the accident hadn't been an accident
at all. That it had been a political assassination attempt, never
mind that there had been witnesses who had seen him step out
in front of the car. Perhaps it made the pain more bearable to
feel that you were a hero, a martyr. What he and his Committee
wanted was a return to a yesterday that she wasn't sure had even
existed outside the history videos. Jewel handed him the water
and watched him gulp it down. Sweat shone on his pale face.
She could smell the water today in spite of the filtering. The city
must be pumping from the shallow well field again.

Carl's face contorted suddenly, and he spilled the last of the water
across his bare chest. "Jewel?"

"I've got some." He hated having to ask her, hated begging.
Especially begging from her, Jewel thought resentfully. She fished
in her pocket for the pain patches she had lifted from old Mrs.
Wosenko. These episodes of pain pierced him without reason, without cause—and there was no prescription from fed-med without
diagnosis of need.

Carl was trembling, and tears leaked from the corners of his eyes.
Panting, he fumbled the patches from her palm. "Give me a minute," he said, his face turned away.

She had hated him once. Jewel went into the kitchen, giving him
privacy until the drugs took hold. Part of her still hated him. And
part of her pitied him because what he wanted was as much illusion
as Alcourt's gardens. Jewel lifted the lid from the pot on the stove.
Bean soup, made with the new high-protein variety that they could
irrigate with seawater. Cheap, but they had a bitter aftertaste that
defied any flavoring.

The front door slammed, and she heard Linda's voice in the main room. Jewel gave the pot a last stir and put the lid back on. Through the kitchen she could see Linda bending over Carl, talking in a low voice. Her hair was as dark as Jewel's, and if she were tanned, they *would* look a little bit like sisters. But she wasn't tanned; sun damage would suggest that she did not take her health seriously. It could cost her a contract. Jewel didn't look at the swell of Linda's belly. She was well into her second trimester, glowing with health. She was paid to glow with health. Monitors embedded in her flesh recorded the progress of the pregnancy, every fetal heartbeat, every nanogram of prostaglandin or HGH or HPL in her bloodstream. If the levels weren't perfect, implanted micropumps would titrate the levels to the ideal.

Pregnancy was messy and uncomfortable, but none of the artificial wombs developed so far had performed well. The human uterus still excelled at its task, and human flesh was cheap. Women who had the money contracted out the discomfort. It was simple to implant a fertilized egg in a strange womb. Under careful supervision, a child would grow and prosper. At the end of nine months a sterile surgical team would remove it and place it in your arms. It would take perhaps half an hour. Three months later Linda could take on a new contract. One infant per year, until her body could no longer perform. This was what Alcourt had wanted from Jewel.

No. Jewel put the lid back on the pot. He had wanted her soul, too.

"Carl, we'll get by." Linda straightened as Jewel came into the room. "We will." She touched his cheek. "Where's Susana?"

Her words were positive, but her tone was so doubtful these days. Linda had never doubted. She had been so sure of herself—more sure than Jewel had never been.

"Tell me how it'll be all right." Carl clutched for her hand, but it was out of reach. "Linda, they've *screwed* me. It's a frame, and you know it."

Desperation in his voice? "What's wrong? Linda?"

"The state refused my insurance claim." Carl turned dull eyes toward her. "That's what the fucking letter was about." His voice sounded like gravel shaken in a cup. "To tell me I get zip. Shit, Linda . . . I'm sorry."

"Carl, it's not your fault." She took his hand with an awkward, hesitant motion, like a stranger reaching for a stranger. "It'll be all right."

"All right, sure." He turned his face away. "You think I don't know how much you've shelled out? For squat." He slapped at his sheeted legs. "For fucking *nothing*. Now we don't even get it back."

"They have to hold a hearing." Jewel retrieved the sheet of post office hard copy from the floor. "The state has to call in witnesses and assign you a lawyer." No one said anything as she scanned the flimsy sheet in her hands.

No, they would not have to call a hearing. Carl's blood, sampled at the emergency room, had tested positive for Synth, a cheap cocaine analogue available at any flea market.

"Don't ask me, Jewel," Carl said softly. "Just don't ask me."

Linda got up suddenly and left the room.

Carl had a drug record. Never mind that it was from twenty years ago, that he hadn't been arrested since. A drug record followed a person forever, and the state paid no accident benefits for drug-related injury. Gently she laid the letter with its damning clinic record down on the bed.

"I want to tell Susana, okay?" His face was still turned to the wall. "Don't you do it. Or Linda."

"All right," Jewel said softly. She had planned to leave when the insurance came through. Her ten thousand had been wasted, and it was only her aide income that kept Linda from applying for partial subsidy. "I'm sorry, Carl." What the hell else was there to say?

He didn't answer.

Linda was in the kitchen, standing in front of the stove, staring into the soup pot. "I have to go back early on Sunday. Eleanor wants me to come with her to a gallery opening. Honestly, she wants to educate Serena twenty-four hours a day." She spoke in a light, brittle voice. "Did I tell you I have to sleep with a teaching program running? I can hear voices in my sleep, like someone's talking inside me. Last night I dreamed it was Serena, that she was telling me something. I don't know if I can eat this. My last toxin screen was up, and Eleanor had a fit. She gave me some microwave dinners to take home for the weekend. And where's Susana? She's never here. I never see her. Every weekend she's gone somewhere, out with friends or getting into trouble, and I can't come out here too often. Eleanor worries."

This wasn't Linda, this woman with the distant eyes and the gushing monotone, like shallow water over stones. "What are you going to do now?" Jewel lifted four bowls down from the shelf.

"I don't know." Linda plopped a ladleful of pale soup into the bowl Jewel held. "Carl wasn't doing Synth." Another plop of soup into the bowl. "The report's wrong."

There was neither conviction nor anger in her tone, just resignation. The old Linda, the real Linda, would have raged and fought.

She would have lost, maybe, but she would have tried. "Don't." Jewel took the fourth bowl from her. "Susana's not here, remember?"

"Oh. Yeah." Linda dropped the ladle into the pot. "She's jealous of Serena." Linda touched her belly. "She's jealous of all of them. I do this for her, to keep subsidy out of her file. Did I do wrong, Jewel?"

Jewel met Linda's eyes. They were clouded and opaque. If the Linda she remembered was in there, Jewel could not see her. Maybe she had died. "No." Jewel grabbed her hand and squeezed. "You did what you had to do, okay? Listen, I'm going to stay with you a little longer. If that's okay. I'm in no rush for my own place."

"Thanks." Linda smiled and picked up two of the bowls. "That'll help a lot."

"Linda?" Jewel hesitated. "Are you there?" she asked softly. "Are you in there?"

Something moved in those shallow-water eyes—a shadow, like a face pressed briefly against a dirty window. Then it was gone. "I don't know what you mean." Linda sighed. "Hand me a couple of spoons, will you. Just stick them in the bowls. Are you going to come eat with us?"

"I think I'll wait. I had a late lunch, and . . . I've got some business on the Net." Jewel watched Linda carry the bowls back into the living room. Her shoulders drooped and her spine sagged around the taut swell of her belly. At night, once Jewel's mother had drowned herself in chemical dreams, she had often sneaked over to Linda's locked and barred house. They had fixed the security mesh on Linda's window, and she could climb over the sill and into Linda's bed. Some nights they just talked. And some nights she cried. She had never cried before she had met Linda. It was something that made you prey, something you didn't dare do.

She could do it in the safety of Linda's bed, face buried against Linda's shoulder. She could talk about where she had been and where she was going to go, *had* to go. Jewel dumped her untouched soup back into the pot and stomped down the hall to the bedroom she was sharing with Linda. They didn't talk in this bed. They just slept. Jewel shivered, feeling the 'burbs closing in over her head like dirty, scummy water—a stagnant pool of resignation, despair, and restless, useless anger. Get out, she told herself. Just walk; there's no reason to stay.

But for a moment, just for an instant, she had glimpsed Linda in those dirty-window eyes.

Next week, Jewel told herself as she pulled her skinthins from the warped chest of drawers. She could handle Carl and Susana that much longer. The skins felt strange as she stripped and pulled them on. This was not hardwired Erebus, and the house didn't have VR access. She dressed slowly, tucking the neck of her skins down inside her tunic, pushing the sleeves up out of sight—walking the 'burbs in expensive skins was almost as dangerous as walking around in a medical uniform. There was a public access booth down by the flea market. She hadn't meant to go into her office tonight, but right now she needed to get out of here. She had gotten another tip from Carolyn . . . if it *was* Carolyn. Jewel flexed her arms, grimacing at the pinch of the bunched-up sleeves. It was still hot and she was already sweating.

If she sold a solid package, she could afford to move out and still help Linda.

Was money all Linda needed?

Some questions had no answers.

Linda was sitting with Carl while he ate. Jewel took the bar off the kitchen door and slipped out that way. Outside it was almost dark and pleasantly cool after the stuffy house. Lights gleamed behind barred windows, and Jewel touched the reassuring lump of the stunner in her pocket. Linda kept a gun in the house; her latest employer had the clout to get her a temporary permit. In the 'burbs, where you traded goods and black-market cash at the flea markets, your assets were real, not electronic. And so were the thieves.

"Boo!"

Jewel gasped and started as a trio of children burst from a clump of bushes. Giggling, pleased with their coup, they dashed away, yelling and whooping. Heart slowing, Jewel watched them disappear into the darkness. She had been a year or two older when she and her mother had moved into the abandoned house near Linda's. She tried to remember if she had ever played like that. If she had, she had forgotten. They had kept moving, she and Mama, riding the refugee trains from city to city, begging, scrounging for jobs, stealing. Running from something—the law, or maybe just ghosts. Mama would never say, but she was always looking over her shoulder. And then they had come to Seattle. To Linda.

Linda had closed the two of them up in their own bright bubble of the present, and it had been all right. For the first time in her life Jewel had felt safe. Linda had taught her how to play.

Jewel shook her head, the stars a bright blur on her retina. What had happened? The stars didn't answer, but they never did. Head down, she took the thorny shortcut to the flea market and the booths.

Chapter Nine

Night could be a dangerous time in the 'burbs, but the long walk down to the platform was uneventful. A man and a woman passed her, but they had their arms around each other and wouldn't have noticed a runaway truck. The flea market was alive with the night-time crowds, lit by solar lanterns and small smoky fires that gave the scene a weird surreal quality. A fire-eater blew gusts of flame onto the hot night air while a girl and a slender youth danced to a complicated drumbeat. Their skin glowed with an intricate filigree of fiberlight tattoos, and the whoops of the men watching them nearly drowned out the drums. For a moment the youth's eyes met hers, glittering and remote, like someone peering through a plastic mask. He reminded her of Flander. Jewel turned away quickly, threading her way past food stalls whose rich smells made her stomach growl. To her relief the fortune-teller wasn't in her usual spot.

The squat column of a public booth glimmered in the light of fire and solar lamps. Its white walls, scrawled with multicolored message icons and gang signs, made her think of the dancers' tattooed bodies. She shut herself inside. It smelled like piss, and the inside walls were as thickly decorated as those outside. "Enter filespace, Jewel Martina," she said, trying not to breathe too deeply. The familiar disorientation clenched her stomach as the dingy walls vanished.

Delicate flowering plants sprouted from cracks in a wall of antique brick. Water trickled over a lip of stone into an earthenware basin. The desk was a slab of pale satiny wood, and Oriental carpets and cushions covered a flagged floor. It was David's custom office design. There was more beauty in this virtual space than she had ever possessed. An unexpected lump clogged her throat, and she swallowed quickly. She would keep this gift, would use it. "Office, retrieve last mail from Carolyn Wasserman."

Carolyn's torso appeared above the desktop, as if she were buried from the waist down in a pale river. "Hi, Jewel." She tilted her dark, curly head, smiling the airhead smile that had always annoyed Jewel because it was a put-on. "Just thought I'd drop in and say hi. Haven't heard from you for a while. And I've got another tip for you. Fed-med's going to require broad-spectrum viral screens for every patient, starting in January. Anything you can do with that? I've got to tell you about my weekend—"

"Office, freeze it." Jewel frowned at Carolyn. She had watched this letter a dozen times, looking for a stranger behind Carolyn's face. Or had Flander been putting her on, playing some convoluted little game of his own?

Her office had frozen Carolyn's image with her face lifted, lips parted to laugh. A shimmering aura of gold-tinged green surrounded her. Her office was reading happiness with an undercurrent of excitement. No warning flag to indicate that this was an autonomous persona rather than a real person messaging her. No flag to indicate that this was not actually Carolyn, but that didn't mean much, because she didn't have any long-term files on Carolyn that were definitely the real person. So her office didn't have a solid reference for running a comparison of body language.

She had taken the chance, set up a package. If it was some kind of trap, she couldn't see it, and she could not afford to pass up the opportunity. "Office, mail to Ishigito." She was through with the Suriyana bitch. Maybe Ishigito hadn't heard about her screwup. Maybe. "Japanese language and formal business mode, very polite, confident, with apologetic overtones."

"Ready," her office prompted in a soft female voice.

Here goes. "Mr. Ishigito." Jewel bowed, hoping that she was projecting the submissive nuances she needed. Her office was editing her every twitch, but there was no guarantee that Ishigito could not read it, no matter how good an office David and Flander had put together. "If you can spare me a few moments, I have a package that might interest you."

Someone knocked on her office door.

"Mr. Ishigito wishes to enter," her office murmured.

"Come in," Jewel said, and winced at her unsteady voice. She hadn't expected a realtime response and fought down a twinge of panic. *Relax.* She drew a deep breath, squashing her excitement and fear. This was not real. Jewel resisted the urge to run her hands through her hair as the door opened.

Ishigito entered smiling and bowed. "You have a new office." He inspected the flowering wall and desk with slitted eyes. "A

Chen design, perhaps? He is famous for his planted-wall motifs. I am very impressed.'' He bowed fractionally deeper. ''You must be doing well for yourself.''

Her office projected an aura that indicated wary caution. Jewel wanted to smile but suppressed it sharply. So, Ishigito-san. It won't be so easy to read me, will it? ''I have information that the federal clinics will require a viral screen for every patient, beginning in January.'' She tapped her desktop, and a security seal appeared. ''A shortage of the tagged antibodies for the tests should drive the price up significantly. I've put together a manufacturing package based in Sumatra. The projected profit is quite attractive.''

Second chances didn't come very often. Incompetency was a lasting brand. Jewel held her breath as Ishigito touched the seal and frowned into space. His own office would be running the numbers from the Token File through his data base, analyzing her projections. Her office was reading wary interest and . . . annoyance. Annoyance? Just a trace, but it was there. Why? Jewel felt her heart sink. It had taken a loan to purchase the Net time needed to put this package together, and she had had to use a personal lien as collateral. If she couldn't sell it, her spare time would belong to the bank for the next six weeks.

Abruptly, Ishigito faced her. ''You have put together a sound package. Epyxx will purchase it.'' He tapped the seal and bowed. ''I am pleased to do business with you, Ms. Martina.''

She read his satisfaction, but that annoyance was still there as a bright orange shimmer in his aura. So what? Jewel answered his bow. He had bought the package. As Flander had suggested, his offer was less than it might have been, but it was still good money. She had been punished, but not as badly as the fox had suggested. She bowed the web node out of her office and let out a sigh of relief.

So there, Alcourt. I did it without you and in spite of you.

Except that she probably hadn't done it in spite of him; he had simply chosen not to break her. Not yet, anyway. She remembered his face as he bent the ivory letter opener between his fingers and shivered. He frightened her. And at other times—when he let his guard down in the solarium or on the massage table, when he let her catch a glimpse of his loneliness—she almost pitied him. Jewel shook her head, banishing Erebus. She was inside. She had made her break into Epyxx, and it would be easier next time. She might make it, after all.

She had enough money now to rent an apartment in the city. Well, on the fringes, anyway. Out of the 'burbs. ''Exit.'' She reached for her lenses.

But she didn't exit to the public booth. To her surprise, she found herself in another virtual. Walls of gleaming ice arched to meet overhead, and a monster crouched on the icy floor, lion-headed, with bared fangs. It had the legs of a goat and a snaky serpentine tail that coiled about its thick haunches. As she stared at it, the creature bared its fangs and lashed out with a taloned paw. Jewel stumbled backward with a cry.

"Relax, lady. It won't bite." A red fox popped up from behind a curtain of ice, teeth gleaming in a canid grin. " 'Bout time you showed up."

"Flander?" Jewel flushed, wondering what her Self was showing him. "What did you dump me into now? Will you stay the hell out of my filespace?" She looked beyond the creature and fell silent. A shadowy woman stood within the wall of ice, arms spread, as if she were reaching out to embrace the icy monster. Her head was thrown back, long hair flowing. By a trick of David's skill, she blurred into the ice so that Jewel couldn't tell where frozen flesh ended and ice began; she seemed to be part of the ice, its soul, perhaps. The ice monster crouched at her feet like a pet dog.

Jewel reached up to touch her own hair. David had made it long, had gathered it into a loose, stylish knot at the base of her neck. She touched the curve of her cheekbone. It was her image in the ice. "This is David's cave." And this was what he saw, how he perceived her? Jewel felt herself blushing again, then shook her head, pissed at her reaction, which the fox could undoubtedly read.

"Yeah, it's his piece. Listen, we got troubles."

"We?" Trapped by that icy Self and the ugly power of the monster, Jewel felt anger rising in her throat. "What do you mean, *we*? I left Erebus, remember? I'm keeping my own head above water. I'm not part of your games with David." She reached for her lenses. "Just stay out of my filespace!"

"What's *she* doing in here?"

It was Susana's voice. Jewel spun around and found herself facing a striped gray and orange cat with a whiskered human face. Oh, yes, Susana. She recognized those angry gray eyes. "What are *you* doing *here*? Let's start with that one." Jewel narrowed her eyes. "That's what the dock skimming pays for, huh? Skins and Net access?"

"I bet you figured drugs." Susana bared cat fangs.

"Nope." Jewel shrugged. "I know what that looks like."

"Knock it off." Flander flattened his ears and glared at them. "I got to talk to Jewel."

"Hey, don't mind me." The fur stood up on Susana's back. "I'll just go back to work. Some asshole smashed my ice woman. I'm going to track that sucker and fix him. See you around, Auntie.'' Tail lashing, she parted the ice-cave wall as if it were a curtain and walked into it.

"How long have you known Susana?'' Jewel stared at Flander.

"A while.'' The fox lifted his shoulders in a very human shrug. "She tags around. I run into her.'' His green eyes glittered. "Yeah, I knew who she was. Small world, huh?''

Too small. How the hell had Susana gotten into the Net? "What's going on, fox? Did *you* leave me that tip about viral screens? Tell me what you're up to or I'm out of here.''

"Hold it.'' Flander snapped at her hand before she could reach for her lenses. "I don't know about any tip, but you listen and you listen good. David's going to get hurt, and it's gonna be your fault. You're the one who spilled it to him about the OD. I told you not to.''

"He needed to know.'' Jewel kept her hands at her sides. "You should have told him yourself.''

"You think I was spaced, don't you? You think I made it up about someone trying to get me?'' The fox's ears folded flat against its skull. "The Complex is like a fucking fishbowl. Shit, they could reach in and just squeeze. So I took off to get this sorted out in a nice safe place, and I didn't tell David, because it's not his problem, and sometimes shit splatters. David knows I always come back, and he gives me space. But this time he's acting crazy. He's *looking* for me.''

"So tell him.'' The ice walls were making her shiver; never mind that the booth was still warm with leftover afternoon heat. "Tell me while you're at it.''

"I can't.'' The fox's fur had gone matted, and its tongue lolled as it panted. "Like I said. Shit splatters, and you don't need to hear it, lady. I can take care of myself. But I can't watch out for David.'' Flander's fox eyes glittered. "You got to tell him I'm safe, that you saw me in the flesh. Tell him if he does anything, I could get hurt. That'll make him back off. If I tell him, he'll know it's a scam. He *reads* me.''

"Why should he believe me?''

"Because you don't like me all that much.'' The fox teeth showed again. "Oh, yeah, lady, we both read that. He'll believe you 'cause he figures you won't do me any favors. But this one you're doing for *him*. He's here in Seattle, staying on one of those fancy islands— Vashon. I downloaded his address to your office. I did a damn hot job on that office, by the way. You owe me for that, too." He grinned.

"I don't owe you anything." Jewel clenched her teeth. "Why don't you tell him the truth about what's going on? Maybe he'll surprise you."

"No." Flander's grin vanished. "Go see him in the flesh. Flesh matters to David. Tell him what I said. Tell him it'll be okay."

"I can't," she said, more forcefully than she had intended. "I'm not going to lie to him, and—I don't have time."

"You have time." Green fire danced in Flander's eyes. "You *better* lie to him, lady. Or he'll end up dead, and it'll be your fault."

Dead? Jewel felt a chill. "Don't give me fault, fox." She clenched her fists. "You're the one who got into whatever mess you're into, not me."

"Okay, screw fault, then." He growled softly deep in his throat. "Go tell him or I'll strip you right out of the Net, lady. I'll leave you naked, got it?" Flander bared his teeth in a silent snarl, leapt into the air, and vanished.

"You're the one he's trying to save!" she yelled after him.

No answer. An address had been carved into the ice where he had been sitting: David's address. Jewel glared at it, cold inside and out now. Water dripped in a single monotonous note, and the ugly lion-headed monster leered at her. "Exit," Jewel said, and shuddered as the scrawled walls of the booth reappeared around her. So David was on Vashon Island. Go see him? No.

He would find out that she was living in the 'burbs. A part of her didn't want him to know.

Which was stupid. If Flander was half as good as she guessed, he could do just what he had threatened; strip her private filespace to the bone. Great. If Alcourt didn't smash her in the web, the fox would clean her out.

But, threat aside, she did not want David Chen to get hurt. He had offered her comfort that night in Erebus, and there had been no price tag. Jewel winced as the cost of her Net time flashed on the wallscreen. Would David even listen to her? She shoved the door open. After the close stink of the booth, the dusty flea market air smelled almost fresh. It was fully dark now. The power curfew had blanked all the city lights, and the flea market burned like a bonfire of light and motion. A man wandered by, head turned up to the pale disk of moon overhead. He rebounded gently from the wall of the booth and wandered on, oblivious—spaced on Synth or something else. Jewel pressed her lips together.

"I figured you went in from this booth." Susana emerged from the shadows, hand on her hip, pelvis thrust aggressively forward. "What'd the fox want? He doesn't play with people like you."

Jealousy? "So you're ghosting around in there. Skimming can't pay for your Net time, so what does?" Jewel stuffed her lenses into her pocket and brushed by Susana, stripping off her gloves as she started walking. "Forget the camps," she said coldly. "Juvenile doesn't save you if you get picked up on piracy. You get the death penalty."

"I'm not pirating." Susana caught up with her. "I've got an in, Auntie, and I'm not telling you what it is, so believe it or not. What do you care, anyway?"

"Linda cares," Jewel said evenly.

"Fuck that. She wouldn't even notice I was gone. Why'd you come here, Auntie? Back to the scum zone?"

Beneath the macho tone those words carried an edge like a razor. Jewel swung around, stopping so suddenly that Susana nearly ran into her. "I came back because you asked me to," she said softly. "Because Linda and I are sisters, and you were right. I'd stopped remembering that."

Susana stood still, her dirty tank top brushing the front of Jewel's tunic, her face turned up so that the pale moon painted it with colorless light and shadow. "I said it, but it's crap," she said softly. "You and Linda aren't related at all."

This kid carried a stone of anger, too. Whose name was written on it? Maybe she didn't know, either. "You're wrong," Jewel said softly. They had used her blade, even though it scared Linda a little that she carried it. They had hidden in the dusty twilight beneath the ruins of a deck, and Linda had made the cuts, carefully nicking first Jewel's tanned wrist and then her own. They had pressed their arms together so that the sticky blood smeared their skin. Now we're sisters forever, Linda had whispered, and had kissed Jewel on the lips. That cut hadn't saved Jewel's life, maybe, but in the end Jewel wondered if it hadn't saved her soul.

"We're sisters." Jewel stared down into Susana's pale, cold face.

"Am I supposed to be impressed?"

"I don't care if you're impressed or not," Jewel said softly. "You asked."

Susana's lips twitched, and some emotion rippled across her face; it was gone like cloud shadow, too fast for Jewel to identify it. "So, you told me." Susana stepped away from Jewel, a vague, sexless figure in the darkness. "I've got business."

"Susana—"

Too late. She had vanished like a shadow. Jewel scanned the

bright, crowded market but couldn't pick her out in the kaleidoscope of light and movement. What had she meant to say to this angry child-woman, anyway? What was there to say? Jewel shrugged and trudged up the dark hill, listening for footsteps, one hand on her stunner.

The house was dark when she finally reached it. Carl was asleep, snoring heavily in the thick darkness of the living room. Jewel felt her way through the darkened kitchen to the bedroom. The shutters were open, and the moon cast a square of pale light through the barred window. Jewel stripped out of her skinthins, the midnight breeze cool on her sweaty skin, listening to Linda's quiet breathing in the darkness.

On the double bed Linda sighed and murmured something. She looked so young, asleep. Her dark eyelashes fluttered, and she smiled. Dreaming what? Jewel wondered. She sat down on the edge of the bed and touched Linda's cheek gently, stroked her shoulder. She was wearing an oversized T-shirt. It had hiked up, and her belly swelled in the moonlight, white and smooth. A scar curved above her hip. Implanted hardware? Jewel took her hand away, shivering. Where was the girl who had cut her wrist and believed in what she was doing? She did not know this woman. What would David Chen read in Linda? Would he see the Linda she remembered, somewhere behind those closed eyes? *I loved you*, Jewel thought, and the past tense wounded her. She buried her face in the pillow and pulled the sheet up over her head. She would go see David. She would give him Flander's message, because—because . . .

Call it final payment for the office package, she told herself. As she fell asleep, her fingers found the tiny ridge of scar her blade had left on her forearm so long ago.

Jewel woke to the hot kiss of the rising sun on her face. Linda curled against her, the swell of her belly against the small of Jewel's back. She stirred as Jewel sat up, her eyelids fluttering.

"I've got to go into town," Jewel murmured to her. "I'll be back this afternoon."

"Okay." Linda yawned, not really awake. "Is Susana home? I'm meeting Eleanor . . ." Her voice trailed away as she sank back into sleep.

She had never waked easily. Jewel had teased her about it. Jewel got up, banishing memory with the small actions of dressing and the nagging ache of a full bladder. Carl would be up. She should check on him before she left. Jewel yawned. She hadn't slept well.

In her dreams Susana, Linda, and Flander had combined and re-
combined in the kitchen or in the ice cave with the fanged, ugly
monster.

She tiptoed down the hall in case Carl was asleep. He was not.
Jewel paused in the hallway. Susana was with him, squatting beside
the bed. Carl was there in the line of Susana's jaw, but hers was
the stronger face. Jewel had always thought of Carl as a strong,
angry presence, but now she wondered if she had mistaken anger
for strength. Or perhaps the accident had used up his strength.

Susana stood and kissed her father's forehead. "I'll be back this
afternoon," she said.

Again, she seemed the adult and Carl the child—a strange rever-
sal of roles for this angry kid. Carl was staring up at the ceiling,
but he heard Jewel as she came down the steps and turned to face
her. "How are you?" Jewel asked. His eyes were full of shadows, and his face looked gaunt this morning. She touched his forehead, wondering if she should put him onto the remotes. They cost.
"More pain?"

"Yeah, I'm hurting, but your drugs won't do shit." He slapped
her hand away. "I don't have a fever. Myron stopped by this morning on his way to work. The Committee isn't gonna fight the Sony-
Matohito plant."

"So maybe it's a good thing." Jewel checked the collection bag,
but it was empty. Susana must have changed it. "Maybe they aren't
planning to cut wages."

"Screw that. Ray sold us out. Oh, shit, who am I kidding?" He
let his head drop back onto his pillow. "People want the damn
jobs, and they don't look any further than that. Sometimes I think
I'm the only one who really gives a damn. The rest of 'em are
sheep. Maybe that's why we're out here." He stared up at the
ceiling as if some kind of answer were written into the cracks and
the water stains. "We got soft. We let everyone else walk all over
us—the Japs, the East Europe Coalition, Little Cambodia, spick-
town, you people all stick together. You do the payoffs. You back
each other up, maybe 'cause you're all related, huh? Maybe we
been doing our own thing too long. We don't know how to work
together anymore. We just keep hangin' on, waiting for the good
old days to come back, and I guess maybe they never will. I ran
the Committee," he went on in a stumbling monotone. "I thought
we had something going, but I was wrong. It was just me and a
bunch of sheep."

You people? Jewel's lips tightened, but she said nothing. What
did he have left? "Maybe it's just a setback." Jewel touched his

shoulder lightly. "Maybe they'll change their minds if they get some solid information."

"No." For once Carl made no move to dislodge her hand. "They won't. I was playing a game. All this time, and look how fast it's falling apart. In a couple of weeks the Committee'll be nothing. I was kidding myself. Yesterday's over. It was over before I was born, and it ain't coming back. I was playing a fucking game."

Truth, and what could she say to that? "Want me to wake Linda?" Jewel asked gently.

"Let her sleep." Carl closed his eyes. "I thought I could fix something. I thought I knew what needed fixing and I could *do* it, like I was some kind of superhero out of a kids' video . . . Get out of here," he said heavily. "Leave me alone."

"Sure, Carl. See you later."

"Jewel?"

She turned back, one hand on the door. Carl had twisted to face her, and his eyes glittered in the dim light.

"I never liked you," he said in a low voice. "You always figured it was because you're a spick, right?"

Jewel shrugged.

"It's not that. It's because Linda cares about you. You meant more to her than I ever did. She married me just because she was pissed at you. I don't know why she stuck it out." He rolled onto his back, arms flat at his sides. "Just get out of here."

No. "Carl—" Jewel groped for words, found none. His eyes were closed, and he wasn't listening to her, anyway. She fled, closing the door very softly, running down the street, down the dusty path through the berries. Carl was wrong. Linda hadn't married Carl because of her. She had decided first, and then she and Jewel had had a fight about it because Carl was such a bigot. He was wrong about this. Out of breath, sweating in the morning heat, Jewel slowed to a walk. Poor Carl. She wondered if he could be right about the wage cut. Labor moved to the cheapest market, and the dozens of little border wars around the globe ensured that somewhere, somebody was willing to work for shit. He was right about LA and the iceberg industry. AllThings had used some very complex legal maneuvering to get Tanaka, one of their firms, a cut on the federal minimum wage. You couldn't apply for an emergency subsidy if you were eligible for an open job. So you didn't have the option to say no and could end up with less money. Whoever said you got choices?

The mag-lev was just pulling up to the platform. Jewel ran for it, swinging herself onboard as the doors whispered closed. No gangies this morning. The guard looked very alert and in a bad mood, as if he would welcome trouble. Good. She slid her card through the register and dropped into an empty seat. She would make up for her extra Net time the previous night by walking to the ferry slip—the rickshaws and electric taxis cost a lot. Everything cost downtown. If you couldn't afford it, you shouldn't be there. Expense created a nice invisible fence, backed up by discreet force—private and public security services were one of the biggest employers. In the 'burbs the public cops rode two to a van, and they went armed. You saw maybe one van a month or less.

Jewel got off the rail at the plaza closest to the Sound. The towers here were lower so as not to block the view of the Sound from the downtown buildings. You could see the Space Needle from here. It had been rebuilt after the Quake, re-created in every detail in a fit of civic nostalgia. Once she and Linda had snuck into it, had played tourist until a smart guard had tumbled and had kicked them out—not very gently. Trees and flowers bloomed in earthenware pots along brick paths. They were artificial. At night fountains of holographic water would play in the empty stone basins. Illusion was for the rich. Reality got left to the poor—reality and the self-created illusions of hope or escape. Like Carl's dreams of political power or the chemical escape of the druggies.

Jewel hunched her shoulders against the harsh lash of the sun. The solar panels that sprouted from every building seemed to soak up the gentler rays. Sweating, she plodded down to the dock, where a ferry was loading for the short trip over to Vashon Island. Jewel slid her card through the slot and pushed through the turnstile window. Upscale place, the island. A historical preserve, rigidly maintained in twentieth-century style. Even the ferry was the original port authority shell. In the old days it had carried cars and buses. The few private cars and a scatter of delivery vans huddled forlornly on its vast deck. A woman boarded ahead of Jewel. She was old, the way Alcourt was old. You could see it in her skin in spite of the cosmetic work that had given her a thirty-five-year-old face.

Her employer, Ruth Wosenko, was old, too. Older than this woman—too old to have grown up with the early surgical interventions, the organ repair, and the cellular implants that imparted youth and health throughout a long life. She could afford to live, but her body was trying hard to die. She spent most of her day in virtual, skiing in the Alps or sailing in the Caribbean with a brown-skinned handsome lover who might or might not have been flesh and blood once. She did not talk to Jewel. Jewel was simply the technician, the servant of the machines that commanded her every breath, that obliged her cells to live, evacuated her bowels, and forced the blood through the failing network of her veins.

Her body wanted to die, and that part of her—the physical Self, the tissue and bone aspect of Ruth Wosenko—hated the uniformed jailers who kept her imprisoned in her decaying flesh. That part of her remained behind while a young and athletic Ruth skied and swam with her dark-haired lover in her electronic never-never land. The real Ruth watched Jewel through those glazed one-way eyes and hated her.

Jewel shook herself, trying to shed her dark mood. The little illusions of the downtown plaza brought back Erebus and her defeat there. Or perhaps it was the thought of seeing David. The ferry was moving, sliding through the contaminated water of the Sound. Reflections glittered on the sluggish swell—watery images of Linda's dreaming face and swollen belly. She blinked, and the mirage vanished into scattered shards of light. Give it up, she told herself. Time to take that apartment and walk away.

Again?

I didn't walk. She married Carl. Jewel's eyes snapped open as the ferry nudged the dock. Her skin was thick with goose bumps from the cool breeze, and she climbed the gangplank reluctantly. Down below in the shadow of the huge pilings dead fish washed in and out with the waves. Something moved in the dark water, vividly orange, groping like blind fingers toward the surface. Jewel shivered and hurried after the small crowd of tourists and residents.

Flander's address led her up a tree-lined lane—no one had cut them for firewood here—to a shabby old house that overlooked the ferry dock and the distant city. Shabby had nothing to do with poverty out here. It was ambience, and you paid for it. These buildings must have been rebuilt after the tsunami that had followed the Quake. They would be historically accurate, with the latest amenities built in. No lousy Net access here. There would be virtual hardware in every room, just like in Erebus; real antiques and the best in medical remoteware. This was the place. Green grass carpeted the sloping yard—engineered stuff, grown over a network of drip-irrigation tubes. Jewel climbed the stairs, her reluctance growing with every step. She had no business here, interfering in whatever went on between David and Flander. None. Except for the business of Flander's threat . . . and the chance that he might be right about David? Jewel scowled at a cracked planter full of straggling flowers. Little fox bastard. She knocked, half hoping David wasn't home. But the door opened almost instantly, as if he had been expecting her.

His silvered skin struck her as forcefully as it had at their first meeting. He wore only a pair of faded blue swim trunks, and the threads of his Net glittered in the sun as he moved.

"Jewel?" His eyes echoed the surprise in his voice. "I . . . didn't expect you." He stepped backward suddenly, swinging the door open. "Pardon my manners. Or lack of same. Please, come in."

"Hello, David." He had expected Flander. "I'm sorry to bother you," she said, wishing suddenly and intensely that he had not been home. *Damn* the fox, anyway.

"You're not bothering me," he said, and smiled. It was a genuine smile, warm as sunlight, and it sparkled in his eyes like light on a dark pool. "You just surprised me. You *did* screen me out, remember? Don't tell me that you live in Seattle."

"I live outside the city." Outside. It should be capitalized. Jewel looked away. "I'm sorry about the screen. I guess I didn't . . . want to tell anyone where I was going." She changed the subject. "This is where you live?"

"Belongs to a friend. I did some custom work for him a while back, and he asked me to house-sit. Would you like some tea?"

"Yes, thank you." Jewel thought she caught a flicker of relief in his eyes. She watched him disappear quickly into the kitchen, and it struck her that he was uncomfortable, too.

That realization made her feel more at ease. His silver-netted presence had brought Erebus into the room, an invisible virtual overlaid on wood flooring, battered wood furniture, and the period sofa. Maybe he didn't want to recall Erebus, either. Brick and board shelves held rows of paperback books that looked as if they might have been read once. Dusty seashells and glass fishnet floats filled any spaces left in the rows. The far wall was filled by a huge window that admitted a view of the Sound and the Seattle towers. Seen from this angle, the towers seemed to huddle together, backs turned to the dry east. The floor was bare in front of the window. Chairs and a small table had been pushed casually against the wall, and a pair of virtual lenses lay on the windowsill. This must be where David did his virtual, Jewel realized suddenly. The walls *were* hardwired. "You were working on something," she said as he came back into the room. "I didn't mean to disturb you."

"Actually, I wasn't inside a piece." David set a lacquer tray down on the table. A white china pot and two handleless cups stood on it. "I was looking for someone, but she doesn't seem to want me to find her." He tossed his head with that familiar sideways twist so that his braid swung back over his shoulder. "This is green tea.'' He handed her a cup. ''A gift from my youngest sister, Shau Jieh. Hand-picked, probably, on some exclusive plantation in the Malay Republic. If it's still the Malay Republic this week.''

He was playing the formal host. Jewel sipped at the pale, flowery tea, wondering how to give him Flander's message. Just *say* it. ''I wanted to thank you for the office,'' she began. ''The Self you created is . . . beautiful. And the office is incredibly powerful. I actually sold a package to Epyxx from it.''

''Shall we stop this?'' David set his cup down very gently. ''We're bowing and smiling and saying absolutely nothing to each other. Did Flander send you? Is that why you're here and feeling so ambivalent about it?''

''Yes.'' Jewel forced herself to meet his dark, intent eyes. *Why do you put up with him?* she wanted to yell at him. *Do you think you really matter to him?* ''I saw him,'' she said. ''He asked me to tell you that he's safe. He asked me to tell you to stop looking for him. Which is a good idea, in my opinion.''

''What else?'' David lifted one eyebrow. ''What aren't you telling me? Did he ask you to lie for him?''

''All right—yes.'' Jewel let her breath out in a rush. ''I was supposed to say that I'd seen him in the flesh and that he'd get hurt if you didn't stop looking for him.'' And to hell with you, fox. Jewel straightened her shoulders with a jerk. I won't play your games.

''It might have stopped me once upon a time.'' David sighed, his eyes dark with an inward stare. ''I appreciate the truth, Jewel.''

''He . . . thinks you're going to get hurt if you keep doing what you're doing.''

David reached out suddenly, his hand closing on hers before she could pull away. His fingers were cool on her skin as he turned her hand slowly palm up. ''Heart line,'' he said softly. ''Life line.'' He traced the deep groove in the skin of her palm. ''What can they tell us, a fold of dermal cells and tissue?''

What, indeed? Jewel shivered. What was life or love but a tangle of illusion? She pulled her hand free. ''He said you could get killed, and he could handle it. You should probably listen to him,'' she said bitterly. ''But you won't, right?''

''I would if it really was his thing.'' He stared out the window, eyes brooding. ''But it's partly my fault. This trouble comes out of the past. You can give your past too much power, turn it into a monster that can destroy you.''

''The ice cave,'' Jewel blurted. ''I saw it there. Your monster.''

''The chimera.'' David looked beyond her, eyes on some distant scene that only he could see. "By definition, it's a fire-breathing monster with the head of a lion, the body of goat, and the tail of a dragon. By definition, it's also a fantasy. A vision." He looked at her, eyes refocusing. "I'm glad you visited the ice cave. What did you think of your image?"

"I don't know." Jewel looked away. "I—do you really see that when you look at me?"

"The strength? The anger? Yes, I see it." David touched her cheek lightly, tracing the line of her jaw. "With a core of fire that might melt the whole cave one day."

"Thanks for the psych profile." Jewel stepped back, embarrassed, wanting to be angry.

"You asked." David's smile had a tinge of sadness to it. "I'm glad you came by. I was afraid I wouldn't see you again. Come by again."

"I will." Maybe. She wanted to, and she did not; she would have to sort that out later. "What are you going to do?

"About Flander?" David sighed, then shrugged. "Keep looking, I guess. I want him to come tell me about this himself. I want him to ask me for help."

"I told him to do that," Jewel said softly.

David waited.

"He said shit splatters." She jerked the door open, stepping out into the hot sunlight that would give a person melanoma even in this upscale, protected place. David would risk his ass for the fox, never mind that Flander probably didn't give a shit. The straggling white blossoms in the flowerpot were real. Jewel looked back at David, framed in the doorway. "You're a fool," she said.

"Very possibly." He didn't sound angry. "I guess I'll find out."

She turned her back on him and stomped down the steps. If David Chen wanted to do this, it was his business, she told herself. His and Flander's. The ferry was docking, adding its bit of twentieth-century ambience to this unreal, exclusive chunk of dirt. She shoved her card into the slot and trudged onboard.

The ride home was the pits. Three Latino gangies were working the cars on the rail, and the guard looked the other way while they shook her down for cash. And pawed her in the bargain. She damn near used the stunner on them, but the odds were bad, and she didn't trust the guard to back her up if things got seriously ugly. It was hot and still in the blackberry scrub, and the thorns left lines of stinging pain on her sweaty skin. The old man was out polishing his car, wiping small tight circles across the rusty fender, talking to himself in a high wandering monotone. In the dusty street behind her a child shrieked in anger or pain. Laughter rose, tinged with cruelty. Someone's joke, and it had hurt. Jewel looked but caught only a glimpse of sunburned legs as the kids fled out of sight around a house. The victim had already gone to ground.

She trudged up the walk and unlocked the door. Linda was gone, off taking her contractor's in utero daughter to an art show. Was this *her* escape? "Carl?" The shutters were closed, and the stuffy twilight of the living room felt too thick to breathe. No answer; he must be asleep. Jewel tiptoed over to open the shutter a crack and caught a whiff of shit on the heavy air. Uh oh. Poor Carl, and he would be stuck with her help. That he would *not* like, Jewel thought sourly. And neither would she, for that matter.

Light slashed in as she opened the shutter. It reminded her of the Antarctic light, harsh and alien—unforgiving of illusion. It fell across the bed, across Carl's still form. He lay on his back, hands at his sides, face turned to the wall. *Wrong!* A small coldness moved in her belly even before she saw the round, lumpy spots on his throat. Drug patches. Jewel dashed to the bed, banging her shins hard as she grabbed his chin. His body resisted. Rigor? Too damn late for remotes, way too late. He must have done it the minute Linda had left.

For a moment her mother's face stared up at her from the bed; waxy and pale, lips slack, eyes staring past her at some landscape that Jewel had never seen. Had her death been accident or suicide? Jewel had never been sure. She clawed at the patches, stripping two, three, four of them from the groove of carotid and jugular. His flesh felt cold, and it was so hot in here. It felt waxy and stiff, not like human flesh at all. The patches clung like round flesh-colored leeches, resisting her nails.

Too late for Carl, as it had been too late for her mother. Patches worked fast. Jewel stripped the last one away. Bluish shadows already stained the lower surfaces of his body—dependent lividity. He had been dead for some time. When had Linda left for the city?

A small sound from behind her made Jewel start. She whirled, heart leaping. Susana stood in the doorway.

"He's dead." Her posture was relaxed, but her knuckles gleamed bone-white as she clutched the door frame.

"Yes," Jewel said softly. "I'm sorry, Susana."

"Are you?" Susana walked slowly across the room, moving with a fierce concentration, as if she were walking a tightrope across an abyss. "You're the doctor." She halted at the bedside and turned cold gray eyes on Jewel. "Don't just stand there. *Do* something."

"It's too late." Jewel looked down at Carl's pale face. He looked peaceful. And a little sad.

Very slowly Susana stretched out her hand to pick up one of the flaccid patches that lay scattered on the mattress. "He told me Linda would be home all day, that he didn't need me to hang around. So I hung out with Coyote and Rat Brat, or I would've been here." She opened her hand, letting the patch fall to the floor. "I fucking would've *been* here."

"He wouldn't have done it if you were here. He would have done it later." Jewel grabbed Susana's arms and gave her a hard shake. "Do you hear me?" Those gray eyes looking into hers were as empty and cold as the Antarctic sky. "It wasn't an accident. He killed himself, Susana. He would have done it later, when you weren't here." As her mother had done. Crouching there, beside her body, Jewel had felt . . . relief. One searing, terrible instant of relief. Jewel shook Susana again so that the girl's teeth snapped together. "You couldn't stop it."

"You're so sure, are you?" Susana said venomously.

"Yes." Jewel met her cold, frozen stare. "You weren't the problem, and you couldn't save him, either." The same way David couldn't save Flander? But could get himself killed trying? "It wasn't you, Susana, and there wasn't anything you could do."

"You don't know." Anger blazed in Susana's eyes. "Don't give me this adult lecture crap. You don't give a shit."

"Yes, I do." Jewel hung on as Susana tried to wrench free. "Because sometimes it all seems so damn futile, and it shouldn't be. It *shouldn't* be." She drew a shuddering breath and released Susana suddenly. Shouldn't be but was. Even in Erebus. Even there, in the middle of money and wealth.

"Why?" Susana stood still now, her shoulders drooping suddenly, looking down at the bed. "Why did he do it?"

She had loved Carl. Jewel put a hand on her shoulder and felt her flinch. "Sometimes love just isn't enough," she said, and heard her voice tremble. "I . . . wish it was."

With a shudder Susana turned away from the bed. Jewel put her arms around her, and to her surprise, Susana did not push her away. Jewel held her tightly, remembering that morning beside her mother's body, seeing Linda's glazed, distant face and David's anguish as he knelt beside Flander on her floor. No, love wasn't enough—are you listening, David? It can't save *anyone*. In her arms Susana gave one choked, hurting sob and was silent.

Chapter Ten

David walked slowly around the chimera, stroking its cold mane, touching a razor edge to the gleaming, deadly fangs. Its dragon tail curled overhead, poised like a scorpion's sting. It had frightened Jewel. It frightened him a little, too. But not enough yet. David snapped his fingers. The monster shook its head, fixed David with baleful eyes, and lunged. Its rear legs were trapped in the ice, and it twisted around, tail lashing, pawing at its hindquarters. Better. David stepped back as it bared its teeth and roared. "Is this what was chasing you, Flander?" he asked aloud. "Yesterday?"

Chasing Flander and chasing him, too? David tugged at his braid, listening to the drip of slowly melting ice. What had he told Dà Jieh in her office? That his fear of failing Fuchin had driven him from the family firm, into the sanctuary of his art. Into Flander's arms? David sighed and turned his back on the chimera. Perhaps, for him, the monster wore his father's face. David left the chimera to sulk and wandered on, observing the new additions to the icy scene. He had hoped that he might find Flander here or some message from him. Someone had pulled a wall into a breaking wave of ice. Nice feel, but it could work better . . . David started to smooth power into the curl, then let his hand drop slowly. What did it matter? The lion tracks still gleamed beneath his feet. He stopped suddenly and frowned. Someone had smashed the woman stalactite, hammered it into random broken chunks. The pieces lay scattered across the floor.

This added nothing to the cave; it had the feel of trivial vandalism: damage for no reason. Petty. He had liked that creation. Whoever had done it had talent. "Broom." David picked the broom out of the air, swept the broken chunks of ice into a pile, and smoothed them into the wall. The woman's face had survived. He merged it into the ice so that it jutted out, bodiless. Thoughtfully, David smoothed the face into a look of sadness. He touched away a crack in her cheek. Who was she mourning? He tossed the broom into the air and it disappeared. When he decided, he would give her a voice.

"Exit," he said wearily. A doorway appeared in the wall of ice, and David walked through into his studio. He squeezed the ice doorway down to a canvas again and racked it carefully. The cat regarded him from the radiator with a yellow, unblinking stare. "I don't know whether it's a good idea, either," he told it. "But I can't think of anything else to do. Studio, request entry to Dà Jieh's Office."

"Requesting."

To his surprise, a door appeared almost immediately in the wall beside the easel.

"Come in." His sister's voice filled the studio.

On the radiator the cat began to wash its face, ignoring him. Maybe he should give the cat a voice, too. David walked through the door and into his sister's virtual office. She was waiting for him behind her desk, her fingers steepled on the polished wood. The vase in the alcove behind her held a single branch of cherry blossoms.

"Thank you for seeing me so promptly." David bowed.

"Such a deep bow, Little Brother." A thin irony edged her voice, although her face was smooth. "You must want something."

"I do." David kept his eyes on the porcelain mask of her face. "I came to ask for your help."

"*My* help?" Dà Jieh's eyebrows rose slowly into twin, perfect arches. "Succor and comfort are Shau Jieh's areas of expertise."

He read wariness beneath that porcelain mask. And, perhaps, curiosity? "I don't have time to play games." David fingered his braid. "Perhaps Shau Jieh is the expert on comfort, but you are the expert on genetically engineered organisms. And viruses. I told you that Flander ODed." David looked beyond her to their father's scroll, with its mountainscape and waterfall. Such a scene of peace. There had been so little peace in their family. "The kicker he used was contaminated with peanut antigens. It nearly killed him."

"What are you asking me, Chen Chih Hwa?" Dà Jieh's voice had gone cold and silky, and she was not bothering to edit out her anger. "Are you asking me if I tried to kill your lover? Are your asking me if I manufactured an illegal virus and did it poorly? Perhaps you had better be more specific, Little Brother."

Which would upset her more, an accusation of murder or one of incompetence? David swallowed bitterness and kept his face smooth because he hadn't invoked any editing instructions for his Self. "I am simply asking you if there is ever reason for a peanut protein to be included in a kicker. Any kicker. This is the lab report." He handed her a white sheet of paper.

Dà Jieh frowned and dropped the paper onto her desktop. It vanished into the polished wood, to be replaced a moment later by numbers and words that David couldn't read upside down. He watched her face instead, catching the tiny telltales of her reaction: surprise and restrained fury. So she *had* crafted this kicker, and someone had tampered with it. She was angry, and she would be angry only if someone had compromised her creation, if someone else had distorted her work. Dà Jieh was possessive. David let his breath out in a slow sigh. Flander had told Jewel the truth, after all: someone had tried to kill him. A new coldness was growing in David's belly. Fear. Jewel had spoken to him only yesterday, he reminded himself. Flander was all right. For the moment. Hiding, probably, which would be why David hadn't heard from him directly. Anyone who wanted Flander's address would monitor David, of course. David felt a small relaxing inside him, the easing of a hurt he hadn't let himself recognize.

He should have taken Jewel's story more seriously. David clenched his fists slowly, then forced himself to unclench them. If Flander had told him, he would have believed, he told himself. They could have dealt with it. But Flander hadn't told him.

Would I really have believed him? David lifted his eyes to the painted mountainscape floating on the white rectangle of rice paper. Or would I have heard a child trying to wriggle out of blame? David sighed and lowered his head.

"Perhaps your friend ingested the peanut substance by accident." Dà Jieh was looking at him, her ambivalence obvious to David in spite of her Self's editing.

She had already compromised herself on his last visit by admitting her complicity in designing kickers, however indirectly she had done so. And by giving David Anya Vanek's name. No security was perfect—you kept that in mind at all times. It was certainly in her mind now.

"He didn't. He's very careful." Flander hated hospitals enough to be responsible about that, at least. "I've been looking for a friend." David tossed his braid back over his shoulder, eyes on the scroll. "She's a midlevel web node, but she's playing hard to get. It's a little game between us, but she's much better than I am in the Net, so I don't stand a chance, and my pride is suffering. I thought I'd catch up to her in the flesh. As a joke.'' He turned his eyes to Dà Jieh, meeting her onyx stare. "I wonder where I should look first.''

"I have no time to waste on flesh games.'' Dà Jieh wiped her hand across the desktop, erasing what was there and calling up new numbers. "You are in Seattle, are you not? You might try Ebenezer's Exchange,'' she said without looking up. "It's quite upscale and very popular with local nodes. If she's local. Personally, I found the place rather boring the one time I visited it.''

"Thank you.'' David got to his feet. "I'll let you get back to work. I appreciate your opinion on the allergen.''

Dà Jieh raised her head, eyes glittering. "I hope you know what you're doing, Little Brother. I am not certain that you do.''

"I don't.'' David bowed. "I have absolutely no idea. Thank you for your help, Eldest Sister.'' He opened the door to his studio and closed it behind him. For an instant he hesitated, thinking that she had called his name, but the door did not reopen and his studio offered no prompt.

Ebenezer's Exchange. Anya Vanek hung out there. He had guessed that Anya Vanek and Dà Jieh had conducted their business in the flesh; it was too risky a transaction to trust to any kind of security system, and Dà Jieh had had to deliver the kicker. She wouldn't have trusted that to a courier service. Vanek might evade him in the Net, but in the flesh world the odds would be a little more even.

Either she had passed the kicker on to Flander herself or she had passed it on to someone else. The person who had given Flander the kicker had wanted him dead. David bent down to stroke the cat, feeling warmth and cat fur beneath his netted fingers as it arched its back against his palm.

Illusion. It could be so believable. Dà Jieh had given him a warning; so had Jewel. David sighed. He could listen to them. He could get back to work and wait for Flander to come home, as he had so many times before. He could believe that this was nothing new, that he had no right to interfere with Flander's business.

Illusion.

David paused as he entered the indoor garden court that his youngest sister, Shau Jieh, shared with their father. Gold and silver fish swam in the green shadows of the lily pool, waving diaphanous fins. The pool was a holo. It had been one of his first holo projects, designed for Shau Jieh's twentieth birthday. David glanced toward her door, half expecting her to emerge, summoned by the sixth sense that she had about family.

The door remained closed, and David wasn't sure if he was relieved or not. Taking a deep breath, he touched the lockplate on his father's door, looking up into the dark eye of the video pickup. "Hello, Father," he said. "Will you let me in?"

Silence. David waited, ambivalent again, wondering if he should simply walk away.

The door opened. His father stood on the threshold: hands clasped in front of him, face folded into a thousand wrinkles, as classically southern as the face from an antique Guangdong scroll, and as expressionless.

"Fuchin." David bowed deeply, his mouth suddenly dry. He looked so old. He looked frail, and he had never been frail. He had been wiry and tough as a stick of green wood. "Thank you for seeing me, Father." He straightened.

"What do you wish from me?" his father asked in rapid Mandarin. "You have no concern for Chen BioSource. You have no concern for the family. Why are you here?"

Why, indeed? "I . . . wished to see you, Fuchin," David said in halting, out-of-practice Mandarin. "May I enter?"

For a moment his father hesitated; then he stepped stiffly backward. The apartment was as David remembered: cluttered with antiques, rich with color and the musty smell of old fabric. A familiar sense of claustrophobia swept over him. For a moment David felt dizzy, as if he had stepped back through time, as if he were here to defend his latest business decision, to take his father's scolding for his real or imagined inadequacies. He shook himself and drew a deep breath. No, that was the virtual David Chen, the imaginary son his father had tried to create.

The son David had tried and failed to be. "It has been a long time, Fuchin." David met his father's dark eyes, looking for ambivalence in his posture but finding only anger. "I think it is time to end our silence."

"The silence was by your choice." Fuchin turned away from David to study a scroll on the wall above a carved wooden desk. "You chose to betray your family. You chose to turn your back on the family firm, to waste your life playing your games, living with that boy of yours. There is nothing more to be said."

"I play my games very well, Father." David did not try to keep the bitterness out of his voice. "Flander is a man and my partner, not a boy. My eldest sister is much better at running Chen BioSource than I ever was or would have been." It had been a mistake to come here. Nothing had changed in the years since he had last stood in this room. It was like stepping back into the past. "I came here to say that I am sorry," David went on slowly. "I am sorry that I walked away. I should have stayed. I should have found some way to make you understand what I could and could not be. I could not be the son that you wanted, but I should not have shut the door between us, Fuchin." His voice faltered. "I would like to reopen it."

"You have made your choices." His father's voice was harsh as gravel, and he didn't take his eyes from the scroll. "Do not speak to me of doors."

David pressed his lips together. He had known it was a waste of time before he had set foot in the atrium. "I apologize for disturbing your evening." He bowed, struggling with despairing anger. The old boy hadn't changed, would never change, would never try to change. The scroll he was staring at was the scroll that hung on the wall of Dà Jieh's virtual office. "Good-bye, Fuchin," David said harshly. "You have your perfect son, if you would only see it. She is your daughter." Then he turned on his heel and marched out of the room.

The bright light of the atrium made him blink after the dim clutter of the apartment. The bench beside the lily pool was empty, and David felt a rush of relief that his sister wasn't there. She would read him, and she would sympathize. He did not want sympathy right now, not from her, or from anyone. He didn't want anyone to know how he felt. All he had done tonight was to replay their last confrontation. Why did I come here? David asked himself as he rode the lift down to the tower's street level. Why did I bother?

Because he was afraid? David shook his head, trying to shake his dark mood. Perhaps he should carve his father's face on the ice-cave chimera. Outside, the streets glowed with precurfew light, and a colored fountain of charged beads leapt into the air with the sound of falling water. More illusion. David signaled a bicycle-powered cab and climbed into the seat. "Ebenezer's Exchange," he said to the muscular woman on the pedals. Time to ask Anya Vanek who she had given the kicker to. Time for her to give him an answer. Silent, grim, David sat back as the cabbie pedaled through the evening streets. This afternoon he had shaped a mangled body beneath the chimera's trampling hooves.

Ebenezer's Exchange turned out to be a bar and VR parlor located on an upper floor of one of the newer downtown towers. The bar area featured live orchids flowering beneath carefully focused lights, small fountains, and a decent view of the Sound. Clumps of ficus and bamboo screened intimate groupings of chairs and small tables. It was a popular hangout. David sat behind a glass of California Pinot that tasted as if it had been cut with cheap tank wine and watched the dynamics. Men and women with faces from twenties to early thirties cruised for partners. By their dress, he placed them as established midlevel web nodes. The rituals were complex and familiar. He watched a dark man and a tall woman in a glittering bodysuit stroll back through the shrubbery to the plain, wood-paneled door at the rear of the long room.

The door would lead to the VR parlor. The man and woman were already wearing skins. They would enter separate cubicles, put on lenses and gloves, lie down on special couches, and make love. Sanitary. Safe. And you could give your partner any gender or physical type you pleased. Some of the men and women went in by themselves. There were hundreds of interactives available—no flesh partner required and as kinky as you could wish. It was a hot industry.

You could do the same thing on the Net, but the hardware to produce the physical sensations of intercourse was expensive, and you could find your midnight acrobatics posted on some board if your security wasn't tight. Most people went to the parlors. David sipped at his wine, wondering if his sister came here. Dà Jieh had never had a long-term lover. If she had regular lovers at all, Shau Jieh didn't gossip about them. So perhaps she came here to touch without being touched. To make love without the risk of loving or being loved. Suddenly sad, David watched a newcomer scan the bar. She was tall and dark-haired, with the stylish glitter of a fiber-light inlay on her left cheek. Not Anya Vanek; she moved with the wrong rhythm.

He knew Anya Vanek. He bought a lot of recordings for use in his art, and some of his sources had less legitimate sidelines. For a stiff price he had been able to acquire a reasonable sample of Anya Vanek in virtual. Her Self's editing was good. It would fool most people and any except a very high-end office. It did not fool him at all.

Flander had tailored it.

He knew Flander's signature, how he shaded skin and hair, how he always gave hands that subtle deftness . . . David swallowed wine that tasted like bile, wondering if the Self had been payment for the kickers. Anya Vanek's flesh Self might look very different from the blond, angular woman he had studied, but he knew how she moved. With any luck, he would recognize her.

David swallowed a sigh. Of course, she might drop in here only once a month or so. She might have met Dà Jieh here because she *never* went here. Dà Jieh might have given him the wrong place just to get him off her back. No matter. Here or elsewhere, he was going to catch up with her, never mind how long it took.

"You look lonely." The dark-haired woman with the inlay had stopped beside his chair. "I'm Reba. Can I sit down?"

"If you'd like. I'm David." First names only here. David studied her face as she sat. Definitely not Vanek. Her brilliant lavender eyes matched the curving abstract of her inlay. Cosmetic work, those eyes. Expensive.

"You're wasting money on the wine. The beer's worth it, if you're into beer. They spike it with Sensate." She leaned across the table, stroking his arm with one fingertip. "Netted skin turns me on," she said. "And I haven't seen you here before. That turns me on, too. Shall we go into the back and get better acquainted?"

That was an up-front line. David watched the silver-haired woman at the next table stand up to meet the pudgy man who had just come in. No, she wasn't Vanek, either. "Maybe another time, Reba." David tinted his smile with regret. "I'm waiting for someone."

"*Quelle* bummer." Reba pouted. "Who're you waiting for? I know a lot of the people who hang out here. Maybe she stood you up for a better offer." She showed her teeth in a quick, hot smile.

"Maybe." David watched her face while he sipped at his wine. "Her name's Anya. Anya Vanek," he repeated adding her last name.

Reba rolled her eyes at his bad manners. "Anya, huh? You know her very well?"

This was the feel of a loaded question. "No." David made his smile sheepish and a little naive. "Actually, I don't even know what she looks like in the flesh. She was supposed to find me."

"Was she?" Reba stretched languorously. "Honey, you been had." She nodded at the silver-haired woman, who was just opening the parlor door. "I guess Anya likes him better, although I can't for the life of me figure why." She grinned. "So, she's got bad taste. I don't."

Anya Vanek? David stared at the silver-haired woman. He watched her step aside for her partner, watched her reach for the door and give it a small push so that it swung slightly wider, watched her walk through. She tilted her face up to laugh at something her partner said as the door swung shut.

No. David leaned back in his chair, absently fingering a branch of the ficus that grew beside the table. This was not the woman who wore Flander's blond Self on the Net and called herself Anya Vanek. Wrong moves.

"Last chance." Reba gave him a sour, sideways look. "Believe me, honey, I don't usually have to work this hard."

"Sorry." David looked up as the waiter approached. "I kind of had my heart set on Anya."

"Anya?" The slender man eyed David's empty glass. "She was here just a few minutes ago." He nodded at the table where the silvered-haired woman had sat. "Another?" He scooped David's empty glass from the table.

"See you around. Maybe." Reba rose lightly, gave him an icy smile, and wandered away.

Ouch. "Yes," David said to the waiter. "Another, please." He would have to wait and approach Vanek as she left. Vanek—or whoever she was. David pushed his braid back over his shoulder, angry and uneasy because—as he had told Dà Jieh—he didn't know what the hell he was getting into. Who was kidding whom here? Ask her, he told himself grimly. If she answered to Anya Vanek, something was strange.

The waiter set David's glass of wine down in front of him. He wore a fiberlight inlay, too, a dagger and a rose. They were in this year. The waiter touched his cheek as if he had noticed David's look, then cleared his throat. "We're not supposed to carry messages for the clients, but this guy in the back asked me to give you this. I guess he likes you."

"This guy?" David swallowed a surge of crazy hope.

"Blond. Kind of skinny. He's in twenty-nine, if you want to know. If you don't, I didn't tell you nothing." He straightened the napkin beneath the wineglass and went back to the bar.

David picked up the glass and turned the napkin quickly over. A fox icon had been scrawled on the back. Flander's icon, in Flander's style. David stood up slowly, wanting to laugh, wanting to wring his bloody neck bare-handed. Melodrama or real danger? David walked casually to the door and pushed it open. This time Flander was going to tell him what was going on. Right here. Right now. From now on they dealt with this together. Twenty-nine? David hesitated as the door swung closed behind him. He was standing in a wide, carpeted hall that was softly lit by holo windows and careful lighting. Pastel doors opened between the windows. Seventeen? David walked slowly down the hall. Nineteen. Twenty-one. He was going in the right direction.

The windowscenes were mostly X-rated. David glanced at a picnic of satyrs, women, and a couple of goats taking place in a sunlit window. Make that an orgy, not picnic. Goats? He walked on, wondering who got turned on by *that* one. The holos themselves were mediocre, lacking in detail and depth.

Twenty-nine was painted pale blue, the last door in the hallway. David pushed it open, breathless. Pale walls and a fold-out couch that would house the sensory hardware for virtual sex. The cubicle was empty. David stood still, confused, almost dazed by that emptiness. He had been so damn sure . . . The door opened behind him. Flander? He started to turn and then stiffened as someone grabbed his arms from behind.

"Freeze, babe," a deep voice purred in his ear. "You're right where you want to be."

Wrong. Major wrong. David twisted, brought his elbow back hard, connected. The man grunted, and his grip slackened. David wrenched free, then gasped as a hard forearm slammed across his throat from behind. More hands on his arms . . . two of them? Struggling for breath, blood roaring in his ears, David lunged desperately, trying to break free. A band of cold pain clamped around his wrists—old fashioned handcuffs? Hands spun him around, shoved. He staggered backward and slammed hard into the wall. The cuffs cut into his wrists as he straightened. Two men faced him: one short and stocky, the other pale and lanky with white-blond hair. The short man was the waiter with the inlay. The tall man was netted. No chance of getting out of the cuffs; his fingers already tingled with numbness. "Where's Flander?" David asked harshly.

"Not our department." The stocky waiter gave him a bored look, then turned and folded the couch into the wall. "You're the one we have business with right now." He nodded to the netted man, who slammed David back against the wall again and leaned a hard forearm across his throat. Smiling, the waiter walked over and held a slender blade in front of David's eyes.

David watched light run down the steel, his mind numb, his flesh full of dead fear. The knife blade dropped out of sight, and he felt its cold touch on his belly. His muscles contracted instantly, tightening for the anticipated thrust. It did not come. Instead, the line of coldness traveled slowly upward to his throat. David was aware of cloth sliding across his skin—his tunic falling loose as the cut halves parted. A new coldness gathered in him, moving downward into his groin as the waiter stripped him. Blackness edged David's vision by the time he had finished, and the room had receded to the bright end of a long tunnel.

When the forearm at his throat suddenly vanished, David stumbled forward onto his knees, black spots dancing in front of his eyes, blood roaring in his head. "What do you want?" he croaked through his bruised throat. This can't be happening, a part of him cried, but it *was* happening. "I don't know where Flander is."

"Neither do we." The waiter looked down at him, impassive. "We're going to do a little damage to you, and he gets a copy. It's a trade. You for him." He jerked his head. "You got the net, Jack. Turn him on."

The blond man squatted beside David, then grabbed his braid and pulled his head slowly back until the cords in his neck stretched tight and David wondered if his neck would break. "Serious pain brings a high price," Jack said softly. He stroked David's cheek, tracing the line of his jaw, his fingers traveling slowly, almost sensuously down his back.

David shuddered.

"Nice that you're netted, too. We get inside and outside viewpoint. Two for the price of one, and the S and M market's always hot, babe." His fingers lingered, exploring slowly across David's buttocks. "We never told our contractor that he'd get the *only* copy." He found the embedded interface above David's right hip, then dug in hard enough to make David wince as he made sure. "Check it," he said, slapping a remote patch onto the spot.

"You got it." The waiter had moved around out of David's sight. "He's recording, and we're getting it. Get him on his feet and let's go."

Jack slid a video band over his forehead. An eyelid node would track the cameras so that they recorded in synch with Jack's eye movement. "Hold his head." He slid another band down over David's forehead, snugging it tight.

"Watch where you hit him," the waiter said. "Don't mess up the sync."

Jack merely grunted.

David struggled as they yanked him to his feet, but it didn't get him anywhere. The waiter held his arms. Jack stood in front of him, pulling on fingerless gloves, his expression pleasant. "Good for you if your buddy comes across soon. Good for us if he doesn't."

He was looking forward to this. David stared into his pale eyes, reading anticipation and an excitement like lust. A cold hopelessness was rising like a tide inside him, threatening to suffocate him. Someone wanted Flander in the flesh. To kill him? To make sure this time?

"I'm going to hurt you a lot." Jack drew his arm back slowly, smiling, watching David watch it. "We're talking serious physical damage. You can beg if you want to. Maybe it'll motivate your buddy.''

David tried to duck, but the fist caught him on the cheek, snapping his head around, filling his vision with exploding stars of red and yellow light. Shock was followed almost instantly by a thunderclap of pain and the coppery taste of blood in his mouth. David gasped and straightened as the waiter twisted his arms. Jack was waiting for him to recover. This was a production for the market. They would take their time, letting the audience savor the nuances of violence and pain, drawing it out slowly.

The next blow split his lip and loosened a tooth. David swallowed blood, full of cold hopelessness. His net was recording the impact of every blow, every cough, every twitch of pain as they beat him. They would get good money for his agony. As the waiter had said, serious pain brought a high price.

It felt like rape.

Jack smashed his fist into David's belly, and David doubled over, retching. A punch to the kidneys drove him to his knees, and he heard someone cry out in a hoarse, animal voice. His voice? He clenched his teeth together, trying to hold it in. Flander was going to watch this. Choice: Take David's place or exit the virtual and walk away.

Flander was so damn afraid of the flesh, afraid of pain.

His brain was filling up with fuzz, his thoughts buzzing with static. Flander! he cried silently as they hauled him to his feet once more. What the hell did you get *into*? Why did you do this to me? Grief and anger struggled inside him as a blow to the solar plexus doubled him over again. David sagged in their grip, gasping for breath as the world blurred to hopeless gray.

Chapter Eleven

Jewel trudged slowly up the hill in the hot evening dust, tired to the core of her being. Old Mrs. Wosenko slipped closer to death every day, no matter what technological tricks they pulled to hold her. Sometimes, watching the monitor measure out the old woman's life in nanoliters of chemicals and electrical spikes, Jewel wondered if the real Mrs. Wosenko had not already escaped. Perhaps she was even now skiing down those sunny, snowy slopes with her young lover. Perhaps the only thing left was the decaying flesh on the bed, the part of her that hated her jailers.

Had Jewel's mother escaped at the end? What landscapes had the drugs opened for her? Had they been full of light or of darkness and nightmare, echoes of the cancer that ate her with steel teeth? Jewel shaded her eyes against the aching glare that not even the sunglasses could dim. Three youths popped up over the crest of the hill on their boards, zigzagging downward, spraying gravel with each tight turn. Jewel slipped a hand into her pocket, closing her fingers around the handle of her stunner. The boarders, on their slender and incredibly maneuverable spring-wheeled boards, were a constant threat out here. They scored off pedestrians, banking past to shove them off their feet and grab whatever they carried. Sometimes the boarders scored hard. On this hill she could end up with a broken leg.

They spotted the stunner and veered off abruptly, spraying Jewel with a shower of gravel. Arm raised to shield her face, Jewel stared after the leader—a lanky girl. No, not Susana. Jewel hunched her shoulders and walked on. Susana had vanished from the house the day Carl died and hadn't been back since. Linda wouldn't talk about it, although she had stayed at the house this week. Her employer had reluctantly given her time off to settle Carl's affairs.

His affairs. Jewel sighed. What did he have to settle except the clothes and memories he had left behind? Linda had spent the last two days wandering through the house, lost in a kind of dark trance, going through his drawers, touching shirts and underwear, then closing the drawers again. Jewel had cleaned out the living room, had turned it from sickroom to living space again. His presence still haunted it, as if his bitter, betrayed helplessness had soaked into the walls and seeped out now like the smell of decay.

Light speared her as she reached the top of the hill. The baleful sun sank into a bloody haze that was dust, not life-bringing cloud. The old man was out polishing the bumper of his useless car again. He gave Jewel a nervous glance and scuttled into the shadows of his garage. The street was empty as people waited out the heat and the dangerous sun. They would come out into the yards after it got dark, spreading beds on the lawns if they felt safe enough or had an illegal weapon. If they didn't, they would stay behind the safe barricade of their barred windows, waiting for the nighttime chill to cool them off.

Jewel unlocked the front door and pushed it open. For an instant, blind in the twilight of the shuttered room, she saw Carl scowling at her from his bed. Blaming her because the old days had vanished—if they had ever existed—and he had to blame someone.

At the end he hadn't blamed her. *Yesterday was over before I was born,* he had said. *And it ain't coming back.* That had been his escape, Jewel realized with sudden clarity: belief in a yesterday that had been over for decades. She felt a pang of sadness for him, for the dream that had turned out to be nothing but dust and illusion.

A crash from the rear of the house made her jump, and the illusion vanished. "Susana?" Jewel pulled out her stunner. "Is that you?" Mouth suddenly dry, she crept up the stairs and down the hall, watching for movement.

The door to Linda's bedroom stood open, and Jewel heard the sound of a drawer opening. Linda. Relief rushed through her as she shoved the stunner back into her pocket. Her back to the door, Linda bent over an open suitcase on the bed, folding clothes into it. "What are you doing?"

Linda gasped as she bolted upright and spun around to face the door. "My God." Her face was pale. "You scared me. Don't *do* that." She spread protective fingers across the swell of her belly. "You'll spike my chemistry right off the scale."

To hell with her chemistry. "I didn't mean to scare you." Jewel looked over her shoulder, at the neat piles of clothes in the battered suitcase. "Where are you going?"

"To stay with Eleanor." Linda stepped back, arms spread a little as if she expected Jewel to grab for the suitcase. "My chemistry has been crazy since . . . since Carl died. Eleanor called here. She's been monitoring me, and she's having a fit. She's so scared it's going to hurt the baby. So I'm moving in there." She didn't meet Jewel's eyes. "She wants to hire me as a nanny. For the baby, when she's born. They have plenty of extra room, and I could nurse her."

"What about Susana?" Jewel said harshly. The look in Linda's eyes was like a wall, shutting her out. "What about your daughter? Don't you care about *her*?"

"I care." Linda looked at her at last. "My daughter has run away, and she isn't going to come back. Carl's dead, and there's nothing else to hold her here." Her voice had gone calm. "I can't stay here." She looked toward the empty living room, and a shadow passed over her face. "It's full of ghosts," she said softly. "They'll eat me."

Full of ghosts? A cold finger seemed to touch Jewel's neck. She shivered, then straightened her shoulders, letting anger warm her. "That's crap, but you don't have to stay here. We can just afford an apartment in the fringe if we put our money together. That should make your Eleanor happy. You'll be out of the 'burbs." It would take every dollar they both made, and there wouldn't be any left for Net time. Jewel shook her head bitterly, angry at herself, angry at Linda—she wasn't sure which. "That makes a hell of a lot more sense than becoming the live-in servant for this woman."

"Does it?" Linda's eyes flashed, and she straightened suddenly. "You think I can't add, huh? You think I don't know how much of your precious money you've poured into my life? You think I can't see how you feel about coming back here?" She clenched her fists. "Don't offer me any more charity, Jewel Martina. I don't want it. Not from you." She turned her back suddenly, arms crossed, hugging herself as if it were cold in the room instead of breathlessly hot. "Just get out," she said in a hard voice. "Go somewhere and do your web thing. I didn't ask you to come back here. That was your choice, not mine, so just leave me the hell alone."

"What—are you talking about?" Stunned by her anger, Jewel stared at her. "No, I don't want to live here. That's what I'm saying, that we can move out."

"We?" Linda said bitterly. "It was never 'we,' Jewel."

"That's not true!" Jewel slammed her fist against the wall. "Damn it, it's not. *You* left, remember? You moved in with Carl, and what was I supposed to do? Move in with you? It was your choice to split, not mine."

"Yeah. I guess it was." Linda picked up a shirt from the bed, then dropped it. "You'd been letting that old bitch put her hands all over you while you were supposed to be cleaning her house. Because she paid you for it and you were desperate for that aide patch, desperate to get out of here. I would've been a drag on you, and we both knew it. I never learned shit on public ed, forget anything private. I was going to be working crap jobs, and I couldn't have paid my share if we moved out of the 'burbs. So you'd have paid and I would've held you back. You think I was going to do that? You think I *could*?"

What had Carl said? That she had married him because of Jewel . . . "That's not the way it was," Jewel whispered.

"Carl loved me." Linda looked down at the half-filled suitcase, her expression indistinct in the gathering shadows. "I thought that would help." She picked up the shirt she had dropped and began to fold it. "Let me finish, okay? Just leave me alone."

"No!" Jewel grabbed her by the shoulders and spun her around. "I care about you, okay? Maybe I did get obsessed, maybe I did lose touch, but I'm back. And what about Susana? What about your daughter? *Your* daughter, not somebody else's? *She* asked me to come back. She cares about you, Linda. She hasn't walked on you—give her a chance. If you leave, you *will* be abandoning her."

Linda slapped her.

Jewel stumbled back a step, her cheek stinging, eyes blurred with tears.

"Don't tell me about my daughter," Linda said softly. "I'll pay you back if I can, but I probably can't, and that's tough. You didn't buy the right to judge me, Jewel Martina. Get out of my space. I don't want to see you again. Ever."

"Linda—"

"You don't understand, do you? You never did." Linda's eyes were as dry and hard as the sun-baked yard. "I loved you. Even when you were in bed with Sam, even when you didn't have time to talk to me because you were so damn busy studying for that damn patch. I *loved* you!" She grabbed a dirty glass from the dresser. "And it didn't mean *shit* to you. Get out, do you hear me?"

Jewel flinched as the glass shattered against the wall beside her.

"Get out of my life. Get *out*!"

Jewel fled, stumbling through the shadowy house. Shapes moved in the living room. Carl's ghost? No, no, she cried silently. We were friends, sisters—I didn't shut you out, it wasn't like that. Something gleamed in the dark, and Jewel cringed back against the wall, seeing cat eyes. Ghosts; there were ghosts everywhere in this place. She flung the door open and burst out into the fading evening light.

Susana stood on the walk, hunched and indecisive. "Yo, Auntie? See a ghost?"

Yes, a ghost of a past that hadn't really happened. Or had it? Whose version was right, hers or Linda's? *Maybe we each live in our own virtual,* Jewel thought bitterly. *We just think we share reality.* "I don't want to deal with you right now." Jewel closed her eyes briefly. "Your mother is about to move out. If that matters to you, maybe you'd better go in and do something about it."

"Why should it matter to me? It doesn't matter to her."

Cold words, so cold that they made Jewel shiver. She opened her eyes, tired suddenly, tired to the core of her soul. "Oh, hell." She stared at the last bloody traces of sunset on the horizon. "I don't know anything."

"You got to get your skins on and come," Susana said, shaking loose hair out of her eyes. "Right now."

"Why?" Jewel sighed, amazed at how much energy it took to push air in and out of her lungs. *I loved you.*

I didn't know, she thought bitterly. *I didn't understand.*

"What does Flander want from me this time?"

"It's his friend the artist. He's in trouble, I guess."

"David?" He had expected this. He had walked into it with his arms open. "I can't do anything." Jewel spread her hands. "I can't do anything for anybody."

"Is it true that this guy did the cave?" Susana asked softly.

Something in her tone caught at Jewel. She lifted her head and tried to read that glitter in Susana's eyes. The wary distance, the cynical look had vanished. "Yes," Jewel said, and let her breath out in a slow sigh. "He did."

"You *got* to come." Susana lifted her chin. "The fox is coming off the wall. I guess this David's in serious shit."

Serious shit. "All right." Jewel rubbed her eyes, tired, tired beyond belief. "All fucking right, I'll come. And I can't do shit, but I've got to prove it to you, right? All right, I'll prove it." She pinned Susana with her glare. "And there's a price. You talk to Linda. I don't care if you spit on each other, but you at least look each other in the face." She would do that much. She would try.

Susana's head had jerked up, and for a moment Jewel thought she was going to refuse. "All right." Her shoulders slumped fractionally. "But you got to come *now.* I'll go face Linda down when we get back.'' She met Jewel's stare. ''It won't make any difference.''

Maybe not. Jewel wasn't even sure why the hell she had said it. She looked away from Susana's dry-sky eyes. David had asked for it. In the name of love. ''I'll have to put my skins on,'' she said through clenched teeth. ''You come face her now.''

Jewel had brought a solar flash along with her, and the yellow pool of light danced across the trodden path as they threaded the blackberry scrub. Susana and Linda had gone into the kitchen while Jewel had put on her skins. If they had said anything at all to each other, they had been damn quiet about it.

''How come you took off?'' Jewel asked Susana. ''I won't even ask where you've been.''

''Good, 'cause I won't tell you.'' Susana tossed her head, then ducked beneath a thorned arch of berrycane. ''Shit, it doesn't matter if you know. I was sleeping with Luis.'' She threw Jewel a challenging glare. ''His dad's not around much at night, so it's pretty easy to sneak in. Look, I didn't want to be in the house, okay? I just didn't.''

In spite of her macho tone, there was an uneasy hunch to Susana's shoulders. ''I'm sorry,'' Jewel said softly. ''You loved your father.''

''Yeah, I guess.'' Susana shrugged. ''Not that he ever really paid much attention to me, but he let me tag along to his meetings and stuff. He was so into it—all his political stuff about making the country great again. For us white folks, anyway. He really believed it. He . . . wanted to make a difference.'' Susana stopped suddenly to look back over her shoulder at Jewel. ''And he didn't. Not really. He thought he was going to change the world, but the rest of 'em, they had their own schemes going. You could see it. That they were laughing at him, some of them. Some of 'em were using him. They figured I was a dumb kid, so they didn't hide it much.'' She shrugged and started walking again. ''I never told him. What good would it do? I never let on that I knew.''

There was an adult compassion in her voice, and Jewel remembered how she had bent over Carl, an adult comforting a child. Had this girl-woman ever truly been a child? I was never a child, either, Jewel thought, and looked up at the cold sweep of stars overhead. Sometimes childhood wasn't in the cards.

They had reached the end of the path. Ahead, moonlight streaked the cracked asphalt of the road with black shadows. The flea market was bright with light and frantic action. Smoke rose from a barbecue pit, turned solid and thick by the glow from a couple of lanterns hung from poles. Strips of meat sizzled on old oven racks above a bed of glowing coals, and the smell filled Jewel's mouth with saliva. Running the booth was an old man, bent and white-haired, with a hard, angry face. He had some kind of black-market connection to the government-subsidized goat herds that were busily stripping the dying lands to the east. The heat from the pit beat against them as they walked past, and Jewel caught a hint of ripe meat odor. The smuggled carcasses didn't come in under refrigeration. If you were smart, you asked for your meat well done.

Susana's posture had changed as they entered the market. She walked straighter, her eyes moving here and there, bouncing lightly on the soles of her feet. This was her turf. There were other kids like her there: striped with tan and white skin, with wired braids or tails of tangled hair, all Caucasian in this market. Conscious of her own questionable profile, watching for trouble, Jewel side-stepped a juggler who was tossing flaming sticks and headed for one of the public booths.

"That one's down." Susana touched Jewel's arm. "In here." She brushed past Jewel, pulling on her gloves, lenses already in place. Jewel followed her reluctantly, blinking in the glow from the over-head light. "Whose ID is that?" Jewel asked as Susana rattled off a code.

"It belongs to Luis's dad. I told you—he's into the parlors. He never notices a little extra Net time. And we've got some others, too. We switch off."

Stealing codes was piracy. No exceptions, not even for the Al-courts of the world. Not if there was proof. So the Alcourts of the world would simply hire someone else to do it. Like Flander. "And if you get caught?" Jewel asked softly.

"I won't." Susana met her stare. "And if I do, so what?" Child-ish macho. She didn't believe in death, this young. But Susana was no child.

Jewel shivered as the ice cave solidified around her. It arched into a blur of distance overhead, too vast to comprehend. They were standing at the edge of a lake of crystal water beneath a tow-ering cliff of ice.

"We're small," Susana said in surprise. She was wearing her cat Self, and she lashed her striped tail. "Cool. He must have stuck some kind of random selector into the program. I wonder what else it does. I wouldn't have thought of that."

She was standing ankle deep in water, and it was cold, damn it. Jewel stepped back, eyes on the cliff. Only it wasn't a cliff—it was the monster, crouched beside the lake, which was really a puddle.

Something lay beneath its paws—a body, Jewel realized with a start. She could see part of the face, but her eye refused to bring the enormous features together into any kind of coherence.

"I thought you'd never show up." Flander emerged from a wall of ice.

"I told you he wouldn't listen to me—" Jewel began.

"Shut up. Just shut *up*!" Flander bared fox teeth. "Yeah, right, he didn't listen. He walked into the middle of a mess, and he's in trouble. Big trouble. They're beating him up, and they're *posting* it. You got to stop it."

The face of the mangled body beneath the chimera's hooves looked like Flander. "What?" Jewel felt herself going pale. "What are you saying? What's happening to David?"

"Two guys are beating him, doing it slow, taking their time." Flander's lips writhed back from his teeth. "They're recording it in virtual, and they're sticking it into the Net. Where I'll find it. You want to get into it?" he snarled. "You want me to call it up so you can watch?"

"Shit," Susana hissed.

Oh, yes. "You bastard," Jewel breathed. "What the hell did you get him into? You and your Net games. This is your fault! If you know what's going on, call the cops. Or is it too much risk for you?"

"Posting a virtual isn't a crime, lady," Flander growled deep in his throat. "These dudes want *me*. They want the flesh."

"So show up." A part of her was turning to cold steel. "How much do you care about him, Flander? As much as he cares about you? How big a fool is he, anyway? Maybe it's time he found out."

Flander's eyes flashed with green fire, and for an instant Jewel thought he was going to leap at her, tear her with his virtual fangs. Then his head drooped, his eyes going dull. "I'd . . . do it," he said in a low voice. "And I don't give a fuck whether you believe me, but . . . I can't. Not in time. You want me to crawl, lady?" Blood dripped from his tongue, spotting the ice. "I'm crawling, all right? They broke his hands, did it one bone at a time. He screamed. He was trying not to, but he did. They're killing him and doing it real slow."

Jewel closed her eyes, sick. You were wrong, David, she thought bitterly. The chimera ate *you*, not Flander. This is what love buys you, and I told you so, but you didn't listen. "What do you think I can do?" she whispered. "What do you want from me?"

"Find out where he is. I can hire bodies to go get him once I know where. They know I'm hot in the Net, so they've been playing cute games, and I can't get a clear trace on him. He's somewhere in the Peten. I know that much.''

El Peten? That was Salgado's neighborhood—Central American and a very closed community. Oh, God, why *there*? That was Sam's neighborhood.

"I hear you got some kind of contact in the Peten."

He meant Sam, he had to, and how the hell did he know about that? "I can't just walk in there." She glowered at Flander. "I don't know what I look like to you, but to the people in the Peten I don't look like I belong. That buys me a knife, real fast. And no, I don't have a contact. Not anymore."

"Suse?" Flander shook himself as if he were wet. "Get out of here, okay? I need to say something to Jewel."

Oh, yeah, Susana. *That* must have been where Flander had learned about Samuel. Linda might have talked about him.

"So say it in front of me." Susana glared at Flander, her cat ears flat to her head.

"Out!" Flander snarled, and Jewel heard ragged desperation in his voice.

Susana heard it, too. "Exit," she said with a scowl, and vanished.

"I can tell you who killed Carl Reyna." Flander's eyes blazed at her. "Go into Peten and I'll give it to you."

"Carl killed himself."

"Yeah, but the car was no accident." Flander laid one ear back. "Don't tell Suse, okay? She'll go ballistic."

He worried about Susana? Jewel shook her head, overwhelmed by all this. So someone had run Carl down, after all. Or was Flander lying to her? Jewel turned over her palm, tracing heart line and life line, seeing Susana's angry, grieving face in her mind. She blamed herself a little, would always blame herself. Because she had loved her father, and it hadn't been enough. *I loved you,* Linda had cried. Jewel swallowed. That love hadn't been enough, either. I didn't *know*, she cried silently. "Do you love him?" She raised her head and looked into Flander's green, glittering eyes. "Do you love David?"

"Yes," Flander said softly. "I love him, and he doesn't understand. Please, Jewel. Please help me find him."

Begging. Flander was begging. She wondered if he had ever begged for anything in his life. "I'll try." Jewel let her breath out in a slow sigh. She closed her hand slowly, squashing life line and heart line into a meaningless wad of flesh. How can I not try? she thought bitterly. Even if it meant talking to Sam.

And she would have to talk to Sam. The Peten was closed and full of violence. Samuel had said something about that once: *There's so much blood in our past. It soaks into a people's soul, and the stain never washes away.* He had painted that onto the rail pylons and walls. He had been such a hot tagger. She had thought he would pair with Linda at first; they painted together once in a while. But he had looked at her instead. They had thought they were in love for a while, but that had been just another illusion. Jewel jerked her head, trying to banish those memories. "I hope I can find him."

"No prob." Susana had reappeared, cat tail flicking as she leapt onto a ledge of ice above Flander's head. "He hangs with Salgado, and I've got Salgado's code. Salgado's doing a party tonight, and Lujan's his numero uno. He'll be there."

Sam had become Salgado's uno? Jewel stifled a pang. "You stay the hell out of Salgado's private space," she snapped. "He won't wait for a trial."

"I can take care of myself." Susana bared cat fangs in a quick snarl. "And we've crashed his parties before, no big deal. So back off." She glared and recited a quick code.

A door materialized in the wall of ice. It was made of stained glass, leaded in a kaleidoscopic explosion of bright geometric shapes. Jewel pushed on it gently. It wasn't locked. Jewel drew a deep breath, afraid of what she might meet on the far side of this door. "Self: body-language edit," she murmured. "Confidence. Translation to street Spanish." Now her every move would be shaded to suggest that she knew what she was doing. Her Spanish wouldn't be quite right—in El Peten—but it would not be English. Even when she had known Sam, she couldn't speak Peten well enough to pass. She said a small prayer that Flander's office was as good as David said. The door was opening, and she looked over her shoulder as she walked through. For an instant she thought that the face on the mangled body beneath the chimera's hooves was her own.

Green leaves slapped her face, and she flinched. The door closed, and she blinked at tree trunks and trailing vines, indistinct in jungle shadow. A black and white monkey scampered up a tree trunk less than a meter from her face. Flicking its plumed tail, it clung to the branches high above her head, screeching and showing its teeth in the green twilight. A security program, announcing her? Something rustled behind her, and Jewel jumped, reminding herself that this was only virtual, that if she stretched out her arm, she would touch Susana or the wall of the booth.

This was happening too fast. She needed time to think about

this, to prepare herself. But David might not have much time. Jewel took a deep breath as jungle shadows resolved slowly into a massive ruin of lichened gray stone. Thick ferns sprouted from the crevices, and roots pried huge, squared-off boulders loose in invisibly slow motion. Overhead, the sky was a lacy canopy of green, supported on the slender trunks of soaring trees. The monkey had stopped scolding her; it was stripping leaves from young twigs and stuffing them into its mouth. Jewel ducked as bits of bark and broken twigs showered down.

"Qué pasa?" A huge jaguar strolled up. "Do I know you?"

"I'm . . . looking for Samuel Lujan," Jewel said, hoping she sounded as if she belonged here.

"He's busy." The jaguar arched its back against her leg. "No rush, eh?"

"I hate cats." Jewel kneed him, her skins giving her jaguar fur and sleek muscle. "Where is he?"

"I don't know you." The jaguar yawned, revealing long white teeth. "I think maybe you better beat it, *muchacha.*"

A man strode up. "I know her." He was naked except for a cotton loincloth and his hair was pulled back from his face, bound with a string of crudely carved jade beads. More jade dangled from his ears. He had a hawklike profile and dark coppery skin. "Beat it, Javier. Welcome to Palenque," he said to her, and showed yellow teeth in a brief grin. "Salgado's on this ancient Mayan kick this week. Don't ask me why."

"Searching for his roots?" Jewel lifted her chin. "Hello, Sam."

"I think his roots are LA barrio, but you don't quote me. Who invited you?" Sam sat down cross-legged on the litter of fallen leaves and stared up at her. "Or did you crash this party?"

"Let's just say I dropped in." She studied his face. A faint orange-red aura shimmered about him. He was pissed, but not very. Well, he had been pissed the last time she had seen him, too. He had been coldly furious at her refusal to come live with him.

"If you crashed, I am impressed. Salgado has good security. Sit." He patted the leaves beside him. "The boss is busy right now."

Purple threaded the aura in wavering streaks; he was lying to her. "I didn't come to see your boss," she said. "I came to see you. I hear you're his main man. I guess you got what you wanted, Sam."

"Did you ever really know what I wanted? And you?" He smiled thinly. "I thought you were on your way smack into the middle of the web, Jewel. Want a better job than the care and feeding of the wealthy and senile? I could maybe find you something."

"Like watchdogging Salgado's drug connections?" Jewel looked away, swallowing hard, wondering what he was seeing and hearing. "We said all this, remember? We threw all these same stones a long time ago."

"Yeah." He shrugged lightly, still smiling. "We did, didn't we? You still got your thing about drugs, huh? Well, you went and did your thing, and I did mine. So why *did* you come here?"

"I'm . . . looking for someone. A David Chen. He's a virtual artist. Someone . . . kidnapped him. I heard he's in el Peten."

"Is he your lover?" Sam's stranger's face was expressionless, but his aura flared crimson.

"No." Jewel felt her cheeks getting hot and hoped her Self hid it.

"So?" Sam's eyebrows arched in mock surprise. "Are you getting paid for this, or do you owe him? Nothing for free, eh, *chiquita*? I know you."

Nothing for free. "I'm . . . not sure why I am doing this." She met his eyes. "Perhaps for no good reason at all. He's . . . my friend."

"You've changed, Jewel." Sam brushed virtual leaves from his perfect virtual skin as he got to his feet. "I'll take you to Salgado."

His aura had faded to blue-green. Sadness? Mild regret? "Can't you find out for me?" Jewel asked, her heart sinking.

"You got to ask the boss." Sam did not smile.

Salgado had absolutely no reason to give away anything to her, and she didn't have much to trade. Nothing for free. Jewel sighed as she followed Sam through a maze of overgrown ruins. In the booth her leg muscles barely twitched, but in this place she wandered through an acre of stones and eerie shadows. Carved faces peered at her from beneath crusts of lichen and moss. Leaning against an enormous stone step was a mask carved of green jade, with staring golden eyes and a protruding cowrie-shell tongue. One golden eye winked at Jewel, and the shell tongue waggled suggestively as they walked past. Salgado was holding court in a painted tomb. Its whitewashed walls were covered with glyphs painted in red ocher, and the roof was gone. A litter of broken bowls and tools lay scattered on the dirt floor, as if looters had been at work.

How metaphorically correct, Jewel thought sourly, that he should hang out in a looted tomb. She would never have expected such subtlety from Salgado. Or maybe it was an accident. He was recognizably himself, reclining on a lounger that didn't pretend to be either ancient or Mayan. Jewel was reminded suddenly of Alcourt

and his holographic illusions. Maybe Salgado laughed to himself
to see people play his games so eagerly.

"Jewel Martina." He extended a hand, grinning. "Did you come
by to visit an old friend?" He leered at Sam. "Does Angelina
know, Samuel?"

His yellow aura meant malice; Jewel didn't need her office to
read *that*. She and Sam had split because Salgado had offered Sam
a job and Sam had said yes. Salgado had tried to recruit her first—
into his bed. He had not forgotten. Salgado was the most powerful
of the neighborhood leaders, and his power grew every year. Carl
had claimed that he was setting up the Sony-Matohito deal to open
a manufacturing plant in the city. Poor Carl. A martyr after all, and
no one knew it. Jewel sighed. "Hello, Salgado. I hear that you're
very big these days." She smiled, confident in virtual, without hope
in actual. "I came to ask you for a favor."

"A *favor*?" Salgado smiled sweetly. "From *me*? How unexpected."

"I'm looking for a friend of mine," Jewel went on doggedly.
"Someone in el Peten has him."

"Name?"

"David Chen."

Salgado shrugged and picked up a broken piece of pottery. "And
what have you to trade for this little favor?"

Nothing for free. Not ever. "I will have to owe you," Jewel said
slowly.

"Is that so?" Salgado flipped the fragment across the tomb,
where it hit the far wall and fell to the floor with a tiny click. "I
offered you a deal once. It was a very good deal, and you turned
me down. I think she was still in love with you, Sam. You must be
very good in bed." He slapped Sam on the arm and laughed. "You
can go," he said to Jewel, and his aura went dusky crimson. "This
is not your party."

As if on cue, the jaguar appeared. It eyed her, rubbing its shoulders lazily against the stonework of the tomb entrance. Jewel wondered if he was masturbating in actual but decided that it would be
exceedingly foolish to ask him just then.

"Let's go." Sam took her elbow, and she went with him meekly.
There was nothing else to do. From this side of the virtual, the
door she had entered by was a curtain of vines. Sam stopped her
as she started through. "Was he telling the truth?"

"He asked me to bed, yes." She looked down at her palm with
its lines of past and future. "I said no."

"When was this?"

She winced and twisted her arm out of his grip. "Before he recruited you."

Back when he and Linda were still tagging, arguing over the details of their painted visions. They would split in the gray dawn, Linda heading home, she and Sam heading off to make love in the weeds. His long hair would smell like paint, and later she would find streaks of bright color on her skin. Linda would be waiting for her as Jewel slipped through the window and into bed. She never said anything, but she would brush the hair back from Jewel's face and pull the covers over them both.

"So how come you turned him down?" Sam asked. "Because he was the drug king?"

"No." I loved you, she wanted to shout at him. Or I thought I did. Why did you do this? Why did you sell your soul to this man? "That wasn't the reason." Ducking her head, she stepped quickly through the door.

Susana was sitting on the ice beside Flander. She had her arm around him, and he leaned his fox head on her knees. The warmth—no, the *intimacy*—of their pose shocked Jewel slightly. How long had she known Flander, anyway?

"Did you find him? David?" Susana scrambled to her feet.

"She didn't." Flander stared into her face, ears flattening.

"No, I didn't." Jewel turned away from their disappointed, accusing eyes. "Salgado threw me out. That means *out*, Flander."

"Don't give me *out*!" Flander snapped angrily at Jewel's face. "You can't quit." His voice was ragged. "David was . . . bad. He can't last much longer."

"There's nothing I can do. Sam was the only contact I've got, and he won't cross Salgado. The Peten is closed to me. Can you understand that? It's *closed*."

"So to hell with David?" Flander snarled.

Jewel tore her lenses from her face, staggering as the scarred walls of the booth reappeared around her. It smelled like piss and sweat and decaying hope. Why hadn't she noticed the smell in the cave? You could even fool your damn nose with illusions. She burst through the door and out into the flea market's light and bustle.

"You gonna just quit?" Susana followed her and grabbed her by the arm.

"I can't find him." Jewel shook her off hard enough to make her stagger. "Damn, damn, *damn!* David, why didn't you listen?" She buried her face in her hands. "This is Flander's fault, and he wants me to save David's ass for him, and I *can't*."

"This David's your friend, too, huh?" Susana's voice came softly from the darkness. "You care about him?"

"Yes." Jewel drew a ragged breath, tasting smoke and roasting meat on the dusty breeze. "I care about him. I wish . . . I didn't." Was someone beating him right now? Was he dying slowly somewhere, in pain? Jewel closed her eyes, her fists clenched at her sides. She had no power to save him, no power to save herself. It was so useless.

Susana touched her arm. "Luis and I could . . . check around."

Jewel flinched, surprised by the touch. Was that sympathy in her tone? She straightened, shoving her hair out of her eyes with a thrust of her fingers. "Maybe you and your friend Luis could skate around in the Net," she said heavily. "Listen for rumors. Anything out of the Peten." Not that residents spent much time in the Net. They were service, not web nodes. Salgado hadn't been into virtual at all when she had known him. "I'd—appreciate it."

"We could do that." Susana was nodding. "Maybe we'll catch something the fox missed."

What had brought about this sudden truce? Perhaps it was because Jewel knew Flander. Jewel finally asked the question that had been bothering her. "How long have you known the fox?"

"Not too long. I ran into him right before you got back. He was kind of hanging around."

Checking me out, Jewel thought bitterly, but she was too depressed to be angry.

"He's cool," Susana said thoughtfully. "But kind of immature, you know."

Jewel swallowed an urge to giggle. "Yeah, he's immature." In some ways Susana *was* older than Flander. "Shit." She groped in her pocket. "I left the flash in the booth."

"Take this if you're heading back." Susana handed her a tiny flash. "Turn the lens to widen the beam. I'm gonna go back in, anyway, and hunt Luis down. He's skating around somewhere, and we can get onto this."

Jewel turned the flash on. The light could be adjusted down to an intense, hair-fine beam. It was standard equipment for breaking and entering. Jewel sighed. "I'll wait for you," she said. "I'm not sleepy yet."

"Suit yourself." Susana shrugged and vanished back into the booth.

Chapter Twelve

Susana stayed in the booth for a long time. Curfew fell, and the distant lights of Seattle's towers blinked out. It didn't make any difference to the market; the 'burbs were a separate world. Jewel leaned against the booth wall, watching fire-eaters and hookers ply the same clientele. A storm was kicking up, and a gust of wind pelted Jewel with grit. Exempted lights winked like yellow eyes on the horizon. Jewel wrapped her arms around herself, cold despite the skinthins beneath her clothes.

Sheet lightning flickered to the west, and thunder rumbled faintly. It wouldn't rain this time of year. The cold wind tugged at Jewel's hair, and it felt like hours before Susana exited the booth.

"Luis'll ask around." She pulled off her lenses. "He's pretty careful, so he probably won't find much tonight." She sounded disappointed and more than a little disdainful. "He doesn't take risks."

"So he's smart."

"Yeah?" Susana shoved her lenses into her pocket and stripped off her gloves. "So he'll play it safe, working for the local boss, hanging out in the parlors for fun. Your flash was still in the booth. You lucked out." Her eyes glittered in the light from the flash as she clicked it on. "He'll end up a nowhere man. Is that so smart?"

"I don't know." Jewel glanced sideways at Susana. The flash's glow highlighted the sharp jut of her cheekbones, giving her an intent, hungry look. Flander had the same look. "What do you want from life?" she asked abruptly.

"Is that something all grown-ups ask all kids?"

"No." Jewel shrugged. "I asked you."

Susana swung the flash in a sharp arc, illuminating a dizzy kaleidoscope of berry leaves, thorns, and brown dust. "I don't know yet," she said after a small silence. "Something that counts. Some-

149

thing that *matters*. I'll let you know.'' She gave a jerky shrug. "This David is Flander's lover, isn't he?''

"Yes.'' Jewel kept her eyes on the flash's pool of light. "He is.''

"I hope he makes it,'' she said softly. "He does neat stuff in virtual.''

She didn't think he was going to make it. Jewel tore her eyes from the yellow beam, staring at the bright afterimage against the darkness. There were lots of ways to cause pain. They were breaking bones, so they didn't much care if he lived or died. Jewel's stomach knotted, and she stumbled into Susana.

"Watch out.'' Susana grabbed her arm. "You okay?''

"I'm fine.'' Jewel closed her eyes, seeing David's face in the Vashon house, remembering his long-fingered hands as he traced the lines in her palm. How much of this was her fault? If she had repeated Flander's lie, if he had believed her, would this have happened?

Damn you, Flander. Jewel clenched her fists. And damn you, David, because you did this to *yourself*. She ducked through the last of the thorns, ignoring the pain. The waxing moon shone down on the dark houses on the hilltop, and the dry wind flung dust into her eyes. Heads down, silent, Jewel and Susana crossed the dusty yards to the unlighted house. The darkness seemed to bulge through the doorframe as Jewel opened the door, thick and heavy with breathing silence. Jewel shivered and reached for the wall switch.

"It's curfew, remember?'' Susana pushed past her, light beam dancing as she went into the kitchen. "Shit.'' Something fell with a heavy thump. "Where'd she put the lamp *this* time?''

Susana sounded uneasy. Maybe this house held ghosts for her, too. Jewel groped down the shallow steps into the living room, thinking that Linda might have left the lamp on the table. Sheet lightning flickered again, and its glow lighted the room in strobed planes of black shadow and colorless light.

It gleamed in the golden eyes of the mountain lion crouched in the center of the floor.

Jewel stumbled backward, groping for the stairs and escape, the afterimage of tawny lion shape imprinted on her retina. No, it wasn't an afterimage. She was *seeing* her, as if the creature were glowing with her own light. Her? Why did she think it was a *her*? Jewel took another step backward and felt the wall against her shoulder blades, as if the stairs had suddenly moved.

"I warned you,'' the lioness said. "This isn't a safe place for you. Get out of here. This isn't your affair.''

I am hallucinating, Jewel told herself, but her hands were shaking. This was no virtual. There was no hardware buried in the walls of this house, and her lenses were in her pocket.

"You are being foolish, child." The lioness's lips wrinkled in a fanged snarl. "Walk away from the fox while there's still time to do so."

The fox? Her mention of Flander diminished some of Jewel's growing terror. Flander, huh? Hardware in the walls or not, this was tech. If it was connected to Flander, it *had* to be tech. "Why should I listen to you?" She drew a deep breath and stepped away from the wall. "Who the hell are you, anyway? You, behind the holo, I mean." She looked around the room. "Tell me or turn it off."

"Such bravery." The lioness's voice held a trace of laughter. "Does it comfort you to think I'm a holo? Perhaps I am." The creature rose to its hind legs, changing, losing shape. "And perhaps I am not, and your certainties about the nature of the world around you are worth so much dust." She had become a woman now, an old woman with gray hair the color of stone, a weathered face, and a jutting nose. "Are you so sure, child? Shall we find out?" She reached for Jewel with long, wrinkled fingers, and her smile revealed the lion's pointed teeth.

Jewel shrank away with a cry, and the old woman laughed. In a fluid rush of motion she dropped to the floor, shifted into lioness form, leapt into the air and vanished.

"Holy fuck." Light flared in the kitchen, driving shadows back across the empty room. Susana stood in the doorway, the solar lantern in one hand, eyes wide in her freckled face. "What the hell was *that*?"

"A holo," Jewel said. But where was the hardware? Alcourt's rooms were lined with projectors. "Maybe somebody projected it through a window." What if the old woman had touched her and she had felt . . . flesh?

"Holo, oh, *sure*." Susana stepped into the room, nostrils flaring, eyes searching here, there.

Jewel stomped into the kitchen, flinching as the lamp swung shadows across the floor, remembering that lion shape in Alcourt's garden.

"Jewel?" Susana's voice skated up half an octave. "It wasn't a holo."

"You believe in ghosts now?" She had looked familiar . . . Jewel snatched Susana's flash from the table and walked briskly down the dark hall, resolutely ignoring the shadows.

The bedroom door stood open. The bed was empty, neatly made. The suitcase was gone.

"She took off." Susana's voice behind her made Jewel jump.

"She wouldn't have." Jewel stared around the small room, as if she might find Linda hiding somewhere. "Not before morning. She wouldn't risk the rail this time of night."

"I bet she called the bitch. I bet she came roaring out here with an armed guard to collect her kid." Susana's voice was thin and cold. "She's not gonna come back. She's been out of here for a long time."

Had she? Had she found her escape in the life in her belly? Jewel leaned against the door frame, wanting only to go to sleep, to wake up and find that it had all been a dream, that she was . . . where? Jewel pressed her lips together. What point in time did she want to go back to? Erebus? That place and its hope had been an illusion, perhaps more of an illusion than the lioness. Back to childhood? To her years with Linda? Time did not stand still. There was no shelter in the past. Only in the future. Maybe. Her lips tightened. "I'm going to bed."

"Okay." Susana watched impassively as Jewel began to strip off her clothes and skinthins. "See you in the morning. Maybe Luis'll find something."

She didn't think he would. Jewel climbed into the double bed. It felt too large, stretched to vast dimensions by Linda's absence. Through the wall, she could hear Susana opening a drawer. Something had changed between them; the needling anger wasn't there anymore. Why? Jewel wasn't sure, and she was too tired to try to figure it out.

I loved you. Linda's words came to her in an accusing whisper from the darkness. Yes, yes, and I loved you, too, and it wasn't my fault that we went our separate ways. Do you hear me? It wasn't my fault. Jewel buried her face in the pillow and covered her ears with her hands.

A touch woke Jewel from dark dreams of David's hands—a shape in the darkness. Jewel gasped in a lungful of air to yell. A hand clamped hard across her mouth, and she clutched her attacker's arm one-handed, grabbing for the stunner beside the bed.

"It's me, Sam," a voice hissed in her ear. "Knock it off."

"Sam?" She gasped as he relaxed his grip. "What the hell are you doing here? Let go!"

"Be *quiet*! He glanced quickly over his shoulder. "You wake anybody and I'm out of here," he whispered. "Some old guy across the street is sitting out on his steps talking to the damn moon. I don't want nobody to know I'm here, *comprende?* Get dressed.'' He rose, receding into darkness. ''I'll pick you up down on the main road in ten minutes.''

''Why?'' Jewel crossed her arms, glad suddenly for the shirt she wore to bed.

''You want this chink artist or not? Get dressed.''

''Sam?'' Silence. Jewel heard a faint footstep in the hall.

She groped for her tights beside the bed and pulled them on. Whatever was going down didn't have Salgado's blessing. She put a tunic on over the light shirt she wore; it was cold at night. Cautiously, Jewel felt her way around to Linda's side of the bed. The gun in the back of the drawer felt heavy and cold in her hand. Linda's gun—a squat, ugly .357. Jewel didn't have a permit, which meant jail time and possibly her license if she got busted with it. She hesitated a moment, then slid its cold weight into her pocket. She could feel death hovering in the darkness, peeking over her shoulder. Or maybe she had heard its echo in Sam's voice. She had to get close to use a stunner.

Shoes in hand, she tiptoed down the hall. Sam had come in through the kitchen door, had sliced the old-fashioned chain and boltlock with a laser cutter from the feel of the edges. High tech, she thought bitterly. They would have to buy new locks now. She shivered in the cold bite of the wind as she cut across the dusty, weed-grown yards. Nothing for free in this world. She knew it and Sam knew it, which meant that there was a price for tonight. And it would be a stiff one. She was a fool to do this, almost as much of a fool as David. Jewel took the path as fast as she dared in the dark, wishing for Susana's light, ducking as many of the thorns as she could. Yeah, she was a fool . . . The moon hung above the horizon, orange and swollen. She looked back over her shoulder, seeing only darkness, feeling lion breath on her neck. A holo, she reminded herself, but out here in the darkness and silence she could believe in ghosts.

Sam was waiting at the bottom of the path in a car without headlights. No light went on as he opened the door for her, and she tumbled onto the seat with a sigh of relief.

''He's in a house on King, just inside el Peten, over the line from Little Cambodia,'' Sam said as he stepped on the gas and drifted down the hill.

Jewel clutched the door, trying not to mind that he still was not using headlights. There was no traffic on the lightless streets. Not out here. If a cop saw them, they would get pulled over just for being on the road. Or blown away on suspicion if the cops were out for scalps. But it wasn't likely that they would meet a cop; it wasn't an election year. The gun weighed a hundred pounds in her pocket. "How did you find him?" she whispered, and cringed as the car swung too fast around a curve. "Sam?" She drew a quick breath. "Why are you doing this?"

He braked so suddenly that she nearly hit the dash. "Maybe I'm doing this because you will owe me and I would like you to owe me." His face was shadowed and indistinct in the darkness. "Or maybe I'm doing it because you turned Salgado down, back then."

He accelerated down the hill, turning on the lights only when they reached a freeway ramp. The car had a lot of power for a converted gas burner. It was low and long, painted a dark color, and Jewel wondered who had paid for a private license. If it was Sam, he was doing very well. The city freeways were still lighted. In their glow, Sam looked older, leaner and harder than the man who had been her lover. His face looked changed. Cosmetic work?

He saw her looking. "We had this little war a couple years back. I got hurt bad." He shrugged. "Salgado came up with the med-credit to cover the face work. Kind of a bonus."

Jewel shivered because she could see the extent of the reconstruction, remembered in spite of herself the feel of his face between her hands as they kissed. Medical credit was solid currency out here, dispensed by local bosses who could lever extra out of the besieged city government. "Thank you," she said. "For doing this, Sam. I do owe you."

"Yes, you do." Sam eased the car off the freeway and onto darkened streets. "I want to tell you something," he said, and there was caution in his voice. "It was very easy for me to find this dude. When I drifted past the place an hour ago, it was quiet. Do you understand what I'm telling you?"

"I'm supposed to find him."

"Or it's a trap. The boss *can* be subtle when he wants to be."

Yes, she had heard the echo of death in his voice. "I'm carrying," Jewel said softly.

"Good." Sam nodded. "What has this guy got to do with Salgado?"

"Salgado? Nothing."

"Wrong answer." Sam swerved the car around a litter of trash in the street. "This is part of that plant deal with the Japs. I'm pretty sure, anyhow. The boss doesn't let me in on all his doings with the web." Sam made a harsh sound in his throat. "If you wanna know, the boss is a little shaky right now. Real paranoid.

This dude tried to take him out at a parlor last year, so he does business in virtual, and that's it. Hey, this ain't a big community for VR.'' Sam spit through the open window. "Lot of people don't like this upscale Net shit, and they don't like him hiding out like he does, like he's some Anglo big shot.''

Maybe that was why Sam was willing to risk helping her. Salgado's power wasn't so certain anymore, and he had an eye to taking over. Maybe he was collecting favors for later. Jewel stared through the window, out at the darkened streets of the Peten. She had walked those streets with Sam long ago. Her face fit well enough to get her by, with Sam. He had family here, and they had welcomed her. It had been a temptation to sink into this place, to put on the identity they offered. To *belong*. She had never belonged anywhere.

To belong here was forever. A forever of service jobs and being scared on the rail every night. Of a future that went so far and no farther. No, she didn't belong here, either. But she had been tempted.

Then she had started cleaning for old lady Delaport, and the old bitch had offered Jewel a full-time position. She was a web node, and she had dangled University Net access in front of Jewel's nose: an aide patch and an entry to a bigger future. The price had been the old lady's hands on her body.

Sam had shit.

Macho Latino pride. Jewel's lips tightened. Sometimes the old lady's spidery fingers had had the feel of prayer; looking back, Jewel wondered if it was youth she had been worshipping. Sam hadn't wanted to hear or understand. When Salgado had offered him a job, he had taken it and had thrown a choice in Jewel's face: choose—me or her. You didn't belong to Salgado's little organization and keep an outside lover.

The choice hadn't been between old lady Delaport and Sam. The choice had been between the Peten and a future in the web.

So it had ended. And all that time Linda had loved her and had never said a word, never gotten in the way. Jewel closed her eyes for a moment. Love was an illusion that faded in the harsh light of the real world. Jewel pushed the past back into its closet, locking the door on it. So what connection did Salgado have to Flander? Did the fox ghost *everyone*? Possibly. The car was slowing, and Jewel touched the lump of the gun in her pocket. The metal was warm now. Warm as her flesh.

This was a bad street. Broken windows gaped in the brick houses, and several had burned. Violence haunted this neighborhood like a vengeful ghost. It had collected here, feeding on itself and on the angry hopeless men and women who answered its call. Weeds rattled in the breeze, and stripped cars looked like the half-eaten carcasses of dinosaurs. "I don't know what I'm into," Jewel whispered.

"That's a new line for you." Sam opened the door and slid out. "If I even *smell* a setup, we beat it. Or I do, anyway. You suit yourself."

Jewel got out, easing the door closed. Her footsteps sounded loud in the darkness no matter how hard she tried to be quiet. In the distance a dog barked monotonously. Dry leaves rattled in the branches of two dying maples in the yard of the gutted house across the street.

"That one." Sam nodded at it. "I'll go around back. You use the trees to check out the front window. Run for the car if anything breaks. I'm not waiting for you." He pressed a small light-beam flash into her hand.

Jewel nodded and slipped into the deeper darkness beneath the trees. Dead grass and weeds choked the lot. The chimney had tumbled into the yard, and the house sagged wearily on its foundations, looking as if a strong shove might push it over. A twig snapped beneath her foot, and Jewel froze, blood pounding in her ears. Death hung in the air like the stench from a pit toilet. Jewel slid the gun from her pocket and thumbed the safety off. It felt heavy in her hand, warm and alive.

Silence, as if the night were holding its breath. She thought she heard a rustle from the rear of the house and prayed it was Sam moving through tall grass or bushes. The big front windows were empty, but shards of glass stuck up from the frame like razor-edged fangs. Very carefully, Jewel peered inside. The narrow beam of her light touched a broken chair, a filthy piece of yellow carpet, and a litter of plastic trash. A broken-backed sofa blocked off a narrow stairway at the back of the room, and a ragged plastic tarp lay tumbled by the front door. The light played over its faded blue folds.

A hand stuck out from under it—long, pale fingers in a slack curl. Jewel clicked off the flash, her stomach tight. "Sam," she called in a hissing whisper.

"He's there?" Sam materialized out of the darkness, silent and graceful as a cat. "It looks clear." He lifted one shoulder. "Let's go. Back door's open."

The back door had been kicked off its hinges long before. Sam was right; either it was too easy or no one cared if David was found. Jewel slipped through the ruined door, aware of Sam close behind her, wondering suddenly just how much he had changed. She was trusting the Sam who had been her lover. That might be a major mistake, but now it was way too late for second thoughts. She held the gun carefully, her ears straining for any sound. If Sam was carrying, it wasn't in his hand.

The small kitchen was cluttered with squashed fiberboard boxes and wads of packing plastic. Someone had unpacked stolen goods here to scrub the security codes before going to the flea markets. A rat scuttled across the floor. Jewel stepped over a pile of flattened boxes and into the narrow hallway beyond, parting the darkness with the muzzle of the gun. A whole section of the ancient ceiling had fallen down.

She picked her way across the pile of lathe and water-stained plaster. An archway opened into the front room she had seen: trash, sofa, and the musty smell of rat shit. Her light beam picked out the blue tarp and the pale hand sticking out from beneath the corner. Her throat tight, she knelt and lifted the plastic. The light glittered on David's silvered skin and she caught her breath. He was naked. Blood crusted his swollen face, and his nose was broken. She touched his hand, seeing the small crookedness in the bones, wanting to retch or cry. He breathed with an uneven wheezing gurgle, and bubbles of bright blood had gathered at the corner of his mouth. Swallowing the sickness and tears, Jewel felt at his throat for a pulse. Broken ribs, a calm, professional corner of her mind whispered. A perforated lung. Internal bleeding. His skin was cool to the touch, his pulse weak and thready.

It was not a trap. Whoever had dumped him didn't care if someone found a dead body.

You can't move him, her training shrieked at her. Jewel shoved the gun back into her pocket. No ambulance crew would come into this neighborhood until daylight. Maybe not even then if this was a really bad street. David drew a gasping breath and choked. For a terrible moment Jewel thought she was losing him. Then he gasped again, coughed weakly, and breathed.

"Still clear." Sam scuffed through the trash. "Let's get him out of here." He hissed softly between his teeth as he looked down at David. "They did a job on him, didn't they? I'll bring the car around back, and we'll carry him through the kitchen. Goddamn it, he's going to bleed all over my seat."

"Probably. Go on—get the car." Jewel yanked the rest of the tarp off David and flung it aside.

They were all dying, the old men and women she bathed and massaged and monitored. It crept up on them slowly, its footsteps muffled by money and medical technology, its face wearing a gentle virtual mask of a lover's kiss or a bright ski slope. This, the damage that one human could intentionally inflict on another, horrified her. It always horrified her no matter how often she saw it. She had a sudden vision of David in his ice cave. What would happen to it if he died? If she went into it, would she find his body beneath the chimera's hoofed feet? A car engine throbbed and died out back. A moment later Sam reappeared.

"Move." Sam squatted beside her, slid his arms beneath David, and lifted him with a grunt. "Kick some of that shit out of the way in the hall," he gasped.

David would be almost as tall as he, but Sam carried him as if he were a child, shoulders bulging with the effort that didn't show on his face. Jewel shoved broken chunks of plaster out of his path and kicked flattened boxes aside, not caring about the noise she made.

"Someone didn't give a damn if he died." Sam grunted as he slid David onto the backseat of the car. "Shit, look at me. Don't let him bleed on the upholstery." He wiped at the blood on his arm and slammed the door.

Jewel slid into the backseat, cradling David's head on her lap. His hair was matted with blood, and the back of his head felt soft, pulpy. Jewel flicked on her flash. His pupils were unevenly dilated, one wide and black, one closed nearly to a pinpoint.

Cranial trauma. Pressure on the brain. "Sam, hurry," she said softly, but it might be too late for that, too late for any kind of help. "Take us to the trauma clinic over on Rosemont." According to the grapevine, they had a good staff. "Fast, Sam."

"I'll drop you off in front." Sam kept his eyes on the road. "It's getting light."

"Fine. Do it." Braced against the sway of the speeding car, Jewel kept her eyes on the uneven rise and fall of David's chest, expecting it to stop, expecting him to die at any moment.

He was still breathing when Sam pulled the car over against the curb at the clinic. A red neon cross fizzed and flickered above the front door. The clinic was in a refurbished two-story house with arched windows and the ruined remains of a gazebo out back. The gazebo was full of bagged trash waiting for pickup, and the windows were covered with heavy metal mesh. The double automatic doors were made of bulletproof glass sandwiching more mesh. From the doors a wide ramp led down to the circular driveway, poured from cheap, rough concrete. A battered ambulance was parked in the weedy front yard. The driver was sitting in the vehicle's open door, eating a sandwich in the glow of the dome light, his eyes fixed on a small laptop screen balanced on his knees. He looked up as Sam opened the car door, snapped the screen closed, and sauntered over.

"Whew." He whistled as he got a good look at David. "I'll get a gurney." He stuffed the uneaten remains of his sandwich into his pocket and sprinted for the doors.

A moment later he was back, trailed by a pair of tired-looking medics in stained greens rolling an ancient gurney. "What happened?" the younger of the two snapped at Jewel. "Got ID on him?"

"He got mugged," she said quickly. "His name is David Chen."

He grunted and wrapped a blood pressure cuff around David's arm.

The older medic was keying an entry into his pocket data link. "Level three care," he said, squinting at the screen. "If it's him. Run a print check on the ID while we're getting him prepped. You." He stabbed a gloved finger in Jewel's direction. "You two stick around. Waiting room's in there. Show her, Harry." He jerked his head at the ambulance driver.

Jewel stepped back as they slid David onto the gurney. The younger man had already started an IV running and was holding the bag aloft as they wheeled the gurney back through the automatic doors. It was an old model, power-assisted but with manual guidance. Its wheels squeaked, and the older of the medics swore as he struggled to keep it on course. Level three care. Jewel let her breath out in a slow sigh. That was two steps up from federal minimum. It was what she could afford: basic health care with a few frills. They would fix what was wrong, but they wouldn't do it fancy. It shocked her that he had only that much health care. She had assumed wealth, perhaps because she had met him in Erebus.

"I'm out of here," Sam said in a low voice. "You owe me. Remember that."

"I will." She eyed him. "It occurs to me that if Salgado didn't care who found David, you didn't run too much of a risk. And if he had wanted to trap me, I would have been right there."

"What are you saying, Jewel?" Sam's eyes were cold.

"I am saying thank you for helping me." Jewel held his eyes. "And we'll discuss exactly how much I owe you."

"No." He smiled. "You haven't changed that much, Jewel. Salgado's going down, and I think it might be time for me to make my move. Think about that, okay?" He leaned forward suddenly to kiss her lightly on the lips.

There was memory in that kiss, a physical buzz like an arc of electricity. Jewel touched his cheek. "I'll think about it," she said, and heard the sadness in her voice. "Do you ever paint anymore?"

"No." He looked at her for a moment, his face as still and expressionless as a stone. "This is a gift—tonight. For back then." He got into the car, slammed the door, and roared away.

A gift. Jewel watched the car vanish around the corner, not sure why she felt like crying. For what might have been? Or for what was? Maybe both. She jumped as the ambulance driver cleared his throat.

"I'm supposed to herd you into the waiting room." He rocked on his heels, eyes on the brightening sky to the east. "If you don't want to answer a bunch of questions, maybe you better beat it, too. I'm an old man." He grinned, revealing stained teeth. "I don't do strong-arm."

"I'm staying," Jewel said tightly. "David's a friend of mine."

"You better take a little walk and think about it, honey." The driver's eyes slid downward to rest on Jewel's pocket.

Linda's gun. Jewel stiffened. Oh, shit, she had forgotten about it.

The ambulance driver had an old face, weathered and wrinkled by the sun, although he probably could have wangled cosmetic work from somebody on staff. His hair was almost white, combed carefully across the bald top of his head. He wore gloves, but his mask dangled around his neck. "It's bad out here at night," he said. "I keep a nine-millimeter under the seat, myself." He nodded and turned his back on her. "Law enforcement ain't my job. I'll show you the waiting room when you're ready to go in."

She went around the side of the building, polished the gun carefully on her tunic, and dropped it behind the scraggly bushes that grew along the front of the house. It might be there when she came out, but it would be better not to look. The driver was back at his screen again, kicking his legs idly. He looked up as she approached, nodded again, and got to his feet. "Moby Dick," he said as he closed the laptop. "Prose version. It's supposed to be the original." He shrugged. "I never got past the graphics version in school." He paused while the automatic doors opened for them, then ushered her through with a polite sweep of his hand.

Those doors wouldn't let her out again. Not until she had answered a lot of questions. Jewel sighed, suddenly realizing how tired she was. She wouldn't answer those questions easily. She could feel the reluctance already, the old wariness she had learned even before she could talk: never say more than you have to. This place was a bridge, carrying her back to childhood and their days on the street and in the transient clinics. The fluorescent light made her eyes hurt. A dozen plastic chairs huddled around a low fiberboard table covered with tattered hard-copy magazines that looked at least a decade old. A reception desk was empty, but security eyes watched her openly from the corners of the ceiling.

The smell was there. It was always there, in Erebus or a fed-med clinic. Jewel breathed shallowly, struggling with a claustrophobic twinge of panic.

"Are you all right?" The ambulance driver was peering into her face. "Want some coffee?"

"Could you . . . ask about David?" Jewel drew a deep breath. "Please?"

"Sure." He patted her arm. "He's a good friend of yours, huh? You sit down, now. I'll be right back."

She didn't sit down. She had spent too many hours sitting in cheap plastic chairs. Pictures hung on the wall-flats, not holos. Painted landscapes of trees and green meadows. In one picture, horses with long delicate legs and too-small heads pranced beneath trees full of red apples. In another, a woman in a red shawl carried a wooden pail beneath unreal trees. Her sleek blond hair was pulled back from her face, and her cheeks were as red as Jewel's mother's when she had been doing street shit. Her mother could have gone into a federal hospice to die. They didn't let a person suffer there; suffering made too much work for the staff. They gave the patients drugs—supervised medication—and plugged them into some pretty virtual so that they could fade away gently, without pain to themselves or anyone else.

They'll find me, her mother had whispered. *They'll steal you.* Always running from her demons, hiding from them and from the pain in the flea-market drugs that had slowly consumed her. Jewel had never meant to come back to the 'burbs. She looked around wildly, trapped by the walls and the blond woman with her pail. She wore a rose at her waist, as red as fresh blood.

"Miss?" The ambulance driver returned, a steaming mug in his hand. "No coffee, but I managed to beg some tea from Greta on dispatch—it's a slow night. Drink it." He pushed the mug at her. "You look like you need it."

"Thank you." Jewel took it, both annoyed and grateful at his insistent kindness. The plastic mug had a crack that wept beads of black, bitter tea. "How is David?" Jewel took a sip and didn't grimace. "Is he out of surgery yet?"

"Not for a while, honey. Takes a long time to fix what's broke in him." The driver scuffed his feet on the worn carpet, not meeting her eyes. "He'll live, don't worry. I've see worse come in here and make it."

"Tell me," Jewel said softly. "Tell me what they aren't going to fix."

"Everybody gets good basic care, no matter what insurance level they carry." His eyes flickered. "He's got a bad head injury. I heard one of the nurses talking. Brain injuries are tricky. You got to be prepared for that, okay?"

Prepared? Jewel knew how to read between his careful lines. The doctors could relieve cranial pressure and let the patient live with the damage. Or, if the patient could afford it, a specialist could go in and do the careful, elaborate, precise work of repairing the human brain. But not on level three care. "If he could pay," she said softly. "What then?"

"You can buy all kinds of stuff—microlasers, those new synthetic neural fibers they make in orbit, cloned fetal cells." He shrugged. "Whatever you need. But you know, they cost. They cost a lot, and head injuries are still tricky. No guarantees." He kept his eyes fixed on a picture on the wall, the one of the woman with her rose and her bucket. "I just thought you should be prepared."

"It would be hell to work here," Jewel said softly. "If you cared."

The corner of his mouth twitched. "Sometimes," he said, and tore his eyes from the picture. "I'm just a pickup man. Dr. Gross'll tell you the whole story when he gets out of surgery."

Maybe it was the job that had withered his skin, not the sun. "Thank you for warning me," Jewel said softly.

"Sure." He pulled the mangled remains of his sandwich from his pocket, stared at it for a moment, then tossed it into a plastic-lined wastebasket. "I'm getting too old for this," he said, and stomped through the doors, back to his screen.

Chapter
Thirteen

It took Dr. Gross a long time to get out of surgery. Or it took
him a long time to get around to talking to her, anyway. Jewel
finally sat in one of the familiar plastic chairs because she was too
tired to stand anymore and there was nowhere else to sit except the
floor. After a while the receptionist came out, young and surly, to
ask the questions that he would pass on to the police. Jewel answered them slowly, too tired to struggle against the reluctance that
this place had summoned from her past. Here she was a transient
again, a grubby kid in dirty, too-large clothes, wary and afraid of
the looming impersonal presence of the clinic. A mugging, she
told him in a street-kid's sullen tone. David had been coming to
visit and hadn't shown. So she had gone looking and had found
him on the street.

The receptionist didn't believe her, but she didn't care; no one
would do anything. If you went in to the 'burbs at night, it was your
ass. If David had enough clout and the desire to make waves, someone might order an investigation. If David was capable of doing
anything at all after this night. Jewel got up and paced to the bulletproof door. Behind his desk, the receptionist glared at her, then
went back to his terminal screen. The ambulance was gone. Jewel
turned away from the hot glare of dusty morning light, wishing the
old driver were still there, wishing suddenly and desperately for
company, for someone. Even Susana's needling would be welcome
now. This place stirred up too many memories, and she kept seeing
David's battered body superimposed over it all.

"Ms. Martina?" A tall, muscular man with pale skin and dark,
curly hair stood in the doorway. He wore surgical greens and carried a chartbook in one hand. "I'm Dr. Gross. You're with Mr.
Chen?"

He sounded impatient. "I am," Jewel said. "How is he?"

"I just came from surgery on him. He's in recovery, so you can't see him yet."

So don't ask. Just out of surgery, huh? Not with those spotless greens and your shower-damp hair. Jewel crossed her arms sullenly.

"He's going to live." Dr. Gross glanced at the chartbook screen. "One lung was perforated; he sustained three broken ribs, fractures to the bones in both hands, and extensive superficial injuries. You told the receptionist that he was mugged." He stared down his nose at her. "Some of his injuries are several days old."

Several days. Jewel suppressed a shudder.

Dr. Gross cleared his throat. "More seriously, the patient suffered a depressed fracture of the skull. We relieved the cranial pressure, and there is no impairment of autonomic function. The long-term prognosis will depend on his condition when he recovers consciousness."

"How much function will he lose?" Jewel glared at his frown. "Which areas of the brain were damaged?"

"I can't make any prognosis—"

"At this time," Jewel finished for him. Bitterness was rising in her throat, threatening to choke her or make her vomit. "Motor? Speech?"

Dr. Gross glared at her. She knew him and all the others like him. He worked in every 'burb and transient clinic, despising the dumb animals who came in with their untreated cancers, drug problems and toxin-damaged children. If he could be anywhere else, he would be. She was wrecking his clean, sanitary speech—the one designed to answer without giving the important things away, the one designed to send the stupid, anxious relatives home and out of his hair.

"It's too early to tell," he said through tight lips.

Which was possibly a yes to her question. Jewel's insides were turning to ice. "If someone could pay, could all the damage be reversed?" She straightened her shoulders, shrugging off the street kid, because street kid wouldn't help David—if anything could help him. "Tell me." She summoned Alcourt's web voice, slapping the doctor in the face with the whip-crack tone. "If you aren't capable of making an adequate diagnosis, then I will have him transferred to the care of a more competent institution."

His eyes widened just a hair. He had been doing this too long to give much away, but she had surprised him. Jewel crossed her arms, waiting, letting her impatience show, as if he were a housekeeper who hadn't finished changing the sheets yet. He had filed her as just another dumb Latina, bringing a beat-up city trick in from the Peten. Now he was reconsidering.

"I'm in a hurry." She glanced at the clock, putting Alcourt's fierce impatience into the set of her shoulders. *One more minute, Doc, and we go elsewhere.* She broadcast the message with her flesh. The bottom line runs your life, too. Your boss'll shit if you lose a really big private-money account. You gonna risk it?

He wasn't. "The prognosis for this type of injury is never certain," he said stiffly. "But I would say that the odds of a full recovery are good. With proper treatment. I'd have to call in one or two specialists, of course. We have some excellent neurosurgeons on referral."

He hated it, talking to her like this, as if she were an Alcourt. He didn't really think she was but he couldn't afford to take the chance. If she had been pushing a package to Ishigito, he would have jumped for it, Jewel thought bitterly. "How much time do we have before the damage becomes irreversible?"

He flinched at the "we" and his face began to darken. She wouldn't have asked that if she had the money to pay. "Treatment should begin as soon as possible." He bared the tips of his perfect white teeth at her. "Within the next three hours, certainly. Would you care to authorize immediate treatment?"

"I may transfer him." Jewel gave him a scant Alcourt nod. "I will let you know." She turned on her heel and marched through the wire-netted doors.

Three hours. She hurried down the dusty drive, her Alcourt confidence evaporating beneath the hammer blow of the sun. Most of the houses were occupied on this block. The yards were relatively uncluttered with junk, and there wasn't much trash. Someone had even laid out a lawn in swirled patterns of different-sized rocks. Good neighborhood. Most of them probably worked as support for the clinic—housekeepers, motor-pool staff, or whatever. Neighbors on the payroll were the best protection against raids.

An ambulance turned the corner as Jewel reached the sidewalk, roaring down the block and screeching into the driveway. Jewel tried to see if it was the old man driving, but it went by too fast. Carrying someone with a reasonable level of care and a fixable problem? Three hours. The sun's heat didn't touch the coldness inside her as Jewel hurried down the sidewalk. There should be a bus stop on the next block, or she might flag one of the 'burb jitneys. Her skins were at the house, and she needed them. Flander would be in the ice cave, and it had only virtual access.

Unlimited treatment. There wasn't that much money in the whole fucking world. Not in *her* world, anyway. She hoped to hell Flander had a different answer.

She caught a jitney, an ancient pickup that wheezed and shuddered. She paid the driver's exorbitant single-fare rate because it seemed like nothing compared to the numbers that had been rolling through her head, and time *mattered*. He stared at her as he pocketed the money. Jewel looked down. Her arms and tunic were blotched with dried blood.

"Bad night?" he asked, full of curiosity that masqueraded as sympathy.

"Yeah, bad," Jewel snarled at him. "I'm in a hurry."

Whatever he read in her face shut him up. He gave her a fast ride home, much faster than she would have thought the decrepit junker could manage. Fast enough to leave her knees a little shaky.

The houses on the hilltop baked in the sun, silent, their windows shuttered. They might have all been abandoned. They looked strange, as if they had changed subtly overnight. Jewel slammed the door of the jitney and ran up the walk to the front door. A brief wild hope seized her that Linda would open the door, but what difference would it make, and what would it change, anyway? Still, she felt a small clench of disappointment as Susana emerged from the kitchen.

"So where the hell did *you* go?" Susana scowled, a plastic container of vat-grown orange juice in her hand. "Jeeze! You get yourself cut or what?"

"I found David." Jewel brushed past Susana. "He's over at the Rosemont clinic. I've got to talk to Flander."

"What do you mean you found him? Like where?" Susana followed her down the hall and leaned against the door frame as Jewel threw off her clothes and reached for her skinthins. "Flander's not around."

"Not *around*?" Jewel glared at Susana as she tugged her skins up over her shoulder. To hell with the blood on her arms. It was dry, and the skins covered them. "Where the hell is he? Either someone authorizes heavy treatment in the next three hours or David ends up . . . God knows how." She shook her head, tears burning her eyes, which was stupid, because she was furious. "That little shit," she hissed. "The little fox bastard, self-centered *shit*!"

"How come you're so into this?" Susana finished her juice. "I thought he and Flander were a thing. What's he mean to you?"

"He isn't . . ." Jewel paused, tunic in her hands. "He's just a friend," she said lamely. He had read her, and he hadn't used his

insights to lever her. He had given her the office, had made it not
a gift so that she would take it. "That's all." She jerked her head.
"I don't have time, okay? I've got to be at Wosenko's in an hour,
and I've got to find the damn fox, or *someone* who can pay, before
then. Shit." She grabbed her gloves and lenses from the dresser.
"I don't even know his next of kin."

"I'll get it for you, if Flander isn't in the cave." Susana grinned.
"Medical files are no sweat, Auntie. I been in and out of the
MedBase for a long time. Boring. They don't even know I'm there."

She was another Flander. Jewel opened her mouth to say no,
then closed it. "All right." She jerked her head. "If he's not there,
you do it. Let's go."

She sweated in the closed confines of the booth both from the
heat and from nerves. She had known that Susana was into serious
ghosting, but knowing and watching were two different things. This
wasn't a case of sneaking Net time onto a friend's account; this was
a flat-out pirate run. She wouldn't get a second chance if she got
caught.

It would be Susana who would get tagged by a security scan, not
Jewel. Jewel wasn't in; she was watching from outside, because
she was no Flander. She was safe. She watched Susana's body
twitch, watched her reach, move her hands and feet as if she were
climbing. It looked so stupid from the outside. What the hell would
she do if the kid got tagged? Run? She would be implicated as an
accessory. All her years of caution, all her survival rules were
crashing down around her in ruins.

The desert had started it—David's desert. It had opened a door,
and this day had rushed through on a wave of yesterdays. Where
the hell was Flander?

Susana made an abrupt tossing motion, nearly smacking Jewel
in the eye, and yanked off her lenses. "Done." She laughed, her
face flushed, eyes sparkling, as if she were high or in love. "Piece
of cake. It's on your desk. Ask for Chen."

Piece of cake? Jewel swallowed relief and a quick surge of anger
at Susana's easy confidence. No time now. None. She pulled on
her lenses, itching, sweating beneath her skins. "Enter filespace,
Jewel Martina," she snapped.

The brick wall formed in front of her. Different flowers were
blooming in the cracks between the bricks—tiny fringed blue cups.
The white blossoms that had been in bloom before had mostly gone
by. David paid such attention to details. Jewel spread her hand

beneath the trickle of water falling into the earthenware basin, watching silver drops scatter. "Chen file," she said too loudly.

They appeared in glowing letters on the satiny surface of her desk: one, two, three, four names. Three sisters and a father. No mother was listed. He had never mentioned family. "Access." Jewel touched the top line of print.

"This access is terminal mode only," her office told her. One wall shimmered, becoming an oversized terminal screen.

No virtual? Jewel blinked. David had to have been netted by his parents, but his father didn't even have virtual access? Before she could pursue this small surprise, a woman's face appeared on the screen. She had black hair and delicate Asian features.

"Who is calling, please?" she asked in a sweet voice.

An answering auto. Jewel's office had already outlined the woman's image in red—a warning that she was talking to an autonomous persona, not a real person. "Jewel Martina. I am a friend of David Chen. This is an emergency."

The screen went suddenly blank. Failed connection? It happened a lot out here. "Reestablish access," Jewel said.

"The connection is still open," her office informed her.

The screen blinked, and a man stared out at her. He looked very old, older than the ambulance driver. His wrinkled face might have been carved from a block of dark, bitter wood. "What is this emergency?" he asked. "What has it to do with me?"

"David was . . . attacked last night," Jewel began.

"I was informed." The old man folded his lips together. "You need not repeat the details. I ask you again: what has this to do with me?"

"He needs treatment to prevent permanent brain damage. His health credit won't cover it. Without it, he may be physically and mentally . . . impaired." Jewel paused, but the old man's eyes didn't even flicker. "Did the hospital explain this to you?" she asked sharply, wondering if he was deaf. "He needs your help."

"My help?" The folded lips got thinner. "He needs my money, you mean. Did he say to you that he is my son? That is a lie. If he has need of money, tell him to ask that boy of his for it. It was his choice to throw himself away on the games, to turn his back on his family. I gave him everything, and he threw it in my face." The old man raised a clenched fist as if he were about to strike the screen. "And now he comes crawling to me? Ha. I knew this would happen! I told him so."

"You're wrong." Jewel met his stony glare, struggling with rising anger. "David didn't ask me to do this. He may never ask anyone to do anything for him again. *I* assumed that he was your son. It was my mistake." No, David had no reason to mention his family. "Exit access," she snapped. "The old *bastard*."

Pale walls solidified around her suddenly; she had dropped into a new virtual. Jewel looked around, half expecting some trick of Flander's. A scroll hung on the wall, and a woman sat behind a polished wood desk. She was Asian, but not the face in the old jerk's auto.

"Ms. Martina." The woman bowed her head so that the dark wings of her hair swung forward along her cheeks. "I apologize for so rudely diverting your access, but I feared that you might refuse any further communication from the Chen family. I apologize for my father's lack of manners." Her black eyes fixed themselves on Jewel's face. "I am David's sister," she said.

"Chen Yao Hwa," her office whispered in her ear. "Eldest of the Chen siblings."

She didn't look like David, but this was virtual and so that meant nothing. She could have two heads. "Were you monitoring our conversation?" Jewel asked, too discouraged and angry for tact. "Did you hear what I told the—your father?"

"The old bastard, you were going to say? Yes, I heard." She steepled her fingers on the desktop. "You are not exaggerating, because I also monitored the doctor's call. I warned David that this might happen." She leaned forward suddenly, her onyx eyes pinning Jewel. "My brother is a fool."

"Yes," Jewel said. "He is." Because he had believed in something that didn't exist, something that had no real meaning in the world of choice and price tags. Just another illusion that carried no weight when it was tossed onto the steel scales of the real world. She closed her eyes briefly, seeing Linda's face against the screen of her eyelids. "I could wish he wasn't," she said softly.

David's sister said nothing for a long moment. "I do not have the funds to finance the type of treatment required." She frowned down at her clasped hands on the polished desktop. "I will speak to the other members of the family, and I will speak to our father. Perhaps we can come to some agreement."

"There isn't much time."

"I'm quite aware of the time limitations." The woman's eyes flashed as she lifted her head. "I can do no more than this. I will not keep you longer." She bowed her head again, and the room vanished.

Jewel found herself staring at David's flowering wall. So much for that. She sighed, her shoulders lifting and then dropping, dragged earthward by fatigue and the stone inside her. Yes, it would keep getting bigger, and one day she would be all stone. Perhaps then she wouldn't care.

Was that what had happened to Linda?

"Exit," Jewel said, and returned to the scrawled walls and stinking air of the real world.

"What's up?" Leaning against the wall of the booth, Susana watched Jewel strip off her lenses and wipe her sweaty face. "Get anything?"

"No." Jewel stuffed gloves and lenses into her pocket. No hope for David, no time to go home and leave the skins. "I've got to get on the rail." She had to report for work; she had used up her personal-emergency allowance when Carl had died. "I need this job." She opened the door, wincing as the sun stabbed her. "Shit," she said, and wiped her watering eyes. "This world is full of shit."

"Yeah." Susana touched her arm. "Look, I'll see you around." She slipped between two empty booths and vanished into the glaring sun and shadow of the empty flea market.

Jewel did not call her back. What was there to say? She ran for the rail that was just pulling in and swung onboard as the warning chime sounded. What was there to say to anyone? She found a seat beneath the watchful eye of the armed guard.

"You're late." Juanita, who had the shift before hers, greeted Jewel coldly as she entered Ruth Wosenko's tower apartment. "I'll go log out while you dress." She marched past Jewel, her back stiff.

Juanita was never early and never late. Juanita Santa Maria had been a licensed aide for ten years, was always on time, and did not approve of anything less. She would undoubtedly file a complaint with the agency. Jewel sighed as she plunked her carryall down on the recliner in what had once been Ruth Wosenko's office and study. She pulled her coverall on over her skins to save time; it was cool in here and they didn't itch. "House, logging on," she said as she stuffed her tunic and tights into the carryall. "Jewel Martina."

"Log on acknowledged. Ms. Santa Maria is leaving. Mrs. Wosenko is engaged in entertainment."

That meant she was in virtual, spaced on prescription hypnotics. Jewel wondered who had programmed the House to use such pompous language. Possibly Mrs. Wosenko herself. She had set up the legal and financial machine that now kept her alive and cared for. Had she been so afraid of death? Had she thought about it as she levered her wealth from the web? Had she meant to use it to buy off death? Jewel had never really met the woman who had lived here. She knew only the sullen, sly flesh that wanted to die. David might be like that when he woke up. A body waiting to follow its soul? Mystical *shit*. Jewel kicked her carryall out of sight beneath the recliner and marched into the living room. Wosenko had so much unused space here. Jewel paused to look through the glass that formed the inner wall of the room.

In these tower arcologies the central core was a vertical garden. Vines, shrubs, and trees grew on a multitude of balcony terraces, and a stream cascaded from terrace to terrace, falling at last into a pool on the ground level. The plants purified the air, and the stream purified and aerated the filtered and sanitized water. Environmentally self-contained; no pollution or toxic waste in the water or air. No melanoma or dust-borne viruses. Old lady Delaport had lived in a tower like this. It had seemed like heaven the first time Jewel had come in to clean with her crew. In that instant she had known what she wanted. It had remained only to discover how to get it. And I found out, Jewel thought bitterly. I did all the right things.

In fifteen minutes the three hours that the doctor had given David would be up. Not that his deadline really meant anything—it was just a guess. It might have been too late five minutes after she walked through the clinic door. Far below, an Asian woman played with a blond toddler on a grass-covered balcony. They were blowing opalescent bubbles that drifted gently on the clean air. The woman held out her arms, and the child ran into them, laughing. Linda would do that in some garden with the child she now carried. Jewel turned her back.

In her bedroom old Mrs. Wosenko lay faceup in the wide water bed. Lenses on her face, skinthins hiding her aged skin, she twitched like a dying rabbit. Skiing? Making love? Jewel went around to the head of the bed, to the console that was tastefully hidden in a carved wood cabinet. Biochem normal—for her. Various drugs titrated to prescription levels in the bloodstream. Jewel did manual vitals, then checked the catheter and the drip lines that led into the permanent ports implanted in her veins. All okay. She logged it in. In the upper left-hand corner of the touch screen time marched past, one digital second after another. Three hours and ten minutes since she had irritated Dr. Gross.

Jewel touched up a new screen on the console and keyed in a timed ending for the virtual that was running. Yes, it was the ski slope. She usually asked for that one. When the virtual ended, she would have to run the exercise regimen. Wosenko hated it. This was what Alcourt faced, Jewel thought suddenly. He was too healthy and too rich to die quickly. He would die gently, in a slow fading of dreams and dying flesh. Jewel shuddered, revolted suddenly, her stomach knotting on its emptiness. Alcourt. Light-headed, Jewel leaned on the frame of the bed.

Possibly. . . . it was just possible. It was also possible that an asteroid might strike the tower, but what the hell . . . He had referred to David as a friend once. Jewel glanced at the console. Everything was normal. Mrs. Wosenko wouldn't walk off the slope for another fifteen minutes. There was time. Jewel groped in her pocket and thumbed on her remote monitor as she dashed back through the main room. It would call her if anything changed.

The study was hardwired for virtual. Breathing fast, Jewel shoved the recliner out of the way, pulled on her gloves, and fumbled her lenses into place. She would never get access, of course. He had no reason at all to talk to a fired employee, and his access was layered deep in screens and security. "House, access filespace, Jewel Martina," she said breathlessly. She fixed her eyes on the blue flowers as they shimmered and formed in front of her. "Office, access Harmon Alcourt, personal." Her heartbeat counted off the seconds: one, two, three . . . of course she couldn't access him. Eight, nine . . . Stupid thought, but she had at least tried.

An archway opened in the opposite wall. Beyond it flowering trees bloomed around a stone basin of water. Alcourt's foyer. Slowly Jewel walked through it, heart pounding. I am afraid, she thought. Why should I be afraid? Last time she had been in this foyer Alcourt had startled her with his silent appearance. This time Jewel was facing his office door when it opened.

"Mr. Alcourt." She bowed, suddenly unwilling to offer him her hand, not wanting to touch him, even in virtual. "Thank you for seeing me."

"My, we're formal." He smiled at her, warm, charming, obviously delighted to see her.

Her office was reading mild irritation and a hint of malice.

So screw the formalities. Jewel tossed her head, realizing with a pang that she had given her Self no editing instructions, realizing at the same instant that it probably didn't matter because his office was undoubtedly good enough to read her editing anyway. "David Chen has been badly injured." She eyed his kindly expression—still irritated, her office cued her. "He will suffer permanent brain damage if someone doesn't pay for treatment. It has to happen right now. Immediately."

"And you want me to pay for it?" His eyebrows rose. He was

thoughtful, his irritation fading. "Why should I, Jewel? Because I'm rich?"

"Because you'd own him." Jewel met his unreal stare. "Even if he never acknowledges it, you'd know it and he'd know it, and that matters to you."

A slow smile spread across his perfect face. Pleased, her office cued her. Trace of malice. "You know, I'm very sorry that we couldn't come to an agreement. You truly are an unusual individual, and you would have made a very worthy heir. Yes, I *would* own him, wouldn't I? And from what I know of David Chen, he would honor that ownership. He wouldn't like it much, but he'd honor it. Yes, I do like that. I'll look into the situation." He bowed. "I predict that you will do well selling your scraps of medical gossip. Now, if you'll excuse me."

"Treatment needs to start immediately," Jewel said quickly.

"I'll look into it." Alcourt was holding out an arm to usher her to the archway.

The thin red outline meant that he had slipped from the virtual, had left an autonomous Self behind. His office was good to shift from realtime to auto that smoothly. "Thank you," Jewel said with quiet irony, and walked through the archway into her own office. Behind her the archway vanished.

So Alcourt had agreed to pay. Or had he? Jewel shook her head, uneasy, disturbed, and not sure why. What have I just done? she asked herself, and had a feeling that she had just signed David's name to a contract she hadn't read yet. Or perhaps she had signed her own name. Something else nagged at her. She had a feeling it was important.

"It's about time, lady!" A red fox leapt from nowhere onto her desktop. "What the fuck's going on?" He snapped at her, fangs clashing together inches from her face. "You didn't do *nothing*."

Jewel flinched backward before her mind could catch up with her reflexes. "You little bastard." She half reached for him, fingers twitching with the desire to grab him by the neck, shake him . . . "*Nothing*, huh? Where the hell have you been? Surfing around? Playing games? You really don't give a shit, do you?

"Knock it off." Flander flattened his ears, panting. "I've been hanging out in the cave, waiting for you to show."

"Don't give me the cave. Susana was there. You weren't."

"You're full of shit. Listen, the guys who have David didn't post anything last night. You get that? Means he's dead—he couldn't take any more." His voice cracked. "So you're off the hook, lady. Does that make you happy?"

Was that really grief in his voice, or was it his Self talking? Jewel looked away from his glittering, tortured eyes. What could you believe in, in here? Too much deception . . . "I found David." She closed her eyes briefly. "He's alive. They fractured his skull, and there's brain damage. Can you pay to fix it?" she asked bitterly. "I can't. Since you weren't around I went begging."

"I was in the cave," Flander snarled. "I was there. Where is he? Fuck it, lady, where's David?"

"Rosemont emergency clinic." she said wearily.

No answer. When she looked, he was gone, vanished.

What did David mean to him? For that matter, what did David mean to her? Susana had asked, and she hadn't really answered. I owe you. You owe me. This has so much value, and this other thing is worth more or less. She had defined the world that way, and it had always worked. Or had it?

She didn't know the rules anymore, and she had *always* known the rules.

Shrill beeping made her jump. Her remote. She had stayed too long, and Wosenko's virtual was ending. Jewel swallowed a curse, snatched off her lenses, and hurried out of the study. More than four hours gone now. Sorry, David, she thought as she pulled off her gloves. I tried. Maybe Alcourt had paid, and maybe he had simply been playing with her. Jewel paused as that nagging bit of memory surfaced suddenly. He had said something about her selling her bits of medical gossip, and he couldn't have known about the antibody package. Ishigito was Epyxx. Alcourt was AllThings. The web nodes didn't talk to each other, and she had put it together after she'd left Erebus. But he had known.

Coincidence, she decided. Or he was ghosting her space? No, Flander's hot office would have warned her. On the balcony below, the woman and toddler had disappeared. The woman had held out her arms to the child as if she were the mother. Jewel leaned her forehead briefly against the cool glass. Perhaps there was too much illusion in the real world, too. "I'm sorry, David," Jewel whispered, and went to stimulate Ruth Wosenko's dying muscles, to buy off death for another day.

Chapter Fourteen

Darkness.

Darkness was safe.

Safe . . . Monsters waited in the light. And pain.

David drifted gently through a black sea, rising slowly toward some unseen surface. The darkness was thinning, and he began to struggle, fear spiking through him, trying to retreat, to sink back into the safe darkness. They were reaching for him . . . hurting . . . He heard someone groan, a distant, awful sound. His voice. He felt his lips move, stiff and clumsy . . . His throat hurt, as if someone had scratched it deep inside.

"Hey, it's about time."

Words, a voice, loud as a thunderclap. It speared through the safe darkness, shredding it. David tried to move, to sit up, felt cloth beneath his hands, suddenly felt his body. It had been gone, or he had been gone, but he was back now. No cuffs. No pain, or not much . . . just distant aches, like a dull glow from dying embers.

"It's all right, dude. Easy."

High-pitched voice. David blinked into darkness. A boy's voice? No. Girl. Not one of them. Not Jack. He remembered that much, that his name was Jack. Netted. He had looked into David's eyes as he worked on his hand, pressed close like a lover. His erection had rubbed against David's leg. He had felt it through the lightning-bolt slashes of agony as Jack broke the bones one at a time.

"Oh, shit, here comes law and order. I'm outta here. Catch you later."

"Wait," David said, but the word came out a croak. He felt a small stir of cool air, an absence. New voices—more than one. David stretched his eyes wide open, ice congealing around his heart, straining to see. He began to pant, his lungs laboring, as if there were not enough air in the room.

175

"Mr. Chen. I'm Dr. Benachim."

Dr. Benachim. Woman's voice. Panic squeezed against the walls of his skull, threatening to burst him wide open. "I can't see," he whispered.

"It's all right, Mr. Chen. This is to be expected. It's not at all unusual."

Calm, comforting words. They soaked into him, dimming the fear, filling him with soft, feathery warmth. Drugs, David thought vaguely. They gave me something. Again he tried to sit up. This time his arm twitched and he felt the cool leaden trail of tubing across his skin.

The tubes were in Flander's arm . . . no, that was in Erebus. Flander?

They had wanted Flander. They had posted the beating to make Flander show up in the flesh. So they could kill him.

"Mr. Chen? Can you hear me?"

The doctor's voice was closer now. Bending over him? "Yes," David said thickly. "I can hear you. What happened?" He swallowed, trying to control his too-large tongue. "How . . . did I get here?"

"You were mugged? Do you remember?"

Mugged? Fingers touched him, lifted his eyelid. David's eye twitched, and he tried to turn his head away. "I don't know." His body didn't want to do what he told it to do. The doctor held his chin still easily and lifted the other eyelid. The fear was a beast inside him, crouched, ready to leap. He had thought that he would die. That they would not stop until they had killed him. They could get a lot of money for death. There were people who would buy it to experience over and over. After a while he had hoped that it would happen soon. David took hold of his fear with both hands. "What's wrong with me?" he whispered.

"You suffered a skull fracture." The doctor's words were soft, professionally soothing. "You're making quite a good recovery, but these things take time. Not all brain functions recover at the same rate."

Brain functions. The words settled into his belly. "But my . . . sight will come back?"

"We used a new implanted fetal-cell technique. The success rate is very high, but everyone responds at their own rate. Let's just take it one step at a time, okay?" The doctor's hand closed around his arm, squeezing gently.

The touch was too professional to feel very reassuring.

"I want you to rest now." Another squeeze. "I've scheduled

you for some physical therapy tomorrow—you need to get back on your feet. You've been on enhanced healing for the last week. It's time to start moving your muscles on your own."

"How long have I been here?" David asked. It was so *black*.

"Eight days." The voice was receding. "I'll look in on you tomorrow."

"Wait." David tried to struggle up onto his elbows but let himself fall back onto the bed, shocked at the instant tremble in his muscles. "Who brought me in?" he asked desperately. "How did I get here?"

"You were transferred here from the Rosemont clinic over on the east side. How you ended up there I can't tell you."

A different voice, another woman. A doctor? A nurse? His head was starting to ache in spite of the drug fuzz. David tried to lift his hand. It weighed a ton, stone-heavy and awkward—tethered to the bed with wires? Fingers didn't move very well . . . oh. Yeah.

"Don't bang yourself in the face." Someone—a woman—took the heavy alien weight of his hand from him and laid it down on the bed. Effortlessly, because he had no strength. "They'll come off tomorrow. These new casts are incredibly clumsy, but that's because of the hardware that generates the bioelectrical field. It works miracles with breaks. You'll be playing the piano in no time."

"I don't play the piano."

"Then you can learn." A smile colored her tone. "Be glad you got to sleep through the whole-body therapy. We don't call it the iron maiden for nothing."

"Don't go." David tried to reach but failed. "Wait a minute."

"I'm not going anywhere." Her hand touched his shoulder, and David smelled . . . cinnamon? "You need to stop worrying, all right? Dr. Benachim is probably the best neurosurgeon in the business. She was one of the pioneers with fetal-cell implants. You'll be fine. She's not worried."

Maybe. Maybe not. David closed his eyes, but there was no difference in the texture of the darkness that wrapped him. "Has anyone visited me?"

"Yes, actually." The smile in her voice again. "You've been pretty popular, for all that you've been asleep."

"Who?" The word dried up his throat, choking off any more speech.

"I don't know their names." Pause. "A dark-haired woman. Nice-looking. And a . . . girl." Hesitation, a hint of disapproval. "A teenager, you know?"

Who? "Anyone . . . else?"

"Not that I've seen." A hand patted his shoulder. "I can ask at the desk. Maybe someone else dropped by when I was off-shift."

"Will you do that, please?" David let his head sink back on the pillow, the last of his strength gone. Flander hadn't come, hadn't sent any kind of message.

Flander was dead.

The woman had left. Silence. A soft hum came from the head of his bed. A console? The console at the head of Flander's bed in Erebus had hummed like that. He would have come or managed to send a message if he was alive. The darkness pressed in on David, heavy as the dirt on a coffin lid.

A soft scraping sound. The door. Footsteps. David tried to focus his eyes on the sound in an automatic, unstoppable twitch of reaction. He couldn't sit up, could barely lift his hands. "Who is it?" he asked, and heard the harsh edge of fear in his tone.

"Yo." A rustle of movement beside him. A presence. "They don't like me much. 'Specially the doc, so I keep a low profile. You're awake, huh? Hi. I'm Susana."

Susana? Familiar name, but he couldn't place it. "Was that you before? When I woke up?"

"Was me. They don't tell me squat, but I've got good ears. I heard 'em say that they were gonna take you out of that tank thing today. Wake you up. Seemed like *someone* ought to be here."

Someone. Yeah. David struggled to place her voice, but his brain felt like a pool of sludge. "I'm sorry." He squashed a new twinge of fear. "I . . . don't remember you."

"No shit." A smile tinted her voice. "You never met me. Or, yeah, I guess you did, kind of. I was into your cave a couple of times. Did some stuff, you know? Dude, you are so hot!"

He kept squinting, as if he could see her if he just tried hard enough. Relax, he told his eye muscles, but they weren't listening. "What did you do?" he asked.

"Nothing much. This chick, kind of growing out of a giant icicle. You didn't wipe it, anyway. I don't know if you even saw it before some asshole trashed it."

"I saw it." David nodded. He could do that much. "It was good. I was sorry that it got broken. Try something else, okay. It added a lot."

"Hey, sure. No problem." Her grin was almost audible. "I been working on something already. You liked it, huh? Hey, I even like what you did with Jewel."

Jewel. Oh, yes. "I do know you. You're Jewel's niece." He remembered the kid who had messaged Jewel in Erebus. 'Burbs-kid dress and chip-on-the-shoulder slouch. She had thrown some kind of gauntlet smack into Jewel's face, hard enough to hurt. And Jewel had left because of it, never mind the official story. "She's been here, too?" Tall and dark-haired. Of course.

"She's not my aunt." Susana's voice had gone cold. "Just keep that straight, okay? No blood between us."

"Okay." David nodded. The chip was still there. And anger. "Listen, do *you* know how I got here? No one's talking."

"Sure. Jewel found you, don't ask me how. Anyway, she hauled you into one of those shit 'burb clinics, and then they sent you here. *Here* is Sisters of Mercy, right downtown. Holo windows in the hall, rugs, and fancy food. I don't fit the decor."

Jewel had found him? Any memory of that was gone, lost in the darkness. He shook his head and felt strangeness as his head moved on the pillow. It was getting easier to move, as if he were getting stronger, or perhaps a muscle-relaxant drūg was wearing off. Some kind of bulky bandage covered his head. What else had happened to his body? He remembered some things all too well, but there were a lot of hazy images that he couldn't bring into focus. David drew a shallow breath, fighting the fear again. He moved one leg, then the other. Everything felt right. Everything seemed to work. "What did they . . . fix?" he asked.

"I don't know exactly." Pause. "Like I said, they don't talk to me. Inside stuff, mostly. Except for your hands. And they fixed up your face in a few places. Looks fine now."

David flinched as cool fingers touched his cheek.

"I guess a mirror's no good even if they had one lying around, which they don't. Maybe you can tell this way, huh?"

Her fingers moved across his face, pressing lightly against the contours of brow, cheekbones, nose (a little tenderness there), and chin. He felt a harder ridge of tissue along his lower lip.

"That was the worst place." She took her hand away. "Hey, dude, I don't know what you looked like before, but you look real fine right now." A grin colored her tone. "I can get the fox to call up an image, tell you if it's the same face, if that's what's bugging you. Me, I'd stick with this one, anyway."

"You mean Flander?" David made it onto his elbows this time, straining to see. "You've talked to Flander?"

"Hey, dude, I'm sorry. I meant to tell you right off. Talked to him, oh, yeah. I can't get in anywhere without him showing up, crashing in like a tank, bugging me about how you're doing." David felt the brush of her body as she leaned close. "He was gonna get us both busted," she murmured softly, and then her presence was removed. "So I figured I might as well hang around here till you woke up, so I could get him off my butt. Dude, the fox is truly ballistic. He says to tell you he's really, really sorry and that he tried but he couldn't stop it, and he's got to talk to you. Man, he's *suffering*."

Flander. He wasn't dead. David lay back on the pillow, a surge of relief rushing through him. But beneath that joy a bitter darkness twisted on itself like a coiled snake.

If he had told me what was going on, it wouldn't have happened. David closed his eyes; the darkness remained the same. If he had trusted me . . .

"They got VR access here like you wouldn't believe. You could run the *web* from one of these beds." She broke off suddenly, and for the space of three heartbeats there was only the sound of the console's hum. "You . . . could get terminal access," she said after a moment. "He could come in on that. Shit. You gotta hurry up and quit this blindness crap."

She didn't sound very certain. David felt a sudden chill, wondering what else she had overheard. He couldn't ask her—the fear clogged his throat, silencing him. Had she just realized that he couldn't do virtual without eyes? He might as well use an old-fashioned telephone to communicate. Virtual depended on visuals. Period. End of story. The fear was getting tangled up with the coiled bitterness in his gut, twisting into a tight, ugly knot.

"No," he said softly. "If Flander wants to talk to me, he'll have to show up in the flesh. He'll have to come to me."

"I'll pass it on," Susana said dubiously. "I don't think he's around. In the flesh, I mean."

"I'm not going anywhere soon." David didn't try to keep the bitterness out of his voice.

"Susana?" A woman's voice. "What are you doing here?"

"Skiing. What does it look like?"

Jewel? Funny how a voice sounded different went you didn't have the visual cues. Maybe because you listened to it with your entire attention. "Is that you, Jewel?" David forced himself not to squint.

David's face looked gaunt beneath the thick cap of bandage on his head. Jewel bit her lip. "Yes, it's me. David, how are you feeling?" She leaned over the bed, putting her hand on his shoulder because he couldn't see her.

He's responding sluggishly to some of the cloned-cell implants, Dr. Benachim had told her. Apparently she had decided that Jewel was in charge, never mind that Alcourt was paying. *Nothing to worry about yet. We'll have to reevaluate the case if his sight doesn't begin to improve soon.*

She had asked her what options David had if the implants failed. The answer was none.

"They've had you sedated and on enhancement since you came in." She had taken to coming by after her shift every day. The hospital was only a ten-minute walk from Ruth Wosenko's tower, and she had no reason to hurry back to the house. "I'm glad you're finally awake."

"Susana told me you . . . found me."

"Flander asked me to look for you, and I got lucky. Someone had . . . dumped you. In the Peten. I—I told the cops I thought it was a mugging, because I didn't know what was going on."

"This place has got security," Susana mused to the ceiling. "They can listen to patients if they want."

Jewel flushed, pissed, but the kid was right. David's eyes were fixed on her face. They looked so *normal*, as if he were seeing her. "Dr. Benachim said they can discharge you in a few days. I guess they want to do some physical therapy while you're getting your sight back." There. Make it sound like a certainty, not a possibility.

He couldn't read her without eyes. Not as well, anyway. Her words seemed to comfort him, at least a little.

"Jewel . . . thank you." His voice had gone low, husky. "That's not enough, but I don't know what else to say."

"I wish . . ." What? That it hadn't happened? That he had listened to her? She sighed. "Flander asked me to give you a message."

She doesn't want to give it to me, David thought heavily. He cut her off. "I know. Susana told me. She'll give Flander my answer." Bitter fatigue was creeping through his muscles. "I'm tired," he mumbled.

"Not too tired, I hope." A cheery new voice from the direction of the door. David strained to see. Male.

"We're going to take a stroll down the hall a little later. The doctor wants you to walk for at least ten minutes this afternoon."

The voice was moving closer to the bedside. David's breath caught in his throat, and his stomach muscles contracted.

"You'll be starting on a regular physical therapy schedule tomorrow. I've been assigned to take you through the program. Here." Sound of plastic being set down on a hard surface. "I brought in your afternoon snack. We've got melon cubes—nice hydroponic stuff from the California coast—and cheese. I brought enough for all of you.''

That voice . . . Oh, God, he *knew* it. He hadn't been into it like Jack. It was just a paid contract and the opportunity to record a pricey bit of S and M. He had done the holding, and he had orchestrated the sessions. David struggled to swallow, his heart pounding. If a familiar voice could sound strange, then a stranger's voice could sound familiar. He wouldn't . . . *couldn't* . . . be here.

''Do you mind helping him?'' The nurse was speaking to Jewel or Susana. ''I can do it if you'd prefer.''

Jewel had been watching David. ''No.'' She shook her head, realizing belatedly that the nurse was addressing her. ''Thanks. We'll be fine.'' David had gone rigid beneath the light sheet that covered him. ''Are you hurting?'' she asked him. He gave a tiny shake of his head but said nothing. His face was turned toward the nurse, and he looked scared.

Jewel studied the man as he took a cover off the chilled fruit platter, feeling a sudden jolt of recognition. He looked like the nurse who had let her in to see Flander in Erebus. He was the one who had rushed in when she had called up the treatment screen on Flander's console to see who had sedated him. She reached for a pink cube of melon, disturbed, watching him from the corner of her eyes. His inlay was covered with makeup, and his hair was red now, but it was he.

Whatever was going on had not ended with David's beating. She knew it as surely as if he had told her himself. And it would be so easy to kill David in here—this wasn't Erebus. Security in this place would be full of holes, and this guy would have access to a lot of drugs. Or maybe she was just paranoid and this guy had quit Erebus, too. Or maybe she was remembering wrong. The door closed behind him.

''Jewel?'' David said hoarsely. ''I think . . . that man was one of the two who beat me.''

Not paranoid, then.

''Shit,'' Susana said softly. Perched on the foot of the bed, arms clasped around her raised knees, she had been staring moodily at them. ''You sure about this guy?'' she demanded.

''No, I'm not sure.'' David let his head fall back on the pillow. He had gone pale, and sweat glistened on his forehead. ''I'm not sure of anything.''

''I think you might be right.'' Jewel drew a slow breath. ''He was in Erebus. A nurse. I met him in the clinic when I went to visit Flander.''

David struggled to a sitting position and swung his legs over the edge of the bed. "I need to get out of here. Now." He turned his head slowly, seeking them. "I walked into this mess blind, and I guess I'm walking out in the same condition," he said bitterly. "I'm alive, and I want to stay alive."

They had meant him to die, whoever had dumped him. Jewel bit her lip. They thought they had hit him hard enough, and they had been careless. They hadn't made sure that he was dead. "You can hire a private guard," she told him. "I'll take care of it." Bodyguards were everywhere in the city, tagging after their contractors or shepherding nannies and children. "Leaving here isn't the answer."

David looked into blackness, his eyes still straining for some tiny speck of light. "I am not going to lie here in the dark, listening to footsteps and wondering who the hell is walking into the room and why. I think I'll be safe if I don't leave a trail on the Net. I'm asking you to help me, Jewel." He drew a deep breath. "I can't do it without you."

Shit. Jewel closed her eyes briefly, hearing a thin edge of insanity in his voice. How would it be to lie there helpless, remembering and listening? "How exactly do you plan to do this?" she said harshly. "Just walk out in your hospital gown and hop on the ferry out to Vashon? Can you even stand up?"

"Not Vashon. Somewhere else. Anywhere else. Yes, I can stand."

"Not yet." Jewel pushed him back onto the bed. "You'll bring the whole nurses' station in here if you start yanking out tubes and wires." She frowned at the console. "I could log you off, but I don't know the access code."

"I do." Susana grinned at her.

"You would." Jewel crossed her arms. "So do it. Quit as soon as you get in or you'll screw something up."

"Yes, boss lady." Susana bowed deeply, still grinning, and darted around to the head of the bed. "That's what they get for not talking to me." She bent over the console. "I get bored, I gotta do *something*. So I watched 'em and picked up the code. The damn numbers show up onscreen as you enter it. Some security. You're in." She stood back, smugly pleased with herself.

"How often were you here, anyway?" Jewel asked, curious.

"Every day." She gave Jewel a sulky look. "Hey, it's a nice place to hang out. And . . . I kind of wanted to meet you, you know." Susana turned to David. "I mean, I've been in your cave enough."

"I'm glad to meet you," David said gravely. "As I told you, I like what you do."

The whole conversation made Jewel want to laugh or scream at them. This was crazy, every last stinking bit of it. Any second someone was going to walk in with a tray or something, and this would all come apart. Ah. Jewel touched up an options menu. The temporary interrupt option was on. A nurse could disconnect the drip and the leads so that he could go piss or take his walk. She touched it, then nodded as a yellow telltale began to wink on the console.

"Okay." She blanked the screen and went around the side of the bed. "Susana, see if there's anything he can wear." She peeled back a strip of tape and slid the catheter from the venous port in the back of his hand.

Susana peered into the tiny closet. "Nope."

"Great." Jewel popped the leads from the enhancement casts, scowling at his flimsy hospital gown. Not exactly street wear. "This complicates things."

"We need a car," Susana said blithely. "No sweat. See you out back in ten minutes. Take the elevator all the way down. The door takes you outside."

"Wait a minute—" Too late. She was already closing the door behind her. "*Damn* that girl."

"What's wrong?" David groped for her arm.

"Leaving here is not a crime. Getting into a stolen car is. Who the *hell* does she think she is? Oh, never mind. We'll get you some clothes," she said grimly. "There's no way."

"Maybe she's going to borrow one."

"Ha." Jewel got an arm around David as he swayed on his feet. He was a little taller than she, and heavy, for all his lean build. She could feel his muscles quivering. "Eight days of enhancement leaves you pretty weak," she said. "If you get dizzy, tell me and we'll sit down. I don't think I can hold you up if you pass out."

"I'll tell you," David said between clenched teeth.

They shuffled slowly down the hall together. His hands hung at his sides, as if he didn't have the strength to hold up the heavy casts. Sweat itched between Jewel's shoulder blades, and she kept waiting for someone to yell, to come running after them. Which was stupid. It was no crime to take a patient for a walk. This was no prison. But she sweated anyway. An aide passed on her way from the elevator to the nurses' station. Preoccupied, she gave them a vague nod. At the end of the hall orchids bloomed in a huge celadon pot— a holo. Jewel touched the elevator plate, and miraculously the doors opened. It was empty. The padded walls smelled of plastic and disinfectant. David staggered as the car dropped. The effort was telling on him. He was trembling, and sweat gleamed on his face. "Susana said the exit door is near the elevator," she told him, hoping she was right.

She was. The wide metal doors were set into the wall directly across the hall. Jewel shouldered them open, leaning back against their heavy weight. At night they would be barred; you couldn't drive a tank through them. Security cameras were recording their exit and she could only hope no one was monitoring this particular camera at this particular moment. Sun slashed them in the face, and Jewel blinked.

"Made it," David murmured.

"Of course. No one was trying to stop us," she said tightly. Not yet, anyway.

They had emerged onto an ugly paved yard. Tall chain-link fenced it, topped with razor wire. Deliveries came in here. A truck baked in the sun beside a huge bale of crushed plastic waiting to be collected for recycling. The blank north wall of a tower shaded part of the small lot. At least the gate was open. This was downtown, and half a dozen wall-mounted security cameras guarded the yard. A rat peeked from behind the bale of plastic, twitched its whiskers at them, and vanished.

"I think I'd better sit," David mumbled.

Yes, and fast. Jewel helped him into the shade along the wall, easing him to the ground as his knees buckled. She crouched beside him, thinking hard. "I can hit one of the tower stores," she said. "I'll get you some clothes and a pair of shoes, at least. After that—" She broke off as a car turned into the yard.

Damn her. Jewel bolted to her feet, but her anger died as she counted two figures in the front seat of the sleek little electric.

"You thought I was gonna lift one." Susana popped the door before the car had quite stopped. She grinned at Jewel. "You got some faith in me, Auntie. It's gonna be tight in this can."

David had gotten to his feet again and was leaning against the wall. Susana put a hand on his arm, tugging him toward the car. "You get in the front, with Mirelle. Duck real low, here."

Her touch was casual, as if she did the same for everyone, as if David's blindness had been noted, filed, and assimilated. Jewel couldn't do it. She climbed into the tiny rear seat beside Susana. She kept seeing it every time she looked at him: blindness, like a mask or a plastic wrapper sealed around him. The driver was petite, black, and a year or two older than Susana. She was netted. The threads glittered on her dark skin like a tracery of pure silver. Her hair had been braided with glowing light fibers of gold and green. She gave Jewel a disinterested, slightly sullen glance. "Where to, babe?" she asked Susana.

"The house." Susana fixed Jewel with a challenging stare. "Why not? If David wants to disappear without leaving tracks, it's gonna take a little time to set up. Better there than some cash-only cockroach hole."

"Fine." Jewel leaned back against the upholstered seat.

Events were rushing along like a river, and she had been swept into the flood. She had no control, had no idea of what was going to happen or how she would deal with it.

"Mirelle's mom owns a bunch of virtual parlors. Upscale dives, huh?"

"You bet, baby." Mirelle sounded bored. "Only the best."

Money here, a lot of it. "You met on the Net?" she asked Susana.

"How else?" Susana shrugged.

Another source of free Net time for Susana? Add a little here and there to Mom's account? And what was the price? In the front seat David leaned against the door, his body moving limply with the sway of the car. Worried, Jewel leaned forward. He flinched at her touch and raised his head.

"I'm still here." He tried for a smile. "I don't think I was quite ready for this much exercise."

"We're almost there. You can rest." And decide what he wanted to do, because *she* didn't have a clue. Jewel leaned her forehead against the window as Mirelle silently swung the little car off the freeway. The temptation tugged at her to simply let go, drift, let this damn flood sweep her wherever the hell it was going—to stop swimming. To let herself drown.

'Burbs thinking. It bought you a long forever out here.

They had passed the dusty, sun-struck flea market. The car growled as it took the hill, whipping past the dusty blackberry jungle. Canes trailed across the road, scratching the side of the car with the sound of steel claws. Mirelle growled something in her throat. Jewel could feel the eyes as they climbed out of the car. People were watching from behind the closed shutters and drapes, alerted by the sound of the car. Not too many cars came up here. David had climbed out and was standing beside the car, head tilted, his posture uneasy.

Jewel put her arm around him and took his weight. "We're at

Linda's house," she said. "Just a short walk and a few steps and you can collapse."

"A few—sounds about right."

"You owe me, babe." Mirelle flicked Susana lightly on the cheek.

"You know it. See ya." Susana caught up with them as Mirelle's little car cut a tight circle in the street and zoomed back down the hill. " 'Elle's gonna find out I don't owe her as much as she thinks," she commented cheerfully. "She doesn't know about the hole I plugged for her yet. It would've been her ass."

"Thanks for finding the car," Jewel said as they reached the door.

"Instead of lifting one, you mean?" Susana raised one eyebrow. "Yes."

"Hoo, Auntie. You got no gratitude." Susana skipped up the stairs and disappeared into the kitchen.

The steps were an impossibility, so Jewel got David as far as the downstairs sofa. He collapsed onto it, breathing heavily, his face frighteningly pale. Jewel grabbed the remotes from the terminal, which had gone unused since Carl's death. She untangled the leads from the neck band.

"Don't." Susana stood at the top of the stairs, a plastic glass in her hand. "It'll leave tracks. Like a fucking flag."

"I'm . . . all right, Jewel." David pushed himself clumsily into a sitting position. "Just tired out."

"I brought you some juice." Susana brushed past Jewel. "Tank-grown orange, but not too bad. You look like shit. Drink it, okay?"

David sipped awkwardly as she held the glass to his lips, then choked. Juice dribbled down his chin.

"I'll do it." Jewel sighed and took the glass from Susana, tilting it more carefully. "We were crazy," she said to David. "Both of us. You should have told them what happened—where those people held you, what they did to you. You should have yelled your head off until they brought in a real, live cop to interview you. You could have gotten one. That was Sisters of Mercy, not some 'burb clinic where they do knife wounds and DOAs. And I should have thought of this," she added bitterly. Only she had not. She had fallen so easily into the old patterns: don't ask for help, because no one's going to come across and you just advertise your weakness. Deal with it and move on before something else comes down on your head. The 'burbs were seeping into her, sucking her into the old quagmire of resignation and endless hopeless todays. She had thought that she had escaped. "So we were both stupid, and now we're here. Time to call the cops, David, before you get in any deeper.''

''No.'' David's lips tightened.

''Because Flander's into something illegal? Because you're afraid it'll come back to him?'' Jewel opened her clenched fists. Life line, heart line . . . *I love him,* Flander had cried. *And he doesn't understand.* ''All right.'' She sighed. ''What do you want to do?''

''I need a place to stay. Until my sight comes back.'' David leaned against the sofa, his face a mark of exhaustion. ''It has to be a cash transaction. So I don't leave tracks.''

''You could hit a cash hotel.'' Susana frowned. ''But I hope you got cash somewhere, because you got to stay out of your filespace. I mean, if someone's looking for you, they've gotta have hooks planted all over your space. Hit one and they'll track you right back to our door. I'm—not sure I can spot 'em if they're good.'' She flushed. ''Flander can. He can run some cash for you, and no one'll know where it came from.''

''No!'' David turned to Jewel, his eyes fixing with eerie accuracy on her face. ''Can you lend me the cash I need? I can pay you back with interest as soon as it's safe. I have that much.''

''Yes,'' Jewel said heavily. She was lost in the flood, without the strength to try for shore and escape. ''I will.'' She walked over to the terminal screen and sat down in front of it.

''Don't,'' Susana yelled. ''Use a public.''

Too late. She had already touched the screen to life. But instead of the usual menu, an explosion of color filled the screen. A fox face so large that only eyes and jaws showed, as if it were pressing its face against a physical window. Jewel recoiled. ''Flander!'' She hadn't expected him here, although he could certainly come in on terminal mode as easily as in virtual.

''David's there, right? That tube set of yours doesn't even have video pickup.'' White teeth filled the screen, clashing with the sound of bone on bone. ''David, are you there? David?''

On the sofa David was staring rigidly at the wall. A small pulse beat in his throat.

''He's here,'' Jewel said. ''He . . . can't talk right now, Flander.''

''You got to get out of there, lady. *Now!* Where the hell do you think they're gonna *look* for you? Are you stupid, or what?'' The oversized fox face was shrinking to screen size. ''Go somewhere, anywhere, and stay out of the Net.''

Oh, yeah—go *here, there,* and do it as blind as David. ''Knock it off,'' Jewel yelled at him. ''I'm through doing *shit* until you tell me what's up. Do you hear me, fox? Tell me who we're running from. Tell David who tortured him and why. You owe him that much, fox, and you owe him right *now*!''

"Jewel." David's voice was low and flat.

"You can't stay there." Ears flat, Flander panted, saliva dripping from his tongue. "David? David, will you *talk* to me? Please?''

"No." David didn't turn his head. "I won't talk to you onscreen. You have to come here, in the flesh. I'll talk to you then.''

Onscreen, the fox opened its jaws and howled a shrill, tearing note. Its image shattered suddenly, exploding, flying apart in a thousand jagged bits, spattering the screen with red blots that dripped and ran like blood.

"Jeeze," Susana said softly. "What's with him?''

"He's right, Daughter.'' A new shape was forming on the screen. Jewel stared into the lioness's eyes, her heart sinking.

"It's time to run, and your only safety lies with me. If you don't trust me, you'll die. You, because you have involved yourself in this, and it is bigger than you imagine—big enough to stretch from Erebus to this place and back. I warned you that you stood on the brink of the abyss, and you ignored my warning. You have to come to me now. I don't want your friends, but you may bring them, too.''

"Who is that?" David asked softly.

"I don't know," Jewel whispered. She remembered dust, thirst, weeping, and a woman's hard, angry face. David's chimera was stalking her through the desert.

"What the hell?" Susana shouldered in beside her. A map had replaced the lioness's face onscreen, showing eastern Oregon and Washington. A thin red line followed highways in a twisting path across the state and down into Oregon. At the end a small star pulsed. "What's this shit all about, anyway?''

"She's a mountain lion," Jewel said faintly. "She's been . . . in my filespace. I don't know what it's about.''

"She's a friend of Flander's." David frowned. "He told me that she was in your filespace. She left a few tracks in my cave. Literally.''

"Whatever she is, she was *here*," Susana said in a low voice. "In this house.''

"It was a holo.''

Susana gave Jewel a sour look and didn't answer.

"This is crazy," Jewel said softly. Neither of them answered her this time. She could see fear behind David's calm. He knew the face of the demons at his heels. How the hell was she going to get herself clear of this? A dizzy lightness was filling her. It was the same feeling she had gotten that day in Erebus, when Alcourt had ordered her to tell him about the desert and she had refused. It was freedom—an "I don't care" freedom, as intoxicating as a drug and maybe as deadly. Back then she had too much to lose. "What the hell." She laughed softly. Time to let go and see where the flood took her. "Shall we go find out what this cat bitch wants, David? Do you want to risk it?"

"Yes." He didn't turn toward her. "What have I got to lose?"

Good question. For both of them.

"So, okay." Susana was staring at her, an odd expression on her face. "I can call in a few favors and maybe squeeze Luis to front a cash-deal rental car for me. No tracks. Then we can get out of here."

"Not you," Jewel snapped. "This doesn't have anything to do with you."

"Your ass." Susana threw Jewel a quick, hot glare as she made for the door. "See you in a bit."

Why the hell did *she* want to be in on this? Jewel winced as the door slammed behind her.

"Jewel?" David said in a low voice. "I'm sorry I had to lever you to help me. I know what I've asked of you. If I could come up with another option, I wouldn't do this to you."

"I have spent my life weighing every choice." Jewel stared at the closed door. "Because I knew where I was going, and nothing else mattered as much as getting there." The rules had changed—or maybe she had changed. "I better pull that port in your vein." she said, and sighed. "It's leaking."

Chapter
Fifteen

The rental car was a battered Ford, all metal and too heavy to get any kind of speed from its cranky, alco-converted engine. *That's what you get when you gotta pay cash,* Susana had said with a disdainful shrug. Jewel had downloaded most of her account to cash, and Susana had gotten Luis to do the rental for them. He had dropped the car off in the late afternoon, a tall, narrow-hipped Latino who had kissed Susana briefly and passionately and had glared resentfully at Jewel before disappearing down the thorny path to the rail.

"I'm going," Susana had said, keys in her hand.

That was the reason for the glare from Luis? Jewel had started to refuse but had shut up instead. There had been a strange, hard look in Susana's eyes. Some kind of line had been drawn. Push too hard and something would happen. "All right," she had said mildly. "Message Linda. You owe her that much."

Susana had done so without argument. That obedience was the most surprising event in the whole day, Jewel now decided. She stretched, clinging to the uncooperative wheel, tired from driving. The moon was just rising, nearly full, spilling pale light over the dry hills and the gray ribbon of freeway that unrolled beneath the tires. They had crossed the Columbia into Oregon half an hour earlier and were now driving east. The freeway was almost empty. She had met only three cars in the last hour and one big truck convoy that had passed them, heading east. They were driving between irrigated fields, rows and rows of crop plants fed by drip irrigation. It was cool, almost chilly, but the dry wind had cracked her lips. She eyed the gas gauge uneasily. This monster ate fuel.

Beside her, David stirred. He lifted the heavy casts awkwardly as he woke, then yawned and stretched. "How are you doing, Jewel?"

He wasn't focusing on her face. Still no sight. "I'm okay." An answering yawn overwhelmed her suddenly, as if to prove her wrong.

"Don't push it. Stop and sleep when you need to."

"I will." She yawned again. "We need to get gas. I saw a sign for a place up ahead." How long until all hope was gone? "I'll get some coffee there, and that'll help."

"I could use something to eat." David sounded mildly surprised. "I'm starving."

"I grabbed some crackers." Susana spoke up from the gloom of the backseat. "That's about all we had in the house."

"I thought you were asleep." Jewel glanced into the rearview mirror.

Susana was sitting with her feet tucked under her, a battered box of crackers in her lap. "Here." She leaned across the back of the seat to feed David a cracker. "Want some, Auntie?"

"Not yet." Jewel scowled at the empty highway. "If I hit anything, you'll go through the windshield without a seat belt."

"If you hit anything in this old boat, we'll all be dead, so who cares?" She fished another cracker out of the box for David.

In his lap his hands twitched. Helplessness added to helplessness. "Your casts were scheduled to come off tomorrow." Jewel said. "I saw the note on your chart. I think we'd better give them a couple more days, just to be sure."

"I can't wait," he said dryly. "Is it a law of nature that you only itch where you can't scratch?"

"It's the enhancement. I didn't even think about it." She grimaced. "They'd have used some kind of local anesthetic in the hospital. Is it bad?"

"Yes."

Lights up ahead, a fuel station. Jewel braked and swung the car onto the exit ramp.

The station was a combination of store, restaurant, and fuel stop, with a small seedy motel out back for the convoy truckers. The buildings looked gray and tired, scoured by the dusty wind and about a hundred years old. The parking lot was empty, but two men in jeans and denim jackets were playing cards on a sagging picnic table beside the door. They looked like old-days cowboys, right down to the silver glint of spurs on their boots.

"I'll stay in the car," David said as she parked at the pump.

Susana was already out, filling the tank. The older of the two men got up and followed Jewel into the store, his boots making a musical jingle with every step. Jewel wondered if he went home at night, put on skins, and rode broncos or roped cattle. Maybe not; this place didn't look like it brought in enough to pay for virtual access. Maybe that was why he dressed. Jewel looked around. Items were clustered haphazardly on the dusty shelves: a stack of folded jeans, dark enough to be new. Replacement chips. A few bits of fake Indian jewelry locked into a cracked glass case. Hard copy maps. Food. The gray-haired cowboy was leaning on the counter behind the terminal, watching her. Undressing her with his eyes. Jewel gave him a brief, level stare and turned her back on him. A hand-lettered sign on the wall beside the rest room door advertised showers for five dollars, towels a dollar extra.

The rest room smelled like piss and methane from the leaking composter toilet. Paper trash had collected like drifted leaves in the corner beneath the sink and there was a pay meter above the faucet. Jewel fished in her pocket and slid a dollar into the cash slot. The meter hummed and gulped it, but the water wouldn't come on. Jewel banged on the thick plastic of the meter and remembered this place.

She kept banging on the meter with the plastic cup, crying because she was thirsty and Mama was telling her to hurry, hurry, or the bus will leave us, and she'll catch us . . .

The water gushed on suddenly, splashing against the stained porcelain bowl, spattering her with wetness. Jewel started. I was *here.* The moment of memory had passed, but her knees wanted to tremble. *I was here.* She cupped her hands beneath the tepid, brownish flow, and the thought of drinking it twisted her stomach with nausea. The cup had been red, a washed-out, sun-faded red, and they had been . . . running away. Not from drug demons but from *someone.*

She. She'll catch us . . . Jewel splashed water on her face, gasping as it ran down her neck to soak the front of her tunic. There was no soap, and the dryer was broken. She dried her face on her tunic and walked back out into the brightly lit store. It looked no more or less familiar than any other such place. She had been mistaken, she decided, and felt a small relief as she grabbed packaged sandwiches from the shelves. She picked up a sealed jug of water, peered at the faint layer of sediment on the bottom, and put it back. You could fake a quality seal. She grabbed a handful of juice pouches from the shelf.

The cowboy raised his eyebrows at the bills she handed him. "Ten percent extra for cash," he said, and leered. "Or you can gimme a kiss and we'll call it even."

He had a bad case of environmental acne. From the crappy water? She gave him his ten percent and ignored his smirk. Outside, the wind raised gooseflesh on her arms. Susana had parked the car over at the end of the building. David was leaning against the passenger side, his face turned toward the dark fields. His bandaged head gave him a stranger's profile. Susana sat sideways in the driver's seat, her legs sticking out, eating the last of the crackers.

"Have a sandwich." Jewel tossed one into her lap.

"Hey." Susana grabbed for it, spilling crumbs into the dust. "You sound so bloody *motherly*."

"No, I don't. I thought you couldn't drive."

"I can park a damn car."

Jewel stalked around the car to David. "I bought some juice." She set the bag down on the car roof and dug out a couple of pouches. "I've got sandwiches, too."

"I'd like some juice. Thanks." David leaned on his crossed arms, his brow creased, listening to the darkness. He could hear it, like a breathing animal waiting to swallow him. "I've never been helpless before—not physically, not financially. Not in any way that mattered." He stared into the darkness inside his head, feeling its density, the weight and texture of it. Permanence? Was that what he was feeling? "Did you grow up on the street?" he asked abruptly.

"I was there for a while." Jewel sounded uncomfortable. "When I was a kid. Before Linda's mother took me in as a foster kid."

"I wondered." He let his breath out in a slow sigh. Every so often she reminded him of Flander. It wasn't language; she was educated, and it showed. It was a composite feeling. Sometimes she reacted to things the way Flander would react. Not often—and not intentionally, he guessed. David lifted his shoulders in an awkward shrug. "Flander talks about it sometimes, how he didn't have any control over his life as a kid. Actually, he *doesn't* talk about it, not enough, anyway. Maybe . . . if I'd known what helplessness feels like, I would have understood him a little better." And maybe had a better feel for what Flander was running from.

Jewel rubbed her eyes, crowded by the darkness, by the ghosts of yesterday that were peering over her shoulder. "Yeah, out there you're helpless," she said softly. "Not all the time, but enough. You get prodded here, there, run down this chute or that one, subsidy or a refugee camp, or whatever. They're all fenced with money," she added bitterly.

Her mother had run from this desert to the streets. Jewel was coming back.

To find what?

David touched her arm with the tips of his fingers. It was a light touch, but there was comfort in it. "I can smell the dust," he said softly. "The smell of green leaves and moist soil twines through it, and every so often you get alcofuel, like a harsh splash of color." He leaned close suddenly, his cheek brushing her hair, his breath warm on her neck. "You smell musky and unique—skin and sweat and hair. It makes a composition, a picture of the night. I think I'll work with scent for a while. No visuals, no tactile—just scent." You could paint pictures on a canvas of darkness, create symphonies of mood. "It's kind of exciting."

He didn't think he was going to get his sight back. This man, at least, had known what he had wanted from the world, had reached out and seized it. And now he had lost it. No, he had given it away. Jewel put her arm around him, weighed down by the stone inside her. David leaned against her lightly, his flesh warm against hers, his face brushing her hair. Then he straightened. "I think I'd like that juice now. If you don't mind holding it for me."

The juice pouches came with an attached straw. She held a pouch for him as he drained it thirstily. Then she unwrapped a sandwich for each of them: soymeat salami on white bread with a soggy slice of tomato. It had a stale, irradiated taste and had probably been on that shelf for a year. But she was hungry enough not to care. Susana had vanished while they talked. She reappeared as Jewel was balling up the empty juice pouches and sandwich wrappers.

"They don't have public access here." She opened the rear door and threw herself onto the backseat. "The old geezer says I can use his terminal, but he wants a wad of cash for it, and the jerk's gonna hang over my shoulder while I'm on, I can tell."

"More likely he'd have his hand down your pants." Jewel carried the trash over to a recycling bin against the wall. The smell of ripe garbage wafted up as she opened the lid, and she closed it quickly. "What about tracks?" she asked as she came back to the car.

"I'm not stupid." Susana eyed David as he climbed awkwardly into the front seat. "I was gonna go check your hospital files, see what they put in about you leaving."

"Damn it, girl." Jewel threw herself into the car. "We've got enough trouble without your Net games."

"I've got a safe route." She met Jewel's stare. "I don't leave any tracks, so they don't even know I'm in. It's not like I'm diddling the bill or anything."

"Speaking of the bill, who paid for this?" David tilted his bandaged head. "It's got to be more than my level of care covers. It wasn't you, was it?" he asked with sudden concern.

"No." Jewel leaned across him to pull the door closed. He was thin. She could feel his ribs beneath the too-large shirt of Carl's that Susana had found for him. "Harmon Alcourt paid." she said slowly. "I asked him to. He's got plenty of money, so why shouldn't he?"

"No, he didn't." Susana crossed her arms on the back of the seat. "I saw it in your file. This Chen Yao Hwa person paid. Whoever he is."

"She." David couldn't keep from squinting, needing to see her, as if she might be joking, hiding a smile beneath that matter-of-fact tone. "She's . . . my eldest sister. Are you sure?"

"Yeah. That's a big deal?"

"Yes," David said. "It is." He wanted to doubt this kid, but he was hearing flat-out certainty in her voice. Dà Jieh. Alcourt, he could believe. The man would consider something like that an investment and would expect payment in kind. Plus interest. "Who told her?" he said out loud. The hospital must have notified Fuchin; he was listed as next of kin. Had he informed the family?

"I told her." Jewel cranked the engine to grumbling life. "I was trying to find someone who could pay," she said quickly. "I didn't think she was going to do anything. I thought she only wanted to know how you were." Acceleration pushed David back into his seat.

She sounded hesitant. David wondered what she was leaving out. "That's very strange," he said softly. Shau Jieh would try to help him, yes. He stared into the darkness, listening to the whisper of tires on asphalt. Perhaps Shau Jieh had begged this favor of Dà Jieh. He had read anger, distrust, even hatred in his sister at various times. So where had this gesture come from? And where had she gotten the money? She had tailored the kicker because she was at the financial brink. Exhaustion was rising like a tide to drown him, as if this unexpected revelation had broken some kind of dam inside him and unleashed a flood. "Jewel, you did . . . a lot for me." He leaned his head against the vibrating window. "More than I thought you would," he mumbled. Tactless words . . . explain them later . . .

"More than *I* thought I would," Jewel murmured beneath her breath. She glanced sideways. David's head lolled as he slept slumped against the door.

That wild sense of freedom had evaporated, and a growing uneasiness had replaced it. Jewel stretched, fatigue and adrenaline clashing in her system. There were ghosts out here. She had met one at that truck stop. In back Susana slept, too, curled up on the seat. The moon rode high in a sea of bright stars, lopsided, filling the car with moving shadows. A million stars up there—you saw that sky from Erebus in the winter midnight, so thick with stars that you could barely see the darkness. You couldn't see that many stars from Seattle, not even after curfew. Maybe they didn't shine for the cities. Maybe they shone only for the empty lands.

Jewel shivered, alone, tempted to shout, to wake up David or Susana because it was too quiet. The hiss and rumble of tires and engine had faded into a curtain of white noise, and behind it something breathed. A lioness? A truck loomed up out of the darkness, spangled with yellow running lights. It roared by them in a rush of displaced air, pulling four trailers. The flow of its headlights filled the car with light, casting David's gaunt features into stark relief, striking copper glints from Susana's hair. Then it was gone, and the darkness returned, breathing softly on her neck.

They passed through Pendleton, dark now, possibly dark even before curfew. A lot of cities had died out here. More fields along the road. Sagebrush. The headlight beams washed light across the gray-green mounds of the bushes. Biomass for the big vat-culture plants, which ground them up, digested them into simple sugars, and used them to grow orange-juice sacs, oil-producing corn cells, or soybeans in huge tanks. In a couple of hours they would turn off and head south. The red line of the lioness's map had burned itself into Jewel's brain. The lioness had stood up and become a woman that night in the house. It had been a holo, no matter what Susana said.

Are you so sure? the old woman had cackled, and she had reached for Jewel with hands that were claws. Jewel shuddered, and the car swerved. Beside her David stirred, murmuring brokenly. Dreaming. His face twisted as if he were in pain.

"David?" Jewel reached across the seat to shake him gently. He started, muscles jumping convulsively beneath her hand. His eyes opened for a second, then closed, and his breathing slowed once more to the rhythm of sleep.

Dark, and she was alone. The highway curved gently, and her headlights washed across the genetically engineered sage. A low ridge thrust up from the dusty green branches. A tawny lion shape crouched patiently on its rocky crest, eyes sparking red in the headlight's glare. It smiled, and its smile was human. Then the headlight beam swept past, and there was only sage, and asphalt, and the faded yellow line. Jewel realized that her hands were clamped tightly on the wheel and forced herself to relax. Perhaps she was not so alone. She drew a deep breath, a cold resignation gathering in her chest. Maybe you had no choices at all in this damn world. Maybe choice itself was another illusion. "We're coming," Jewel said softly, and rolled up the window.

She turned off the interstate just before dawn, driving south through mountainous land covered with sparse trees—live or dead or dying, she couldn't tell. The slopes flattened out slowly into expanses of flat land as the moon set. She met no other vehicles, which was a good thing; the two-lane road was crumbling, and huge chunks had cracked away, narrowing it to one lane. Susana and David slept on. Nightmares had troubled David once or twice, but for the last hour he had slept peacefully. Jewel stretched her shoulders. Her muscles ached dully. She knew she was tired, exhausted actually, but it was a distant knowledge—vague sensations sealed away from the here and now. Somewhere ahead of them the lioness waited.

Jewel braked as the road they were on ended at another empty road. The car bumped across a sunken, broken cattle guard flanked by rusty tangles of barbed wire. The sky was turning yellow and rose above the dark line of distant hills, and Jewel blinked in the growing light. Sparse clumps of wild sage dotted a landscape of dust and gray rock. The dust was the color of a mountain lion's hide. Beside her, David stirred. In a little while they would turn off onto a dirt road. The map glowed against the screen of her eyelids when she closed her eyes. The lioness waited at the end.

"Jewel?" David yawned. "How are you doing? And where are we, anyway?"

"I'm okay." Southward, an isolated bluff of tawny rock thrust up from the sage. In the uncertain light it looked like a ruined wall left by some vanished race. "We're nearly there."

"I feel sun. You've been driving all night?" David's face was creased with concern. "You should have stopped. You should have gotten some sleep."

"I'm not sleepy." Jewel noticed suddenly that he was squinting at her. "Can you see something?" She held her breath.

"No." His shoulders drooped fractionally, and he sighed. "The muscles keep trying to make it work. Habit." He grimaced. "I've got to piss. Is this a good place to stop?"

"Sure." She braked and pulled off the road, although she could probably have parked right smack in the middle. Sage stems scratched at the underside of the car with the sound of claws.

"Huh?" Susana blinked sleepily, her face screened by her tangled hair. "We there?"

"Potty break." Jewel turned off the ignition, and a thick quiet rushed in to fill the car. Cooling metal ticked, and the sound of the car door opening was as loud as a thunderclap. Wind whispered in her ear, and small stones grated beneath her feet as she went around to David's side of the vehicle.

He stood with his arms at his side, his face lifted, nostrils slightly flared. "Desert?"

"Yes."

Yellow fire burned on the eastern horizon, streaking the sage and rock with light and harsh shadow. Jewel unzipped the too-large jeans, and David pissed a long steady stream into the dust. "That's better," he said, and sighed.

His penis had stiffened in Jewel's hand. David sucked in a small breath, and for a moment Jewel stood still, hand still closed around him, aware suddenly of his scent, of the warmth radiating from his silver-threaded skin.

"Nice timing." David laughed, his erection wilted, and she zipped his jeans for him, ignoring the unexpected tingle between her legs, too tired even to try dealing with it, thank you. The sun had nearly cleared the distant mountains. She could already feel its heat, and the harsh yellow light cast sage stems and rocks into harsh, vivid relief against the dusty, familiar landscape. Jewel caught her breath, her stomach contracting with a rush of memory.

"Jewel?" David's fingertips brushed her arm. "Are you all right? This is your desert, isn't it?" he asked in a low voice. "The one you saw in Harmon's garden?"

"Yes," Jewel whispered. "I don't know." This land had not changed—not in years, maybe not in centuries. She could feel it, the past, like layers of dust on the ground. "We're driving into yesterday," she said softly, and *she* was out there, crouched in the sage, tawny coat invisible in this lion-colored land. "I'm . . . scared."

"Why?" David's arm went around her, clumsy and comforting.

"Mama was . . . running away. From something. I thought it was the drugs." Jewel swallowed. "I thought it was just . . . craziness. Now—I don't know."

"Hey, the car's turning into an oven." Susana wandered over, her tangled hair unbraided and loose on her shoulders. "There's a couple of juice packs left. I'll hold yours for you," she told David, tossing the other one to Jewel. "I saw it," she said to Jewel. "Our mountain lion. It was lying behind this bush watching me piss. Want to tell me it's a holo, Auntie?"

"She," Jewel whispered. "Not *it*."

"Yeah?" Susana yanked at a knot in her hair. "You know her name now, huh?"

"No." After a moment Jewel finished her juice and crumpled the packet. "Let's not keep her waiting."

"Speak for yourself, Auntie." Susana gave her a hard sideways look. "I'm in no hurry to meet any damn ghost."

"Why not? Where else have we got to go?" Jewel yanked the car door open.

Neither of them answered her.

The road bent slowly southeastward to hug the foot of a knife-sharp rim of gray rock that marched south like a wall. *Soon, now,* the wind whispered in Jewel's ear. *Soon.*

They had passed through the abandoned ruins of two towns, gas stations with gaping, glassless windows and battered, useless pumps, sagging houses that stared at them with forlorn resignation. In a weird way the land reminded Jewel of Antarctica; it was the sense of alienness, she decided. Humanity had never really *lived* in either land. Humans had marked them, yes, damaged them, even, but their presence had been shrugged off, ignored. We don't belong here, Jewel thought, and for some reason that comforted her.

A dirt track led off to the left, two faint wheel tracks that disappeared up the gentle slope below the rim. Eyes burning, brain numb from the oven-breath wind that blew through the window, Jewel braked and turned the wheel.

"Hold it." Susana leaned on the seat back, scowling. "We're supposed to go through another town, remember. Then turn left at some kind of crossroad."

"This is the road," Jewel said softly.

"No way, lady."

"Do you remember it?" David asked.

Jewel didn't answer. Inside her, words had solidified into silent waiting. For what? She slowed the car to a crawl as it bucked and scraped its way across rocks and sage.

"So get us stuck. Jeeze!" Susana clutched the seat.

They were following the dry fold of a creek bed back into the rimrock. Sweat trickled down Jewel's side and belly, and when she leaned forward, her tunic felt cool and damp on her back.

"We should have bought more water," Susana spoke up. "We were stupid. Hey, Auntie, are you deaf or what?"

"Jewel?" David groped awkwardly with one imprisoned hand.

She ignored them both. She had no words left, no energy, none beyond what was required to fight the wheel as the car climbed the steep slope. A big lizard sunned itself on a rock, and she shuddered violently.

"Goddammit. We're gonna get stuck. Turn *around*!" Susana leaned across the seat back. "Shit!"

They had reached the top of the rise. The car groaned, wheels spinning as it fishtailed up and out. A shelf of land pierced the rimrock above the narrow creek bed, invisible from the main road. A house stood on the shelf, built of desert stone, backed solidly into the canyon wall. Beyond it a stone fence enclosed a small barn also built from stone. A tethered goat browsed nearby on tufts of grass. It lifted a shaggy gray head and bleated at them.

The familiarity of it overwhelmed Jewel. The car lurched as a wheel dropped into a low spot, and the car tilted, sage crunching.

"Watch out!" Susana yelled. "You're off the road."

The engine coughed and died. Silence. Jewel became aware of the whispering wind and a distant bird call. The goat stared at them with its strange yellow eyes.

"You're trembling." David's fingertips brushed her arm. "Jewel, what is it? What's out there? Where are we?"

"There's a house," Jewel whispered. "And a barn. A goat. I don't see anyone around . . ." Her voice trailed away as the house door opened. "People are coming out," she said, and felt a crashing surge of relief. This wasn't yesterday—she didn't remember this. "I see a couple of men and two women. One of the men is carrying—" She squinted. "A goat kid, I think."

"Great." Susana snorted. "Livestock, how nice."

Jewel didn't answer. One of the women was walking toward them, sunlight gleaming on her gray hair. David had opened his door, was getting out. Susana had gotten out, too. Jewel pushed her door open. The woman stopped to pat the goat. She wore loose tan pants and a too-large man's shirt embroidered with bright colors. She was smiling, her face weathered into a thousand brown folds, her gray hair pulled into a twisted knot at the back of her neck.

"Hello, Jewel," she said.

Her face was the face in the ice cave, weathered and aged. It was the face on the Self that David had designed for her. It was the face she saw when she looked into the mirror.

Her smile was the lioness's smile.

Jewel took a half step back, dizzy, hearing a roaring in her ears like a storm coming. The old fortune-teller in the flea market had warned her about this moment. Change, danger, and the past in the shape of . . . her mother. "No," someone said in a strange, strained voice.

The ground tilted up suddenly to bang her solidly on the shoulder. She felt gravel against her cheek and wondered dimly why it didn't hurt. Then darkness swept over her in a wave and washed her away.

Chapter
Sixteen

Jewel woke slowly, unsure for a moment where she was. Erebus? No, that was over. But it wasn't the bed she shared with Linda—the mattress was hard, and it smelled wrong. Then a goat bleated in the distance, and memory rushed back: the drive, the stone house.

The woman who had come out to meet them wore her face.

Jewel's eyes snapped open. She was lying on a piece of foam in a dimly lit room, covered with an unzipped sleeping bag. David was sitting on the floor beside her. Still blind; his eyes seemed to focus on a point just above her left shoulder.

"Good morning," he said gravely. "Serafina said you'd be waking up soon. How are you feeling?"

"I'm . . . not sure yet." A dream, that woman's face? She almost asked him, then swallowed a bitter laugh at the thought. She brushed hair out of her eyes and winced. Her cheek stung, and when she touched it, she felt crusty, scabbed skin. "I . . . fainted, didn't I?"

"You sure did." David's expression was quizzical. "And scared the shit out of me for a couple of minutes. Considering you drove all night, I guess it wasn't too unexpected. At least it didn't faze our hostess much. She seems to be some kind of local wise woman or healer or something. Here." He fumbled for a mug on the floor beside him. "You're supposed to drink this—herb tea. I had some. Tastes awful, but my headache went away, so I'm through scoffing."

She blinked as she took the cup. "Your casts are off."

"Serafina said it was time." He flexed his hands, smiling. "They work fine."

Serafina. The name fell softly into her mind. Yes, that was her name. Serafina . . . She sipped the tea and choked.

"I warned you." He smiled, and then his expression went sober. "What happened, Jewel? It wasn't just the drive, was it?"

"I . . . lived here." Amber tea slopped over the rim of the cup as she set it down. "You asked me if I grew up on the street." She took a deep breath. "I did—but that isn't all of it. We were running. All the time. We rode the refugee trains and went from city to city. I think Mama had . . . forgotten why; we just did it. Or maybe she didn't want to remember. Looking back, I think she was . . . kind of crazy, even then. Running was just the way we lived, like the sun coming up or going down. We'd stick around a while, maybe she'd pick up some street-labor job, and then we'd move on. Until she got sick and got into the drugs." Until the burned house, and Linda, and the window she had climbed through to be comforted for the first time.

"You're scared." David groped for her hand.

"Yes." She took his pale hand gently, grateful for his comfort. "I think—this is what Mama was running from. This is my desert." Jewel's voice trembled as she looked around the room.

Thick, coarsely woven blankets covered most of the stone walls, patterned in shades of brown and bright red. A tattered topographical map had been pinned to one of the blankets, and a rumpled bed stood against the far wall beside a chest of drawers. Jewel stared at a holo-picture in a frame on the chest. In it a young woman laughed, head thrown back, her face full of wildness and light. She looked vaguely familiar. Serafina looks like me, she wanted to tell him. She's got my face, so who is she? What happened here?

Jewel let her breath out slowly, unable to do it, unable to speak the questions out loud. "How long was I asleep?" she asked instead.

"Almost twenty-four hours." David's fingers tightened on hers. "It was a long time ago, whatever it is or was. I'm here. And Susana. You're not in this by yourself, okay?"

His words startled her a little. "I'm that easy to read?" she said bitterly.

"Yes." He squeezed her hand. "Oh, there's breakfast. Are you hungry?"

"No." Jewel eyed that blanketed door. "Not yet."

"You need some food, anyway." David stood, hauling her to her feet with surprising strength. "Serafina is gone. A bunch of goatherds showed up just before us. They're camped down in the creek bed, and I guess they've got some kind of medical troubles. Anyway, our wise woman is pretty busy right now. There's no one here but the three of us."

Jewel swept the blanket aside, exasperated and comforted by his accuracy. He held her arm lightly, not clutching at her as they walked. She could feel his hesitation, though, and she slowed her steps. Was it too late to hope for sight? The main room of the house was larger than she had expected. A massive wooden table stood in the middle of the room in front of an open fireplace. One end of the room was a kitchen with an old-fashioned sink set into a wooden counter and what looked like an antique wood-burning cookstove. The floor was made of rock slabs filled with gray cement. One corner had been partitioned off into a small room with walls made of weathered gray boards and an ancient paneled door. Taking it all in, Jewel shivered with memory.

That table had been so high. She had stood on a chair seat to reach . . .

"Yo." Susana appeared from behind the wooden wall, gloves and lenses in her hand. "No running water in this dump, but the old witch's got access up the butt. We're talking full virtual and all the hardware." She did a little dance on the stone floor. "You know what she is? She's a serious operator, probably a hot pirate. Has to be. Hooo, boy, who'd go looking for her flesh out here in this shithole end of nowhere? Clever place to hide the bod, if you could stand it." Susana grinned. "Yeah, I bet she's hot. And she's got some kind of major lock on the system, but I bet I'll get past it before she gets back. I want to check in with Luis and find out what's going on. Don't shit, Auntie." Susana rolled her eyes at Jewel's expression, still grinning. "I'm just talking access. I'm not stealing any Net time from her, and *I* don't leave tracks. I'd have asked her to let me use it, but she took off before I woke up, okay? What does she care if I use her access? I'm not billing to *her* account." She vanished back into the small room.

Jewel opened her mouth to protest, then closed it. "Fine." She clenched her fists. "If you want to screw around, go ahead. If this Serafina throws us all out because of it, so what?" *Yes,* a part of her was crying silently. Yes, yes, get us *out* of here. She spun away from the virtual room, full of rage suddenly, shaking with it—or was it fear hiding beneath a mask of anger? David was sitting at the table, his head tilted in a listening position. "Leave me alone," she snapped at him. "Just don't say anything. This is your fault."

"There's a plate of biscuits on the counter." He nodded toward the sink as if she hadn't spoken. "Water's in a pottery jug beside the sink."

"I see them." Jewel stomped over to the wooden counter.

Yesterday's giddy freedom seemed like such a joke now. How

long had this woman prowled her Netspace? All her life? Had Serafina watched her scuttle here and there like a rat in a maze? Had she guided her along? It occurred to her to wonder if her University Net access had really come from old lady Delaport. Or had the lioness arranged even that? Jewel shivered. Mama would never use a terminal. She had babbled about demons in the Net, and Jewel had heard only craziness talking.

An operator couldn't find you if you stayed out of the Net.

She shivered again. Perhaps there was no real freedom in this world, just layers of invisible mazes. If you escaped one, you fell into the next.

The jug David had mentioned stood beside the sink: big, rough, shaped by hand, with a metal tap at the bottom. A plastic pail stood on the floor beneath the tap to catch the drips. The kitchen wasn't as primitive as it looked. An electric cook surface had been set into the wooden counter, although the ancient stove looked real enough. A microwave stood beside the cooktop. Solar power? Jewel hadn't noticed any panels. She took a thick glass down from a shelf and filled it at the tap, her anger draining away. The tap dripped. She grabbed a lumpy yellow biscuit from a plate beside the jug and stalked back to the table.

"I'm sorry." She set the glass down with small thump. "It isn't really your fault. It was my idea to come here, not yours."

"So it's my fault for asking you to do this and your fault for saying yes." He smiled crookedly. "Shall we split the blame fifty-fifty?"

"Sure, why not." Jewel bit into a biscuit, expecting soy flour or corn. Grain, yes, but neither soy nor corn. It had a soft licorice flavor that tickled her memory. *Crumbly mouthful of cookie . . . hunger and saliva rush of eating . . .* Ghosts. She put the rest of the biscuit down. This house was full of ghosts. "David? What now?"

"I've been working on that one." He leaned his elbows on the table. "I need to figure out what Flander was into. I need to know who's behind this." A shadow passed over his face. "I've worked for a lot of inside people in the web. People with a lot of power. Some of them would do favors for me. If I know what's going on, I might be able to get us out of this mess. Whatever this mess *is*."

"So ask him."

They both jumped as Susana tossed gloves and lenses onto the tabletop.

"She was *laughing* at me." She threw herself into a chair. "When I finally got in, this auto jack-in-the-box pops up and tells me how

I coulda got in easier and then jumps me through these hoops so nobody can track me back. Like I'm some day-care first-timer and she's gotta hold my hand." She glowered. "Rude, and I don't give a shit if she's the hottest ghost in the Net. So go ask the fox if you want to know what he's into. He's in the cave, waiting for you to show. Shit, man, he's in meltdown."

"I'll talk to him in the flesh." David's face might have been carved from stone.

"Lay off." Jewel glared at Susana.

"*You* lay off. He doesn't need you to protect him. You were giving him shit a minute ago." Susana shoved her chair back and stood, glaring down at David. "They're after his flesh, too, whoever worked you over. Why do you think this bitch hides out here in the dust? You got to hide the flesh if you operate. And yeah, it's truly bad that you got hurt, but his ass is on the line, too. And they don't kill clean in this game. You're a really cool artist, you know? I get into what you're doing, and I can't do anything that good, and I don't know. I guess I feel like maybe . . . your stuff *means* something." She shoved loose hair back from her face with a savage swipe of her hand. "But shit, the fox can't show up in the flesh. Someone's out there waiting to gut him. He's on his knees, man. You want his blood, too, or what?" She turned her back on the table. "So maybe you'll get it. I'm gonna go get the damn car out of the hole it's in because I want out of here."

"Susana!" Jewel winced as the door slammed. She glanced at David, but his head was bent, his expression invisible. "I'm . . . sorry." Jewel gulped the last of her water, awkward in the face of his silence. "I'm going to help her get the car out."

"Fine." David didn't raise his head.

Damn that girl, anyway. It wasn't any of her business. Jewel shoved the heavy door open and winced as the heat slapped her. She hadn't appreciated how cool it was inside the stone house. Hot sun licked her face, making the scrape sting. No sunscreen. She had packed it but forgotten to use it when she woke up. Later. Squinting against the glare, Jewel searched the shelf. No goat today. It wasn't stupid enough to be out in the full sun. No sign of goat herders or Serafina. David had said they were down in the creek bed. Not far beyond the house, the car's left front wheel hung over the edge of a deeply eroded gully that the sage had hidden. Jewel swallowed, frightened by how close she had come to rolling the car right into it.

Suddenly the engine roared to life. Brown dust fountained from beneath the rear wheels, and the car shuddered like a live thing, rocking violently, as if it were struggling to right itself. Slowly, ponderously, its rear end slid toward the edge.

"Stop!" Jewel ran through the sage. "Cut it out." She pounded on the fender. Behind the windshield, Susana clutched the wheel, face set, her eyes wild. The car shuddered and slid again. "Goddamn it." Jewel stuck her head in through the passenger window. "You're going all the way in. This isn't how you do it."

The car slid farther, wheels spraying dust, tilting.

"Turn it off!"

The spinning wheels caught on something. The car leapt like a frightened animal, slamming Jewel backward into the dust. With a cough, the engine died and the car shuddered. Shaken, Jewel picked herself up. Her elbow ached where it had hit the car door, and she felt a bruise on her leg. It had been close; both wheels hung over the lip of the gully, and the car canted dangerously. Susana still clutched the wheel. Jewel leaned through the window and snatched the keys from the ignition. "So now we need a tow truck." She shoved the keys into her pocket. "You got to do everything yourself, huh? Even when you don't know squat about how to do it. Nice going, Susana. Real nice."

"Get off my back." Her voice shook just a little. "If you're so hot, *you* get it out."

"You better climb out carefully." Jewel sighed. "This thing looks like it could go all the way in, any second."

"So what?" Susana threw the door open. She caught her foot as she climbed out, lost her balance, and slid to the bottom of the gully in a shower of gravel and dust.

"Are you all right?" Jewel scrambled down after her, terrified that the car might come down on top of her. "Get out of the way." She grabbed her arm and yanked her to her feet. "You stupid, goddamn *idiot*!"

"Get off my case." Susana shoved her. "Just get *off* it. I *hate* this desert." Angry tears tracked her dusty face. "*You* brought us out here, and I *hate* it." She swung a wild fist at Jewel's face.

"You little shit." Jewel grabbed her wrist, sliding in the gravel, and they went down together. "Are you crazy?" she gasped as Susana elbowed her in the ribs. It hurt. Furious now, she got Susana by one wrist and twisted her arm up behind her back. Want to play rough, kid? I know how. She straddled Susana, shoving her face into the dust. Susana was strong for all that she was small. Jewel nearly lost her grip as she struggled.

"Fuck." Susana gasped and went limp. "That hurts," she said in a muffled voice. "Fuck it, let go."

"You don't try to hit me again." Jewel said between clenched teeth. "Got it?"

"I got it." Susana yanked her arm free as Jewel got off, then rolled over and sullenly sat up.

"What the hell's wrong with you?" Sweat trickled down Jewel's belly from beneath her breasts. "What's your problem?" Then she got it suddenly, saw it in her eyes. Fear.

"You're scared of it," she said softly. "The desert. Is that it?"

"It's so fucking *big*." Susana wrapped her arms around herself as if she were cold. "I mean, the Net's big, but *I* run the Net. I make it do my dance, you know? Out here we could just die. Who'd even know? I mean, it always seemed like we mattered, even if it wasn't any big deal. But we don't." Her voice caught. "You can feel it out here. That we don't matter. That's what he did to Carl, the fucker who ran him down. The bastard made Carl see it. That he wasn't any hero, that no one really gave a damn about what he said, that it didn't mean shit. He didn't *matter*, and that's why he used those fucking patches. And no one cared."

Susana had cared. And Carl had told her loud and clear that her caring didn't matter when he had plastered those patches over his jugular. "Is that why you came down on David?" Jewel asked softly. "Because Flander cares?"

"The fox is really hurting." Susana's voice trembled. "It's like he's crashing. I mean, he can't even do it anymore. Virtual. He keeps fading out, messing up his visuals, losing it. He's . . . my friend. I can say things to the fox, and he . . . I don't know." She blinked, her eyes full of the desert emptiness. "He hears me, if you get what I mean. Shit, I don't know. Maybe it doesn't matter. Maybe nobody really gives a shit about anyone." She wiped her face on her sleeve, smearing the dust and tears to a film of mud. "I just want to get out of here," she added in a small, hard voice.

"Maybe Carl couldn't see it." Jewel got slowly to her feet. "How you felt about him."

"Maybe." Susana scowled down at her dust-covered clothes. "He was so deep in his Committee stuff. But he was there."

And Linda wasn't? Jewel sighed. "Linda cares too much. She always did."

"Yeah, she cares. About those fucking tadpoles in her belly. They aren't even *hers*."

"I think she's hiding." Jewel looked away. Linda could love those babies she carried, and they wouldn't hurt her. She could hide inside her own flesh with them and be safe, the way Flander hid in the Net. And how much of that was Jewel's fault? Jewel peered at

Susana's face. "You didn't put anything on your stripe, did you? You're red."

Susana touched her cheek and grimaced. "Yeah? So now I get the cancer lecture? Gimme a break, Auntie." She spun on her heel and stomped away, slapping dust from her tunic.

She was hiding, too, behind the tough-kid macho act. And maybe Susana was just a bitch, Jewel decided sourly. She had been the same way once. She winced a little as she scrambled up the side of the gully after Susana. It had been a necessary wall, but Linda had reached through it. Oh, hell . . . Jewel stopped suddenly. A few steps ahead of her Susana had frozen statue-still, eyes fixed on something on the ground in front of her. Cautiously Jewel moved closer. A sharp buzz stopped her in her tracks. The snake coiled in the shadow of a rock, less than a meter from Susana's ankles. Eyes wide, the girl stared down at it, rigid with terror, ready to bolt.

Oh, shit. "Stand *still*," Jewel hissed, but it was too late. Susana spun on her heel, panicking. Idiot! Jewel lunged, shoving her so that she stumbled down the slope, staggering, scrambling for footing. She yelped as something sharp snagged her ankle, fell flat on her face, and flinched as the rattler arrowed across her outspread hand to vanish into a crack between two rocks. A slow, hot ache was spreading up her right ankle.

Sucking in a quick breath, Jewel worked her dusty tights up around her calf. Twin punctures seeped bright beads of blood, and the area was already starting to swell.

"It bit you." Ashen beneath her tan, Susana dropped to her knees beside Jewel. "Oh, jeeze, now what?" Her voice quavered.

"I think it was pretty small." She didn't have any idea, but it made her feel better to say it. Jewel drew a shallow breath, sick to her stomach, wondering if the nausea was from the venom or was just a reaction. "Give me the tie from your hair." She snatched the woven cord and tied it around her leg above the bite, not too tight, not for too long. "Go find Serafina." The nausea was trying to climb into the back of her throat. "Quick!"

Susana ran, showering her with pebbles as she scrambled up the gully wall.

It's all right, Jewel told herself. I'm an adult. It was a small snake. Maybe. But this was *nowhere*. Surely Serafina would keep anti-venom out here? Surely. She could die—it could happen. Jewel shivered, couldn't stop shivering even though the sun blazed down on her. Shock, a calm corner of her mind announced.

Pebbles and dirt slid down the gully in a small avalanche as Susana slithered down to her again. Behind her Serafina climbed easily, without disturbing a single stone. "I was already on my way," she said. The skirt of her loose shift hiked up indecently high on her stringy, muscular thighs as she leapt down to where Jewel lay.

Jewel stared at her, unable to look away, seeing her own face overlaid with years and sun damage and confused, briefly, because Serafina had been so *tall*. I was little, Jewel thought dizzily. Her pulse pounded in her ears, and fire was seeping into her leg through the bite.

"How large?" Serafina's tone was brisk.

"This big." Jewel measured with her hands. "Maybe a little smaller."

Serafina unzipped the belt pack she wore around her waist, tore open a plastic packet, and wiped stinging cold across the punctures. "Hold very still." She fumbled in the pack again. Silver glittered between her fingers, and Jewel gasped as the scalpel blade sliced a deep gash across each wound. She dug her fingers into the dry soil, trying not to flinch.

"The old, crude ways work." Serafina applied a small suction cup to the wounds.

It hurt. Jewel clenched her teeth, icy sweat chilling her face. No way she was going to faint again. No way. The pain ended at last, and Serafina wiped the thick blood away with another pad. "This will help fight the venom." She smoothed a thick paste onto the swollen cuts. "I don't want you to walk, so we'll carry you back." She raised her head suddenly and clucked her tongue at Susana. "Don't look so frightened, kitten. She won't die. Did you find your way onto the Net?"

"Yes, and I know my way around." Susana's chin lifted. "I didn't need your yellow brick road."

"I live here." Serafina zipped the pack and tossed it at Susana. "Carry this. I like living here. I have no desire to move just because someone has discovered where I hide my flesh. So you'll follow that yellow brick road, like it or not. Grab my wrist." She reached for Susana's hand. "We'll make a chair."

Susana ducked her head, silent and sullen as Jewel eased herself onto their clasped hands. The sick feeling was getting worse, and the blood buzzed in her ears. So Susana was right about Serafina being a pirate. Pirates traded in stolen information or damage done; if you had a pirate in your space and legal means were too slow or not a choice, you did your damnedest to find out where the pirate lived in the real world. And then you hired a hit.

If Serafina was that sort of Net ghost, she had access to the kind of hardware that could put a mountain lion holo into Linda's living room. In spite of her discomfort, Jewel felt a small relaxing inside herself. Lion visions in the dark after twelve straight hours of driving she could explain. This woman was flesh, after all. "Who are you?" Jewel forced the words past the nausea. "We lived here, my mother and I. I remember you."

"Yes, you lived here. Lean back. So." Serafina's withered cheek brushed her hair. "We'll talk about it later."

Susana made a small, rude sound.

"I can foretell the future. At least the goatherders say I can." Serafina raised her head, eyes glittering. "Shall I tell you your fortune, my little lynx kitten? Shall I tell you how long you're going to survive in the Net, rash and full of pride as you are? Not long." Her smile was the smile of a lioness—a flash of white fangs and the scent of blood in the air. "Your skill doesn't match your nerve, kitten."

"Don't . . . give me *kitten*," Susana panted, struggling with Jewel's weight.

"The fox has already saved your cat skin for you. Did he tell you? I watched him watch you while you were into that Epyxx broker's personal space. That was a stupid choice, kitten." Her smile widened, and Jewel sensed the scent of blood growing stronger. "That one has been bitten before, and he decided a long time ago that death is the simplest and best antidote to piracy. He has very good security, and he would have followed you—if the fox hadn't covered your tracks."

Susana flushed, opened her mouth as if to speak, then closed it.

"It was my little score on the fox, to know he did that. I thank you." Serafina nodded, amusement gleaming bright in her eyes. "I'm not sure that the fox was quite so pleased." She nodded at Jewel. "When you've rested, we will discuss the future with your blind artist. I do not particularly want any of you here for very long."

"Then how come you invited us?" Susana growled.

"To save Jewel's ass. Not yours."

Susana grunted something that was probably obscene and shut up. Jewel's leg hurt, throbbing with the beat of her pulse as they carried her slowly back to the house. Susana panted and staggered, but Serafina seemed unaffected. Her muscles were knotted like cables on her lean arms. Jewel had the giddy notion that if she wanted to, Serafina could lift her into her arms like a child for all that they were the same height and build—that Susana was helping only because Serafina had reasons of her own for requesting help.

And maybe she was just suffering from snakebite, Jewel told herself. Imagining things.

David met them at the door, frustrated, angry, frantic with worry. "I can't help. I can't do *shit*," he said raggedly. "Jewel?" He squinted in her direction. "How are you?"

"Feeling shitty but not dying." She leaned her weight on him as Susana and Serafina let her down. "It's all right." She only wanted to be let alone, to curl herself around the sickness inside her and sleep away the pain in her throbbing ankle.

David helped her into the bedroom, unwilling to let go of her—needing to do something? Jewel eased herself onto the rumpled sleeping bag and burrowed into it, wanting him to go away.

"Artist." Serafina's voice cracked like a whip. "Leave her alone."

Jewel heard him suck in his breath as if to snap back at her, but he said nothing, and she heard the hesitant shuffle of his retreating footsteps. Rest, Jewel told herself. It was hard to do. Her ankle pounded like a drum, and tiny pains shot upward clear to her hip. Sweat plastered her hair to her face, and her teeth wanted to chatter at the same time.

Footsteps scraped on the stone floor. "Jewel?"

Susana's voice. Go away.

"I brought you some tea. The old bitch says drink it or else."

Anything that might help . . . Sitting up made her head hurt. Jewel took the cup, tasted it, and made a face. Yikes. She gulped it down.

"The old—Serafina said that if I'd stood still, the rattler wouldn't have struck." Susana's voice was oddly subdued. "She says you knew that. Is that true?"

"I know that rattlers don't usually strike unless you move." And where had she first learned it? Here, long ago? Jewel put the empty cup down.

"How come you pushed me?" Susana picked up the cup and stared into it. Her loose hair straggled over her face, hiding her expression. "How come you didn't just stand back and let it get me?"

"I'm bigger than you." Jewel sighed. "Adults don't usually die from a rattlesnake bite. And you . . . you were scared."

"I was." Susana spoke so softly that Jewel could barely make out the words. "Weren't you?"

The temptation was to shrug it off and play macho. "Yes." Jewel met Susana's pale eyes. "It scared me a lot. I'm not sure I could do it again, okay? So don't trip over any more snakes."

"It's a deal." Something flickered deep in Susana's eyes. "How do you know Sam Lujan, anyway?"

Jewel blinked at the sudden change in subject. "He used to tag with Linda. Didn't she ever tell you?"

"She tagged?"

"She never told you?" Jewel stifled a twinge of pain. "She was good. She and Sam were the best. They worked together sometimes, and the other taggers let their stuff alone. Even the gangs laid off. I just hung out with them. I'm no artist." And even back then, in the warmth of their shared excitement, she had known that it was no way out of the 'burbs, that it was not for her. "I can't believe she never told you."

"She doesn't talk about the time . . . before Carl. Luis told me Sam tagged, but he never said anything about Linda. Maybe Sam doesn't talk about her, either."

"Luis? What's Luis got to do with this?"

"Sam's his dad."

Jewel felt as if her mouth were hanging open. Susana was in bed with Samuel Lujan's son. The pang that speared her at the thought was too complex to identify. "Did Luis get you into the Net?" she asked with sudden comprehension.

"Yeah." Susana shrugged. "I go in on his access a lot. Like I said, Sam doesn't watch his bill too close."

She understood now. Jewel stared at the woven hangings without seeing them. This was Sam's private gift to Linda's daughter: a little free access to keep her from getting busted. Ah, Samuel . . . "I see," she said. Yes, she thought. The University Net access had come from Serafina in the guise of old lady Delaport. The hands had been something else. A small anger stirred in her. Why couldn't you have just done it? she thought bitterly. Whoever you are, why didn't you just *tell* me?

"I'd better go." Susana stood up, the empty cup clasped in her hands. "The old bitch told me not to stay long." She started for the door and then paused. "Thanks, Jewel," she said softly.

"You're welcome." Jewel met her eyes. Tears? Susana vanished through the door before she could be sure. It could have been a trick of the light, she told herself, and lay down to sleep.

Chapter
Seventeen

David listened to the silence in the house, full of sullen anger.
Serafina had brushed off his questions, then had dragged Susana
off to the goatherders' camp to help her treat sick children or whatever. It said something about the woman's power that Susana had
gone with her. She had been less than enthusiastic. David smiled
sourly. Jewel was asleep. He had groped his way into the bedroom
a few minutes before and listened to the gentle rhythm of her
breathing. It sounded okay, but if anything happened, what the hell
could he do? He leaned his face in his hands, listening to the whisper of his own blood, staring into the darkness that had become so
terrifyingly familiar. Flander was in the cave, waiting for him to
show up. *Do you want his blood?* Susana had demanded. Did he?
Was that what he really wanted—an eye for an eye, agony for agony? Street kid, scarred man, needing, afraid to need. David let
his breath out slowly. How many times had Flander tried to run
away or make David throw him out? But he had offered understanding and comfort when David's doubts had eaten at him.

"You could have told me," David said softly. *You could have
asked,* the silence whispered. Too late to change the past. It was
gone in an instant, out of reach; you only had the moment as tomorrow rushed into yesterday. Seize it or let it go by. David got
slowly to his feet, pushing his chair back with a scrape of wood on
stone that sounded deafeningly loud in the quiet. Wood creaked
somewhere—not a step, just the house talking to itself.

Susana had come from over there. David let go of the table,
edging through blackness, one hand groping. His flesh was still
hesitant, wanting to flinch from unseen obstacles. He had to force
himself to step out and take a normal stride. Susana was another
Flander, and she scared Jewel. They were so alike—maybe that
was why they rubbed at each other the way they did. David's fingers

brushed stone. The wall. He turned right, his left hand brushing the roughness of plastered stones, anchoring him in the void. Ah. His outstretched fingers bumped splintery boards and explored them. A wall built out at right angles to the stone wall. Another room? He found a door handle—rough, as if it were old or rusty—pulled the door open, and went inside.

Was this Susana's virtual room? David swallowed. "Access," he said, and his voice sounded shaky. "David Chen, studio." Blindness did not affect his vocal cords. The system should get a clean voice match. If it asked him to palm a screen, he might have trouble.

It was taking too long. Realizing he was straining to see, he forced himself to relax. Susana had said that this was a protected access. She might have the skill to worm her way in, but he didn't, not even with sight. So he couldn't get into the cave. A small relief tickled him, and he pressed his lips together, angry at that revelation.

Meooooow.

The sound startled him. His studio cat. Sometimes it jumped down from the radiator and yowled at him. He was in. David felt a faint tingling at his ankle. His Kraeger was feeding him sensory input: a virtual cat, rubbing against him. There was a bitter irony here. His studio saw *him*, even if he couldn't see *it*. So it reacted to him. My creation lives on without me, he thought. Too much ego in that, and too much fear. The tingling around his ankles waxed and waned. He would feel cat fur if he could only see the cat. David closed his eyes out of habit and tried to imagine it rubbing against his ankle. Its back was arched, and it looked up at him with reproachful yellow eyes.

Closing his eyes made the darkness feel intentional. He could almost feel it, the brush of silky fur against his skin, the bump of a feline shoulder against his shin. David bent slowly, stretching out his fingers. Tingling . . . he tried to feel cat, feel its head shoving at his fingertips, wanting its ears scratched.

It almost worked.

David straightened and took a step forward, then another. How far to the wall and the racked canvases? He walked across this space every day, sometimes so lost in thought that he didn't even see it. He swallowed bile. He had walked away from Fuchin, from his family, for this—a handful of darkness. He had thought of it as so solid, so wholly real. The only threat had been his own ambivalence or his doubts about his talent. They seemed so damn trivial now.

It was fragile, this medium. He hadn't understood how fragile . . .
like a spiderweb. A careless brush of the hand and it was gone.

David's outstretched palms tingled. The wall? His storage rack?
He took another step, then winced and pulled his hand back slightly.
The amperage increased if you tried to put your hand through a
solid surface, and he had set the gain high for realistic pain. So was
this wall or rack? He had cleared voice access from the file years
before; he didn't use it, and it took up space. Silly conceit, all these
visual metaphors. David clenched his teeth, trying to clear his mind.
See what you're feeling. Pain there, so this was wall or the frame
of the rack . . . but not there. He moved his hands slowly, and
slowly pain and no-pain began to take on shape in his mind. He
was standing in front of the rack. The ice-cave canvas was in the
end space. If this was the end space. If he wasn't standing in the
corner playing silly mind games with himself. He bit his lip, starting to lose the picture. Think about something else, about how the
chimera doesn't quite work. He reached, thinking about the curve
of those fangs, sketching out a better shape in his mind, letting his
muscles move with their own memory, palms tingling . . . and then
he *had* it, he had picked it up. He stretched it, muscles knowing
just how far. He imagined the doorway opening, looked through,
and made himself see ice and soft bluish light. He stepped forward,
holding his breath, and felt a subtle tingle that meant cold in this
file.

"David! Son of a bitch, where have you been? Where the hell
have you *been*?"

Almost-pain here, there, exploding unexpectedly across his chest,
arms, hands, face, confusing him . . . "Flander, stop." David
staggered, losing his balance in the sensory flood. "I can't see you.
I can't react. Just hold off a minute, okay?"

The sensations ended abruptly. "What do you mean, you can't
see me?" Flander's voice was hushed. "David? What are you saying?"

Susana hadn't told him. "I'm . . . blind. It might not be permanent." Silence. "Flander?" David held out his hands. "This is
kind of a visual medium, but I can still feel my way around a little
bit." His palms tingled faintly. Flander's hands against his? The
tingle moved up the inside of his arms, spreading to chest, shoulders, cheek, as if Flander had put his arms around him.

"David, I'm sorry." Breaking words, harsh and close in David's
ear, raw with pain. "Oh God, oh God, man, I'm so *sorry* . . ."

Slowly David closed his arms, skin tingling with the invisible
presence of Flander. In Serafina's desert house his arms curved

around empty air. In the ice cave Flander embraced him. Which is more real? David wondered, and wasn't sure. "Why didn't you trust me?" he asked softly.

"*Trust* you? Oh, shit, David, it's not that." Flander's voice quivered. "Don't think that, please; don't even say it. If you know what's going down, you're dead, okay? I tried to tell you enough so that you'd stay clear, but things weren't working, and you were pissed at me. For the kickers—and you were right, so I couldn't get you to listen. It's my fault. I fucked up, and it's all coming apart and I don't know why. Where *are* you?"

David hesitated, the answer on his tongue. Flander sounded like Flander . . . and he sounded wrong. He sounded different somehow, but David couldn't put his finger on that difference. Everyone sounded strange without the familiar visual cues, he told himself.

If he could see Flander, he could read him. He would know. No one could fool him with an auto of Flander.

He couldn't see.

He wasn't sure.

"I'm safe," he said, hearing the evasion of his voice. Come to me, he wanted to yell. Right now, in the flesh. Come here and tell me I'm going to see again. Not even Dr. Benachim could tell him that. "Flander, tell me what's going on. Who's behind this?"

"You don't trust me!"

Pain flared along David's arms, and then the tingling stopped, as if Flander had shoved him violently away.

"Man, you can't fool me. You think I'm *lying*. You think I stood back and let you take the fall for me to save my own hide? You think maybe I just exited so I wouldn't have to know what they were doing to you? I couldn't *get* there in the flesh. I would have, David. I would have walked in there and let them do it to me, but I couldn't make it. Not in time. I tried, man. Oh, God, I tried, I tried, I triiied!"

David covered his ears, hunching against Flander's earsplitting shriek.

"David?" Flander's voice was uneven, fading suddenly in and out, as if the connection were failing. "Forgive me, okay? Say . . . you forgive me . . ."

David closed his eyes, and the darkness did not change, might not ever change. "I've always forgiven you, no matter what you pulled. I think maybe that was wrong. I think you were asking me for something else, and I didn't understand. It's my fault, too. Flander, I love you." he said softly. "But I don't know if I can forgive you."

No answer, no touch except the all-over tingle of simulated cold. David raised a hand to his lensless face and felt moisture on his cheeks. I'm crying, he thought with a dull sense of surprise. When did I start crying?

"He's gone."

Serafina's voice, close beside him. David jumped, not sure if she was there in the flesh or in virtual. "Don't *do* that." He felt himself flushing, wondering how long she had watched them.

"You can tell the fox that you're with me," she went on in the low, throaty growl of a cat. "Knowing where and finding that where in the flesh world aren't the same thing. You will *not* describe this location. My security will screen your words well enough unless you make a serious effort to fool it." Fingers closed on his arm, flesh and human. "I would not make a serious effort to fool it, artist."

The nails that dug briefly into his arm had the feel of cat claws. "I'm not going to give anything away." David wiped his face on his sleeve, sighing.

"Do you have any doubts that you spoke to your friend?" A frown colored Serafina's voice. "I didn't eavesdrop, by the way."

"Thank you for that." David frowned. "I . . . wasn't sure. Flander sounded strange, but everything sounds strange to me right now. No." He shook his head, remembering that tortured cry. "It was Flander." He sighed. "I *think* so, anyway."

"You're not sure." Serafina made a sound like a harsh cat purr in her throat. "I'm not, either. It wasn't quite the fox's style—or he's slipping, and it shows. Which may be. He was very upset. My Security didn't read it as a false Self or an auto, and my Security isn't usually wrong. Come on." The fingers tugged at him. "We're going to sit down, the four of us, and sort out this mess you've dumped on my doorstep."

She kept her hand on his arm, guiding him back to the table. He almost didn't need help; he remembered where it was, walking to it easily, a half step ahead of her. He summoned an image of the room and reached for the chair he remembered. It was there. As he sat down, he felt Serafina's hand on his shoulder.

"You've accepted your blindness." Her fingers touched his face, light as a breath of wind. "When you stop denying a thing, sometimes you can change it."

The words resonated inside his head. They had an intimate feel, as if she had spoken only to him. But Jewel and Susana were already there; he heard the small sounds of their breathing. "How's your ankle?" he asked.

"Better. I can walk on it."

Her voice sounded a little weak, and there was a contemplative note to it, a hint of sadness.

"The kitten and I looked at the car." Serafina's voice was serene. "Perhaps one of the herders will pull it out with a truck. Chen Chih Hwa?" Her voice hardened. "Tell us what's going on."

"Not much." It startled him to hear her use his Chinese name. It told him how much she already knew about him, as it was intended to, he guessed. "In Erebus someone gave Flander a contaminated kicker." He frowned, re-creating the twisted path that had brought them here. "The kicker had been custom designed to the specifications of a midlevel PanEuro node named Anya Vanek."

"Tailored by your sister, Chen Yao Hwa," Serafina interjected smoothly. "You don't have to trust me, but you will give me every piece of this puzzle. Or I will abandon you, and you will almost certainly die."

"Why should we believe you?" Susana burst out suddenly. Her voice had gone high and tight, making her sound younger than she was. "Stop playing this mystical goddess shit and give us some solid info. You could be pulling our strings. *You* could have set this whole thing up. How about if you tell us why *you're* into this thing, anyway."

"You can leave, kitten." Serafina's voice was silky. "Feel free."

"Fuck that 'kitten,' " Susana growled. "Don't worry. The minute we get the car unstuck, we're out of here."

This was going nowhere. "Shut up, Susana." David turned his face in her direction. "I'm the center of this mess, not you, and I'm the one who has to end it. I'll trust you, Serafina. I don't have much choice."

"You don't. Good decision, artist."

Susana made a rude noise.

"My sister did tailor that kicker," David said slowly. "I went in to ask Flander who was behind this, but . . . I blew it. He got upset and exited, and I don't know if I can reach him again." He could feel their eyes on him, or maybe it was the pressure of their unspoken questions. David pressed his lips briefly together. "I want you to answer one question, Serafina. Why *are* you helping us?"

"To protect Jewel." The cat purr was back in her voice.

"Thanks for shit," Susana growled.

Ditto, but he would take what he could get. David bowed stiffly in the direction of Serafina's voice, "I went looking for Anya Vanek last week. She evaded me in the Net, so I tracked her in the flesh.

She lives in Seattle, and I went to see her. The woman who is known as Anya Vanek in the flesh world is not the person behind the Anya Vanek Self on the Net.''

"Why do you think so?" Serafina snapped. "The flesh Vanek's Self might be too good for your office to read."

"*I* read that Self." He could feel Serafina's stare. "I'm . . . talented. I guess that's as good a word as any. Sooner or later I can read any Self, no matter how good the editing. The flesh and virtual Vaneks are two separate individuals."

"Interesting." Doubt shaded Serafina's voice. "And unlikely."

David shrugged. Not even Shy-Shy, Flander's wild creation, had fooled him for long. Flander was such a talent—a crazy genius, sometimes walking the edge of sanity. What had he wanted with his testing and his needling? What had he been asking for? If I had known, David thought bleakly, maybe I could have saved us.

"So what?" Susana was tapping one foot impatiently against her chair leg. "I don't get it. So you got two Vaneks? Who cares?"

"In the web you always worry about being fooled," Jewel said thoughtfully. "If you talk to someone, you need to be sure that it's them and not someone else hiding behind their face. You don't want to give information to the wrong person. If someone has created an extra Self that's good enough to fool the best offices, she or he can work for more than one web—play each one off against the other and make some good money at the webs' expense. Don't you see?" Jewel sounded like she was frowning. "If someone has created a fake Self, they need someone to play the flesh role. That way, a chance Security sweep won't reveal that the extra Self has no flesh body behind it. So this Anya Vanek Self is probably controlled by someone who openly belongs to a different web."

"All right, all *right*," Susana tossed her head. "I got it, Auntie."

"I think that's the game," David said softly. "And I think Flander designed the Vanek Self. Whoever commissioned it paid Flander in kickers, covering their tracks by having the flesh Vanek deal with my sister." He frowned. "It feels wrong, though. It's a very big chance. Why waste the effort to create a midlevel node like Vanek? The payoff doesn't match the risk." He sighed. "I have no idea how to find the person behind the Vanek Self."

"David?" Jewel was frowning again. "Did you ever have any connection with Salgado, one of the big city bosses? He runs el Peten and does labor deals for Epyxx. At least he was setting up a wage scam for Sony-Matohito, and they're part of the Epyxx web."

"Salgado?" David shook his head. "The name doesn't click."

"A friend of mine is one of his lieutenants. He's the one who found out where you were.'' Jewel hesitated. ''He said the beating was Salgado's doing. That it had something to do with a new plant opening in the 'burbs.''

Salgado. David stared into darkness. He hated Jack and the name-less waiter, hated them with an intense, personal hatred—a primitive gut-level desire to kill them, to get their blood on his hands. This Salgado, this was different. This was the man who had sat back and issued the orders, who had not been there to listen to him scream or get spattered with his blood. Maybe he hadn't even watched the tapes. A new hatred was taking shape inside David. This one was colder, darker. Uglier. ''I don't know anything about a new plant.'' With an effort, David forced his mind back to the issue. ''He could be it. He could be wearing Vanek in PanEuro, Salgado in Epyxx.''

''I could check it out.'' Susana was trying to sound casual. ''I could drop in with Luis, see what he knows. He's always after me to do sex games with him. So we'll do it. When he's got his mind on his dick, I could pump him dry and he'd never tumble.''

Serafina made a sound in her throat that might have been laugh-ter. ''You're too sure of your nine lives, kitten. I think they'll outlive you. But I think I will let you do this.'' Her voice had gone low and thoughtful. ''I haven't been able to track the shadow who's pulling these puppet strings, and that bothers me. Someone this good is dangerous, and it's no one I know. I want the name of this shadow.''

''No.'' David leaned forward. ''The risk is mine, not Susana's. It's not true that I can't find Flander—I've been hiding from him. I've been telling myself that he had to show up in the flesh to prove that he loved me. *I'm* the one who put up a wall between us.'' His voice shook because these words were truths and they hurt. ''Love is a kind of helplessness, and I was afraid of being helpless. I'm too much like my father,'' he whispered. ''I wanted to control it all—our relationship, my feelings. If you'll help me get back into the cave, Flander will find me. He'll tell me who's behind this.''

''David,'' Jewel said softly. ''Don't be so hard on yourself.''

Tears in her voice? What had she said about love once? There were tears in his eyes, too, hot as scalding water. He brushed them away, remembering Flander's anguished cry in the cave.

''David?''

He imagined her leaning forward, her face turned toward him. It took him a few seconds to realize that he wasn't imagining it, that the shadowy vision was *real*, that it vanished when he blinked.

Dear God.

He held his breath, his heart suddenly pounding, frightened that the slightest movement might banish it, this fragile, precious light. "I can see," he whispered. "Don't touch me. Just wait." He was terrified, more afraid than he had been when he had awakened blind. To have it again, sight, and lose it . . . If it went away, if the darkness closed in around him again, he would go crazy.

"David, is it really coming back?"

Jewel's face was blurry, but he could make out her concern. It was a little better, wasn't it? A little clearer? She reached for his hand, and he grabbed it. "It's coming back." His voice was unsteady. "I can see you."

"Shit, okay, man!" Susana dashed around the table in a blur of motion, her arms going around him the way Flander had thrown his arms around him in the cave. "Okay, I knew you'd get it back— I mean, you *had* to."

"I told you," Serafina said softly. "When you stop denying something, you can change it. Sometimes."

The skin prickled on the back of his neck. "Was it Flander?" He faced her, afraid of her suddenly, struggling to bring her face into focus. "If I was blind, I couldn't go into a virtual. I didn't have to face him. Was that it? Was it me?"

"Ask yourself, artist. You have the answers." Her eyes glittered in the brown blur of her face like backlit chips of onyx.

"You're right. I do." He drew a slow breath, dizzy and drunk with sight. I'm sorry, Flander, he thought, and grief seized him by the throat. I fucked up more than you did. But maybe it isn't too late to fix it. "I need to leave here." He drew a deep breath. "By myself. I'm the lightning rod in this storm. If I'm out of here, you'll be safe."

"Not true." Serafina's voice was harsh. "None of us will be safe until we know the identity of our shadow."

Her face was coming into focus at last. She sat at the end of the table, her arms crossed, face weathered and old. David stared at her, shocked. She could be Jewel's twin. She was old, yes, but she even crossed her arms and carried her shoulders the same way. As if Jewel had suddenly aged fifty years. He turned his head slowly, wanting to laugh out loud at the beautiful shape of Susana's arm, the pristine, perfect grain of the tabletop. Oh, yes, they looked alike. He smiled at Jewel. "You're related," he said. "You didn't tell me that."

"No," Jewel whispered, but her eyes were frightened.

Oh, shit. She was scared of yesterday, remember? David reached for her hand, guilty, but she must have noticed the resemblance.

"Wow." Susana stared openly. "You two really *do* look alike.

Hot shit. I never noticed, I guess 'cause you're so old,'' she said to Serafina. ''What are you, her granny?''

''Oh, no.'' Serafina didn't smile. ''She's my daughter.''

Jewel's chair fell over with a clatter as she scrambled to her feet. ''We ran away.'' She faced Serafina, her face pale. ''I remember. You fought, you and Mama . . . Elaine, I mean. She isn't my mother. I *knew*. I guess I always knew; I'd just . . . forgotten. She was running away from you. And you knew about me, didn't you?'' Her eyes were wild, full of bright, crazy light. ''You stood back and let me end up in that fucking camp. You let the old witch paw me, let me think it was payment for the Net access, when it came from *you*, didn't it? You didn't care if she put her hands on my breasts, did you? You didn't care if I had to leave Linda behind, if I had to . . . oh, *shit*!'' She flung herself away from the table.

''What the fuck?'' Susana stared after her.

David shoved his chair back and started to follow. What the hell had he done here? ''Jewel? Wait!'' The door slammed behind her.

''Stop, artist.'' Serafina grabbed his arm, yanking him to a halt.

Either he was still weak from the enhancement or this was one strong lady. ''Let go.'' He clenched a fist.

''Don't.'' Serafina bared her teeth at him. ''She won't do anything stupid, artist. She's a survivor. Like me.''

''*Are* you her mother?'' David stared into her flat, unreadable eyes. ''You did what she said, didn't you?''

''You're perceptive.'' The stone-chip eyes did not waver. ''But you don't know everything. So be quiet and sit down.'' She bared her lion smile again. ''Enjoy your rediscovered sight and let my daughter throw her tantrum in peace. Since you've decided you can see, we're going back to your cave. You'll ask the fox who pulls the strings in this game, and he'll tell you. *Then* you may go comfort her.''

''You're a bitch.'' Still standing, he met Serafina's implacable stare. ''Even if you did save our lives.''

''I am, and I did. Don't forget it.'' A shadow passed across her face. ''Sometimes the simplest path twists into darkness.'' Her face smoothed once more, and her fingers tightened on David's arm. ''We need the fox, and fast, before our shadow finds you.''

David hesitated, wanting to follow Jewel, wanting to tell Serafina to go to hell. But she was right. David blinked: light, dark, light, such a precious sequence. He could sit here and simply *look* at the world. ''I'll go find him,'' he said heavily. ''I'll need a pair of lenses.''

''*We* will go find him.'' Serafina nodded. ''I have extra lenses for you.''

David sighed, afraid of this confrontation, afraid of the things he needed to say. ''We'll start with the cave.''

Chapter
Eighteen

Meooww . . .

The black and white cat leapt from its radiator perch, tail in the air. David leaned down to pet it, feeling fur beneath his palm, his throat tightening with the memory of darkness and the buzz of his net as he struggled to feel a cat. It looked so damn good. He straightened, examining his studio, amazed by the bright, clean conjunction of colors and shapes, smiling at the familiar easel with its sunflower painting, at the racked canvases. A bubble of lightness was expanding inside him, pushing against the shell of his body, filling him up until he thought he might drift into the air. He pulled one of the canvases from the rack. It was the gallery piece he had started months before with Flander, a theme of nebulas and birthing galaxies. I almost lost this, he thought, and struggled with sudden tears.

Between his hands clouds of gleaming dust and young stars twined into a skein of millennia. Loss and rebirth . . . He eyed the canvas, knowing suddenly how it would work, how he would do it. Emphasize the darkness . . . space without light, yeah, and size-shift so that you were suddenly tiny, drowned in this sea of light and future life . . .

"Cool," Susana breathed over his shoulder. She wore a cat Self with a feline/human face. "Truly cool. Can we go in there? I mean just to look; I won't touch." She clasped her hands behind her back in a little-kid gesture of promise.

"Later, okay?" David racked the canvas—reluctantly, because he wanted to work on it, too, wanted to give his newborn vision free rein and go where it took him. "Want to see what you can do with stardust instead of ice?"

"You're kidding!" She twitched the whiskers that sprouted from her cheeks, a little wary, sitting hard on her excitement. "I mean, what's the catch, man? What if I mess it up?"

"No catch. I can undo anything I don't like." David shrugged and pulled the ice cave from the rack. Flander had been about the same age when he had started to work with David. "Drop in when I'm working on it."

"Hey, *dude*. You don't gotta ask twice." Susana lashed her tail and grinned. "No prob."

Why had he just offered to let this kid play? David ran his fingers along the edge of the canvas, feeling illusory fabric between his fingertips. He was groping for yesterday, for the wary, admiring Net-ghost genius who had haunted his space. This girl wasn't Flander, just as Flander wasn't the kid who had worked on those early pieces with him. Not anymore. David yanked the ice-cave canvas to door shape. No fox flung itself at him as he stepped through.

"Flander?" David swallowed disappointment, then cupped his hands around his mouth and shouted: "Flander!" His studio translated that metaphor into a call to whatever access Flander had set up. If he was monitoring in realtime, he would show up. If he wanted to. Realizing that he was holding his breath, David let it out in a rush. Flander was in and out everywhere, all the time. Messages didn't always catch up with him immediately.

He lowered his hands, looking around in the dim blue twilight of the cave. The lightness inside him was increasing, a pressure that threatened to burst out in song or tears. He had thought he would never see this again. Half-frozen into the ice, the chimera lowered its head, glaring at David, its lips writhing back over icy fangs. A mangled fox lay between its paws. The creature's head was twisted back, eyes glazed and sightless, darkened tongue lolling. Blood glued the fur at its torn-out throat into stiff, sticky points and spread across the ice in a glossy pool.

He recognized the characteristic shading of the hair, the minute detailing of eyelashes and claws, the slightly too-white teeth. Flander had done it.

"Shit." Beside him, Susana flattened her cat ears. "Don't bust me for that, okay? Last time I was in here, it was a body. Human, you know, and the face kept changing. Every time I looked at it, I saw myself. *Truly* weird."

"I know you didn't do it." David stretched out a hand, snapped his fingers once, and grabbed the eraser that appeared in the air. He erased the dead fox with a few strokes, disappeared the eraser, and restored the androgynous mirror body he had put there originally. It immediately assumed his own likeness, naked and dead beneath the fangs of the past, penis slack on its sunken belly, blood streaking the silver-netted skin. David shivered and turned his back on it. "There's been a lot of traffic in here." he said harshly.

"Some jerk's been trashing the place." Hackles had risen on Susana's furred shoulders. "Just smashing stuff, like my carvings. If I catch him, I'll ghost him good. I'll post his kinky sex life all over the damn Net."

"Relax." David managed a faint smile. The dead-fox image had hit him harder than he wanted to admit. "Sometimes you get your best leads from vandalism." He glanced at the new carvings in the ice—some worthless, some good, most indifferent, like scribbles on the walls of an old building. He raised his hands to call Flander again.

"He's not listening." A mountain lion leapt down from no-where, landing lightly on the ice.

Serafina. David recognized the eyes and the way she moved. "He can hide his access pretty well," David said reluctantly.

"Not from me." The lionness shook herself, ears flattening. "He didn't receive your message. I don't like this absence."

David glanced involuntarily at the body and looked quickly away from its silver-netted sprawl.

"Let us drop in on Señor Salgado. I want you to look at him with these clear eyes of yours." Serafina didn't hide her skepticism. She bared her teeth at Susana "*You* will behave."

"Shit!" Susana glared at the neon red manacles that had appeared on her wrists. She stretched her arms apart, and the manacles stretched, too, shortening as she brought her fists down to her hips. "What the hell is this?"

"A little visual reminder." The lioness smiled. "You're in my space, no matter where you think you are. You're a spectator only, kitten, and you're my guest."

Susana lashed her tail and glowered but said nothing.

A door appeared in the ice-cave wall. David eyed it. "You know your way around my file pretty well, don't you?" She must have to have left footprints that he hadn't been able to erase.

Serafina didn't bother to answer him. She reached for the old-fashioned china knob on the plain wooden door, her lion paw metamorphosing suddenly into furry human fingers. The nails were a lion's claws.

Jungle? David blinked as the door opened onto soft shadows and tangled foliage. He had expected . . . what? An office setting, he supposed, and wondered if Serafina had accessed them into a recreational file. He followed Serafina through the doorway, unhappy about crashing filespace—ghosting. Susana had already bounded ahead, was peering intently between vine-tangled tree trunks. David stepped onto a deep litter of rotting leaves and fallen twigs. But something was wrong. He looked down. His feet didn't sink in, didn't disturb a single twig. He felt nothing. Before he had walked through a virtual without sight, by touch alone. Now he had sight without sensation. It was a little eerie not to feel the brush of leaves and bark against his skin. That lack increased his nervousness.

He could smell his own sour sweat stink, but at the same time a part of him was lost in the sheer beauty of the thousand shades of sun-dappled greens and browns. Flowers bloomed among the leaves, glowing gems of purple and dark magenta. Had colors always looked so beautiful? he wondered. Had the implanted cells altered his perceptions, or was it simply the contrast with that recent darkness that made them look so new and different? A monkey chattered overhead: a flicker of black and white movement in the canopy, showering twigs and torn leaves. This virtual was good—top quality.

A spotted jaguar prowled into sight ahead of them, head low and swinging, as if it were sniffing the ground for a trail. As if it were hunting. Security? Serafina had stopped, her lion body pressed hard against Susana. David froze, his heart pounding, adrenaline flushing through him like chemical lightning. The jaguar wandered on, vanishing like mist as it prowled through a patch of sunshine, and David sagged with relief. Serafina looked back over her shoulder at him, tongue lolling, sly laughter in her golden eyes.

David glared back at her. Flander did this kind of thing. *He* did not. David slowed as Serafina stopped suddenly. Gray stone showed between the tree stems. A ruin? He could make out a vast pyramid of tumbled rock thickly furred with ferns and creeping plants. A Mayan temple? He paused, impressed by the detail work. He had similar recordings in stock, raw takes purchased from a Guatemalan free-lancer who had recorded hours of half-buried stone, tree shadows, and the vandalized ruins of Chichen Itza and Río Azul. The free-lancer was Tzultzil Mayan and had made a personal connection to those echoes of past glory; it had scored her takes like music. Someone had finally shot her—a coca farmer or a soldier fighting one of those little wars that never ended anymore. He missed her work.

Serafina had stopped beside a ruined wall of gray stone. David edged up beside her, looked over Susana's shoulder, and froze. Framed by a wide gateway in the old wall, men and women lounged in a flagged courtyard. David sucked in a quick breath, wanting to duck. Obviously they weren't visible, but it was damned hard to keep that in mind. All except one of the three men and two women present wore dark-skinned, native-looking Selves dressed in white loincloths or shifts, wearing bright collars of feathers and strings of jade. Period costume or fantasy? No one seemed to notice them, and David began to breathe again.

One man lounged in a modern recliner that jarred with the native ambience. He wore a modern tunic; his face was Hispanic, but without the stark Mayan profile of the others. He was the center. David watched the others orbit him like planets, arranging and rearranging themselves within his range of vision, subtly jockeying for attention, faces turned to him like sunflowers following the sun. Salgado? David examined him, cold gathering in his belly. Did you give Jack his orders, you bastard? Strong face, perfectly muscled body that probably had very little to do with the flesh reality. Did you watch what they did to me? Did you enjoy it, you son of a bitch? Did you get off on it, or did you forget about it and go home to bed? David let his breath out in a soft hiss as the man leaned over to whisper in a slender woman's ear.

The Salgado Self was Flander's work. The cold was turning to ice inside of him. Look at his arms—Flander always put a shade too much definition into muscle. And the skin tone . . . Something else nagged at him. David took a deep breath and put Flander and hatred away. Eyes narrowed, he watched the man talk, watched him gesture impatiently at something someone had said, watched him get up from the recliner, slide an arm around the woman's waist, and open a door in the stone wall. Opening a door . . . Yes!

A jaguar stalked into the courtyard, lifted its head, and stared directly at David. Its hackles rose suddenly, and its lips drew back in a snarl.

"Time," Serafina growled.

David flinched as the ruins dissolved, dripping like melting plastic, running across his field of vision in a disorienting avalanche of texture and color, as if the universe itself were dissolving. His skin buzzed with sensory static, and David staggered, his sense of up and down shifting wildly, his stomach twisting with a brief clench of nausea. He heard Susana gasp, and then the walls of Serafina's VR booth blinked into existence around him. Up and down were back where they belonged. David drew a deep, relieved breath and planted a sweaty palm against the comfortingly solid wall.

"Shit, lady." Susana snatched off her lenses, face pale and angry. "What'd you do? I think I'm gonna throw up."

"You'd rather I left your friend my address?" Serafina pulled off her gloves, her expression mildly amused. "He picked us up, our jaguar Security. So I left him enough tracks to keep him hot and running for at least an hour. None of those trails will lead him to us. Sometimes it's better to leave misleading tracks than to leave none. Remember that, kitten. It would have saved the fox the trouble of covering your ass." She turned her piercing stare on David. "So? What did you see, artist?"

What, indeed? David drew a slow breath as he followed Serafina out into the main room. "Flander designed Salgado's Self." He leaned his palms on the tabletop, frowning down at the battered surface, feeling Serafina's stare like a prodding finger in his back. "Jewel was right. Salgado and Anya Vanek are Selfs for the same person. I'm sure of it."

"So." Serafina paced across the long room, moving with the prowling grace of a restless cat. "For the moment I will believe that you possess this talent of clear sight. You say that the flesh Anya Vanek doesn't wear the Vanek Self, but Jewel knew this Salgado from the flesh. So he is behind both Selfs."

Salgado was Epyxx. Vanek was PanEuro. The flesh Salgado would have inside information from two separate webs, could use it to set up packages that would benefit him at the expense of either or both webs. That was exactly what offices were designed to prevent. But Flander was a genius. David let his head droop, suddenly exhausted. What he wanted to do was go into his studio, get out the nebula canvas, and go work on it. Screw the web and all the power dances. David let his breath out slowly, shoulders sagging. "Flander designed both the Vanek Self and Salgado," he said softly. "Which means he'll have some way to expose the scam." The web didn't forgive scams, so Salgado had his back to the wall. His flesh Anya Vanek might expose him if she was faced with serious prison time. And he would get no second chances, no matter how big he was. Maybe Flander had tried a little blackmail already, or maybe he had simply let Salgado find out that he had kept a key to the Selfs. David tried to banish a vision of Jack's creamy patience as he waited for him to recover enough to anticipate the next blow. "Salgado . . . needs to kill Flander in order to keep his scam secret." David looked away, at the gray slabs of stone that made up the wall of the house. Who had built that house? Homesteaders back in the last millennium, full of hopes and dreams that they could make the desert bloom? "I'm the key to finding Flander."

"You may be right about all this." Serafina halted her catlike pacing, her eyes dark with thought. "It agrees with my own discoveries."

"I think I can deal with this." David tore his eyes from the stones. "Harmon Alcourt is big enough to step on Salgado." For a price, and Alcourt would make a very accurate assessment of exactly how valuable that service would be. "I think he'll handle this for me."

"Possibly." Serafina frowned. "Alcourt is very powerful. He might be able to save you, if he'll do it for you." Her eyes pierced him. "The herders are dealing with measles. I need to go back to my duties as local healer." She gave David a cold smile. "We'll continue this discussion later."

The door closed behind her, and the house filled with silence. It wouldn't be so bad belonging to Alcourt, David told himself. He was good at the kind of work Alcourt liked. A headache speared through his skull, a scary stab of pain that made him squint, as if he could cling to vision. He would not lose it again, he told himself, but the assurance felt thin, unreal. The silence in the house weighed on him until he realized that Susana had gotten very quiet.

She was curled up on the swaybacked sofa that stood against one wall, arms around her shins, chin on her knees. Brooding. She looked up as he dropped onto the sprung cushion beside her. "He had those guys beat you up, didn't he? Salgado?" Her eyes glittered, flat and hard as blue agate. "You want to get him for that?"

There was hatred in the set of her shoulders, in those hard blue eyes. It tugged at him like a dark moon. "Yes." David shivered at how much he wanted it. "I would like to kill him," he said softly. "With my own hands."

"He killed Carl. One day I'm gonna kill him. That's a promise, man."

For a moment something crackled in the air between them: shared emotion, like an electrical current or a touch, more intimate than sex. "I'm sorry," David said. "About your father."

Susana shrugged jerkily.

She reminded him of Flander, self-contained and too well defended. "What does it mean to you?" David asked softly. "The Net?"

"I'm cool in there." She gave him a quick sideways look. "I mean, I do what I want. No one shits on me, you know? No one pushes me around 'cause I'm just some number. I'm *someone*. And *I* made me someone."

"It's power," David agreed softly. "You've got control in the Net."

"You got it." Susana scowled at nothing. "It's all pretend in the 'burbs. You're shit. Nobody. Carl found that out finally."

And the Net was real. Or maybe it wasn't. Maybe that was at the root of Flander's drug use: he needed it to be real, and he thought he could make it real. David got to his feet. "I'm worried about Jewel," he said. "I'm going to go look for her."

"Is the old bitch really her mom, do you think?"

"I don't know."

"She's gonna hate it if it's true," Susana said softly. "She doesn't want to owe anybody for anything."

Perceptive kid. David looked at her, measuring the shadows in her face. "You okay?" he asked gently.

"Oh, yeah, sure." She bounced to her feet. "Look, I'm gonna go to sleep before the bitch drags me off to help her stick needles in babies again. There's nothing else to do around here." She shouldered through the curtain that covered the storeroom door.

Maybe he had imagined the weight and depth of those shadows. David hesitated, then pushed the heavy door open and went out into the searing, wonderful sunlight.

Jewel stumbled along the narrow shelf, her feet carrying her blindly, finding their own path through sage and rock. *She's my daughter. She's my daughter.* The words beat in her head with the rhythm of wheels rolling along an endless road. *She's my daughter.*

She had known it. It had nestled inside her like an egg, an enclosed moment of future that had dragged her back from Erebus, had tugged her out to this godforsaken place of dust and heat as the moon drew the oceans. That egg was hatching . . . into what? *She's my daughter.* No, no, no, how can you say that to me? Jewel stumbled, her feet sliding in loose rock, gravity tugging at her, dragging her forward. The path had brought her down over the canyon wall and onto a ledge of cracked rock. Jewel looked around. At this time of day the ledge was shadowed by a bulge in the canyon wall. Someone had built a crude wooden bench here. A handful of wilted flowers lay on a shallow niche in the rock above the bench, along with a milky blue lump of agate. Like an offering? To some god or goddess of this dusty place?

Jewel shivered suddenly and walked to the lip of the shelf. Beyond the mouth of the narrow canyon the desert spread out in an endless plain of gray and ocher, every detail bright and clear in the afternoon light. Faint bleating rose from the creek bed below, and Jewel looked down. Gray shapes milled in the canyon bottom, raising clouds of brown dust. Goats? Jewel spotted four pickups, three of them capped with battered camper shells. A water tanker stood beside the dry creek bed, and people stood around it.

Serafina's goatherders. As Jewel leaned out to look, the ground suddenly shifted beneath her feet. A slab of rock gave way, sliding downward, taking her with it. With a cry Jewel twisted around, groping for a handhold.

"Look out!" Fingers clamped on her arm.

A woman was clutching at her, surprise on her face. Jewel scrambled back up onto the ledge, kicking a small rock slide of dust and pebbles down the slope. "Thanks," she gasped as she brushed dirt from her clothes, taking in the woman's dusty jeans and faded tank top, tanned, dark skin and hair that had been bleached almost white in the sun.

"You gotta be careful up here." The woman's teeth flashed white in her dark face. "You slide down on your ass, you'll be lucky not to break a leg." She held out a hand. "I'm Cheri."

"Jewel." A little shaky-kneed, Jewel returned the woman's strong clasp. She looked young, no more than Jewel's age, but the sun had already etched fine lines into her face. Her collarbones and ribs pushed against her tanned skin, and her muscles lay in knotted ropes along her bones. "Thanks—for grabbing me," Jewel said. "I wasn't paying attention."

"You said it. Good thing I came up here. Are you waiting for the healer, too?"

She capitalized the word with her tone. "The healer?" Jewel tried to collect her scattered thoughts. "You mean Serafina?" . . . *my daughter.*

"Yeah." Cheri nodded at a ragged daypack on the ledge where she had dropped it. "Where's your water?" She frowned at Jewel's look of surprise. "You don't go *anywhere* without water. Where are you from, anyway? The city?"

"Yes." Jewel looked down at the milling herd below. "I wasn't going anywhere," she said, wishing this stranger would go away. "I was just out for a walk."

"Oh." Surprise showed on Cheri's lean face. "You stayin' around here? We didn't see your rig." She shaded her eyes to glance up the path Jewel had taken. "I hope she's around. We got another kid with spots, and we gotta be movin' on soon. Last circle through we got a little water here, but not this time. The tanker's low, so we got to keep pushing if we want to make it over to the aquifer at Nyssa before we run dry. Shit, the rain's been bad three years running."

Jewel had heard about the caravans, the nomadic goatherders who followed their herds across the desert lands. They were supposedly the descendants of the cattle ranchers. The genetically engineered goats ate the sage, getting fat on it, and needed little water. The herders sold the young animals to government yards along their circuits, providing fresh meat for the luxury market.

"She's at the house," Jewel said, and watched relief flood Cheri's face.

"I'm here." Serafina's voice came from behind them, and they both jumped.

Jewel looked over her shoulder into Serafina's gently smiling face. She stood at the end of the bench, as if she had materialized on the ledge—or had come down another path at the far end. Jewel felt a sullen annoyance at the theatrics. Drama for the hicks. A little pretend magic, maybe? Backed by tech? And the hicks paid for it, probably. She glanced at Cheri, lips tightening at the look on her face.

Huh.

"I expected you, Cheri." Serafina held out her hand. "I wouldn't let you·leave without taking your pain."

Pain? Jewel looked, recognizing it now—the shadowed tightness of Cheri's face.

"It's getting bad again." Cheri's gaze flicked from Serafina to Jewel and back again, eyes widening suddenly. "Rink . . . sent me up to ask you if you'd come down tonight." She was staring openly at Jewel now. "Marty's boy is down now. A few spots, hundred and two temp. He sent another cheese as payment." She pulled a cloth-wrapped parcel from her pack and handed it to Serafina.

"Of course I'll come." Serafina set the wrapped cheese down in the strip of deeper shadow beneath the bench. "Close your eyes, child." She took Cheri by the shoulders and sat her gently on the bench. "Let your mind go, let it drift . . ." Her voice was low and gentle, and Jewel found herself wanting to yawn. Cheri slumped on the bench, relaxed, eyes closed as Serafina stroked her gaunt face. Her breathing deepened, and she didn't even twitch as Serafina smoothed a drug patch over her jugular vein. "Embrace your pain," she murmured in that low, hypnotic voice. "Accept it, let it soak into you."

Cheri whimpered softly, eyelids closed, her hands palms up and relaxed in her lap.

There was a vivid intimacy in their tableau, as if the two were lovers. Cheri whimpered again, and Serafina made a low purring sound of comfort in her throat.

"Take a deep breath, child, and hold it within you. Let the pain flow into that breath, into that bubble of air within you, let it go until you are clean and the pain and air mingle in your chest. Now release it, breathe it out. Let the pain flow out with it so that the wind may scatter it like dust.''

Cheri was breathing out in a long slow breath that seemed to go on forever, far beyond the capacity of human lungs. Her shoulders slumped as if she were collapsing into herself, deflating like a punctured balloon.

"So, my child," Serafina murmured. "Empty yourself of the pain. Release it and let it go. And now you may wake. The pain is gone.''

Cheri yawned and opened her eyes, an expression of dreamy peace on her face. "Thank you, healer," she said softly. "I'll tell Rink that you're coming tonight." She smiled at Jewel, turned, and started lightly down the path.

Serafina bent stiffly to retrieve the cloth-wrapped cheese. "The caravans trade dried sausage and cheese when they stop here," she said conversationally. "I don't eat the meat, but it brings a very nice price on the local black market.''

"And you play magician." Jewel's lip curled. "What was in the patch? A painkiller?''

"I gave her a slow-acting sedative." Serafina's smile was cold. "Cheri has cancer. She got her diagnosis at the Nyssa clinic two years ago. She's on Basic, so they can only offer her drugs, and she can't herd goats on their drugs. I help her out when she comes through. Tonight, when I go down to the caravan, she'll be asleep. She won't feel anything when I implant a drug pump in her thigh. It contains Synth. At low sustained dosages, it's a very good painkiller. Illegal and ultimately harmful, but she won't live long enough to worry about side effects.'' Serafina lifted her shoulders in a slow shrug. "Even so, the Synth couldn't keep her free from pain for the months between visits. But she believes in me." Serafina's eyes held Jewel's. "She believes that I have power, that I can walk in the wind and reach into her body to still the pain, if not heal her. So she won't hurt—because of Synth and her belief together. Never underestimate the power of the mind. Boundaries exist only because you make them boundaries. Look beyond them and they vanish." Serafina sighed. "I don't think I'm going to see Cheri again. It'll be six months before the caravan comes back this way. She won't be with them.''

Jewel looked away, remembering her mother's—no, Elaine's— slow, dark dying. "I'm sorry for her," she said softly.

Serafina said nothing, and the silence expanded, filling the ledge, enclosing them in an invisible bubble. She was waiting for Jewel to speak. Jewel stifled a twinge of panic, wanting to run, to flee back to the house, back to David's comfort and Susana's needling. She wondered what would happen if she tried to run. Would the skin of this bubble snap her back onto this ledge? I'm as bad as Cheri, Jewel thought, and lifted her chin. "I called her Mama. Elaine. She told me she was my mother. All her life she was running away from you. *We* were." Her voice cracked like breaking stone. "Why?"

"I never said I was your mother. I said that you're my daughter." Serafina lifted her head, and the yellow light of the setting sun painted shadows beneath her high cheekbones. "I looked for you, but I couldn't find you. Elaine never showed up on the Net. For a long time I thought you were dead."

"And then I got into the Net," Jewel whispered. "What the hell do you mean, you're not my mother? Are you or aren't you?"

Emotion rippled across Serafina's face like a cloud shadow sweeping across the desert floor. "Elaine Martina carried you in her womb. She bore you, and she loved you. I could see how much she loved you. When she took you, I let her go. Because of that— that she loved you."

A surrogate. Her mother . . . Elaine . . . had been a surrogate, like Linda. Such a twisted closure. Jewel closed her eyes. *She loved you.* "Do you know what I remember?" Her words tumbled out like an avalanche of broken stones. "I remember running. Always hungry, always afraid because we were new in town. That's what it was like—running and hiding. From *you.*" She gasped for breath, wondering if she had used up all the air in the invisible bubble that enclosed them. "I think she finally found a place to hide. In the drugs." And in the slow removal of dying. "What did you do to her? Why did you let her take me? Why did you lurk around in my filespace, fix up little mazes for me to run, like with the Delaport woman? Why didn't you just *tell* me?"

"I loved her. Elaine was my lover." Serafina stared out at the far wall of the canyon. "And . . . I was afraid."

Love. Jewel looked away. "What were you afraid of? Me?" She laughed bitterly. "You can't leave this place, can you? Someone will find you and kill you for piracy. So you're trapped here. Too bad if your lover and your kid wander off, huh? You'll just sit around and wait for her to wander back." Which she had done. Jewel felt a twinge of fear.

"You think you've got it all figured out?" Serafina's eyes flashed. "You are so sure that I abandoned you? That it was too much trouble to search for you, that I didn't care?" She took a step closer to Jewel, seeming to grow taller, her eyes expanding into dark pools full of moving shadows. "I let you go. Because Elaine loved you. And yes, because I was afraid . . . of you."

Brilliant flecks sparkled in her eyes like stars glimpsed in some distant sky. Jewel tried to look away but found that she couldn't. "Afraid of *me*?" She tried to laugh but managed only a breathy exhalation. "What the hell could I do?"

"I was afraid of how much I wanted you, of what you could become for me." Serafina touched Jewel's face, a feather-light stroke of her fingertips that made Jewel shiver. "You're so sure of your little reality. You don't even know the boundaries of your own world. I could envy you that ignorance." She laughed softly and took her hand away from Jewel's cheek. "Me, I'm not so certain. I lost certainty a long time ago. Anything is possible if you don't blind yourself. Ask your artist. I think he's beginning to understand." A shadow crossed her face. "Death is the one absolute we can't escape. We can hold it at bay for a while, but in the end it gets you. With every passing year it becomes harder to let go of life." Pale light woke in her eyes. "I thought I could find my immortality in a daughter. You're *mine*, gene for gene. I paid to have one of my gametes split and rejoined in a private lab. You're mine and no one else's." Her voice dropped. "And in you I found immortality, yes, but not what I had expected. In you I can live on. Elaine knew it, and I knew it. She was . . . afraid for you. And, I think, jealous. She was possessive, Elaine." The light in her eyes died suddenly, and she looked away. "When she stole you, I was angry. After a time, I stopped being angry, but I still couldn't find you. Elaine . . . knew me. I didn't have the strength to turn my back on a chance to live forever, and she knew it."

Jewel recoiled, the breath catching in her throat. Serafina *shimmered*, as if Jewel were looking at her through clear, shallow water. She was melting, flowing, her arms shortening, thickening, her legs curving strangely, her face elongating, her nose broadening into the flat muzzle of a big cat. Almost before Jewel could focus on the terrifying change taking place before her, a mountain lion stretched lazily on the ledge. She bared her teeth, looking up at Jewel with Serafina's eyes.

"Are you still so sure of your world, Daughter?"

It was Serfina's voice, inside her head. Jewel took a step back, her mind blank. Not believing this.

"Myself, I have found that there are no certainties. You may do anything if you are able to grasp the possibility. Are you still so ready to judge me, Daughter?"

The lionness paced toward her, head lifted, rounded ears pricked.

Her whiskers quivered, and a gust of wind fanned the golden fur on her flanks. Her eyes glowed like molten gold, full of hunger. She sank onto her haunches suddenly, one paw slashing out, a golden blur of motion. *"You are myself, Daughter."*

Jewel stared at a landscape of rolling green, wondering for one shocked moment what had happened to the desert. Humid air lay thick and dank against her skin. Her dirty cotton shift stuck to her sweaty back, and the hoe handle felt smooth in her callused palms. Almost sunset. In the next field over Mama was working the mule, getting in the last of the plowing. Got to finish the rows or Mama would scold. She chopped at a leafy sprout of pigweed, but it was hard to work. A breeze was picking up, nosing through the thick summer air, breathing a promise of coolness on her neck, coaxing her. She spread her hand, and the wind caressed it. She leaned on her hoe, bonnet pushed back on her head, watching the wind play with the new corn plants. She put out her hand, commanding, and it came to her, almost visible in the still air, swirling around her, coaxing, playing, and . . . untamed.

Power. It rushed through her like a wave, lifting her. She could call the wind. She let her hoe drop into the crumbly red dirt. She could see it. She spread her hands, her nipples hardening as it flattened her shift against her, rubbing like a dog.

"What else can I do?" she whispered . . .

. . . and found herself back on the ledge, receding like the vision a wave, leaving her stranded on a beach of years that was studded with memories like broken shells . . .

"This is why I let Elaine steal you," Serafina's voice whispered in her ear. *"Even now, I'm tempted."*

Jewel blinked. No mountain lion stood on the ledge in front of her. There was only sage and dirt and the long shadows of afternoon.

For a moment she had been . . . someone else.

Serafina.

I was *remembering*, she thought with a twinge of panic. It felt so *old*, that memory. She had been wearing a bonnet, like in a visual from a history text. But this was the real world; illusion belonged to the Net. Mountain lions might prowl the virtual corridors of her world, but flesh hid behind the fur—normal flesh. Jewel shivered, her skin flushing cold, then hot. If she had touched the lioness, what would she have felt? Below her, shadows were beginning to fill the creek bed, although yellow light still washed the canyon walls. Goats bleated. Cheri was down there somewhere, tending them, dying without pain because she believed that Serafina was the healer, with magic in her hands.

Immortality.

The ledge was empty, but shadows crept up from the creek bed, stalking her. She had seen such hunger in the lioness's eyes. *Even now, I'm tempted*, the lioness had whispered. Panic seized her suddenly, and Jewel ran, scrambling up the path, falling to her hands and knees, wanting only to get away.

She did not go back to the house, afraid that Serafina would be there. Instead she walked away from it, along the shelf, toward the mouth of the canyon, where she could see out over the desert. Out there, beyond the blue rise of mountains, lay the cities, the endless shuffling nothingness of the 'burbs, and the towers with their Mrs. Wosenkos. Jewel sat on a gray boulder that jutted out over the rim of the shelf, squinting against the orange flare of the setting sun. Where did reality end and illusion begin? She flexed her hand, remembering the feel of the wind nudging her palm, the sense of power.

Remembering. She balled her hand into a fist, nails digging into her palm. Yes, remembering. That memory was as real now as her memories of Linda's mattress and her mother's drug dreams. No. Not her mother—Elaine. The wind brushed hair back from her face, and Jewel imagined that it touched her with a questing curiosity. Or was it recognition?

If her mind was filled with another's memories, who would she be?

The sun had sunk behind the horizon, leaving a chaos of orange and pink, streaked with the bruise purple of high clouds that never brought rain. It struck Jewel suddenly that this was a virtual—that she had wandered in here somehow and had forgotten. She leaned out over the stony rim, looking down the rocky slope. Illusion or reality? One step and she would know. There was a heady lure in the thought of falling without control, drifting swiftly downward to a dark place where nothing mattered. If this was a virtual, she could leap from this ledge and float, or fly, or whatever the designer had programmed in.

"Jewel!" It was David's voice close behind her, harsh and startling in the quiet. "Wait!" The scrape of feet sliding in rock, the shock of his weight as he grabbed her arm with both hands. It hurt.

"Stop it." She twisted free, angry, her anger dying suddenly as she understood. "I wasn't going to jump," she said, and didn't laugh, because for a moment she had been tempted.

"Good." His smile didn't make it to his eyes. "I was worried about you."

"You're really seeing again." She watched his eyes track her face. "David, I'm so glad."

"I am, too. Very glad." His eyes narrowed. "What happened to your arm?"

Jewel winced as he seized her left wrist, gently this time. A thin line of blood curved down her forearm, precise as the mark of a pen. The shallow slice might have been left by a scalpel blade. "It's a cat scratch." She swallowed a hysterical giggle. "A mountain lion did it."

"Tell me," he said softly. "About Serafina."

"I'm . . . her clone." Jewel swallowed. "It's illegal, but you can do it—recombine a dividing gamete, stimulate it to divide and grow like a fertilized egg. The daughter's genes are identical to the mother's."

David said nothing, but his eyes never left her face.

"She turned into a mountain lion right in front of me. She made me . . . remember. Her childhood, I think. And while I was remembering, I was *her*. David, she's *old*. I don't know how old; I don't know what she *is*. If she . . . gives me her memories, I'll drown. I'll be lost, do you understand? She'll be here instead of me." The words tumbled out in a rush, and she kept her eyes on his face, waiting for skepticism, for laughter, for the comforting sanity that would make her realize that it had all been pretend, a real-world virtual that could somehow be explained if you only knew the hidden tech behind the illusion. "I'll be her," she whispered. "That's what she wants." Immortality. "Goddamn it, this is *stupid*." She slammed her fist down on a rock, the shock of impact rushing up her arm, turning into pain. "Stop looking like you believe me," she said in a shaky voice.

"You believe it," he said softly.

"No, I don't. My God, I can't believe I'm really saying this." The dying embers of the sunset stained her skin with ruddy light. "I remembered how the wind is alive and now—" She steadied her voice with an effort. "Now I feel it, too." The night wind nudged her gently, and she shivered, clasping her arms around herself. "What's happening to me, David? Have you got any idea? No. Never mind." She stepped closer, laying her fingers lightly on his lips. "You can't have any idea, because this is all crazy. So just don't say anything, okay?" Sunset had softened into twilight, and Jewel imagined the slink of a prowling lion in the shadows. She put her arms around him, suddenly needing his physical warmth.

He held her tightly, his flesh full of comfort. ''You're not crazy,'' he said softly.

Which meant what? That what she had experienced had actually happened? Cold comfort. The desert frightened her. It was too big, too full of possibilities. Jewel shut it out, focusing on the warmth of his body. She breathed the musky scent of his skin, welcoming the sudden rush of desire that tightened her muscles. He was surprised; she felt it in his brief hesitation. But then his arms tightened around her, and when she lifted her head, he opened his mouth to hers.

His fingers explored, working slowly, sensuously down her back, evoking quick, hot ripples of pleasure that dimmed the shadows and drove back the night. He was not hesitant anymore. She arched against him, pressing her body against the quick beat of his heart and the hard bulge of his erection, her eyes closed, hiding in this sweetness. He drew back a little, cupping her face between his palms, his eyes glittering as he looked into her face. He smiled, and there was a trace of sadness in it, but he said nothing. Instead, he stripped his sweat-stained tunic off over his head and reached for her.

His net glittered in the fading light, spreading like silver lace across his shoulders and chest, vanishing into the dark curl of his pubic hair as he finished stripping out of his clothes. Jewel tossed her own onto the pile of tumbled fabric and reached for him, closing her hand around the thrust of his erection. He sucked in his breath with a soft hiss, then scooped her into his arms. For a moment he held her, muscles tight with strain, his face a stark profile against purple twilight. Then he set her gently down and kissed her.

They made love on their tumbled clothes. The subtle gleam of David's silvered skin above her and the shared rhythm of their movements protected her, drove back the ghosts and the desert. There was no rush. Time had stopped, past and future were held at bay by this moment of pleasure and skin and sweat, and she didn't want it to end. Slowly, however, their rhythm quickened. David breathed harshly, in quick shallow breaths, and she locked her legs about his narrow hips, gasping as she came, lifting him as she arched her back, night blurring away for a moment into an endless sweet now.

Afterward they lay entwined, sweat drying in the cooling wind, watching satellites fall like slow-motion meteors across the starry sky. Erebus sky. The stars didn't shine like that for the cities. He had taken off the bandage, and the surgery scar on his scalp had healed to a thin line. ''I'm so glad you got your sight back.'' Jewel traced it lightly. "I felt like it was my fault, your blindness. If I had just walked away, not gotten involved, maybe it wouldn't have happened."

"It would have happened. One way or another." David half rose on his elbow so that he could look down into her face. "Are you okay?" He brushed her hair gently back from her face. "She scared you."

"Yes." Jewel moved restlessly, not wanting to talk about it. "I was being silly." She laughed, a light, breathy note. "You know, this woman's been playing witch queen to these nomads for God knows how long. She's got the routine down pat, and all the electronic aids she needs to pull it off. Out here you forget about tricks like holos. Everything seems so immediate. So real." She covered her eyes with her forearm. "Susana would have seen through it in a minute."

"Would she?" David pulled her arm gently away, his face close to hers, sober, not smiling. "Tell me that it wasn't true," he said softly. "Look at me and tell me that you were making it up, that it was a hallucination or a trick."

She could not. Jewel tried to roll away, but he was leaning across her, pinning her to the ground. "Tell me if it was real or not, Jewel." His eyes were full of shadow. "Tell me right now."

"I'm . . . not sure." She stopped trying to push him off and lay still. "All right. It was real. It was real, and I don't know what's happening, okay? Are you happy now? How come you've got this need to know? You don't pry." She meant the words to sting. "Flander does that."

"You're right." His expression was unreadable in the darkness. "I don't pry. I stand back and tell myself I have no right to interfere with anyone's life. That nice, safe distance lost me Flander and maybe lost Flander to himself. He was begging me to save him, and I probably couldn't have, but I didn't even try. I wanted you to say it out loud so we'd both know what was going on. So we could face it."

We. Jewel looked down at the tunic wadded in her hands, a faint hope stirring in her chest. Let David share this load. Let him help. The wind touched her face gently, and she shuddered, because it was a caress.

"Don't do it." David twined his fingers in hers. "Don't shut everyone out, Jewel. You don't have to do this alone."

But she did. It was she and Serafina, and no one could help. Her throat clogged with an unexpected lump.

David sighed. "All right." He squeezed her hand gently, then reached for his clothes. "I guess we'd better get back."

Jewel suppressed a pang of regret as she dressed. But what could he do? Overhead, the Milky Way was a white sweep of nebulous light across the arch of the sky. Hand in hand, they picked their way back through the sage, stumbling on the rocks, listening to the soft breathing of the desert. And the wind caressed her, touching her as David had touched her, ruffling her hair. This was hers to deal with. She withdrew her hand, afraid of the wind's touch, afraid of herself. Of what she was or might be. The house was just ahead, its windows glowing with yellow light, bright beacons in the endless darkness.

"I think I've found us a way out of this mess," David said softly. "Salgado's behind it. Harmon's big enough to get this guy off our backs, and I think he'll do it for me. So we'll be all right."

So Salgado *was* the one. Sam had said as much. Something nagged at her, something else he had said, but she couldn't dredge it up.

"Jewel?" David faced her, his eyes full of darkness in the shadow-streaked light from the windows. "I'm part of this, too, even if you think I belong on the sidelines. Keep that in mind, okay? Besides, I need to keep track of Susana." He gave her a crooked smile. "The kid has a lot of talent."

He was telling her something, but she wasn't quite sure what. She almost asked him, but then the door crashed open, flooding them with light. Jewel's heart jumped in her chest.

"Where the hell have you been?" Susana glared, one hip cocked against the door frame. "Fucking in the bushes? Next time, tell me, okay? I thought all three of you fell off the damn cliff."

Jewel flushed, unable to stop herself. But for all the angry tone, Susana had been scared. It showed, even to her. "I'm sorry," she said, and meant it. "I thought Serafina was here."

"Well, she isn't." Susana glowered at the darkness, then retreated into the house. "And I'm starving. Where do we look for food around here, and what the hell happened to your arm, Jewel?"

Chapter Nineteen

Jewel woke to darkness, pain in her arm, and a thin, distant howling. Dog? Coyote? She tried to remember if coyotes still lived in the desert. Her arm throbbed with the beat of her pulse. She touched it and winced, a little frightened by the puffy heat of the long scratch. She had found a tube of antibiotic ointment in a cupboard, but cat scratches could be ugly. What about the scratch of a lion woman? Jewel sat up, goose bumps rising on her skin in the nighttime chill.

David was asleep beside her, one arm sprawled across the edge of her sleeping bag, as if he had had his arm around her. His face looked pale in the moonlight that seeped through the open windows. He had said "we," had offered to share this burden. She reached to touch him but drew her hand back. She carried Serafina's genes, and the wind nudged at her, questing and alive. She had seen a terrible hunger in those lion eyes yesterday. Hunger for immortality.

For her soul.

He couldn't help her. No one could. Jewel touched his face lightly, then slid out of the bag and pulled on her tights. A few feet away, curled against the wall, Susana snored softly. Jewel leaned over her, hesitating, reaching out to wake her. But then David would wake, and he wouldn't want her to go, and Serafina might hear. Another abandonment? Jewel clenched her teeth and yanked her hand away. "No," she breathed. "I'll find you when it's safe. I promise. I'm sorry."

Thin words, empty and hollow as dried-out weed stems, they mocked her. *You'll never stop running away,* a voice whispered in her head. Linda's voice? David's? Jewel shook her head. No, no, she told herself. David would tap Alcourt to save him, and he would take care of Susana. Jewel would catch up with them as soon as she was out of Serafina's reach.

Sure.

It occurred to Jewel as she fumbled for the pack that held her skins and her clothes that he had said just that outside the door the previous night. Because he had guessed she might run.

David's eyelids fluttered, and he stirred, murmuring Flander's name in his sleep. Shouldering her pack, Jewel tiptoed across the floor. The curtain hung like a wall in front of her, and she hesitated. Was Serafina on the other side? She imagined her waiting in the darkness, eyes shining with yellow fire. The rings clacked softly as she drew the curtain aside. Darkness and silence mocked her. Maybe Serafina spent the night prowling the desert, chasing deer or whatever a mountain lion would find to chase out there. Maybe she was still down in the herders' caravan.

That made her pause, but there was nowhere else to go. Not without the car. Jewel crossed the room, her muscles tensed enough to hurt, expecting every second to hear Serafina's soft laughter in her head. The door creaked as she pushed it open, scraping loudly across the floor. Jewel cringed and left it open. An owl hooted somewhere, and the wind touched her neck.

Jewel ran, holding her scratched arm stiffly, her pack banging her shoulder. The waxing moon hung low in the sky, and a faint hint of gray showed in the east. Almost morning. She reached the lip of the shelf and searched for the path Cheri had taken, panicking briefly because everything looked so different in the darkness. She found it finally and scrambled downward in a shower of pebbles and stones, discovering too late to slow down that it was steep.

She was sliding, scrambling, making enough noise to wake everyone in the caravan, barely able to stay on her feet, losing it; her momentum was pulling her forward to that critical moment when her center of gravity would be too far ahead of her feet and she would fall . . . Abruptly, the slope leveled out. Jewel ran three long, jarring, out-of-control strides, the impact jolting her teeth together, and then, blessedly, she got her balance and was able to stop. Dusty, gasping for breath, she dropped her pack. The wind brushed her hair gently back from her sweaty face.

"I know you." A shadow rose from the sage. "I met you on the ledge yesterday."

"Cheri?" Jewel stiffened as she focused on the rifle in the woman's hands. It didn't quite point at her, but it didn't point away, either.

" 'S me. I went to sleep early, so I took the last shift on watch.

You're lucky.'' Her teeth shone briefly. ''You would've gotten a different hello if you'd come charging down on Ellie's head.'' She looked over her shoulder suddenly. ''It's okay,'' she called. ''She's a friend of the healer's.'' She turned back to Jewel, frowning a little this time. ''So what're you doing here? We're just on our way down the road.''

Jewel looked beyond her and saw that people were moving around in the caravan. A camper door slammed, and someone laughed. Goats bleated in the distance, and the wind brought her the sound of bells. ''I'm glad I caught you.'' Jewel was getting her breath back slowly. ''I came to ask if . . . I could go with you. As far as the next town.''

''That's Ryo.'' Cheri frowned, her expression dubious in the growing light. ''It's only two days away, but it's not much of a town. Mostly it's a big vat-sage plantation. They tapped into some good water.'' She shrugged. ''You might be able to hitch a ride with someone if they're going into town for supplies or something. I'll have to ask Rink.'' She eyed Jewel's pack. ''You can't have much water with you, and we're awfully short.''

''Can you get some more in Ryo?'' Jewel glanced up at the rim of the shelf. The gray dawn light was growing, and she felt a gnawing urgency, as if Serafina might appear any second and order Cheri to send her back. Which was stupid. She was no prisoner of Serafina, but she couldn't shake the feeling that she was a fugitive. This was what her m—Elaine had lived with. Jewel shivered. ''I can pay,'' she said quickly.

''That should suit Rink.'' Cheri's smile lighted her face like a shaft of sunlight. ''You can ride with me. I drive the water truck, though I'd rather be out herding.''

In the growing light Jewel could see how thin Cheri was—fragile, as if the cancer were eating the flesh from her bones. ''Thank you,'' she said. ''I appreciate it.''

''You don't leave people behind out here.'' She pulled a strapless wristwatch out of her pocket. ''My shift's just over. Let's go find Rink.'' She cocked her head as she led Jewel toward the parked trucks. ''Are you . . . related to the healer?'' she asked hesitantly.

''Yes.'' Jewel looked away. ''Can we talk to Rink?''

Cheri gave her a sharp look, then put a hand gently on Jewel's arm. ''He's over there. And then we'd better put some stuff on your arm.'' She nodded. ''You got a really nasty cut.''

''She's gone.'' Susana prowled across the room, shrinking it with her restlessness. ''She just got up and fucking walked away.

Serve her right if she dies of thirst out there. She doesn't give a shit about anybody but herself, you know that?'' She spun to face David, arms crossed beneath her small breasts, hands tucked into her armpits. ''Nobody does, if you get right down to it, you know? You watch your own ass, carve your own slice out of this shitty world, and to hell with everyone else.''

''That's true for a lot of people.'' David leaned his elbows on the table, stifling a sigh. This kid wore anger like a set of skins, but the hurt showed through anyway, raw and red like a bloody wound. What had Jewel meant to her? Something major. He wondered if Jewel knew or if she had only picked up on the anger. ''Jewel's scared.'' David watched Susana fill a glass from the water crock and drain it in quick, angry swallows. ''She's running from something, Susana. She didn't just walk away.''

''Yeah, sure. You think Serafina's really her mom?'' Susana shot David a quick sideways look. ''I heard different, but jeeze, she looks like her.''

''I'm . . . not sure what's between them.'' He had offered help the previous night, had thought it might make a difference. It had not. He traced the grain of the battered wooden tabletop. She had told him a story of magic and cloning. She had believed it. What was real? He pushed his chair back. Sometimes it was damned hard to tell. ''I'm going to go see if Harmon will talk to me.''

''You don't need me, do you?'' Susana threw herself onto the sofa. ''You can get in okay, right?''

''I'm fine unless Serafina locked the access. Susana, Jewel didn't want to leave you behind,'' David said gently.

''Hey, it's cool.'' Susana didn't look at him. ''I could give a shit. So you can drop the bedside manner, okay?''

''Yeah. Okay.'' He touched her shoulder lightly. ''I'll yell if Serafina's yellow brick road loses me. It doesn't take much of a lock to stop me.''

''No prob.'' She didn't smile. ''I'll help you out.''

Ah, Jewel, what did you do here? David sighed as he pulled on lenses in Serafina's chamber, less than certain about his call to Alcourt. There was no guarantee that he could even get through. Alcourt's space was well defended, and just because he had had access before, that didn't mean he still had it. ''Access,'' he said. ''David Chen, studio.''

But instead of his studio, the ice cave materialized around him. Someone had left the file open. David opened his mouth to call Flander's name, but the word died in his throat. An enormous eye bulged from the ice: brown iris, pierced with a black pupil larger than he was tall. Reddish fur surrounded it, fading into the blue-white wall of ice. A fox's eye. Fox paws were scattered across the floor like the prints of a prowling fox, only these were *paws*. Embedded in the ice, they had been sliced neatly off at the top of the foot to show red flesh rimmed with blood-stiff hair and neat white bone. Strips and scraps of fox hide stuck to the walls of the cave, as if a pelt had been blown up like a balloon until it had exploded into a thousand bits. A foxtail wagged solemnly from a stalactite of clear ice. Vertebrae ran through the column like a spine, and white fox teeth sprouted from the ceiling, making it the arch of an enormous pale mouth.

David pivoted slowly, taking it in, his stomach contracting. "Flander?" It came out a whisper, his throat thick with horror. No answer. He had expected none. "Exit, studio," he said hoarsely.

The familiar walls appeared around him. David let his breath out in a gasp, sweating, feeling as if he were going to vomit. Flander had created those images, just as he had created the dead fox carcass beneath the chimera's hooves. Visual metaphor was Flander's primary language. They both used it, overlaying words like a melodic line above the complex harmony of the visual messages. What David had just witnessed felt insane. Oh, God. David prowled his studio space, searching for any message from Flander. Nothing. No message, no trace that he had been there at all.

The message was in the cave. He bowed his head, grief a weight in his heart, dragging at him. He didn't want to read it, couldn't help but read it. "Studio," he said harshly. "Access Harmon Alcourt, private and personal." Time to end this craziness. Maybe there would be something left to salvage.

Yeah, sure.

"Attempting access," his studio announced.

David ran through the other inside web nodes he knew. There were several, but none of them wielded the power that Alcourt did. Still, they could perhaps do something.

"David?" Alcourt's voice boomed too loud in the studio. "Come in, come in."

An archway opened in the studio wall—the entrance to Alcourt's foyer. David stepped quickly through, into the fountain court he had designed. Had it been only a few months ago? It felt like years.

"David?" Alcourt was waiting for him, sitting on the stone bench David had put beside the pool. He stood, holding out his hand. "How are you? I heard that you'd had an . . . accident, but when I tried to reach you, the hospital said you'd checked out with no forwarding address."

"I seem to be fine now." He clasped Alcourt's hand, his net giving him dry, warm flesh and firm pressure from Alcourt's fingers. "Thanks for calling. I know how busy you are."

"Yes, yes." Alcourt fanned the air as if waving away gnats. "This is all small talk, and since I'm busy, why don't you tell me why you're here? What can I do for you, David?"

Harmon Alcourt's Self always jarred him a little, even though he had originally created it. Although he had designed the package to shade heavily for ruthless and aggressive body language, the virtual Alcourt went beyond the edit manager. He kept that ruthless side hidden, in the flesh. David cleared his throat. "I don't know what you heard, but my accident was a bad beating."

"Police report called it a mugging."

David shrugged. "I didn't have a chance to correct it. The fact is, a local politico with ambitions is trying to murder Flander, and he's probably going to kill me in the process." He nodded slowly, reading excited anticipation behind Alcourt's outward reserve. Yeah, Alcourt had just figured out where this conversation was going and was already calculating the price. David swallowed a sigh. "I need help, Harmon. I need someone with your kind of clout to get this bastard off me."

"Flander is a punk." Alcourt picked a pale rose from a twining climber. "I'd dump him." He began pulling petals from the rose, tossing them one by one into the pool. "He's more trouble than he could possibly be worth."

"Maybe." David shrugged, shading his body language to suggest he was truly considering Alcourt's advice, shutting out memory of the cave. "I've still got my back to the wall even if I do."

"Who is this politico?"

"A Seattle hotshot named Salgado. He's associated with Epyxx, from what I've heard." David drew a deep breath. "He's running a scam in the web, using a created PanEuro identity, a midlevel node named Anya Vanek. The Self is good enough to get by Security. Who knows?" David shrugged, projecting casual certainty. "He may be running another fake in AllThings."

"That good? You're kidding. No, I know you, David. I know you have your facts straight." Alcourt tossed the tattered rose into the water, then paced across the court with his hands clasped behind his back. "Let me guess who created the Selfs. No, don't say anything. That punk of yours is good, I'll give him that." Alcourt spun to face David. "So you want me to get Salgado off your back, right? And I'd guess that you want me to keep Flander out of this if I blow the scam?"

"Yes." David met his eyes. "I'm not asking you to do this for free."

"I didn't think you were." Alcourt showed his teeth briefly.

"Knowlege of that scam is going to be valuable in the web," David went on doggedly. "I know *you* too well to think that you won't use it, so we'll subtract that from the price."

"Of course." Alcourt was matter-of-fact. "I'll make sure this Salgado leaves you alone, and I'll do my best to conceal Flander's role in this web scam. In return, I get an unlimited call on your talents for one year, starting today. Do we have a deal?"

It was what he wanted and the price was less than he had expected, but David hesitated. Something was bothering him, some nuance of Alcourt's body language or tone. David groped for the source of his uneasiness, but it eluded him. Alcourt was waiting, and Alcourt did not wait patiently. David had no trouble reading that. "I agree." David nodded. "Thank you," he said with sincerity.

"You're welcome." Alcourt's eyes flickered slightly, as if he were reading a display that David couldn't see. "Where are you?" he asked abruptly. "You're not at your Vashon address."

"No." David hesitated. He hadn't foreseen this particular question. "Our host requested that I not give away the address here." He frowned. "It's very safe, Harmon."

"I'm sure." Again that infinitesimal flicker.

David stifled an urge to look behind him; there wouldn't be anything there. Alcourt's office would be displaying it for his eyes only.

"If you want me to eliminate your problem, I have to know where you are." Alcourt was frowning now. "You'll have to trust me on my methods, since I'm not about to discuss them with you on this TinkerToy access you're using. I guarantee you I can match the security any Net rat can give you."

He intended to use David as bait. David's stomach clenched. That would be almost as bad as sitting blind and helpless in the hospital, waiting for someone to kill him.

"David? You follow my orders or I don't touch this." Alcourt's voice cracked like a whip. "I know what I'm doing, but I have to be able to do it."

Anger and absolute confidence on the surface, but underneath was Alcourt anxious? David rubbed his face, pushing at the lenses, which didn't quite fit and were starting to bother him. Maybe he was, and maybe it didn't have anything to do with this. Again, what choice? "We can meet you," he said, trying to remember the map tacked to the wall in the storeroom. "There's a town in southeast

Oregon. Ryo. We'll be there in two days.'' If they couldn't get the
car out, they could hike that far. It occurred to David that Jewel
might have headed for Ryo. Maybe they could catch up with her.

"Ryo?'' Alcourt wandered over to the stone basin and stared
down into the still pool. "I suppose that will do for now. I may
send you elsewhere, depending on what I put together. Use your
own name so my people can find you.'' He plucked another rose
from the climber and began to strip the petals again. "I'll take it
from there. 'We,' you said? Flander's with you?''

"I've got Susana Walsh-Reyna with me,'' David said stiffly.
"Jewel Martina's niece.''

"I see.'' Alcourt gave him a sharp glance. "You finally lost the
guy?''

"I don't know.'' The conversation had assumed an uneasy, on-
hold feeling, as if they were both waiting for something to happen.

Alcourt grunted suddenly and stripped the last petals from the
rose. "I'd better make my arrangements.'' He tilted his palm, scattering the petals evenly across the surface of the pool. "I'm tired
of this foyer. You can design me something a little more dynamic.
Someone will contact you in Ryo.'' He turned his back on David
and disappeared through his office door.

Dismissed. David frowned down at the bruised petals drifting
gently on the surface of the pool. Alcourt had agreed to save his
ass. Why did David feel so ambivalent? He tugged at the ill-fitting
lenses, squinting as the foyer warped and distorted. "Exit.'' He
pulled them off as the walls of Serafina's chamber took shape around
him.

"The next time you tell someone I'm her fucking niece, I'm
going to kick you right in the nuts.'' Susana leaned against the door
frame, glowering. "So what's doing? I take it this Alcourt dude
said he'd squash Salgado? I hope he does it slow and ugly.'' She
showed her teeth briefly. "Is this Ryo a city? God, I hope so. I'm
so *sick* of all this empty space. How come we're going there, anyway?''

"It's probably a gas station and a bar.'' David tossed the lenses
onto their shelf and sighed, deciding to ignore her earlier questions
for the moment. "We're going there so I can be bait.''

"Oh, great.'' Susana grimaced. "You trust this guy that much,
huh? Not me, baby.''

"I'm a little short on alternative options. If you've got a better
idea, I'd sure like to hear it.''

"Hey, don't get pissed at *me*. You're the dude who said yes.''
She shrugged. "It just seems a little iffy. I mean, I'd like to hang

out in that awesome space piece of yours. I can't do it if you're dead.''

That was one hell of a backhanded compliment. David's lips twitched. ''I'll do my best to stay alive.''

''Good. She's back, by the way.'' Susana either missed his ironic tone or chose to ignore it. ''Cat woman. I didn't tell her Jewel split.''

''I'll tell her.'' David eyed Susana. ''So what do you think? Is our mountain lion a holo or some kind of ghost?''

''It wasn't any holo in the house.'' Susana shrugged. ''You tell me.''

She sounded as if she believed it and accepted it without qualm. David brushed past her, surprised and a little thoughtful. This was another kid who had escaped into the Net. Maybe it was easier to believe in ghosts and spirits when you spent most of your life in the unreality of virtual. Maybe the boundaries between real and unreal began to blur after a while. And maybe Susana was just pulling his chain. She was sharp enough to do it.

Serafina was in the kitchen end of the room, stirring something in a ceramic pot on the cooktop. She didn't look up as he approached, but her body language acknowledged him. ''If you're coming to tell me that Jewel took off, I already know.'' Her voice was without emotion. ''I doubt she'll return.''

David leaned a hip against the counter so he could look directly into her face. ''Are you her mother? Why is she so afraid of you?''

Serafina shrugged. ''She has reason.'' She took a jar of cracked grain from the shelf and measured a handful into the simmering pot. ''And, no, I'm not her mother, artist. As she told you.''

''She said she was . . . your clone.'' David narrowed his eyes, trying to read that weathered, folded face. It was like trying to read emotion on the face of the desert. ''She said you possessed her.''

Serafina stirred the pot. ''This is your business?''

''Yes.'' David's lips tightened. ''Jewel's my friend.''

''Is she?'' Serafina looked at him at last, her dark eyes as flat and opaque as desert stones. ''You don't believe what she told you. Oh, yes, I know you that well. So I see no reason to answer you.''

David gave up. ''Is there any way we can haul the car out of that ditch? Weren't the goatherders going to do it?''

''They left.'' Serafina's eyes narrowed. ''Why do you want the car?''

''We need to get to Ryo, Susana and I.'' David wanted to squirm beneath that impassive stare, suddenly unsure of his arrangement with Alcourt, hearing Susana's sour doubts all too clearly. ''We're meeting some of Alcourt's people in Ryo. He's going to lean on Salgado.''

''You told Harmon Alcourt you were here?''

''No.'' David flushed at her icy tone. ''I didn't mention your name, and your security didn't edit me.''

''He'll know.'' Serafina stared past him, frowning at some vision in the air. ''You are so *innocent*. Innocence is dangerous, artist. It's willful blindness, and you should know how limiting it is to be blind. Harmon Alcourt knew you were coming in on my access. He knows my signature, oh, yes.'' Her teeth showed briefly. ''And now he knows that I live within a short distance of Ryo. I'm going to have to move, and it's your fault. I could be very angry with you for this.'' Her eyes flared briefly, then she sighed and lowered her head. ''Too late now. I'll let it go because you're important to my daughter. Get your things together and I'll show you the road to Ryo. And don't apologize to me, artist. I don't want to hear it.''

David bowed silently and left, chastened and angry, remembering the indelible tracks in his cave. He did not want this woman for an enemy. Had it been a willful blindness? He should have guessed that she had pirated Alcourt; Flander could have told him. An image of the cave intruded, and David detoured into the virtual closet, pulling on his lenses to enter his studio. The cat leapt down from its radiator, then yowled its outrage as he brushed it aside. No message, no sign that Flander had been there since his last visit. There was no time for more searching. He exited, worry a growing weight in his chest.

Susana was in the bedroom, closing up her pack, getting ready to leave. The room had a forlorn air, as if it had already been abandoned. David touched one of the blankets that covered the walls, noticing the uneven texture of warp and woof. Hand-spun and handwoven? Primitive crafts brought big money in the city galleries. He wondered if Serafina would take them with her. Whatever lay between Jewel and Serafina, he had given her a bitter return for her hospitality.

''Are we leaving?'' Susana slung her pack onto the bed. ''Is she gonna get us a truck so we can get the car out?''

''We're going to walk.''

''Walk—you got to be kidding.'' Susana planted her fists on her hips. ''Jeeze, man, you can see forever, and there's nothing there. You're talking *miles*.''

''So stay here.'' David squatted to roll up his sleeping bag, tired of her attitude. ''Your choice.''

''Yeah, sure,'' she said in a more subdued tone. ''So, okay, we get to do healthy exercise. Look, I'm sorry if I'm a bitch.'' She avoided his eyes. ''I'm just like that, I guess. I don't mean anything by it, okay?''

''Okay.'' David managed to keep his surprise out of his voice. She was rolling up her bag clumsily but doing it herself. He wondered if she would ever let anyone get far enough past her guard to touch her. Maybe not. She reminded him a lot of Flander that way. David sighed and began to stack the rolled bags against the wall.

They had to wait out the midday sun before Serafina would let them leave. It was a silent and uncomfortable few hours. Serafina withdrew into herself, curled catlike in a chair, her tension showing only in the restless flick of one foot. Like a cat's tail, David thought. He could imagine her a mountain lion prowling the desert hillsides. He almost asked her if she could change into a lioness. But in the end he did not; the words sounded too silly to throw in her face when he had cost her her peace and security. Susana acted out her restlessness, pacing the room, sitting on every piece of furniture in the house, until David was about ready to take a chance on the sun.

He was nervous, too. Bait was not a role he was looking forward to. And something still bothered him about his interview with Alcourt. The harder he tried to pin it down, though, the more elusive it became. He checked into his studio once more. Nothing from Flander. So what? he told himself. The ice cave could be a tantrum and nothing more. Flander came and went at unpredictable intervals. *You want his blood, too, or what?* Susana's hard, angry words came back to him like a slap in the face. *Maybe you'll get it.*

Maybe he had. David tried to put that fear aside. Unsuccessfully.

Sometime in the late afternoon Serafina decided that they could hike without getting sunstroke. ''There is a shortcut,'' she told them as she handed them each two plastic jugs of water. ''It is an old RV track. It will save you several miles of walking, and if someone is looking for you on the main roads, they will be less likely to find you. I will go that far with you, and then you are on your own.''

The goat, tethered in the shade of a scrubby juniper, bleated as they approached. ''All right, little one.'' Serafina scratched between its horns, then unbuckled its collar. ''You can go eat where you will today. I filled the water bucket beside the door.''

The goat followed them a short way down the track, ears pricked. It finally stopped, calling after them for a while, a forlorn figure against the dun hillside. It occurred suddenly to David that Serafina was not coming back here—that she was taking only what was in her pack, on her way to search out a new hiding place for her vulnerable flesh. Security was that precarious for a pirate. He hadn't understood.

He felt like shit.

The sun seemed frozen above the western horizon, and the dust hung in the still air like a trail as they trudged along. Sweat trickled down David's face and stuck his shirt to his back. It was easy walking except for the heat; the main road was unpaved but relatively smooth. Susana stayed close to David, her head down, scowling at the ground as if it might be laced with invisible booby traps. Serafina walked with lithe grace, her head lifted as if she were sniffing the air.

Like a mountain lion.

She halted finally. The faintest trace of wheel tracks left the main road and vanished into the sage. The sun hovered above the horizon, streaking the land with rich yellow light and stark shadow. "This is the shortcut." She pointed. "It takes you through that notch. Stay on it, and it'll bring you back to the main road about three miles this side of Ryo."

"Thank you." David faced her. "I'm sorry. I didn't know what I was costing you when I accessed Alcourt."

"I told you." Her expression didn't change. "I don't want your apology."

"You get it, anyway." He met her opaque stare. "I owe you a large debt. It won't go away."

Serafina's eyes flickered. "Who can say how the future will turn out?" She inclined her head in the barest of nods. "I'll remember your debt." She turned away suddenly as the sound of an engine broke the quiet.

A chopper? David shaded his eyes as a helicopter swung into view around the jutting shoulder of the low hill to the south of them. It was following the road, running low and fast.

Serafina hissed softly through her teeth.

"Yo." Susana shaded her eyes, hopeful. "Hey, it's coming down. Friends of yours? I could sure use a ride."

"Maybe we'd better run?" David asked, his eyes on Serafina's face.

"The sage farmers hunt coyotes from the air." Serafina watched the chopper descend, her face unreadable. "They use high-powered rifles, and very few animals escape once they've been sighted. I am no coyote." She slid her pack from her shoulders and straightened slightly. "No, kitten. They're not *my* friends."

"What the fuck does *that* mean?" Susana shouted over the thunder of the blades as the copter settled into the sage. "So what's going on?'' She stepped nervously sideways, dumping her pack onto the ground.

"We're about to find out.'' David lifted an arm to shield his face from the blast of wind that whipped the sage and filled the air with grit. Cold crawled in his gut. This could be Alcourt's pickup. Or not. The machine was big enough to carry cargo and was painted in desert-camo splotches. Smugglers? David took an involuntary step backward as doors popped open on both sides. Two men swung down, dressed casually in scuffed jeans and faded tees.

"Yo.'' The taller of the two men, gray-haired and weather-beaten, ducked casually beneath the slow swing of the rotors. "I'm supposed to pick up a David Chen.'' His eyes traveled deliberately from David to Susana to Serafina and back to David again. "You him?'' He addressed David as if the other two had evaporated.

"Maybe.'' David took a step forward. Behind him Susana was hunched and tense, ready to bolt. Serafina stood still and tall, hands at her sides. Her earlier tension had vanished, and her expression was almost dreamy, as if she were listening to music. "Who sent you?'' David asked the man harshly.

"We got a contract.'' The gray-haired man shrugged. "I'm supposed to tell you that Harmon said it's okay.'' He spit. "That make it better?''

Alcourt's pickup? Two days early? Maybe something had come up. But why hadn't he found a message in his studio? David's earlier sense of wrongness intensified, tightening the skin at the back of his neck. The other man, a blond muscle junkie with a twenty-year-old face, was opening the cargo hatch.

"Let's go.'' The gray-haired man jerked his head at the door. "We got a schedule. Load up.''

Wrong. This felt *wrong*.

"Well, all right, great.'' Susana relaxed suddenly and grabbed her pack. "C'mon, man, it's our ride, right?'' She took one long step toward the helicopter and froze.

The blond man had turned around, the squat ugly shape of an Uzi in his hands. He lifted it smoothly, his face creased in concentration as he fired. The Uzi stuttered briefly, bucking in his hands, the noise incredibly, shockingly loud. Serafina spun backward with a cry, and then the blond man was turning, his eyes tracking Susana, not angry, not excited, just making sure of his aim.

They wanted David. Period. The muzzle of the Uzi was slowing, centering on Susana's chest. David flung himself forward, his arms going around Susana as he slammed into her. She gave a cry, rigid, fighting him as they staggered backward together. David struggled to keep his footing as the sage stems snagged his ankles, afraid that they'd fall and break apart and the gunner would get a clear shot. "Hold *still*!" he hissed in her ear. Catching his balance at last, he clutched her like a lover, half-turned so that neither of the two men could get a clear shot at her.

The gray-haired man grunted, obviously annoyed. He started warily forward, staying out of his partner's line of fire, watching for a weapon.

"Hold it." Think fast, damn it. "Right now." He put authority into his voice, the certainty that they would not dare disobey him. To his relief, the smuggler hesitated. "You better check with your boss, and do it fast," he snapped. "If you kill her, I don't cooperate, and that's what he's buying. My cooperation. If he doesn't get it, he's going to blame you. So check. Now!"

For a moment it all hung in the balance. David doubted that his cooperation meant much to whoever was behind this—and if these guys knew it, Susana was dead. He was gambling that they were what they had said they were—contract labor—and didn't know enough to make judgment calls. That might buy some time if they were the cautious sort. Maybe. The blond man had his eyes on the older one, waiting for a cue.

The older man scowled, weighing his options, his posture mirroring his brief indecision. "She goes." He jerked his head. "Like I said, we got a schedule."

Safe. For now. David's knees wanted to buckle. "Come on." He tugged at Susana's rigid body, his arms still around her, still shielding her as they moved awkwardly toward the cargo hatch. The older smuggler stepped back as they sidled past him. There was nothing to do but get in.

"Watch out!" Susana jerked sideways.

He tried to dodge, tried to turn, but light exploded suddenly in his skull, bursting into a shocking blossom of crimson pain. For a stunned instant he disconnected, and then he was on his knees in the dust, blinking at dead sage twigs and brown pebbles beneath his palms. His muscles tensed, waiting for the racket of the Uzi, knowing that he had lost, that he had blown it. Jean-clad legs moved into his field of vision and David raised his head, wincing as a lightning bolt of pain speared his brain. The gray-haired man looked down at him, holding the big handgun he had just hit him with, making sure David saw it. "That was for causing me trouble," he said without heat, and looked past David.

The blond man was walking back to the copter from where Serafina had fallen, the Uzi still in his hands. He nodded.

Serafina was dead. David's fault. Remorse stabbed him as Susana crouched in the dust.

"You okay?"

"I think so." He got to his feet, momentarily dizzy and glad for her steadying hands. It scared him to have gotten hit on the head again, and he fixed his eyes on a clump of sage, a part of him terrified that it would suddenly vanish into darkness. Warmth tickled the side of his face. Blood?

The gray-haired smuggler twisted David's arms behind him, slapped cable cuffs around his wrists, and locked him tight. Susana yanked her arm free as he grabbed her and spit at him. He backhanded her across the face, grabbed her wrist as she reeled, and spun her around. "You're on the edge, honey." He slammed her against the side of the helicopter, leaning hard against her. "Give me trouble and I'll beat the shit out of you. Got it?" He locked her cuffs and jerked his head at the cargo door. "In."

It was an awkward scramble into the copter's cargo bay, but neither of the smugglers offered any help. Susana, shorter than he, leaned across the threshold and swung her legs onboard, ending up on her belly on the floor. Her face was pale beneath the pink of new sunburn, but her eyes were cold with anger as she scrambled over to sit beside him on the floor. The door slammed closed, cutting off the harsh flood of evening light, and a moment later the copter leapt into the air.

The cargo space was crowded with plastic boxes. Insulated cold-storage containers for black-market meat? The space had a faint carrion smell. Maybe they bought from the goatherders. Or stole from them. David braced himself as the copter tilted. Susana was leaning against him, her feet planted against the anchored cold boxes.

"They shot her." Her voice came to him faintly over the roar of noise. "Like it was some drive-by in the 'burbs. Just *bang-bang-bang* and she's so much meat. I don't know, man. I guess it's the same all over." She stared at the stacked boxes, her face bleak. "There's nowhere to go, you know? To get out of this shit. Where're we headed?" She looked at David. "Got any idea? These aren't Alcourt's people, so who are they?"

"I don't know." David's shoulders slumped with his sigh. Were they Alcourt's or not?

They had used Alcourt's name as a password, which meant that whoever it was had tapped into David's conversation with Erebus. Which meant that they had gotten through Serafina's Security, not to mention Alcourt's.

Or else they were working for Alcourt. That scared him—that Alcourt was the shadow behind all this. It couldn't be true. David leaned back against the metal wall of the copter, breathing shallowly, feeling as if a giant fist were closing around him, crushing him. Alcourt's fist? He tried to imagine Alcourt walking in his desert garden, admiring the holos as the two men beat him. A part of him would not believe it, because they were friends. He couldn't have read that wrong. Blood trickled into his eyes, warm and sticky. Serafina had overestimated his knowledge of the world she and Flander moved in, and she had underestimated their adversary's resources. And so she had died.

What a shitty epitaph.

"You're really bleeding." Susana crowded closer. "Or you were. I think it's stopping. What happens next? Any idea?"

He heard the fear underneath her light words. "I don't know." He wiped his face on his shoulder as best he could, leaving red smears on his tunic. "We'll just wait and see. I've still got an ace to play." Which was shit, and from the look on her face, Susana guessed it.

It was hard to pretend right now.

"I guess we'll find out." Susana settled herself close against him. "I guess we don't have much choice, huh?"

Truth there. Oh, yeah, truth.

Chapter
Twenty

She could have walked to Ryo in one day. Jewel clutched the water truck's door as it lurched across a broken stretch of pavement, arching forward to let the oven-hot air from the window dry her sweaty shirt. The seat was covered with the same handwoven fabric that had hung on Serafina's walls. The caravan adults all worked on it, weaving it from the tufts of silky insulating wool that the children combed from the goats while on herd duty. They traded the weavings for supplies and water in the towns they passed through. Jewel guessed that by the time they made it to a city market, they would sell for ten or twenty times what the caravan members made on them.

But that barter was their edge. From what Cheri had told her, the caravan didn't make much on its sale of goats each year. The government subsidized its water with a priority-use permit but in return paid less than black-market price for the stock. Jewel leaned back against the seat, her shirt already dry, the descending sun hot on the side of her face. On either side of the faint track they were following the stubby little goats spread out across the landscape, browsing their way through the sage. The caravan zigzagged across the desert, moving just far enough each day to let the herds catch up with it by nightfall. In the morning they moved on again in an endless, slow-motion game of leapfrog.

"We camp just beyond this playa. It used to be a lake once, although I think that was before anyone here was born." Cheri nodded at the flat salt pan to their left. "We're only a couple of miles outside of town." She steered the lumbering truck around a massive boulder. "We have this story for little kids, how the mountain spirits play ball with big rocks when it thunders, and that's how these whoppers end up down here." She smiled. "The desert spirits get mad, but they aren't big enough to throw them back."

Part of Cheri believed in that tale, at least a little bit. Jewel could hear it in her voice—a half laugh, a concession. The caravan people saw spirits everywhere out there. Maybe we all need our fantasies, Jewel thought suddenly, escape from the gritty reality of dust and weather or 'burb streets and despair. Maybe. But it scared her a little how much Cheri believed in her weather spirits. If Serafina walked into the middle of camp and changed from woman to lioness in front of them, no one would blink. That scene had kept her awake the previous night: Serafina prowling into camp, eyes fixed on Jewel, demanding her return.

Demanding her soul.

Jewel laughed, but on a harsh note that drew a sideways quizzical look from Cheri. Oh, yeah, sure, her soul. But even in the harsh hot light of day she couldn't laugh it away. She remembered the worn-smooth feel of a hoe handle too well. The snake bite was still a little swollen, and it itched. She scratched it, made herself stop, and huddled back on the seat, oppressed by the cracked, sterile salt pan glittering in the sun, suddenly understanding Susana's fear. Technology had always defined the world for her. Not here. Out here too much was possible. Tech couldn't save you. Yes, this land reminded her of Erebus.

"Almost there," Cheri announced. "The main road's on the other side of that rise. You walk south, and it takes you right into town."

They had reached the southern end of the lake bed. A low ridge blocked it, resembling the remains of an enormous dam. Cheri pulled the truck along the base of the ridge to a shallow creek bed clogged with willow brush and parked at the edge of a barren stretch of ground. The blackened circles of old fire rings dotted the rocky soil.

The campers were pulling in alongside them, arranging themselves in a loose circle. In an hour they would have their camp set up and would be cooking dinner. The herders would come in at dusk, and the night teams would go out to keep an eye on the goats. No one gave orders much, not even Rink, the official leader. They just did things. Jewel opened the door and slid down to the ground, stretching in relief. The wind teased at her, flicking her sweaty hair into her eyes, tugging at her shirt. Jewel reached behind the seat of the truck to yank out her pack.

"Wait a minute." Cheri caught up with her as she started around the back of the truck. "You can't go hiking off with just a swallow of water—not even if you know where you're going. You got to get that through your head." She took Jewel's jug, filled it at the small tap in the back of the water truck, and handed it back. "So come on." She grabbed another pack from behind the truck's seat. "I'm on cleanup tonight, so I've got to be back before dinner's over."

"You don't have to come with me," Jewel said awkwardly. "I can find it."

"You owe us water, remember?"

"Oh, right." Jewel blushed. "I wasn't trying to run out on that, honest. I forgot."

"I figured that." Cheri smiled, squinting a little as the wind skipped around them, kicking up dust. "You sure are city. I hope you make it out of here in one piece. You just don't *forget* water out here. You can get yourself killed if someone thinks you're stealing."

Beneath her smile she was serious.

"I'll try and remember," Jewel said soberly, telling herself that the teasing wind was just air, Coriolis force, and imagination. But she wanted *out* of here. "Thanks."

" 'S okay." Cheri slung the empty pack onto her shoulders. "So let's go."

The sun was sinking toward the western horizon, but it was still oven-hot. Sweat stuck Jewel's hair to her face and trickled down her belly as the wind died. Heads down, they plodded doggedly along the dirt and gravel track that was the main road, not talking much because the hammer blow of the sun smashed conversation out of them. Jewel almost missed that damned unsettling wind. Slowly Ryo emerged from the sun haze, bleached colorless by the sun, blurred and deformed by rising heat waves. Closer, the blur resolved into the squat shape of a fuel station built of scabby, whitewashed concrete block, a couple of weathered houses, a feed store, and an incongruously new post office.

"The Gilsons got the government to put in the post office." Cheri seemed unaffected by the heat. "They grow this new type of supersage all over the place out here and ship it to the big processing plant up in Burns. They kind of own this part of the state, and they don't like us goat people much. They think we're going to sneak our goats into their sage or something." She made a face. "Anyway, it keeps Ryo alive, 'cause the main ranch is just back in that creek bed there. You can even rent a room up over the store. I guess it's not too bad. They fly in and out of Burns for supplies, and they kind of offer taxi service. For a price." She wrinkled her nose. "I hope you got money."

The main street was paved, a stretch of three whole blocks, maybe less. A small spray plane was parked in front of the fuel pumps, and one of the three houses looked abandoned, its windows broken and forlorn. Jewel followed Cheri past the plane and into the dim recesses of the store. No air-conditioning, but it seemed cool compared to outside. Crude wooden shelves overflowed with foodstuffs, stacks of jeans and shirts, boxed electronic hardware, batteries, and a bewildering chaos of odds and ends. Solar panels were stacked along the wall, and big storage-battery banks sat on pallets outside. A small brown bird chirped in a handmade rat-wire cage above a grimy Formica counter cluttered with dusty jars of dried sausages and hard candies. A stringy woman with dark, gray-streaked hair nodded behind a grimy counter, her eyes half-closed.

" 'Lo, Jenny.'' Cheri raised her voice as she slid her pack from her shoulders. "I need water, please. Three gallons okay?'' She raised an eyebrow at Jewel.

Jewel nodded, having no idea what was fair or not.

The old woman popped stereo plugs from her ears. "Three gallons of water, coming up.'' Her voice was surprisingly young. She unscrewed a cap on the top of the pack and propped it beneath a tap on the wall.

The pack itself was a water carrier mounted on a frame. Jewel fished her card from her pocket, the sweet sound of running water making her suddenly thirsty.

"Three gallons.'' After a minute or two the woman recapped the water pack, then slung it easily onto the counter. She had muscles like braided cable, and Jewel realized suddenly that she *was* young, aged by sun and chronic malnutrition. Jewel handed over her card and watched the woman zip it through the reader behind the counter. "Is there public access somewhere?''

"Yep.'' The storekeeper laid the card on the counter. "Right over in the post office. They got virtual, even. Brand-new, and they can rent you the suit and stuff.'' She beamed. "I never tried it before the post office moved in. You can go wade in the *ocean*. I coulda swore I was there—half expected to be wet when I got done.'' She shook her head, her eyes bright. "You don't have to set foot out of your house with one of those things, you know? You could live your whole life inside someplace nice and cool. Just never go out and still see *everything*. Shit, I'm twenty-three, and I've never been farther than Pendleton.''

Pendleton. Jewel looked away from her old-young face.

"Oh, yeah.'' Cheri hoisted the sloshing pack to her shoulder. "Any chance Jewel can catch a lift with one of the Gilson planes? Anybody heading to Burns or Boise for supplies?''

"Not for a while.'' Jenny stuffed her plugs back into her ears.

"Sanders just come back with a full load." Her eyes went dreamy and unfocused. "You can rent the upstairs room if you're gonna wait—it's empty. And do the ocean thing. It's neat."

A while? A sense of urgency clenched like a fist in Jewel's chest. Not *here*, not this close. "What about renting a car or something?" she asked desperately.

Jenny shrugged and shook her head, swaying to her unheard music.

"Too bad." Cheri ushered Jewel outside, sympathetic. "Don't worry, it won't be a long wait. The agplex flies stuff in and out every few days."

A few days, all of them spent waiting for Serafina to show up? Jewel looked up and down the three-block stretch of civilization, a tide of desperation rising in her. The light had gone yellow, and evening shadows were beginning to creep across the landscape. The wind was back, riffling her hair like invisible fingers. Jewel wondered if it would tell Serafina where she was.

"You can come with us," Cheri said softly.

Jewel shook her head.

"I'm sorry you got stuck here." Cheri tilted her head, eyes dark with concern. "You're running away from the healer, aren't you? You didn't say, so I didn't want to ask."

"Yes." Jewel bit her lip, afraid of the wind's familiar nudge. "I am."

"We all sort of wondered." Cheri sighed. "You look like her. The healer scares me a little, you know. Not for anything she's done—she's done wonderful things for us—but for what I think she maybe could do. Does that make any sense?" She touched Jewel's arm, her face full of questions. "Anyway, I hope it works out."

"Me, too." Jewel looked away, not willing or even able to answer those questions.

"Take care, Jewel. If you change your mind about coming with us, we'll be around until dawn." She touched Jewel's arm again and started back down the street, her heavy pack sloshing with each step.

"Good-bye." Jewel stifled an urge to run after Cheri, to say she was coming along. Would it be so bad to live out here, following the goats, sinking into the routine of camp and move and camp again?

Yes, it would be. Jewel looked around, squeezed by the horizon of dust and hills. Cheri didn't have any more choices than Jewel had had in the 'burbs. Herd goats in the heat and dust to pay for your water to herd goats . . . It was just another treadmill to nowhere, with no way off. And Cheri would probably be dead by the time the caravan reached this town again. Arms crossed, hugging herself as if she were cold, Jewel marched up the street to the post office. Time to take hold of her life again, put the last weeks behind her. Time to reactivate her status on the employment roll. Toss the dice and see what turned up. Take it, the first job opening, no matter where it was. If Serafina was the Net operator Susana suspected, no place on Earth was safe. Jewel marched through the post office doors as they whisked open.

The cool, dry air raised instant goose bumps on her skin, and the familiar interior comforted her. A row of private full-access booths lined one wall. Touchscreens and hard-copy slots lined the other wall. It could have been the inside of any urban PO, and that familiarity shut out the hot, dusty reality outside. Holoed surf curled and broke across the end wall—an ad for Jenny's travel virtual?

A bent man with a withered, sun-dried face lounged in front of the fake waves. He gave Jewel a sharp, penetrating look. His eyes were such a pale blue that they seemed almost white in his dark face. Jewel paused in front of a screen, noticing suddenly that the man was casually positioning himself so as to be able to read over her shoulder. Yeah, gossip was probably a hot item in this godforsaken place—prime trade goods. Jewel gave him a cold glare, but he stared blandly through her and didn't move. Feeling the stranger, alone and unsure of the rules in this alien place, she turned her back on him, stomped into one of the full-access booths, and slammed the door. Seething, she yanked off her tunic and leggings, fished her skins from her carryall, and began to pull them on. What the hell—full access was better, anyway. Employment was posted for any access, but the screen-only files were trimmed to the minimum.

"Access, office, Jewel Martina." She pulled on her lenses, blinking as color and light wavered, distorted, and solidified into strobing blue and white light so bright that it hurt her eyes. David's cave? Jewel lifted a hand in an automatic gesture as the cave walls flickered with ice-white brilliance. Some sort of system crash? Or another of David's artistic tricks, like the monster? The brilliant flashes began to resolve into kaleidoscopic shapes that merged, separated, overlapped, and separated again.

Eyes suddenly filled the space around her: a universe of eyes, perfectly spaced in three dimensions, disappearing into an endless distance, millions of eyes. Green eyes rimmed with fur, veined with bloody capillaries, pupils contracted to points of blackness.

Fox eyes.

"Flander!" Jewel struggled with dizziness as the eyes began to resolve around her, turning faster and faster. "Stop it. Now, or I'm going to throw up!"

A high-pitched yipping filled the booth, distant and shrill and full of frantic pain.

"Flander, knock it *off*!" Jewel reached for her lenses.

The eyes came together in a sudden implosive rush and combined for a second in a squashed mass of white and green and bits of red fur. Then, suddenly, Flander was standing in front of her in his usual fox form, head cocked, ears pricked. "Shit, lady. What's your problem?" He leapt at her, and his jaws closed on her hand. "Not so fast."

"Ow!" Jewel snatched her hand out of his mouth. Illusion, maybe, but her skins gave her the experience of pain. "David's fine, he's safe, he got his sight back. Didn't he tell you?" She glowered at him. "So you can stop playing games with my file-space."

"What games?" He flattened his ears. "I've been hanging out here *forever*. No, David didn't tell me nothing. He won't come into the damn Net, won't answer his access, and I don't believe you about him seeing again. He would have told me."

"You're shitting me." Jewel gave him a cold stare, which he got full force because she hadn't given her Self any editing instructions. "David was back in the Net at least twice that I know of. One time he was looking for you and said you weren't around."

"You're lying." Flander bared his teeth, crouching to spring at her again. "Go get him."

"I can't. He didn't come with me." This conversation was costing money. Jewel tossed her head. "Look, I need to update my file in the registry. If you don't mind . . ."

Flander was staring at her, his eyes twin emeralds full of flickering fire. "What the hell do you mean, he didn't come *with* you?"

"When I left Serafina's."

"So that's who was hiding his damn access. I figured it might be her. Shit, lady." He snapped at her, his teeth clashing with the sound of a brass cymbals. "How come you're running out on him so fast? You guys only got there yesterday."

Reflexively, Jewel covered her ears. "Don't *do* that. We were there more than two days, and I left two days ago. What's your problem? You can't tell time?" She meant to make it sarcastic, but her voice faltered. Flander's image was wavering, distorting, fading in and out in random blotches. A shoulder going translucent and pale, then reappearing, a leg stretching to a rubber-band caricature.

''What's wrong with you?'' She drew back a little, cold creeping up her neck. ''You having trouble with your interface?''

''Four days? You're shitting me, lady.'' Head lowered, strobing like dying neon, the fox crept toward her. ''You're *shitting* me! More like twelve hours, give or take a few minutes.''

''Access him yourself.'' Jewel forced herself to stand still—this was only virtual. ''He might not even be there anymore, okay? I left two days ago, and I don't know what his plans were. Harmon Alcourt was going to give him some kind of protection; that's all I know. Maybe they got the car out and headed somewhere else—it's not my problem anymore, fox. Got that?''

''Alcourt?'' Flander's eyes expanded, full of green fire, and the rest of his body vanished. ''You told Harmon Alcourt where he was? You bitch. You fucking *bitch*.'' The eyes contracted suddenly, shrinking down to twin points of emerald light that pulsed in the air. ''He's *behind* it. I told you he did it. I told you, back in your office, that Alcourt was the one. That he asked for the stuff, that he paid me in shit, set it up so he could watch me die. And you fed David to him—'' The lights dove suddenly at her eyes.

''Stop it! You didn't tell me, Flander. Do you *hear* me?'' She flinched as the eyes halted just centimeters from her face, sweating and afraid suddenly, never mind that this was virtual. ''I asked you who was behind this, and you wouldn't tell me.'' The eyes pulsed with baleful light. ''You said you didn't know, that you couldn't remember. Flander, what's happening to you?''

''Nothing. What the hell do you mean?'' In a nanosecond he was the fox again, staring up at her, ears flat. ''I told you, lady. Don't shit me.'' But he sounded less certain.

''You didn't. It was David who called Alcourt. Will you shut up and let me think?'' Jewel closed her eyes, her mind reeling. Alcourt—Harmon Alcourt had ordered David's torture? Could he do that?

The flesh man she had known, no. But Jewel recalled that afternoon in his office, the broken letter opener. *He* could do it. She had thought all along that the virtual Alcourt was the real man and the flesh version was the illusion. ''See if you can get into their access,'' she said. ''Serafina's.'' She opened her eyes.

No Flander. The cave was back to normal. Angrily, Jewel glanced around. The body beneath the monster's hooves was her own, bloody and trampled. She shuddered. ''Flander?''

No answer.

He was crazy, mirroring his insanity in virtual. She shuddered again, her skin thick with gooseflesh, freezing suddenly. At the far end of the cave her buried image watched her from the ice, the beating heart of a glacier, face full of contempt.

"Exit." Jewel yanked off her lenses.

The sudden disorientation of the exit nearly did it for her unsettled stomach. Jewel leaned against the booth wall, breathing deeply, fighting nausea. David and Susana were at Serafina's house, waiting for rescue, only it wouldn't be a rescue. Alcourt might want David, but he didn't need Susana. Death could be so clean from a distance. He could kill Susana from Erebus, and it would be no more real than a virtual. Less real, perhaps. She pulled on her lenses again and found herself in her office, to her great relief. "Access—Serafina." Serafina *what*? She didn't even know if Serafina was her real name. "Access Serafina," she repeated more loudly.

"Searching." Ten seconds passed, then thirty. "No such access exists in public files," her office told her.

So much for that. New buds were opening on the wall David had designed so carefully. "Exit," Jewel whispered. Now what? If she went back, if she got in Alcourt's way, she might die, too. That wasn't what scared her. Hand on the booth door, Jewel hesitated. If she went back, Serafina would devour her. She had to keep on going. Get a new assignment, walk away, and never look back. Eventually she would make it in the web.

Yes, she would make it. Jewel could see it, past and future stretching out all around her like an invisible landscape. She would make it, small at first, then getting more and more inside, until she was secure. The price was David and Susana.

Once the price had been Linda. Jewel opened her hand. Life line, heart line . . . She wouldn't have had the money for Net time if she had shared with Linda. Linda would have held her back. She had let Linda see that, and Linda had moved in with Carl, because then Jewel would have to walk away. She had done it because Jewel had wanted her to. Because Linda had loved her enough to do what Jewel had wanted. She shoved her way out of the booth, past the surprised local.

The woman looked up from behind her counter as Jewel burst into the store. She was chewing gum now, her stare placid.

"I have to rent a car." Jewel controlled her voice with an effort. "Right now." Her fingers twitched with the desire to yank the plugs from the woman's ears and throw them at her. "It's an emergency. Look, I just need to drive out and see someone."

"I hear you just fine. You don't got to shout." Jenny cracked her wad of gum and shifted it over to her other cheek. "We got the shop loaner. I'm not supposed to just rent it, but you promise to bring it back tomorrow, I guess you can use it. Thirty bucks and mileage, and you get it back here by ten tomorrow.''

"That's fine, sure. Here.'' Jewel held out her card.

Jenny peered at it, stared at her briefly, then fished under the counter for a dog-eared pad of paper. She turned through the yellow leaves with painstaking slowness, ignoring Jewel. "Fill this here out.'' She slid the pad across the countertop. "I got to have a real address or I can't rent it. None of this electronic address stuff.''

A white page and an identical yellow page were separated by a rumpled sheet of carbon paper. Primitive. Swallowing her impatience, Jewel filled out the lines, using Linda's address. Linda, Susana's dead, and it's my fault. She tried to imagine herself saying those words to Linda, but her mind would not summon a vision of Linda's face. Hurry up, Jewel wanted to scream. Teeth clenched, she handed the pad back, jittering while the woman tore off the white page with careful perfection.

"Here's the keys.'' She tossed a ring with two battered keys onto the counter and picked up Jewel's card. "I've got to run a deposit on this. Three hundred.'' She stuck the card in the reader. "I deduct the charge when you bring the car back and cancel the rest. Okay?'' She handed the card back.

"Okay.'' Jewel shoved the card into her pocket. "Uh, I need directions.'' She met the woman's skeptical look. "I'm looking for a friend's house. She lives off this dirt road that runs north to the highway. She's old, about my height.'' And she looks like me. "Serafina's her name.''

"Yeah, I figured you meant her.'' The woman's eyebrows were rising slowly as she examined Jewel's face. "You take the road north out of town, turn right just after the cattle guard. You got to watch for it. The road's hard to spot. You know where her road takes off?''

"Yes, yes, I know it.'' Jewel turned her back on the woman to cut off her surmising stare. "The car's out back?''

"Yep. An old Bronco. Got a high center and good tires. Just don't take the curves too fast, hear? What is she? Your grandma?''

Jewel left without answering her. The car sat out back, baking in the hot sun, white with lake-bed dust. The passenger-side window had been broken out, and small chunks of glass remained in the frame. Jewel slid behind the wheel, shoved the key into the ignition, turned it, and held her breath. She half expected it not to start, but the engine roared easily to life.

Take the road north out of town. There was only one road through

this place. Jewel backed out into the main street. Jenny was standing in the door, jaws moving rhythmically, shading her eyes against
the setting sun. Jewel hit the gas and headed north. She found the
turnoff, grateful for the cattle-guard landmark. It looked like any
other wheel track cutting through the sage. What a place to hide.
Who would look for a Net wizard out here in this wasteland?

Surely Serafina had been monitoring David's conversation with
Alcourt. She wouldn't let him give her away, so they were safe.
Surely.

She kept seeing the broken pieces of that letter opener neatly
arranged on her underwear. The light was fading, and she pushed
the Bronco harder, bouncing across unexpected washes and rocky
stretches. Shadows spread across the landscape, and she turned on
the headlights, half expecting to catch the glitter of a cat's eyes in
the dark.

All she saw was sage, and rock, and deepening darkness.

She missed the road in the dark. It wasn't until the dirt track ran
into the larger county road, paved with the cracked vestiges of
asphalt, that she realized her mistake. Raging at herself, Jewel
wrenched the car around and started back the way she had come,
forcing herself to drive slowly even though she wanted to floor the
accelerator. It was midnight by the time Jewel topped the rise onto
the shelf. It felt later. The headlights swept across the dusty rental
car, still canted into the ditch. So they hadn't left yet. Relief softened her spine, but fear squeezed her at the same time. Serafina
waited for her. *Run*, a voice whispered inside her. *It's not too late.*

Yes. It *was* too late. Jewel shut off the engine. She had spent her
whole life running. David knew it. Metal ticked softly, and the
desert night rushed in to fill up the space: whisper of windblown
dust and stirring sage stems, the soft chirr of insects. The slam of
the car door closing sounded as loud as a thunderclap, and Jewel
tensed. No lights in the house. They must all be asleep. The moon
was down, and it was dark in spite of the glittering sky. The wind
nuzzled her, raising the hairs on the back of her neck. A flash was
clipped to the front of the seat. Jewel grabbed it and thumbed it on,
grateful for its weak yellow beam.

A shape moved in the darkness near the door, and something
moaned.

The voice was not human. For an instant terror overwhelmed
Jewel, turning the darkness pregnant with moving shapes. Breathless, she swung the beam toward the sound. Strange eyes flashed
deep ruby, then resolved into nothing more terrible than Serafina's

goat. It bleated again—a low, sad murmur—then trotted up to rub its head against Jewel's arm.

"Hey. Don't." She pushed it away.

It followed her to the door, its nose bumping her back as if it, too, were afraid of the dark. A small unease began to grow inside Jewel. The door was closed tight, not locked. Jewel pushed it open. "Susana? David?" Her voice seemed to echo in the vast, dark space.

Silence.

She stumbled through the room, tripping over the leg of a chair. It fell over with a crash as she shoved the curtain aside. The light beam picked out sleeping bags, rolled up and stacked against the wall. They were gone, after all. The light trembled in Jewel's hand. Maybe they had walked to Ryo; she could have passed them on the road in the dark. Or Serafina could have found them a ride and they could be halfway to Pendleton by now. They could be anywhere. Jewel threw herself onto the bed, trying to think. Leave a message for David, routed to his personal access? She should have done that in Ryo—idiot, *idiot*. The damn primitive landscape denied technology—you stopped thinking about anything except flesh out here. Leave a message in the cave, too. Do *something*. She swung the flashlight beam around the room, hoping against hope for a message. But David would not expect her to come back here. No reason to leave one.

The small holo portrait on the chest of drawers beside the bed caught her eye. The woman looked at the camera with a tilted, fey smile, her sun-bleached hair blowing in the breeze. Jewel reached for the picture, recognition coming to her in a rush.

Mama—no, the woman she had called Mama. Elaine. There was a hint of wildness in her face, or maybe she was only imagining it, seeing the future in that smile. She looked so happy, so different from the woman Jewel remembered. She had been Serafina's lover. Jewel swallowed, trying to ease the sudden knot in her throat. This house was full of ghosts. Leave a message for David and get out. What if Serafina came back?

Jewel set the picture down very carefully. Her flashlight beam was weakening rapidly, and she hurried to the table in the main room, groping for the switch on the solar lamp that hung above it.

"Jewel?"

Jewel froze as soft light flooded the center of the room, beyond terror, then turned slowly to face the voice. Serafina was sitting in one of the chairs at the edge of the light, the planes of her face cast into stark relief by the lamp's glow. I am lost, Jewel thought, and fear squeezed her like a vise.

"Daughter." Serafina's voice was low and dry, like the rush of wind through the sage. "I did not expect you to return."

"I . . . had to come back." Jewel wanted to start shaking. "For Susana. And David."

"Why?" Yellow light glittered in Serafina's eyes. "You're afraid of me."

"Because Susana matters. And David's my friend." And I've run from you all my life, and from the 'burbs, and from love. And it's time to stop running. Jewel twisted her fingers together to hide their trembling.

A spasm of pain twisted Serafina's face. "I was loved once." She let her breath out in a slow sigh. "You don't have to be afraid." Her face was full of shadow. "I'm not going to hurt you. If you'll bring me the picture from the bedroom, I'll tell you a story."

She watched me look at it, Jewel thought, but felt no surprise, only acceptance. She bowed her head without speaking and went to get the picture. The door lay only a few steps away, but she felt no urge to run. The time for running was over. The universe had contracted to the here and now, and Jewel had the dizzy feeling that everything hung on this moment: David and Susana, herself, Linda. Jewel picked up the holo frame, carried it back into the main room, and handed it to Serafina. Side by side, grasping the frame, their hands were identical.

"I suppose Elaine was always a little crazy." Serafina looked at the picture for a long moment. "That's partly why I loved her. Reality for Elaine was a very flexible thing. She could accept me without question. Only the who mattered to her, and she loved me. It surprised me, that love." She laid the picture down on her lap. "I had stopped believing in it long before."

"What are you?" Jewel whispered. "What am *I*?"

"You need a label?" Serafina smiled at Jewel with gentle irony. "I haven't come up with one yet. I'm simply a woman who discovered many, many years ago that the world didn't work for me the way it worked for others—or perhaps it does but others don't let themselves see it. I discovered that I could *do* things, that reality is as manipulable as the Net. Do you have any idea of what it means to be truly unique?" Her sigh was the sound of the desert wind blowing over empty miles. "To be unique means to be truly alone," she whispered.

"Elaine never stopped loving you," Jewel said with sudden insight. That was behind the drugs, the escape. It wasn't just the pain. "I don't think she ever stopped hating herself for running," she said softly.

"I . . . could wish you were lying to me." Serafina touched the holoed face of the woman on her lap. "She was the only person who has ever loved me, and I sacrificed that love. I didn't understand what I'd lost until it was too late."

And Jewel had sacrificed Linda for escape, for success. "Oh, yes," Jewel said bitterly. "You're my mother, my sister. Oh, yes, we're alike." She straightened, aware of Serafina's hunger, like water pressing against the walls of her mind. "Where are Susana and David? Alive?" Her voice shook in spite of herself. "Does Alcourt have them?"

"You might be stronger than I." Serafina closed her eyes. "I think I can be proud of you, Daughter. I think you're safe from me." Serafina opened her eyes. "Harmon Alcourt has them. The artist accessed him, asking for help. I think he asked the wrong man. Smugglers picked them up in a helicopter. They weren't what the artist expected."

Too late. Too late. The words beat like a gong in her head. She had come back here too late to do any good—the story of her life. Bitterness overwhelmed her suddenly, banishing her fear. David, Alcourt would keep. But Susana? "What can I do now?" She clenched her fists.

Serafina sighed with the sound of the desert wind. "I don't know what comes next. Daughter? Will you look at me?"

It was a plea rather than a command, and something in her tone made the hair prickle on the back of Jewel's neck.

"I thought I could live forever. Reality is just another Net, and why should we die? I stayed young for a long time, but—" She broke off. "The fox thinks he can transfer his memories, his thoughts, his soul into the Net. That's his hope of immortality. I could do that, transfer myself into you—perhaps because you're me. I almost did, down on that ledge. Because I was afraid." For a moment Serafina's eyes glittered with that terrible hunger; then they darkened. "I'm sorry, Jewel. I'm still afraid, but I'll stop hiding from death. I'm tired of being alone. I loved Elaine." She stretched out her hand, her fingers brushing Jewel's cheek like moth wings. "Please remember that for me."

Her fingers were cold, and Jewel shivered as Serafina slumped back in her chair. Her head lolled sideways onto her shoulder.

"Serafina?" Jewel reached out to her. Her skin was cold—too cold. Way too cold. Heart hammering, throat tight, Jewel touched her face and felt for a pulse at her throat. Nothing. Already Serafina's flesh was stiffening, as if rigor were setting in at an accelerated pace. Something white glistened at the corners of her mouth. Jewel bent closer. Fly eggs. She straightened with a choked gasp. The embroidered tunic had hidden the stains, but she saw them now, saw the dark holes that were bullet wounds. Jewel stepped slowly back, numb, knowing that this could not be, that she must be dreaming, hallucinating.

Knowing that it was real.

"I'm not so certain anymore," she whispered. "Do you hear me, Serafina?" Her voice trembled, and she heard the lurking hysteria behind her words.

She was dead.

Alcourt had David and Susana.

I am *she*. Jewel shivered. What does that make me?

What the hell do I do now?

There was too much here, and her mind shut down, refusing to deal with any of it. Moving automatically, she went into the bedroom to get the spread from the bed and cover Serafina.

Chapter
Twenty-one

David leaned his forehead against the window of the jet, eyeing the thick floor of clouds below. According to the sun they were flying south and had been flying more or less south for the last several hours. South to where? A part of him didn't want to answer that question, didn't want to believe that Harmon Alcourt had sent those smugglers to pick him up.

Alcourt had been their first big commission, back when he and Flander had been struggling with the occasional stationary gallery showing and bills for a lot of Net time. They had become friends. Or David had thought so, anyway. He let his breath out in a slow sigh. He had always admired Alcourt's ability to make the decision that needed to be made with seamless and casual confidence. Once it was made, he never looked back. He learned from his mistakes, but he never regretted them. That was perhaps what had brought him into the center of the web.

If it was in his best interest to order David's torture and murder, would he have done it? David stared down at the cloud floor beneath the plane, searching for answers in the gray and white shadows. No, he decided finally. Not the Alcourt he knew personally. Or did he know Harmon Alcourt as well as he thought?

Harmon knew about Flander's allergy; David had told him. Beside David, curled up on her reclined seat, Susana stirred in her sleep. Across the aisle the uniformed security guard glanced at her impassively and went back to her little laptop screen. She was following some kind of graphic novel. David caught a glimpse of figures darting across the screen—pretty good visuals for a flat. Her eyes flickered at whatever was coming in over the plugs, and her mouth twitched as though she wanted to smile. It didn't mean that she was not watching his every twitch; she and her partner sitting at the front of the plush cabin were coldly professional.

The last pair—the ones who had picked them up from the smugglers—had been pros, too. People didn't ask questions when they saw you were being herded around by someone in a uniform. He had tried to run, remembering last time too well to walk through this farce passively. The three members of the ground crew who had been within range of his yells for help had looked startled. Kidnap! he had shouted. Call the cops. Don't let them take off. Susana had joined in. It hadn't flustered the guards. They had shoved them along, miming exasperation with the behavior of these obvious losers, the image of patient legitimacy.

The airport employees had stared briefly, then ignored them. David's hands had curled into fists with the humiliation of it. One man—a kid really—had at least looked doubtful. Maybe because Susana was so young. But in the end he had turned away, too, perhaps embarrassed by his own momentary and tentative belief. Uniforms and badges pushing bedraggled, handcuffed street types around—no big deal. People saw it all the time, and they simply did not question it. Not seriously. David leaned his head back against the seat and closed his eyes. In the privacy of the plane one of the guards had used an electric stun wand on him twice. It had hurt like hell. The man hadn't said a word, but the message had been quite clear.

And then the same man had cleaned up the cut on David's scalp, taken off their cuffs, and served them dinner. The plush leased jet had a shower, and clean clothes had been laid out for them. The clothes fit. That final detail had depressed David enormously. People were so damn accessible. Every detail of their lives was recorded somewhere in Flander's electronic universe, right down to their shoe sizes. David rubbed at his wrists where the cuffs had chafed him, swallowing the urge to get up and pace, yell, throw himself at the guard across the aisle, *do* something.

There was nothing to do, not against two armed guards. Except try to guess their destination. They were headed south, and that was all he knew. The urban airport where the helicopter had grounded had looked like any city airport in the dark; the leased jet could have flown in any direction during the night. They had changed planes and escorts again just before dawn, and again they had done so out on a concrete runway. This time the crew servicing the plane had spoken Spanish. Mexico? Central or South America? David tried to figure hours and airspeed. Their new uniformed escorts left the cuffs off, but they escorted David and Susana between planes at gunpoint. Not at all sure what orders they had, afraid that they would shoot Susana, David didn't try any melodrama this time. He didn't speak Spanish, anyway. Neither pair of guards would say who had hired them. David doubted that it would be the real person behind this kidnap, anyway—it would be another go-between, another level of distraction and security. Whoever was behind this was big. It cost a lot to lease two jets, a helicopter, and a small army of mercenaries ready to commit murder.

To reach Erebus travelers flew from Christchurch, New Zealand. Or from Punta Arenas, in Chile.

Susana stirred again and sobbed once, a harsh, heartbroken sound. "Easy, Susana." David stroked her face gently, pushing tangled hair back from her forehead. "It's just a dream."

She didn't wake, but she sighed in her sleep, and her fingers curled around his. Her cheek was puffy where the smuggler had hit her, and her eye was darkening to purple. She was scared—closed up inside with her fear, like a cornered dog with its teeth bared. David yawned suddenly and uncontrollably, his jaws stretching until they felt as if they would crack. He was tired but didn't want to sleep. Sleep felt too vulnerable, and he was afraid he would dream about Jack.

Beyond the window the clouds were breaking up, shredding away to streamers of white mist. An ocean glinted blue far below, looking flat and hard, a wrinkled sheet of plastic spread across the world. White glittered in the distance: ice. Bergs spotted the sea, tiny from this height, floating mountains in reality. Ahead, a rising line of white floated on the rim of the world. David felt a small sinking in the pit of his stomach.

He had known where they were headed. He just hadn't wanted to face it.

Susana gave a choked cry, and her fingers closed convulsively on his hand. She sat up suddenly, her eyes wide, staring around in confusion. "Where the hell are we?" Her eyes focused suddenly, and she glared briefly at the impassive, watchful guard. "What are we doing, flying around the damn world?"

"Only halfway." David nodded at the window. "To Antarctica, to be precise."

"So it is him. Alcourt. He's behind all this, right? He had those shitbags off Serafina." She looked down and released his hand abruptly. "What the hell for?"

"Flander pulled some kind of illegal scam for him." David fought the bitterness that rose into the back of his throat. "Now he wants to kill Flander, and I'm his link to Flander. You were just in the vicinity. I'm sorry."

"Me, too." Susana glowered at the guard.

David leaned back in his seat, filled with a strange stillness. Harmon Alcourt. He wondered suddenly how long Flander had been working for Alcourt, if Alcourt had given David his commissions only to keep Flander's talents within easy reach. Possibly. David stared out at the ice-dotted sea, the bitterness threatening to choke him.

"You know, I was pissed at you. Because the fox was hurting and hiding and you wouldn't talk to him." Susana spoke hesitantly, frowning out the window. "But he *walked* on you. I mean, he did it, even if he had a reason. He walked, and you caught the shit. What you said at Serafina's about it being your fault—your distance—did you forgive him?"

She was wrestling with something. David dragged his gaze from the fanged horizon. "We both messed up. He wanted love and was scared of it, and I was scared to give it." Fatigue was catching up with him now, dragging at his shoulders, making his head ache. If he had stayed with the family firm, could he have forced his father to accept his art, to accept him as the man he was? Perhaps not. Perhaps Fuchin was as crippled as he. "I guess I forgive us both," he said with an effort.

Susana had gone very still, her eyes on his face. "I don't know," she said at last. "When someone, like, walks on you . . . I mean . . . fuck 'em. That's it. It's over, man." She tucked her feet up onto the roomy seat, chin proppped on her knees, frowning. "Only Flander didn't really walk away, you know? I mean, I know that. He was truly suffering, but . . ." She shook her head, scowling. "Shit, *I* don't know."

Was Susana's black and white world blurring into shades of gray? David got the feeling that she had grown up with absolutes: do or don't do. Survive or die. He would have called it a primitive attitude before knowing Jewel. Now he wondered if it was not a matter of survival. Shades of gray, compromise, and doubts entailed risk. Maybe you had to have some security before you could afford the luxury of taking risks. "Sometimes people have complicated reasons for what they do," he said slowly. "Sometimes they don't even know themselves."

"You're talking about Jewel." Susana shot him a hard, sideways look. "You want me to let her off the hook for running out on us like she did."

"Yes." Pushing aside the evasion that came to his lips, David met her glare. "Yes, I'm asking you to let her off the hook. Be pissed at her, sure, because she deserves it. *I'm* pissed at her, because I offered her help and she walked away from that, too.

Look, she didn't just forget to wake you up. She was running, and she thinks it's for her life. I don't know if it is or not, but there's something between her and Serafina. Something old and ugly.'' So ugly that she had to turn it into magic in order to deal with it? ''She's running from herself,'' he said in a lower tone. ''She could spend the rest of her life doing that.'' Like Flander hiding in the Net? How about yourself, Chen Chih Hwa, hiding in your art? ''Hell, maybe we're all running from ourselves. Maybe that's the mainspring that drives the whole damn race.'' Yes—*that* was the nature of the chimera in his cave. David felt a rush of excitement. When you looked at the monster, you saw your whole self: the mangled body and the monster both.

''Huh. You may be running from shit, but I'm not.'' Susana was watching his face, her eyes narrowed. ''I know right where I am. Or where I was before Jewel started messing things up.'' She hunched her shoulders, not ready to forgive anyone yet. ''Are we going to land right in that fancy hideway?'' she murmured.

''Not in this thing.'' David shook his head. ''We'll probably land at the McMurdo airstrip and come in by 'copter. Only they call them heelo's down here.''

Susana grunted. ''I'm not walking up to this rich scumbag and doing a curtsy so he can off me without putting himself out, okay? I figure this is our last chance, so if we get a crack, I'm through it. Come along or not.''

She had a hard pride, this kid. And maybe not enough sense of her own mortality. Or maybe she didn't care all that much. Her universe did not have a lot to offer her, and he guessed she didn't have any illusions about it. ''Let's see what happens,'' David said, and hoped to hell he could stop her if she tried something stupid.

It turned out that he needn't have worried; their escort let Antarctica itself guard them. The jet landed and taxied to the far end of the runway, out to the high-security warehouse where supplies bound for Erebus were unloaded and inspected. A heelo was already waiting, the rotors idling—a slick private passenger job.

The woman had put away her laptop. She tossed them each a hooded jacket, nearly as flimsy as a sweatshirt. ''This'll get you to the chopper if you move it.'' She sounded mildly bored. ''Don't try for the terminal. By the time you get there—if you get there— you'll be so frostbit that a body doc'll have to start from scratch on a rebuild. Keep your hands in your pockets and your head down.'' She popped the hatch, letting in a blast of freezing air. ''Go!''

Her partner prodded them forward, his gun out. David's flesh cringed as the cold reached in and grabbed him like a clawed fist.

When he had been outside before, suited, protected, he hadn't really taken the measure of it. "Don't touch anything with your bare hands," he said to Susana, and stumbled down the stairs after her. Side by side, they ran for the waiting helicopter. The distance had looked so short from the warm safety of the jet, but now, they seemed to move in slow motion, not getting any closer. The cold dug its claws slowly through David's chest, piercing him so that he gasped for air, feeling his lungs burn, breathing through his nose because the cold made his teeth ache. He was freezing from the inside out. A step ahead of him, Susana hesitated, her head swiveling toward the impossibly distant terminal. David shoved her hard in the direction of the heelo, terrified that she would try it and he would chase her.

She stumbled, put her head down, and ran for the hatch. The pilot popped it, and they scrambled up into the tiny passenger compartment. Warmth like an oven's breath wrapped them as the hatch *thunk*ed automatically closed. David's ears and face flamed with instant fire.

"You didn't have to push me." Susana glared at him. "I'm not totally stupid, okay? Shit, that *hurts*." She rubbed her ears. "Does that mean they're frozen?"

"Just cold, I think." David looked around the small, plush space. "I hope so, anyway."

Four recliner seats filled the carpeted cabin, and a small, sleek kitchenwall took up the rear. A permaglass wall divided the cockpit from the rest of the cabin. The pilot and copilot had their backs to them, but a voice reached them over a hidden speaker.

"The kitchen is stocked with drinks and snacks. Please help yourself. It's a short flight, and there's no weather today, so we should make good time."

He knew that voice.

"Hey, pilot!" Susana banged a fist on the permaglass. "This is illegal, man. This is a kidnap. Let us out of here right now."

The pilot didn't even twitch; he probably wasn't listening to the cabin channel. The copilot turned around, however. "I'm sorry, sir. You'll have to schedule a return flight from the Complex." He gave them a sleek professional smile.

"You stupid shithead." Susana pounded a clenched fist on the wall between them. "Can't you understand English, or what?"

"He works for Harmon." David eyed the man's blond, expensively perfect face, trying to remember his name. Casper? Castor, that was it. The other aide—the VR junkie. "I've got to go along, anyway."

"Shit!" Susana flung herself into the seat beside him as the cop-ter lifted smoothly into the air. "What do you mean, you've *got* to go? You got a serious death wish or what?"

"How else can I get Harmon Alcourt off my back?" David looked out the window. Bergs dotted the cold blue surface of the Ross Sea, and the copter bucked in a sudden wind. That was hard reality out there. No, no virtual could ever do it justice. "I work in the Net. Where do I hide?" He shook his head, still unable to do it; he couldn't overlay the Alcourt he knew with the man who had hired Jack and his partner, who had paid the smugglers to shoot down Serafina and Susana. "The only way out is this way," he said softly. "If there's any way out at all."

She gave him a sideways, doubting look, hands clenched on the padded arms of her seat. "Shit, I'm scared," she said softly.

That was a major admission for this kid. "Me, too." David put a gentle hand on her arm. "I'm scared shitless."

She gave him a tentative grin for that and didn't shake off his hand. David watched the copter's shadow skim across the surface of the icy sea, a part of his brain reshaping the chimera in the cave, a part of it wondering if he would ever enter the cave again.

They left the ocean to fly across ice and black, frozen rock. Eventually the helicopter drifted gently and precisely down to land at Alcourt's private pad in the rocky flank of Erebus. It seemed like years since David had last been there. Or another life. It had been another life, cut off from this one by a solid wall of darkness.

The voice over the speaker again. "Parkas are in the locker be-side the kitchen."

The hatch popped, admitting a breath of freezing air. David opened the locker and tossed one of the two neon-orange parkas to Susana. "There are gloves and a face mask in the pockets," he said as he shrugged into his parka and sealed it closed. "Put them on."

She didn't argue with him. Her eyes had a cornered look, and she stayed close beside him as they climbed down the steps and hurried across the packed-down path to the entry. The brittle snow squeaked under their feet, and their breath plumed white in the air, frosting their balaclavas with crystals of ice. Security watched them with its video eyes, judged them, and checked them off on some data base. A diamond-dust shower of ice crystals drifted to the ground as the door opened for them, then closed behind them, sealing out the alien cold.

Back in Erebus.

Full circle.

David stripped off his gloves, pulled off his mask, and unsealed his parka. "You can take your stuff off," he said to Susana. She was standing in the middle of the floor, her nostrils slightly flared, staring around at the walls covered with hand-glazed Italian tile, the real-wood locker doors. She jumped as he touched her arm.

"Yo." She pulled off her gloves and fumbled with her parka, her movements stiff and clumsy.

The inner door opened for them, and she jumped again, dropping her parka in an untidy heap on the floor, following him stiff-legged into the main room. This room had been decorated with rosebushes the last time he had been here. Now wisteria vines twined on beautifully crafted trellises, heavy with drooping clusters of purple blossoms. White snapdragons bloomed in antique Chinese pots set here and there between wrought-iron chairs and cushioned loungers. Adequate holos, but not an outstanding job. Susana edged around a pot, wide-eyed and tense. It occurred to David that this was almost as alien an environment to her as the ice outside. Perhaps more frightening.

"The greenery is all holo," he said to break the silence. "The furniture's real—most of it, anyway. But you might want to check before you sit down."

"You're kidding." She touched a purple wisteria cluster, wiggling her fingers inside the projection. "Well, shit. Fancy job."

She eyed the plants, relaxing a little. Visual unreality she could handle. That was familiar ground. David looked toward the door just as Harmon Alcourt walked into the room. He always looked good, but David could see age in the way he held his body, as if he were fighting an extra tug of gravity. Fighting and losing—slowly, but losing all the same. Castor was with him, now wearing his licensed-aide uniform.

"David." Alcourt smiled, a real smile, as if this were a visit, a pleasurable moment and nothing more. "It's so good to see you again."

"Like we had a fucking *choice*." Susana shoved forward, fists clenched. "Shut it down, okay? Who do you think you're kidding? Hey!" She twisted violently as Castor stepped up behind her and seized her arms. A muscle jumped in his cheek, and Susana gasped suddenly, her face going white with pain.

David chopped his hand down on Castor's wrist, breaking his grip on Susana. Castor took a quick step forward as she wrenched free, his face darkening.

"Stop!" Alcourt glared at them. *"You."* He pointed at Susana.

"You are a guest in my house, and you will behave like one, please. Castor, show her to her room."

"Guest?" Susana clenched her fists. "Don't give me 'guest,' scumbag. Just 'cause you hide behind your muscle doesn't make you *clean*. Come near me and I'll kick your fucking nuts off." She showed her teeth at Castor.

David winced. Alcourt's expression was shaded with outrage and disgust. He was staring at Susana warily, as if she were an exotic, unpredictable animal. Castor was poised, waiting for a cue, a hungry look in his eyes. This was getting out of hand. Beyond this civilized facade Serafina lay dead in the hot desert sun. The step from this scene to that one might be very, very short.

"Susana?" David laid a hand on her arm, putting urgency into his grip. She was scared, although she was hiding it well enough. "I need to talk to him," he murmured. "I need to do it alone, okay? Will you go with this guy? You'll be all right."

"You're so sure, huh? Since when did you get elected boss?"

Tough words, but she was trembling a little. "Susana, please?" He did not want her to hear whatever was going to be said here. Knowledge could be dangerous, as deadly as a poisoned kicker. Susana's eyes were on his face. They flickered suddenly, and she looked away, her shoulders slumping.

"Have it your way." She jerked her head at Castor and stalked past him.

David watched her leave, then turned his eyes on Alcourt at last. "She'll be all right? I told her she would be."

"David!" Alcourt's outrage was real. "What do you think? I asked Castor to show her to a room since she can't behave. I didn't ask him to strangle her. Where did you find her, anyway?"

"Let's not play games, Harmon. The men who picked us up in the desert shot the woman who was with us." The words gave him a breathless sense of falling, as if he had just stepped from a cliff. "They would have shot Susana—and you know that, because they checked with you for further instructions." How far was the drop? "What exactly did you tell them? Pick up David Chen but make sure there are no witnesses? Or did you actually say 'kill anyone with him'? Did you put it like that? In so many words?"

"My God, David." Alcourt took a step back, his expression a mixture of shock, anger, and hurt. "I rescue your butt, and you walk into my house and throw this, this . . . *accusation* in my face?" His voice trembled. "You asked me for help, and I helped you. How can you say such things to me?"

Truth. He could swear that Harmon Alcourt was telling the truth.

For a dizzy moment David wondered if he had fallen into a virtual Erebus where none of this ugliness had ever happened. He realized he was fingering the bristly hair on his scalp, feeling for the faint traces of surgery. Alcourt was that convincing. "Too bad you don't design Selfs." David took his hand away abruptly. "You'd be the best on the market."

Alcourt stiffened, then relaxed visibly. "David, you're tired. I won't pretend that what you just said doesn't make me angry." His eyes flashed. "Part of me wants to throw you out right now. I'm tempted." His lips thinned, then relaxed. "Hell, we've been friends too long for me to throw your friendship away so casually." He put a hand on David's shoulder, his face slightly averted. "Come have a drink and something to eat. You're tired, and you've been through hell. I know that. Yes, I checked into the hospital report." He guided David gently toward the door. "That kind of horror could skew anyone's perspective."

David let himself be guided, his feet lead weights, fatigue dragging at his flesh. The normality of this conversation, Alcourt's genuine concern, scattered his anger, leaving him dazed and floundering. He had walked into this room ready for confrontation and perhaps death. He was fingering the scar again. David took his hand away from his scalp, noticing suddenly that Alcourt was steering them carefully around his holoed plants, as if they were real.

Maybe they were. He was losing his grip on reality in this place. Alcourt ushered them into the library, where a tray of cheese and fruit lay on the table. David stared at the perfect globes of nectarines nestled among polished black grapes, all dirt-grown and carefully tested for toxins. He wondered if Susana had ever tasted dirt-grown fruit.

"David, you can stay here as long as you need to. I've got some projects in mind that I'd like to have you do." Alcourt handed him a glass of wine. "But I don't want you to take too much time from your own work." He lifted his own glass. "California Pinot. To your continued success, David."

David lifted his glass. Light from the antique Tiffany lamp on the carved wood desk filled the wine with sparks of ruby. Red as blood. Serafina's blood would be dry now. Crows would have picked out her eyes, and the scavengers would be eating her flesh. David set his glass down on the desktop, careful not to spill a single drop. A letter opener lay on the satiny wood: a delicate leaf of carved ivory. It had been broken in half. "Flander worked for you. You had a go-between pay him off in custom kickers," David began, and then it came to him suddenly, like a cascade of icy water down his spine. "*You're* the flesh behind the Anya Vanek Self," he said softly. "You're behind the Salgado Self, too. Flander did it. He created Selfs that even I have a hard time detecting." The clues had been there in both the Vanek and Salgado Selfs, the hints of Alcourt's rhythms and the nuances of his body language. But they were so subtle that he hadn't noticed. He would see them now—but only because he knew. No office made was likely to catch it, no matter how good. "And no one knows about this except Flander," he said softly. "How many of these undetectable Selfs do you have, Harmon? One in each major web so you can gather inside information, play one web off against the other?" That was what Security was all about—preventing just that from happening. "I don't understand." He shook his head, struggling to make sense of it. "These are only midlevel nodes. You don't need the money. Harmon, *why*?"

"Don't be ridiculous, David." Alcourt sipped his wine. "No one can create a Self that can get by really good office Security." He laughed sourly. "When you're as inside as I am, every office in the web carries your profile, and believe me, they check. You have a rather inflated opinion of your little lover's skill."

Once upon a time David had believed that one of Flander's creations was a real person. He swallowed bitterness. Shy-Shy had fooled him for quite some time. That was when he had realized that he was dealing with talent on a scale he could never hope to equal. Genius. Ah, Flander, couldn't you see this coming? No, because Flander was naive in some ways. He would have been seduced by the challenge and possibly by the temptation of the custom kickers. "Did Flander try to blackmail you?" David asked softly. "Or were you simply afraid that he might do it one day?"

"I've had enough of this." Alcourt drained his glass. "You're tired, David. You're upset—and understandably so, after what you've been through. But I'm tired of being insulted. Get some rest, and we'll try this again later. Castor?" He didn't raise his voice. "Show Mr. Chen to his room."

Alcourt's body language had changed subtly, had gone harder, straighter. It had a ruthless feel, and his eyes revealed nothing at all. It was like watching someone put on another Self. This was the Alcourt who operated in the web. This man could have ordered Serafina's murder and his torture. This was not the man who was his friend. David shivered suddenly, wondering which one was the real Alcourt and which was the put-on Self.

Castor had appeared almost instantly in the doorway, summoned by his link. He stood easily, his feet spread a little, watching David.

Expecting a struggle, by his posture. Anticipating it with enthusiasm. This was Erebus. David stood inside Harmon Alcourt's virtual universe.

"I'm not going to make a fuss." David turned on his heel and started for the door, unable to take the charade anymore.

"David?"

An echo of pain in Alcourt's voice stopped David at the door.

"I didn't intend you to get hurt. That was an accident."

"An accident." David shook his head, trying to banish Jack's smile. "Did you enter the sessions?" he asked softly. "Did you watch while they broke my bones? Did you listen to me scream?"

"I'm . . . sorry, David." Alcourt licked his lips, face averted. "I really am."

"Go to hell." David marched out of the room, followed closely by Castor.

Despair sat like a stone inside him as Castor herded him down the hall. He had gambled that the Alcourt he knew was the real one, that the ruthless web node was the Self, the mask.

He had been wrong. Now he knew about the scam. Flander knew. And Alcourt—the web Alcourt—would not be safe until they were both dead. David glanced into the desert garden as they passed it. Jewel had seen Serafina here. Did her ghost haunt it? Bizarre notion. And where was Jewel? Safe? Alcourt would be hunting her, too. No, she wasn't safe. He closed his eyes against the image of Serafina falling backward into the sage, arms spread, embracing death like a lover. She had known that she would die before the helicopter had even touched down. *I am no coyote,* she had said. The coyotes would give her her funeral.

Castor had opened a door for him, obviously hoping he would resist. He reminded David too much of Jack. David pushed past him to find himself in an elegant suite decorated in ivory and pastel turquoise. Nothing but the best for the condemned. An adjoining door opened, and Susana burst through. For a moment David thought she was going to throw herself into his arms, but she spied Castor and stopped in the middle of the room.

"Are you all right?" David touched her arm lightly.

"Yeah. I guess." She watched Castor leave, a trapped look in her eyes. "The door's locked. Mine is, anyway, and I bet yours is, too. There's no access, no voice response, no terminal anywhere in this damn place." She prowled into the bedroom and stood glaring at herself in the mirror wall at the foot of the bed. "It's a fucking cell."

"Alcourt doesn't use terminals for casual access. Everything is virtual."

"You got a set of skins I can borrow? How 'bout a pair of lenses?" She stuck her tongue out at her reflection. "There aren't any in here—that I can find, anyway." Susana picked up a statuette from the small table beside the bed. A naked girl bestrode a dolphin, carved in milky jade. "So." She hefted the figurine. "What happens now?"

He knew too much to lie to her. "I don't know." His shoulders slumped. "I'm still his only connection to Flander. I guess I'm a hostage to keep Flander in line."

"You listening?" She tossed her head and stared straight at the ceiling-mounted optics. "I know, too, okay? About the fake Selfs. I know as much as David does, so just keep it in mind, scumbag."

"Shut up!"

"No." She faced David, eyes flashing. "I'm in this, too, got it? He killed Carl, and he gutted him first. Don't give me any of this protective shit, David Chen. This is my score, too, okay?"

Big talk for a skinny 'burbs kid. But David felt no desire to laugh. "I'm sorry." He bowed. "Yes, you're in this, too, and I apologize for forgetting that." And it was too damn late to change it now, anyway.

"It's his ass if Flander spills it, huh?" Her voice rose sharply, edging toward hysteria. "So we're all three dead? Is that it? Oh, *shit*." She hurled the statuette at the mirror. "Fuck you, Alcourt! Are you listening, you prick?" Glass shattered, scattering across the carpet, and the dolphin bounced off the wall with a *thunk*. "That's what I think of you and your shitty games!"

"Susana, take it easy."

She flung herself away from his touch, lost her balance, and fell onto hands and knees amid the shards of glass. "Damn it," she gasped, and began to cry. "Goddammit."

A concealed hatch opened in the wall, and one of the little housekeeper beetles popped out. It scuttled across the carpet as David helped Susana to her feet, sucking up the glass with musical clinks and a satisfied hum. Someone was guiding it via the video pickups. A little reminder that they were standing in a fishbowl, that the walls were an illusion of privacy only. Susana leaned against him, weeping onto his shoulder. David patted her back, murmuring soothing words.

It was an act, the tantrum and tears. Good, but an act nonetheless. David held her and watched the carpet beetle eat glass, wondering exactly what her game was and if it could help them in any conceivable way.

Chapter
Twenty-two

She was *heavy*, as if death had settled like lead into her bones. Jewel struggled with Serafina's dead flesh, panting, sweating, her eyes dazzled by the bright morning sun.

The wind touched her as she half carried, half dragged Serafina's body through the sage, stroking Jewel's face with the intimate touch of a lover, whispering in her ears. Whispering longing. Whispering need, and envy, and hunger . . . Serafina's voice. Jewel bent her head, shutting her mind and her ears to the lost whisper. What did a soul sound like, scrabbling at the gates of life, wanting to come in? She remembered a mother singing lullabies in Creole French, crooning stories about when she had lived in the city, where she wore frilly dresses and all the men begged for a look or a toss of her head and she laughed at them all. But that was before she came home swollen and pregnant to her papa's farm, to walk behind the mule and grow brown and coarse in the sun. She had sold the frilly dresses to dress her baby daughter and herself in plain calico. Now all that remained of the city and her youth were the stories.

Serafina's memories of her mother. Jewel's memories now—as real as the memories of the distant, dreaming woman with the lost eyes. How many years had Serafina kept death at bay? Jewel shook her head, trying to clear the fog from her brain. She should sleep. Not here, a part of her cried. Who will you be when you wake up? She shivered as she found a shovel in the goat's shed. Serafina was still here in the wind and the sky, waiting. Waiting to slip inside Jewel, to slide into her head on the grease of those memories.

Jewel stabbed the shovel into the rocky soil, trying to block out the feel of red clay beneath her bare feet, the cracked leather reins as she plodded after the mule, driving him home after a day behind the plow. The memory was like an open virtual in her mind. She could walk down that corridor of yesterday to that long-ago red clay field. If it happened, if she let Serafina in, she would drown. Her handful of years would dissolve in Serafina's sea of yesterdays. She would *be* Serafina, overlaid, perhaps, with a gloss of Jewel.

No!

Jewel!

Jewel dug the shovel blade again into the stony soil, scraping up a bare handful of dirt and rock. The sun was high now, and she welcomed its lash on her back, fighting exhaustion, focusing on the bite of the splintery handle against her palms. David and Susana were lost. She was lost. It had all gone to hell, and if she blinked, if she let it, the wind would rush in and blow her away. Flies buzzed around the wrapped bundle that was Serafina's cold skin.

Don't think about her. Just dig.

Shovelful by shovelful the grave deepened. Shadows moved, tracking the burning eye of the sun as it moved across the sky. Her shadow grew longer until it stretched across the shallow grave. Her hands were bleeding, leaving smears of bright blood on the handle. Jewel stared at the shallow grave at her feet, mildly amazed because it was deep enough at last and she could quit. Her muscles ached and her arms flared with sunburn, but the pain was a necessary thing, a shield to keep ghosts at bay. She bent her knees, gasping a little as her muscles trembled and her legs threatened to buckle, flinching at the touch of Serafina's dead flesh.

The body slid into the grave in a small avalanche of dust and pebbles. The wind had gone away, and silence pressed down on her—an enormous, empty silence as big as the sky and the horizon. She was so thirsty. Jewel picked up the shovel again, staggering, aware suddenly that her body was on the verge of rebellion, that in a minute she would fall down and not be able to get up again. She dug the shovel into the soil and tipped a trickle of dust into the hole. Another. It was important . . . what she was doing . . . very important. Another shovelful, another. Someone was standing at the edge of the hole, watching her.

Linda? Jewel squinted, dazzled by the sun. Or was it Susana, come to accuse her? "I came back," Jewel croaked. "I did."

It was Serafina. She held out both hands, her face stark with longing.

"No." Jewel stumbled backward, nearly falling into the partly filled hole. "I'll never let you in. Never, do you hear me?"

No answer but the hiss of wind on sand. No Serafina, no Linda. No Susana. Nothing but harsh sun and heat. Hallucination. Jewel licked her cracked lips. Dehydration, she told herself with her aide's knowledge. Fatigue. Maybe sunstroke. The grave was full enough.

She let the shovel fall because it was too heavy to carry back to the house. Leave it here. Who cares?

Who cares?

Serafina had created her out of need. Elaine had stolen her out of love. In the end, what difference had it made? "Maybe nothing matters," Jewel said out loud. Far above, a hawk circled in the dry sky. And maybe . . . you had to *let* things matter. Jewel straightened slowly, feeling for strength, finding it like a thin, tough wire running through her, never mind that her flesh was trembling with fatigue. She picked up the shovel and went back to the house.

Serafina's shawl trailed across the chair where she had sat. Where her body had sat. Jewel picked it up, folded it carefully, and hung it over the back of the chair. She still had her skins on; she hadn't stopped to take them off after running out of the post office. They were filthy now, dusty and sweaty. She got a drink of water first, her flesh crying in relief, then dug her gloves and lenses from her pack. As she got them out, the wind pried the door open and came questing into the room, touching her with Serafina's fingers, prying at her. Never. Jewel slapped at it, hurried into Serafina's virtual chamber, and slammed the door closed behind her, shutting it out.

Flander was not in the ice cave.

"Flander? Where the hell are you?" Jewel cupped her virtual hands around her mouth, needing to yell, furious that he wasn't there, desperate. "Flander!"

His name echoed from the ice cavern's walls, and the chimera gave a gurgling snarl. Jewel stared down at her mangled body beneath the creature's hooves. It had torn out her throat, severing jugular or carotid, judging from the amount of spilled blood. A white gleam of mangled trachea was visible in the carnage, and the monster's goat hooves had left blood-edged bruises on the body. Realistic. Jewel stared at the pale, blood-streaked image of her face. Yes, you got it right, David. I let my past eat me. "Flander?" she said out loud. "Alcourt has him—David." And Susana, who had looked at her with Linda's eyes. "If you give a damn, get the hell in here."

"I'm right here." Flander blinked into existence in front of her, paws spread, fox nails digging into the ice. "You don't have to yell. Shit, lady, what do you mean, he's got David?"

"What I said." He had split into three images—a blurred redundancy of red fox fur, overlapping slightly, all staring at her, all panting, tongues lolling. "Smugglers picked him up in a 'copter. They shot Serafina." And Susana? Was she still alive? I ran out on you, kid, just like I did to your mother. I did, and I'm sorry, but it's too late now, isn't it? "Maybe David's already dead." She flung the words at Flander like icy stones, intending to hurt, wanting to smash him with their ugly truth. "Or maybe they're going to torture him again, fox. Are you going to watch if they post it again? This is your fuck-up, not his, so why don't you go put *your* body on the line this time? Time to decide, fox. How much does he mean to you?"

Flander twisted his triple heads into the air, and Jewel tensed, expecting him to leap at her face. Instead, his lips writhed back from his fox fangs, and she clapped virtual hands over her ears as an inhuman, shivering wail filled the cavern.

"Stop it!" She jerked her hands away from her face because, of course, that didn't block the sound. "Just *stop* it!" she screamed at him. "I'm so sick of your neat images, I could puke! David's in this because he loves you. Or he did. I hope to hell he knows better by now. You could give a shit, you spoiled jerk! You just play your games and do some really cool grieving in virtual, and you don't risk one hair off your ass. You said you loved him. So turn your body over to Alcourt or get out of here and stop pretending that it matters. Just *stop*." A sob caught in her throat, and she turned away, yanking off her lenses, blinking at the blurred walls of Serafina's virtual chamber.

"Jewel, wait. Please."

Flander's voice in her ears, because she hadn't exited yet; she had simply pulled off her lenses.

"Please, Jewel, help me. I'll stop, I'm all right. Don't leave me."

Her mouth open to exit, Jewel hesitated. Another game, she told herself, but there was a desperation in Flander's voice that she had never heard before, and it tugged at her. She couldn't touch Alcourt on her own. Maybe Flander couldn't, either, but . . . She let her breath out in a noisy rush and jammed her lenses back down over her face again.

He was human this time, the Flander she remembered from Erebus, skinny and small, the blond tail of his hair trailing down his back.

"You got to help me help David." He wavered in front of her, the icy wall just visible through his body, as if he were a transparent overlay on the cave. "I'm having trouble. In the Net, I mean. Things aren't working for me. I keep losing track, crashing, and I don't know why."

"I don't want to hear it." Jewel crossed her arms, feeling like stone inside. "You turn yourself over to Alcourt on a trade. I'm not going to talk about anything else."

"I can't." He held out his hands, imploring. "You don't understand. I've . . . lost it. I can't find it. I've tried, Jewel. I swear it, but it's gone."

It? Jewel felt a cold tickle at the back of her neck, even though she knew he was manipulating her again, playing his clever games. "What the hell are you talking about, Flander?"

"My flesh." He looked away, fingers knotted. "I've been trying to do it for a long time, you know—get out of myself. The flesh one, I mean. Get into the Net for real. I mean, I figured you could pull it off if you put enough of yourself into a complex matrix. We're just a bunch of stored information in a flesh Net, right? There had to be a way. And this kicker, it really cut me loose, you know? Like on your floor. I mean, I was okay. Sure, the stuff he'd stuck into the dose screwed up the body, but *I* was fine. So I, you know, got this friend of mine to make a connection with some bio dude, and he cleaned up the stuff. And anyway, I did it again. And . . . I don't know." He spread his hands in a jerky, half-ashamed gesture. "I can't go back. I just can't feel it anymore, you know? I'm *here*. Period. Only I'm not holding it together. I mean, all of a sudden you tell me a couple of days have gone by, or something. Only it hasn't—Not for me. But then I check, and it has, so I don't know what's going on. Jewel?" Flander held out his hands, then let them drop slowly to his sides. "If I could do it—go back into the bod—I'd do it. I'd give him the key to those Selfs. I'd walk into Alcourt's arms if he'd let David off. Anything he wanted. Only I can't. I think . . . I died. Jewel?" He touched her this time, a thin groping of fingertips against her upper arm. "Jewel, will you believe me? Please? For David? We can't do anything unless you understand."

Jewel shuddered because her skins simulated the touch of flesh fingers on her arm. "You're telling me you're dead," she whispered. "You're telling me that you're some kind of electronic ghost or AI or something. That's crazy. You know it, I know it, so you're shitting me again."

"I'm not."

He was the master of virtual Self. He could give her any expression, any nuance of tone or gesture that he wanted.

So why the hell did she believe him?

Maybe because the wind waited outside to whisper in her ears with Serafina's voice. Maybe because she remembered plowing with a mule. "Hell, why not?" she said softly. "I just talked to a

dead woman with fly maggots in her mouth.'' She wanted to laugh
at his uncomprehending expression. ''What the hell? Why shouldn't
I believe that you're a ghost?''

''Will you talk straight?'' His image shimmered, and red fur
coated him briefly before he refocused in human mode. ''I don't
give a shit about ghosts. I just want to spring David, okay?''

''What did you do?'' she said flatly. ''Why does Alcourt want
to kill you, Flander? For pirating?''

''No.'' Flander tossed his head, his expression sulky as a child's.
''I don't pirate. I told David I'd quit, and I did, okay? Even if he
didn't believe it. I guess he had reason not to believe it.'' His
shoulders slumped suddenly. ''I guess I gave him enough reason.
No, I did some work for Alcourt. I made him a bunch of Selfs.
Really good ones.'' He gave her a sideways look. ''When I want
to, I can do a hot Self. Not even David can tell right off, and these
were better than I'd ever done. They'll get by any office out there.
For a while, anyway.'' He shrugged. ''I did one for each web, by
my count. It was some job, you better believe.''

Oh, shit.

If Flander was the crazy genius that David had claimed, if he
could do a Self that no one could detect . . .

Then Harmon Alcourt had access to *all* the webs.

''Why?'' Jewel stared at Flander, not really seeing him, seeing
the holo-filled rooms of Alcourt's Erebus retreat. ''Doesn't he have
enough?''

''Enough what? If you're talking about Alcourt, I bet that dude
never has enough *anything*, lady.'' Flander tossed his hair back
over his shoulder. ''What now?'' His image was beginning to blur,
splitting into multicolored shadows. ''What the hell can I do? All
he wants is my flesh.''

''Flander, you're losing it. Flander!'' To Jewel's relief, he solidified again, and she closed her eyes, struggling to think. What *could*
they do? No way they could get close to Erebus, even with Flander's
talents. ''What does he really want?'' she said softly.

''Me, dead.''

And he already was. The craziness of the entire conversation hit
her and made her want to laugh or maybe scream. Jewel took a
deep breath. ''He's afraid you'll expose him.'' She frowned, struggling to think, her brain buzzing with feverish energy, shifting from
possibility to possibility in a frenzied staccato. ''Can you?'' She
snapped her fingers. ''You fixed them, didn't you, you sly little
bastard? You've got some way to mess him up.''

''Well, yeah, but I've got to get into his access first, you know?

I've got to have, like, direct connection to one of 'em or I can't do it. I had to pull something like that to get it by him, and he guessed, anyway.'' Flander grimaced.

"So he knows.'' Jewel chewed her lip. "That's why he wants you dead. So you can't use the key and expose him.'' If Alcourt's trick was discovered, he would be out, blacklisted by every web, ostracized. Everyone would know. The Alcourt who had broken that letter opener would not risk it. Better to be dead than the target of general laughter? "Where did you leave it?'' Jewel asked gently. "Your . . . body. Where did you do your last access?''

"I was in our room,'' Flander said softly. "David was kind of pissed at me, so he was working a lot on Alcourt's garden thing. Obsessing, you know? And I . . . went out on the ice. I did that, sometimes, to sort of clear my head. Only it didn't, this time, and I had this cleaned-up stuff back from my friend, and I really wanted to try it. And I knew David was going to be into that desert all night, 'cause that's what he does when he's pissed, so I did it.'' He looked away from her. "I figured I'd be up again before he got back, or he'd figure I fell asleep on a job and just go on to bed. Only I didn't come up. Not that I remember.'' He looked at her, his eyes haunted. "I had a lot of blackouts on that stuff. That's how I ended up in your room. 'Cause I was there just before, remember? Sort of checking you out? So I think maybe I went back out on the ice, like sleepwalking. And I've got all these gimmicks tucked into Erebus Security. Because they think they're so hot down there. So I kind of fucked around, and the pricks never even tumbled. I could go in and out through the locks, and it didn't show on the pickups. I had this editing loop in place. So . . . I think maybe my body's on the ice.'' He ran out of words suddenly and hunched his shoulders.

"David was right,'' Jewel said softly. "He said you were trying to commit suicide.''

"Bullshit.'' Flander glowered at her. "He didn't understand. I'm here, right? Do I sound dead to you, lady? Huh?'' He dropped into the fox again, tail low, hackles raised. "It's the flesh—lose the flesh, that's all I was after. What's it good for? Gets you hurt, lady. Lets people cause you extreme pain. David was too much into flesh to understand. That's all.'' He metamorphosed into a man again, his face sad, his green eyes full of shadow. "I tried to make him understand. I lived with this operator, you know? She picked me up off the street when I was, like, six, and she just took me in. Just like that. She was truly hot, Shy-Shy. Truly.'' His eyes got darker, as if someone were turning down a lamp behind windows of green glass. "I was there the day this muscle team busted in. She told me to hide, and she meant it, lady. They were a retribution squad from some node she'd burned. They took her apart. A little at a time." His eyes had become holes of darkness in his face. "I lay flat, played dead, listening to her scream. I puked, lady, I shit myself, and I just lay in it, too scared to move. Too fucking scared, because they'd off me, too. That's it," he said softly. "That's what flesh gets you. That's what it got David. I bet he understands now." A spark of fire kindled in his eyes as he faced her. "I don't regret it, okay? Cutting loose, I mean. I'd do it again right now."

"David understands." Jewel looked away from Flander's tortured face.

What is real, and what is illusion? She had thought about that a lot down in Erebus. Real, to David, was flesh. Touch. Outside the wind cried in Serafina's voice, and Jewel shivered. If the fake is good enough, is it still a fake? A model of an atmosphere is not a real atmosphere, but if the model of a human mind can think and grieve, what is it?

Can you model a soul?

"I think I see a way out." She stared at the chimera and its bloody prey. "It's a risk for David and Susana. It's a risk for you." Because if he was alive, he could still die. His death was the only bait Alcourt would rise to. "It could work. Maybe."

"So we do it." Flander's voice was low and harsh. "We do it right now, because I don't know how much longer I can hold it together. Okay, Jewel?"

"Okay." Jewel let her breath out in a slow sigh. "I hope Harmon Alcourt is willing to believe in ghosts." She glanced at the chimera and looked away. The mangled body beneath its cloven hooves was Flander's. "We need money to pay for the best secure archive in the Net. And you need to trust me."

"Jewel, my dear." Harmon Alcourt lounged on the stone bench beside the pool David had designed for him, trailing his virtual fingers idly in the water. "I'm a very busy man, as you well know. I allowed you access because I had a lot of respect for you as an employee." *Had.* He stressed the word slightly as he flicked drops of water from his fingers. He frowned. "Don't jerk me around."

"So don't give me shit." Jewel lifted one eyebrow delicately. She had keyed her Self to confidence and veiled greed. Flander had done some very fast diddling with it because he knew Alcourt's office and had inserted a trick or two. Even so, she did her best to project right along with her Self.

It wasn't easy. A part of her wanted to shout agreement with the assessment that she was jerking him around. He would be crazy to go for this, and now he would know where she was. Flander had warned her about that.

Don't even think like that. It'll show.

"If your security was so good, how come you never found out that Serafina was my mother?" Jewel let her smile carry just a trace of smugness. "If you don't believe me, check with the smugglers you hired—the ones who gunned her down. We look very much alike, she and I. And I am very much her daughter in my Net abilities. Which is why you only found my official history."

"I don't know what you're talking about. Smugglers? Cut the melodrama, please." Alcourt grimaced. "As I recall, you couldn't find your way around the outermost fringes of the web. And I have never believed in ghosts, dear. Not the ectoplasmic variety, anyway." His smile was warmly humorous, but her office tinged his aura with faint green.

Doubts? Good. Jewel kept her smile in place. "Go look. I think you'll find it." Maybe.

"Flander's body?" Alcourt waved the words away. "Security would have a record of his leaving and not returning."

"Security?" Jewel loaded her voice and posture with scorn, trying to *feel* it. "We both know that the little prick was playing all kinds of games with your Security down there."

"I thought he was a friend of yours?"

His surprise read genuine, and maybe it was. "He thought he was." She met his stare. "You have what I want."

For a long moment Alcourt was silent, studying her, considering whatever his office was reading from her Self. "Tell me again. Exactly what you are offering?" he asked finally. And although his Self showed a skeptical frown, Jewel's heart leapt. Got him.

She snapped her fingers, and a stuffed animal appeared in her hand; a red fox with green glass eyes. The crimson blob of a security seal hung around its neck on a green ribbon. "He's in here. Check the Token File if you want." She shrugged. "I put a copy of the Security certification into it. This is *Flander,* Harmon—all there is of him. One copy only. Erase this file and he's dead." She tossed the toy fox in the air and caught it. "Think about it. Check around for him. Only don't send your animals here." She let her smile slip, not even needing her Self to augment her expression. "If you try anything, this gets released." She lofted the toy gently once again. "And then he's loose with a vengeance. He's not a real stable personality, Harmon."

"I know." He ignored her use of his given name. "What you're telling me is, of course, impossible." He reached out and touched the seal, frowning at something she could not see as the Token File downloaded to his office. He was there—Flander, file, electronic soul.

Without warning, Alcourt's hand shot out like a spear. It went right through the toy fox, and he yanked it back with a cry, glaring at her.

So you don't believe me, huh? "Surely you didn't think I'd toss it at your feet without Security?" Jewel smiled. Flander had been right that he would try to crack the file. Good thing Serafina had set up the layered protection that she had.

"Pretending for one moment that this insanity might be truth, how did you get that jerk into his present state?"

Genuine curiosity. Jewel let her smile go and met his cold, virtual eyes. "He trusted me."

"You know, I'm sorry that you didn't take me up on my offer." Alcourt bowed his head fractionally. "I'm afraid that it's too late now, but I will never underestimate you as an adversary."

Threat? Jewel felt a chill but tried not to show it. It wasn't a threat; it was a promise. That's what the web was about, wasn't it? Continual polite war? Bloodless virtual wounds given and received, and occasionally the real thing, carried out from a safe virtual distance. Civilized violence.

"I left an access open for you." She swallowed bile, wanting to spit on his virtual floor. "Thank you for your valuable time." She bowed formally and exited before he could dismiss her.

"Fuck him," she said to the rough walls of Serafina's chamber.

He hadn't told her whether Susana and David were even alive. That would be next, after he had checked out her story. It would be his move, then: a cautious showing of his hand, just a glimpse, to elicit an offer from her. If they *were* alive. They had to be. Believe it. Jewel sighed. Her story that she had been in collaboration with Serafina was a fragile tissue of lies, a virtual fabrication that might, if she was very lucky, come across as reality. Where does reality end, Harmon, and virtual begin? I hope to hell you can't find the seam . . . Jewel pulled off her lenses and tossed them onto a shelf.

Harmon Alcourt would snap his fingers and call in some labor. He'd tell them to go look for a body. On Erebus, he could do that, and if they found one no one else would know. Unless Alcourt wanted it that way. Erebus was beyond any law save that of the web. Jewel stripped off her gloves and laid them on the shelf beside her lenses. Would they find Flander's corpse, frozen stiff and white?

She held out her hand, staring at her empty palm as if the stuffed fox were still in her grasp. Flander's Self—the program, the complex matrix of information that made it walk, talk, and smile his fox grin—was contained within a Secure File. If what Flander had told her was the incredible, impossible truth, she *did* hold his life in her palm.

If Alcourt found a body on the ice, he would make an offer. Heart line, life line. She traced them on her palm. He had believed her because she had told him the truth. And because a part of her could do it—hand over the fox, sell Flander, David, and Susana for the price of an inside-web perch. His office had read that, too. Yes, Harmon. Jewel closed her fingers slowly into a fist and lowered her hand. I could make it in your world.

Chapter Twenty-three

David lay on the bed, staring at the faint mark that the vanished mirror had left on the ivory wall. An electronic sketch pad that he had discovered in a drawer lay beside him. David wondered if Harmon had ordered Housekeeping to leave it there for him. He pushed the pad away with one finger. He had been doodling designs for a new piece—a crude task in 2-D, but at least it gave him something to do. Alcourt had ignored them for the past twenty-four hours. The outer doors remained locked; each room had a kitchenwall and its own bathroom. David had explored every square centimeter of the suite, searching for something that might help them escape. If they could get out into the public corridors . . . David glanced up at the ceiling, at the nearly unnoticeable flaws in the walls that marked the video pickups. Someone was undoubtedly watching them over the monitors. As Susana had said, it was a cell. Plush but a cell all the same. And if there was a way out, he had missed it. He sighed as a door opened in the main room. "Susana?"

"Yo." She stuck her head through the door, her eyes darting around the room as if someone might be hiding in the closet or under the bed. "Anything doing?"

The words sounded brittle, as if they might shatter like glass. "Nothing." David sat up. "You look like shit. Did you eat anything today?"

"Thanks a lot. I don't remember. I don't want anything." Susana sat down on the foot of the bed and began to bounce gently up and down. "If we don't get out of here pretty soon, I'm gonna come unglued."

She looked bad, pale and pinched, and her eyes glittered as if she had a fever. He touched her skin, but she felt cool, almost too cold. She had been prowling the space like a caged animal.

"How can you stand it?" she asked in a breathy whisper. "Just sitting here, I mean. Waiting for him to do something. He's so fucking *polite*. How can you handle it?'' She broke off abruptly, lower lip clamped between her teeth, her muscles as tight as wire. ''Shit,'' she hissed. ''I'm gonna start screaming or breaking stuff for real.''

''Take it easy, Susana.'' David put a hand on her arm, half expecting her to brush him off. ''If we get a chance, we try for a public corridor and make a major fuss. I know a few people who spend time here. That should help.'' But how to get into a public corridor? Alcourt's Security opened and closed doors. David picked up the pad. I've given up, he thought, and felt a twitch of anger at himself. It had been growing on him ever since the door had locked behind him: helplessness as crippling as his blindness. More crippling, perhaps. At least he had been able to feel his way around his studio when he was blind.

Blind . . . ''That's it,'' he said, and immediately clamped his lips together. Eavesdroppers, fool. Shut up.

Susana looked at him from the corners of her eyes. ''Is it?'' She reached for the sketch pad in his lap. ''Show me. What is it, anyway?''

Sharp kid—sharper than he. ''It's an idea for a new piece. Look.'' He took the stylus, trying to stifle the leap of hope that was probably far too premature. ''I'm going to use a volcano background.'' *I had a personal access here,* he scribbled across the pad. *If Security didn't purge it, it's still open.* They might have missed it. It had been a convenience while he had worked on the desert garden—a direct access into his files, keyed to him alone. It was an in-house access only, so it wasn't a Security risk. They might have overlooked it.

''I don't get it. You mean like this?'' Susana took back the stylus, shaking her tangled hair forward over one shoulder and raking her fingers through it absentmindedly. She hunched over the pad like any kid with bad posture, her loose hair and the curve of her shoulders hiding the pad from the video eyes no matter what their angle of view might be. *No lenses,* she scribbled.

David shrugged. ''Close. This is the focus, here.'' *If I remember the visuals, I can go by touch.* Maybe. He hadn't been into Alcourt's House menu much—twice? Three times? David closed his eyes briefly, trying to remember the visual layout. Alcourt used a simple 3-D menu: icons were residents of a tropical reef. If he could get into a file, he might be able to get voice access to the Net. Alcourt's House was complex, the newest and most elaborate on the market. That might work to his advantage; a simpler system would simply have denied him voice access, period. This one might recognize him if he addressed it from an established access.

If he could access the Net and get into his studio, he could contact some of the inside nodes he knew—people here who could go head to head with Harmon Alcourt. Erebus was not entirely beyond the law. And he knew a few nodes who would love to get a chance at Alcourt. David smiled crookedly, aware of Susana's eyes on his face, of her suppressed hope.

I'll need a distraction. The invisible eyes were watching. They could stop him fast enough once they guessed what he was trying to do. David touched the erase key, blanking the pad without saving their scribbles. "I'm starving." He tossed the pad onto the bed, stood up, and stretched. "Let's get some lunch."

"I hate the food here." Susana hunched her shoulders even more, suddenly sullen and angry. "Do you hear me?" she yelled at the invisible watcher. "I *hate* the fucking food!"

Nice job. David hid his appreciation behind rolling eyes and resignation. One watcher; he would bet on it. Let the watcher keep his or her electronic eyes on Susana.

"Do you hear me?" She stomped past him to order a bowl of noodles from the kitchen wall. "I hate it," she yelled, grabbing the bowl.

Oh, yeah, their eavesdropper would be watching her, waiting for that bowl to hit the wall, maybe even amused. More fun than they had had all week. David closed his eyes, heart pounding. Do it. He snapped his fingers twice, and the familiar gesture brought the desert garden back in a rush. If he took two steps *that* way, he would stub his toe on the rock Alcourt had had flown in from the Grand Canyon Preserve.

In, he told himself, although he didn't know that for sure at all. Ceramic crashed and broke in the main room. Noodles all over the walls? "House, access main menu," he said, and closed his eyes, praying that their watcher was enjoying the little scene Susana was creating.

He felt the shift. Funny how he had never noticed it when he had sight—that tiny change in skin tone as his Kraeger reacted to a new environment. So, he *was* in. Desperately he tried to relax, to summon up a vision of the menu: bright clownfish, anemones, a purple starfish . . . Main system over there, a yellow and black fish. Library that pink-shelled mollusk, communications that branch of coral right *there*. He reached and his palm tingled. Got it? "House, access David Chen studio." Hurry, hurry. More crashing and banging from Susana.

"I'm sorry." Alcourt's House voice had a faint accent, although David had never been able to place it. "You must choose Communications in order to access outside systems."

Shit! He had blown it. David groped, one hand on his current icon as an anchor. Nothing, nothing. Where the hell were the other icons? "House, unlock all guest room doors." A desperation move.

"Guest rooms are all unlocked."

Better than nothing. David opened his eyes and bolted through the main room. Noodles and stir-fried vegetables clung to the walls. Susana had just reached the door and was slapping her palm against the plate. It opened, and they dashed through. "Turn right," David gasped, but it was too late. She dodged left, didn't hear him, was racing down the corridor.

"Susana! Wrong *way*." He followed.

She heard him this time and skidded to a stop in front of the solarium doors, her eyes tracking beyond him, narrowing. Someone was in the corridor behind him? David threw a quick glance over his shoulder. Castor, damn. He shoved Susana through the doors, ducking into the changing room just inside. Robes and clothes hung on hooks or lay folded on shelves. Extra skinthins. Lenses. Three or four pairs lay in a tangled heap next to some gloves. David grabbed a pair, yanked them on, snapped his fingers into the desert access, then dropped into the main menu again. No time for Communications. He grabbed the icon for door security. "House, lock solarium," he panted. "My pass only."

"Solarium locked," the House informed him. "Harmon Alcourt cannot be denied entry."

Well, maybe Harmon was busy. Whoever was outside banged twice on the doors, but they didn't open.

"Let me know when I can get into an access," Susana said from outside the virtual. "Maybe I can find a way out of here."

"In a second." David grabbed the Communications icon—

And fell into another virtual.

The sudden transition made him briefly dizzy. He caught his balance, his mind registering leaves and water, recognizing the garden foyer he had created for Alcourt. Harmon sat on the rock bench beside the pool, and Jewel stood in front of him, a plush toy fox in her hands. They both looked up in surprise as David appeared in the virtual.

"David!" Jewel's eyes widened. "What are you doing here? Where's Susana?"

"Right here with me. She's fine." David read the tension her Self was hiding and felt a chill. "What's going on?"

Alcourt scowled at David. "Nothing that concerns you. How did you get in here?" He was masking outright rage with a face of mild annoyance. "Never mind. If you'll excuse us, I'd like to finish this private interview. I'll talk to you later."

"Stop playing games, Harmon." David stepped forward, eyeing the stuffed fox in Jewel's hands. What the hell did the metaphor represent? What was going on here? "I'm not a guest, and you know it. Susana and I are prisoners in your guest room. How about if we end this charade right now."

"You already seem to have done so." Alcourt's eyes shifted up and left, reading a heads-up display that David could not see. "How can you be a prisoner when you're in the solarium? Stay and listen." He smiled at Jewel. "I don't mind."

Jewel minded. David read it through her Self. The solarium doors whispered. David tensed, but no one grabbed him. Another whisper as they closed. "Susana?" he murmured. Silence. Damn her. If he exited, Harmon could lock him out permanently. "What's going on?"

"A trade." Alcourt smiled, but he was as cold as Erebus's flank. "Jewel is going to sell me your fox lover in return for a considerable chunk of money and power."

"What?" She would not do this. David tried to reach through Jewel's Self, but she wouldn't look at him and he got nothing but tension from her. She wouldn't do it, but she had run again, and maybe this was a way of shutting doors behind her, shutting friendship away behind a wall of betrayal. "Serafina's dead," David said urgently. "Alcourt's hired help shot her as we were on our way to Ryo."

"I know." Her tone was flat and cold. "It doesn't change anything." She held up the fox toy. "You found the body, Harmon. You know I'm telling the truth, no matter how impossible it seems. I'll strip the Security on this as soon as you meet my terms. You transmit the signed agreement, and I'll give you the access code. Erase the file and you're safe."

"Except for you," Alcourt said pleasantly. His rage smoldered like buried coals beneath the calm, amused veneer of his Self.

"Except for me." Jewel gave him a thin smile. "I'll take my chances."

Body. Destroy the file. The words tolled like funeral bells in David's head. Flander. This had to do with his death. That was what Alcourt wanted, and nothing else. And Jewel was about to give Flander to him. She meant it.

David flung himself at her, clutching for the fox-toy icon. His hands went right through it, but Jewel staggered as he crashed into her. Her skins told her *contact*, and her flesh was fooled. She stumbled sideways, losing her balance as he grabbed again for the fox.

"David, *don't*!" she screamed, but he wasn't listening; he thought she was was selling Flander out. He believed in that betrayal because he knew that a part of her could do that, could sell him out if it got her what she wanted. That was why Alcourt had believed her. Because it could be true.

Only it wasn't.

With a cry she clutched at the toy, needing to strip the security seal so that Flander would be released inside Alcourt's access. David grabbed again. This time, to her horror, he yanked the toy away from her. He had accessed the web from Serafina's house, she remembered too late. Serafina must have exempted him from her security file. Neither Jewel nor Flander had thought of David; he wasn't a threat. But his access was from Alcourt's system, which meant Alcourt now had access to the fox. Jewel flung herself at David. Too late.

An enormous cartoon hammer had appeared in Alcourt's hand, and he slammed the fox from David's grasp. David lost his balance as the fox fell to the flagstones underfoot. With a cry of triumph, Alcourt smashed the bizarre hammer down on the toy. Cloth split, and white stuffing spilled out like guts. Stunned, Jewel stared at the stuffing on the stone floor. One of the fox's green glass eyes had cracked straight across, and the broken piece glinted on the floor. What was that hammer? It had to be some kind of killer access. Alcourt had blasted his way into the archive the minute David had crashed the Security. Alcourt never hesitated.

"David?" Jewel sank to one knee, not wanting to touch the ruined fox. What happens when you die in the Net? "I wasn't . . ." Her eyes stung with burning tears for Flander, who was truly dead this time. For herself and Susana and David, who would die. Too late for explanations or salvation.

"I'm afraid you have no bargaining position anymore." Alcourt looked from her to David and back again.

He might not dirty the web with blood, but he would spill it in the flesh world. Jewel clenched her teeth, groping dully for something, anything to save them.

"Good-bye," Alcourt said coldly.

In a second, a half second, the foyer would vanish—

Daughter . . . The word was a whisper of desert wind, groping through the cracks in the virtual chamber, laden with dust and the smell of sage. *Daughter* . . .

No. Jewel focused on the foyer, desperately trying to shut out the flesh world and the gritty taste of dust on her lips. Not now, oh, God, not *now*. On the virtual floor in front of her the broken fox toy twitched like a dying animal but was actually a dying man— Flander in the only existence he had, because Alcourt had found his frozen corpse out on the ice, curled up in a hollow in some rocks.

Daughter . . . The desert whispered to her with Serafina's voice and Serafina's memories, prying at the walls of her mind.

Through a hot blur of tears, Jewel watched David kneel and reach for the fox, his face twisted with grief as if he knew, even though she hadn't told him.

Daughter . . .

She could feel those memories, those years of life plucking at her soul. Serafina, Net operator. Serafina could have saved them, reached through the ruin of Flander to find what he had hidden: the key, the thread that would unravel Harmon Alcourt's pretty tapestry of power and deceit and death. Serafina could do it. The wind stroked her face with Serafina's fingers, wanting life, wanting entrance. Jewel shivered, hating Alcourt suddenly and intensely— hating him because he didn't have to touch, because he didn't care that the 'burbs had eaten Linda and would eat Susana even if he didn't kill her. Because he had everything and it was not enough, would never be enough, and she wanted vengeance for Carl, and Flander, and David.

That heady sense of freedom seized her: freedom to choose, to fly, to die. For everything, a price—for love, for hate . . . Vengeance is mine. *You are stronger than I,* Serafina had said. If it wasn't so, the price would be her soul.

Maybe she had already sold it, years before, when she had sent Linda into Carl's bed.

Maybe it was time to find out.

Jewel laughed with the sound of a cat growling. From the corner of her eye she saw David turning toward her, his eyes narrowing with surprise. She spread her hands, her fingers curving like cat claws, tasting dust on her tongue in that distant desert room, letting Serafina in . . . Mother. Sister. Self.

Vengeance is mine.

Of course he's not dead. The fox *always* keeps a copy. She raked the toy image open with one razored claw, seeing what was there in spite of the havoc wreaked by Alcourt's assault. Links—yes— hidden well enough to fool even a high-end archive sweep. Ah, you sly, talented little fox, you. Do this, and *this*, and this. She plucked threads, followed them back to their sources in a handful of nano-seconds, darting through the Net from here to there to there because she knew how the fox's mind worked, piecing together the few bits of thread into one long string.

Got it, node! Let's just see what kind of mischief the little fox pest had in mind.

Back in an instant; long in the Net, short in the flesh. No one had moved in the virtual foyer. In and out between heartbeats. The node still looking smug—they all think too much of themselves. The artist grieving—well, he should be. Death in the air? The scent of blood to spill soon, but whose death? Whose blood? All right, fox, I brought you back. You've got something up your sleeve be-cause that's your style. It's your show now, so *do* it!

David sucked in his breath as the torn fragments of the fox toy twitched. Unbelieving, he watched as they shivered, hesitated, then gathered in a sudden implosion, wavering, distorting. ''David?'' Flander looked at him, eyes pleading—fading, brightening, solid-ifying in an instant into his normal fox form. ''David, I'm sorry. I am, but it'll be okay, I promise.''

With a cry, Alcourt swung the hammer again.

''Look out!'' David threw himself forward to try to block it but fell to his knees, powerless in Alcourt's virtual. ''Get out of here, Flander. Get *out*!''

But Flander crouched instead, snapping here and there as the hammer descended and slowed, resisted briefly by Flander's Se-curity. Eyes full of green fire, he snapped one last time, then bared his teeth as Alcourt's killer program touched him. ''Gotcha, you bastard,'' he hissed. ''I love you, David.''

He exploded, fragments of fox fur flying in all directions, his eyes winking out.

''Flander!'' He was gone. David looked around wildly, but noth-ing remained, no toy pieces, no scraps of fur or fox flesh. Nothing. He was dead. David bowed his head, feeling the tears begin to gather.

''He saved you, artist,'' Jewel said in Serafina's voice.

Out in the web every one of Alcourt's fake Selfs was changing, altering, right in front of business associates, nodes, virtual lov-ers—taking on Alcourt's face, readable by any office, no matter how cheap. This is Harmon Alcourt. Not who you thought, huh?

''No,'' Alcourt cried hoarsely. He stared at them, past them, his wild eyes seeing something they couldn't see. ''You bastard. You little fox bastard, you've killed him. They'll know. They all know, and now they'll *laugh* at me." His voice trembled.

He had changed. David stared at Alcourt. His Self had eroded away, dissolved by Flander's ghostly command. The man who stood in front of him was straight visual, the flesh Harmon Alcourt—the man who had been his friend.

"David, how could you let Flander do this—kill him?" Alcourt buried his face in his hands. "He's dead; it feels like I'm dead—how can I do it without him? But it doesn't matter, does it, because they won't let me in. Because they know, don't they? And they'll turn on me, like the jackals they are; they'll eat me. He showed them . . ." His words trailed away into a choked sob.

Flander had somehow blown the scam? *Something* had happened. "Harmon." David pitched his voice with firm warmth. "Will you unlock all the doors, please. We need to leave."

"Leave, leave, you can't help me. No one can help me. How could he do this?"

There was no editing. Alcourt's face was softening, aging in front of his eyes, melting into lines of loss and childish fright. David got slowly to his feet. "Unlock the doors, Harmon."

The lock on the solarium door clicked.

"Don't be mad at me, David." Alcourt held out a shaking hand. "He did it. I didn't; he wasn't me. I had to let him do things his way or they'd have eaten us. The jackals. You've got to have an edge to stay in the center, and I was losing it. David?" Alcourt's face was full of pleading. "I'm sorry for what he did. I couldn't control him. I'm sorry. I am."

He wasn't me. David took a step backward, his scalp prickling. Alcourt meant it, believed it. Had he really split the ruthless web node so cleanly from himself that he could believe in his own innocence in this mess, deny any guilt?

"Leave, artist." Jewel faced him. "Do it quickly. I've made reservations for you and the kitten. A shuttle leaves for McMurdo on the hour."

David tore his gaze from Alcourt, coldness creeping up his neck. This was not Jewel talking. This was Serafina, wearing Jewel's Self.

Serafina was dead. *She wants to possess me,* Jewel had told him. And he hadn't really believed her.

He believed her now. "Jewel?" he said, dry-mouthed. "Jewel, are you there?" The words died in his throat as Susana popped into the virtual in her cat Self.

"Yo, Harmon Alcourt." Light glinted on her needle teeth as she smiled. ''I want a word with you, and we're gonna do this in public.''

Alcourt didn't seem to hear her. He stood with his head down, his fingers twisting together in endless patterns.

''Salgado was one of your fake Selfs.'' Susana moved closer, her tail twitching as if she were stalking something. ''He was you, and *you* killed my father. Did you give a shit when that fucker ran him down? Or were you into some party, or thinking about a little hot sex, or how much money you were making? Did it matter to you at all, you scumbag?''

Alcourt looked down at her finally. ''I didn't kill anyone.'' His mouth twitched. ''He did that, not me. I'm very sorry about your father.''

''Are you?''

''Susana?'' David took a step toward them. He guessed it suddenly—she was *there*. That was why the solarium door had opened. She had gone to find Alcourt in the flesh.

''Look at this.'' Susana stood up, metamorphosing into human shape, but with her fur-covered cat's ears flattened. She touched one clawed fist lightly to his belly. ''Don't move,'' she purred as he flinched away. ''My hand's empty, see?'' She glanced down at her fingers curled around an empty space of air. ''Funny about that, huh? Your virtual doesn't know how to translate a long, thin piece of broken mirror, so it just leaves my hand empty. No default metaphor, I guess.'' She bared more of her white teeth, grinning up at him, cat tongue lolling. ''If you twitch, I'll gut you. This thing cuts like a razor, baby; you better believe it. And I'm gonna cut you anyway, but it'll be quicker if you hold still.''

''Don't.'' Alcourt stared down at her empty palm, his eyes rimmed with white. ''Oh, my God, it hurts. You're *here*.'' His voice skidded up an octave. ''You cut me. You're *real*!''

''Am I? Hold still!'' Susana's hand twitched, and he choked back a cry. ''You so sure you can tell anymore, scumbag? We could find out. I could stick this into you. What's your default metaphor for guts and blood, huh?''

''Susana, don't.'' David took a useless step forward, halting as she tensed. ''We exposed him, and he's out of the web for good,'' he said urgently. ''If you kill him, you're screwed. No matter what he did, you'll get death for killing him. Don't do it, Susana.''

''He killed Carl.''

The kitten was foolish. The node was already dead . . . *No!* Jewel shook her head, dizzy, floundering. Not ''kitten.'' Susana— and she was going to stab Alcourt in the flesh, and David was right;

it would be suicide. The kitten is a fool, but that is her choice . . .
No! No! I'm Jewel, not her . . . "Susana!" Jewel struggled, sinking, drowning in a sea of yesterdays.

Jewel . . . me . . . Serafina . . .

No!

She groped for a memory of Linda, holding her in the dark, loving her—and Jewel knew it, had known it back then, had run away from that love. Remember Susana's face when she asked, *Why did you get in the snake's way?* Remember Jewel . . .

She seized those memories, clutched them, then reached out and touched the wind, gathering strength from it because she knew how to do that, too, because she was . . .

Me. I.

"Susana?" she cried. "Don't do this."

"What the hell do you care?" Susana didn't look at her.

"I didn't want to care." She held out her hand, thousands of miles away, only a scant few meters from this poised balance of life and death. "I ran away because you scared me as much as Serafina did. And . . . I came back to Serafina's because . . . I had to." She shivered, terrified by the weight of the words. "I care about you, and that scares me, because I've never let myself care about anyone." Yes, I'm like you, Serafina, do you see? And like Alcourt, too. "Susana, please don't do this," she whispered.

For a long moment, Susana stood motionless, as still as if she had been carved from stone. Then her face twisted suddenly and the muscles corded on her arm as she clutched her invisible knife, hand shaking. Jewel sucked in an agonized breath, expecting Alcourt to scream, to crumple. Instead, Susana opened her hand and tilted her palm. Her shoulders slumped, and she looked away from Jewel. "So, okay," she said. "I didn't do it." And vanished from the foyer.

David exited, too, quickly and without a word to her. That left the two of them, she and Alcourt, face to face in the beautiful garden that was as unreal as a dream of tomorrow.

"Why?" Jewel asked him softly. "How much money did you need?"

"It wasn't money." Alcourt looked into the pool as if searching for an answer. "I controlled it. Nobody knew, but I was pulling their strings, making them dance. It was me." He looked up into her face, his eyes flaring suddenly. "I'm going to die soon. You know it better than anyone. These young snots with so many years left, they think they've got it all. They know I'm old, and they look down their noses at me. As if it's my fault. As if they're immune from age. But I made them dance." He laughed softly. "And they didn't even know it. Jewel?" He stretched out his hand to her. "I wish . . . you had stayed."

Jewel shivered at the loneliness in his bleak eyes. "Exit," she whispered, and reached up for her lenses.

Chapter
Twenty-four

David dropped back into the solarium, yanking off his lenses as he shoved the door open. Alcourt would be in his private virtual lounge, where he worked the web. He ran down the hall, wondering where Castor was, hearing banging on the closed door of the library as he ran by. Aha—Susana must have managed to lock him in after she left the solarium.

He burst through the door of Alcourt's lounge, relieved to see that it was unlocked, terrified of what he might find. Alcourt was alive. David halted just inside the door, heart hammering, panting as if he had run a mile. Alcourt was still in virtual, talking with someone in a strange, broken voice. Susana stood with her head down, half-turned away, her left hand cradling the right. Blood welled between her closed fingers to drip slowly, brightly onto the carpet. A bloodstained sliver of mirror lay at her feet. She flinched as David reached for her hand but didn't raise her head.

The glass had slashed her palm nearly to the bone. David glanced down at the ugly shard of broken mirror. He wadded up the hem of her tunic and squeezed her bleeding hand around it. "Hold on tight until we can get something on this. Let's go." He glanced anxiously at Alcourt. "We've got a way out." Courtesy of Jewel, or had it been Serafina? At the end, it had been Jewel talking.

Susana offered no resistance as he put his arm around her and led her out of the room. Alcourt was mumbling to himself or to someone in the virtual with him. Out in the corridor Susana finally looked up. "I didn't kill him." Her tone was as fragile and razor-edged as the glass that had sliced her palm. "Was she shitting me?"

"No." David met her empty gray eyes, searching for something, for a flicker of warmth in that desolation. "She wasn't shitting you," he said gently. "Give her a chance. Okay?"

In those still gray depths something moved. "Maybe." She sighed a long, weary breath. "I'll try. Can we go home?"

Home. He couldn't remember ever hearing her use that word. Come to think of it, Jewel didn't use it, either. Maybe that could change, too. "Yeah," he said. "I think home is a good idea."

Chapter
Twenty-five

Jewel trudged up the hill past the midday desert of the flea market, her carryall slung over her shoulder. The sun hammered the road and the dusty blackberry thicket, filling the air with the dry smell of dust and hot asphalt. Berry canes clawed at her as she took the path up to the development, their thorns forged by the heat into steely hooks that snagged skin, hair, clothes. Jewel shouldered through the last clump and stopped, shading her eyes against the glare. The dozen or so houses baked silently in the heat, their shutters closed, the dusty yards empty except for a couple of little girls playing quietly in the sparse shade beneath a dying shrub.

Nothing had changed. It shocked her a little; something should look different. Her life had cracked apart in the invisible earthquake of the past weeks, and it seemed that that earthquake should have left its mark in the physical world. The two girls turned identically grimy, identically curious and wary faces to watch her as Jewel walked slowly up to Linda's door. David and Susana had returned from Erebus ten days earlier. David was at the Vashon house. Susana was—somewhere. Jewel touched the sun-hot wood of the door, tired with a weariness that went beyond her walk up the hill.

David had heard through his web connections that Alcourt had retreated, ostracized, wounded, and passive. He had messaged her when he and Susana had first returned, asking if she needed any help. She had told him that she was going to stay in the desert. The day before yesterday she had driven the overdue rental back to Ryo and had endured Jenny's tongue-lashing. She had hired a man to winch her car out of the ditch, and then she had left, driving back along the roads they had taken on their midnight flight. Now Jewel pushed the unlocked door open, listening to the dry creak of the hinges, hearing emptiness in the hot silence. She had stayed to challenge the ghosts. She had stayed because she *remembered* living there—the smell of the desert after rain, the feel of the goat's lip on her palm as she fed it salt. The touch of Elaine's hands on her body. She remembered it, and part of her had wanted to run from that remembering.

She was through running.

So she had slept in Serafina's bed, rummaged through her cupboards and drawers, worn her clothes.

And remembered.

Her past and Serafina's. *Are you there?* she had whispered, sitting on the rimrock beneath the starry sky. She had received no answer but the soft touch of the wind on her face. It had whispered of cotton fields and red clay with a voice of sage and stone. It had whispered of goat lips and rain and the touch of the lover who was also her mother. And on the morning after she had talked to David, she had wakened in Serafina's bed and had known that she could go.

She was who she was. Jewel Martina.

Jewel stepped down into the sunken living room, embraced by heat and silence and the familiar smell of the house, feeling centered, poised on the uneven shift of here and now. She dropped her pack onto the sofa where David had sat. Even blind, he had been able to read her. She smiled, wanting suddenly to see him, to tell him about the desert and her communion with Serafina's ghost, who was nothing more than herself. He would understand. He had sculpted the chimera. She wondered if she could make Susana understand. Jewel sighed, pierced by a sudden pang of grief—for Elaine, eaten by her fear of life, and for Serafina, eaten by her fear of death.

"Who's there?"

Jewel whirled, her heart contracting, thinking of thieves or squatters. "Linda?" A sudden rush of emotion pushed tears into her throat. "You didn't move out? You're back?" She took a single step toward the stairs and stopped, squeezed by sudden awkwardness. "I was going to call you," she said shyly. "I thought you were living with the Ikikos. Susana's back, too. She's fine."

"I know. She messaged me. I am living with them. Eleanor is so worried about the baby." Linda patted the smooth swell of her belly, her voice too bright. "I just came back for some things I forgot. I have to be out of here by the end of the week, and . . . I wasn't sure what to do with your stuff. I'm just going to leave the furniture, so if you want it, help yourself. I've got my own apartment at the Ikikos' house, you know. It's back behind the pool, really nice, with its own little garden. All rocks and raked sand, with a little statue. It's very pretty. You'll have to come see it some-time; I'm sure Eleanor won't mind. She wants me to stay on as nanny, and she wants another daughter in two years.'' Linda looked nervously over her shoulder. ''I've got to finish. I've got this boy coming with a truck at three. Don't be angry with me, Jewel.'' Her eyes flickered. ''It's a long-term contract. It's a good deal, and I want to do it,'' she finished softly.

Jewel stood at the bottom of the stairs, leaning forward a little as if an invisible barrier blocked her path. It was real, that barrier—made up of years and silence, like thick solid glass between them. I can see you, she thought bitterly. I can't touch you. Not now, maybe not forever. ''You're right.'' She managed a smile. ''It's a good deal.'' She drew a slow breath. ''I . . . knew you loved me, Linda. It wasn't the money. It wasn't your holding me back. I loved you, too, and it scared me. What you wanted scared me. I couldn't be what you wanted, but I shouldn't have shut you out like I did.'' She swallowed. ''I lost something important. We both did, I guess. I'm sorry.''

Something moved across Linda's face: a tiny flicker of sadness, perhaps, or regret. Or maybe it was just the light. ''I'd better finish.'' Linda edged down the hallway. ''I've got this boy coming . . .'' She turned her back on Jewel, walked quickly down the hall, and disappeared into the bedroom the two of them had shared.

Jewel leaned against the shaky banister, one foot on the bottom step, not moving, not trying to go after her. What was left to say? Yesterday was over, with its mistakes and its victories. You could turn it into a monster to trample you forever, or let it go. With a jerk, she turned and left the house. She would not come back here again. She was wearing her skins, and there was nothing in the house she really wanted.

Love could be so damn resilient, or it could be as fragile as glass. And like broken glass, it could cut you so you bled to death. She shifted her carryall higher on her shoulder and hurried back down the hill, fighting her way through the clawing berry canes, welcoming the sting of the scratches because that gave her a reason for her tears.

David knelt in the cave, his Kraeger giving him cold and slick ice beneath his knees. Gently he teased ice from the wall and shaped it into a desperate curve of spine. The figure was taking shape: a fox growing out of the wall, twisting back on itself to snap at its own hindquarters in a frenzy. Ice struggling to escape ice. The desperation of that struggle raised the hairs on his arms. The chimera brooded over his shoulder, huge now, its perspective twisted, playing tricks, until you were inside and outside the creature at the same moment, victim and monster, one and the same. And in the center that was not the center, a desperate fox struggled to escape.

"Shit, David. This is *unreal*."

Flander's voice. David's hand froze, and he stopped breathing because he could not be hearing it. Flander was dead. His body had been dead for a long, cold time.

"David, are you . . . still pissed at me?"

He turned around at last to face the slender blond man with the green fox eyes. "Flander?" The words came out hoarse and harsh, blocked by the lump in his throat. "I thought Harmon killed you. When he destroyed the Secure File."

"Not me, man. I *always* keep a backup. Not even Serafina could find this one." Flander walked into David's arms.

Flesh, warm and alive, and no more real than the ice. Only the grief was real . . . "No, I'm not pissed," David murmured. "I wish I'd understood. I wish it could have been different. I thought . . . you were gone." And you are, he cried silently. You're dead, and that's forever, no matter how much of a genius you were. He closed his eyes. "I miss you."

"Yeah, me, too. I'm sorry, David." Flander buried his face against David's neck. "It's not enough, but I am."

It wasn't enough . . . and maybe it was. There were no words. David could only hold him, eyes closed, letting him be real for this moment, this fragment of time and space and illusion.

"You let Suse into the stardust piece." Flander sniffed. "She's not as good as me."

"She's different. She looks at things differently." David opened his eyes and touched Flander's face lightly. "She's not you, and I don't know if she even wants to work with me."

"Nobody's me. And if she doesn't jump for the chance, then she's brain-dead and why waste your time?" Flander winked, but his eyes were sad. "I couldn't be what you wanted, David. I tried, I really did. I know it didn't show much."

"I couldn't be what you wanted, either." David blinked back tears. "We both tried." He kissed Flander gently. The warm flesh beneath his hands was fading, dissipating into the ice-cave virtual like a wisp of smoke. "Flander?" He let his arms drop to his sides. A ghost, he thought. An electronic ghost haunting a virtual world. Where does reality end and illusion begin? Maybe everything was illusion, and that was all you would ever have. "I love you," David said out loud, and thought he felt the faintest brush of invisible fingertips against his cheek.

"Excuse me," his studio interrupted. "Chen Mu Lung wishes to enter."

Chen Mu Lung? David stared at the ice fox. Fuchin? His father did not do virtual, had never done it. He had netted David so that he would never have to do virtual. And now he was here. Requesting entrance. David opened his mouth to exit to his office. No. "Come in," he said, and faced the door that opened in the nearest wall.

Fuchin was himself, a basic Self, recorded by realtime video pickups and projected into this world. He stood stiffly on the doorstep, staring around the cave.

"Fuchin." David bowed, bound suddenly by formality. "Please come in."

The old man took one careful step into the cave. "It is slippery." He scowled at the wet ice beneath his feet. "How can this be?"

"Your eyes are misleading you." David resisted the urge to drop into Mandarin. "It is only an illusion."

"This is all illusion." Fuchin scowled. "How can you deal with such unreality?"

"Is this illusion so different from the flesh world?" His father's name meant Chen Wooden Dragon. And in this cave, embraced by the chimera, he made David think of a dragon—a small dragon carved from dark wood. Yes. He would use this. "Father." David straightened and held out his hand. "I am . . . honored."

Fuchin stared at David's outstretched hand for a moment, then clasped it with his withered fingers. "I wished to see one of these . . . games of yours." He turned slowly, eyes narrowing. "Your sister informs me that you are—well."

"Yes, Fuchin. Thanks to Dà Jieh. If she hadn't intervened, I would be blind." He still dreamed of darkness without end, then would wake up and sit with the light on for a while. "I owe her a tremendous debt." Dà Jieh had accepted his thanks without explanation, and Shau Jieh had claimed no knowledge of the paid hospital bill. So it hadn't been a family thing, after all. David sighed. A meter of virtual space separated him from Fuchin—a gulf of years and silence perhaps too deep to cross. "I'm sorry," David said softly. "For all the pain I have cost you."

Fuchin nodded slowly, stiffly. "And I." He stared past David at the struggling ice fox. "This place disturbs me. Your games are not what I imagined." He bowed. "I prefer to greet my visitors at my door, to serve them tea that they can taste." He paused at the

doorway, looked over his shoulder. "I am pleased that Dr. Benachim's technique has restored your sight. I have heard that you have
great talent, that the Chen name is respected in this field. I am . . .
proud." He walked through the door and closed it behind him.

David stared at it, speechless.

I am proud. Of me? David stroked the fox's shoulder gently,
smoothing away a small imperfection. His father didn't ever do
virtual. It occurred to David suddenly that his father had invited
him to visit. In the flesh. And it also occurred to him that he had
mentioned Dr. Benachim's name to no one in the family. Only the
person who had paid the bill would have seen it. Which meant Dà
Jieh might have told him.

Fuchin possessed the money to have payed David's hospital bill.
That would explain Dà Jieh's stony silence when he had thanked
her; she would not have liked acting as go-between in this matter.

Susana could find out for him.

He reshaped one of the fox's ears, gently stroking the delicate
curve. He wouldn't ask her. It was Fuchin's choice to tell him or
not to tell him if he had done this.

David discovered suddenly that he very much wanted Fuchin to
have done it. He would go to drink tea with Fuchin. And perhaps,
one day, he would ask him.

Jewel went into the booth near the flea market to leave a message
for David that she was back. On a whim, she dug out her lenses
and gloves and entered the ice cave. It had changed, and the change
took her breath away. Inside and outside? *I am* the chimera. She
shivered because her body still lay beneath the chimera's hooves,
but she reached out to touch the icy curve of its powerful shoulder.

No fox eyes threatened her today, no strangeness, no hint of
Flander. She wondered if he had finally died that day in Alcourt's
foyer. He could have escaped, but he had stayed to expose the scam.
To save David.

Love could be resilient, too.

Movement caught her eye, and Jewel realized that someone else
was already here, half-hidden by shadows and a trick of perspective. She started to exit but paused as she recognized the figure.
David. He was leaning against the shoulder of a carved fox, and
Jewel thought he was crying. But as she started to withdraw, he
straightened suddenly and nodded at her as if he had known all
along that she was there.

"Jewel." He held out his hands. "I'm glad you're back safe."

His eyes were dry, or maybe his Self had hidden the tears. Jewel took his hands, her mind and her skins giving her the feel of his flesh warm against hers. He was netted. She tried to remember if his Self had been netted before and thought that it hadn't.

"I wanted to tell you that Salgado is dead," she said softly.

"The flesh man?" David had gone very still. "He didn't really do it—order my torture. But a part of me hates him. It's still out there on the Net, the beating. It's still—going on." He caressed the frozen fox gently. "Sometimes, late at night, I wake up and I think about it. That I could go into that file. Be there again." He shivered. "Maybe the barrier between reality and virtual isn't so solid after all."

Maybe not. Jewel looked at the snarling chimera. She had messaged Sam from Serafina's, had told him that Salgado had sold out to Alcourt, that he had fronted a flesh body for Alcourt's web scam. She had suggested that the new plant might benefit others besides the residents of El Peten. A cryptic note had come back from Sam via e-mail: *Good-bye to S. It's mine now. We're even.*

Good-bye to S. The lines had reeked of death. So you are revenged, Carl, Jewel thought bitterly. Revenged on the flesh and on the virtual spirit, both. And Sam had what he wanted: control of El Peten. A lump closed her throat. Tears? For Sam? Or for those angry, vivid poems he'd painted on the dirty concrete face of the 'burbs?

"How are *you*?" David touched her hand gently.

"I'm . . . all right. I think." She met his eyes. "I'm her, too. Serafina. But I'm me. I don't see the world the same way anymore." She groped for words to explain how it really felt, how the wind and sky and earth worked. "I'm not sure what I can do with it yet. Serafina told me that reality is . . . like the Net. Does this make any sense at all?"

"Yes." He kissed her gently. "You're not running anymore."

"No. I'm not." Not from Serafina or from Linda. And not from herself. Jewel tried to swallow the lump that clogged her throat. "I'm sorry about Flander, David. I never had a chance to say that."

"He was here. He's in the Net." David looked down at their clasped hands. "He'll always be a part of me. Part of my talent, part of my art. Maybe *he's* the chimera."

Part of him. Jewel shivered. As Serafina was part of her, and Elaine's pain, and the Linda who had loved her. We are all so many people, Jewel thought dizzily, a patchwork of our past. Whether we want to be or not.

"I got a message this morning that Alcourt died last night."

"What?" Jewel blinked. "Are you sure?"

"Apparently he had a heart attack. The monitors were turned off, but no one knows why," David said softly. "That's the official version."

And would remain the official version, because Erebus was exempt from anyone's law. If Alcourt had chosen to commit suicide, it was his prerogative.

"I wonder." David touched his sculpture lightly. "Did he kill himself because he couldn't live with what he'd done, or was it that he couldn't live without the virtual Self? It's so easy to put on a Self and give that Self life, let it be the part of you that you're afraid to be. Flander . . . went one step farther."

Jewel looked at the desperate fox struggling to escape the ice. Perhaps she had been right. The virtual Alcourt had been the real man, and he had died. Alcourt's flesh had simply followed, the way Mrs. Wosenko would follow her skiing Self one of these days.

"I offered to take Susana on as an apprentice." David's eyes were on her face. "She's not Flander. She has her own talents. I . . . laid down some rules this time." His eyes flickered. "About priorities. About choices."

"What did she say?" Jewel discovered that she was holding her breath.

"She told me she'd think about it." David looked away, frowning a little. "I think she's working something out. Or trying to. I haven't heard from her since."

"I haven't, either. She disappeared." Jewel pulled her hand free from his. "How can she just walk away from an offer like that?"

"Jewel?" David touched her face gently, his dark eyes full of compassion. "It's not your fault. Partly, maybe. But not entirely."

"It *is* my fault." Jewel took his hand, wishing suddenly and intensely that this were flesh and not virtual. "I walked out on her in the desert. Like Linda did to her. Like Carl did. She'll never forgive me for that."

"I don't know," David said with sad honesty.

Jewel sighed, because this was virtual and she could smell the stale piss in the stuffy public booth. "Thank you," she said. "For trying. And for understanding."

"The offer's still open if she wants it." He stepped back, face full of sympathy. "I'm sorry, Jewel."

"Me, too." She exited back into the hot, stinking reality of the booth and the sun and the flea market.

She had sacrificed everything to escape this world, only to find the same people living in Erebus, the towers, and the desert. Outside, the rail platform was empty. Thirty minutes until the next train. The midday runs were risky. Not too many people traveled that time of day, and the city cut security to a minimum. The gangs worked the midday runs.

She would risk paying the gang toll, because she could not stay here any longer. Jewel peered down the track to where the rail merged into the shimmering heat haze. A couple of boarders were working the far end of the platform, skimming off a homemade ramp, doing slick turns and fancy flips, their faces and arms barred with dark tan. One of them cut off and headed her way. Too late Jewel realized that he was focused on her, one hand out to hook her carryall. She skipped backward and caught her heel on the vandalized remains of a plastic bench, struggling for balance. He was going to hit her. He had misjudged her movement, or maybe he *wanted* to cream her.

Jewel flung up an arm and, in a vivid moment of déjà vu, caught a blurry glimpse of flying limbs and copper hair as someone darted between them. The boarder ricocheted off the figure's outstretched arms, stumbled, and nearly lost his board. With a twist of his hips he regained his balance, mouthed something obscene, and rocketed on down the platform.

"You need a keeper, Auntie." Arms akimbo, Susana glowered at Jewel.

"Where have you *been*?" Breathless, Jewel faced her. "I was worried. How come you turned David down?"

"You sound like a mother. Jeeze. I've been around, okay?" Susana gave a jerky shrug, avoiding Jewel's eyes. "I didn't turn him down. I told him I had to think, is all. Through with the lecture now? Can I go, please, Auntie?"

"No." Jewel blocked her path, her mouth dry. "It's a way out for you, what David's offering. Better than some, worse than others. Not a sure thing at all." She drew a deep breath. "I meant what I said. I walked out on you both, and I'd be stupid to expect you to believe that I won't do it again. But . . . I won't." She looked away, realizing that she was afraid. "Would you like to move in with me?" The words sounded so awkward. "I'm leasing this place over on the north side of town, near my new client. It's big enough for two, and it's got access."

"You gonna try and play mother?" Susana's eyes were on her face, unreadable as a cloudy sky. "Is this supposed to make up to Linda somehow?"

"No. It's not." Jewel met her stare. "And we're going to piss each other off, because we're too alike and too different at the same time. But I think we can be friends."

Susana's nostrils flared slightly, and Jewel waited for her to walk away. It was too late, and she had blown it back there in the desert.

"Friends, huh?" Susana's shoulders slumped suddenly, and she looked down at the filthy concrete of the platform. "I don't know. It might be okay, living with you. Sometimes . . . you're a cool lady." She raised her head, scowling. "Sometimes." She changed the subject abruptly. "I went into the cave. Did you *see* what David did to the chimera? Flander was there." She tossed her head. "He's gonna be a royal pain if I start working with David. Who says *he's* the hottest artist on the planet?"

Susana had no doubts that Flander was real. Perhaps there was no dividing line between the Net and the 'burbs for her. She, too, might be able to understand what Serafina had been. "I was there." Jewel looked into the distance, out at the shimmering heat haze that blurred the city towers. "David said Flander was the chimera." Perhaps he had meant that Flander was a fantasy, a ghost made up of love and loss. Reality to David was flesh. Or maybe he had been hurt too badly to let Flander become real. Jewel sighed. "He's right," she said softly. "The chimera's a patchwork monster—part goat, part lion, part snake." Where does reality end and illusion begin? "Flander's a patchwork, too: memories of flesh, thoughts formed of electrons in silicon, and his soul . . . of whatever dreams are made."

Susana was staring at her with an odd expression. "Yeah, Auntie, sometimes . . . you're okay." She held out a hand. "You really sure about this? About my moving in?"

Was there a hint of longing in those eyes? "Yeah, I'm sure." The words caught in Jewel's throat and came out halfway between laughter and tears. "Deal?"

Yes, she was afraid. She stuck out her hand, and Susana clasped it, flesh warm against flesh. Real flesh, not a virtual. Jewel swallowed. She was afraid of what she had just done: saddled herself with this kid, this obligation, this complication in her life. But she pushed the fear aside and squeezed Susana's hand. "We'll do fine," she said, and wondered if that was a benediction, a prophecy, or maybe just a hard, solid hope.

"Yeah, maybe." Susana gave her a tentative grin. "I guess we'll do okay. And I guess I ought to tell David I want to do it, huh?"

"Yeah, you ought to." A weight was lessening inside her, as if that stone she had carried so long was beginning to dissolve. They would do all right.

Make that a prophecy.

Also by
MARY
ROSENBLUM

Available in bookstores everywhere.